T0029961

Antoinette's
Sister

"The political landscape of Southern Italy during the period of the so-called Kingdom of the Two Sicilies is one of the most complex and daunting in the history of the Italian peninsula. But Diana Giovinazzo weaves a clear path for us through the historical minefield in her latest historical novel, *Antoinette's Sister*. Though the eyes of Maria Carolina Charlotte, queen and de facto ruler of Ferdinand I's kingdom, we experience the personal struggles, tragedies, and triumphs of one of the most remarkable women of the eighteenth century. A fascinating biographical portrait as well as an engrossing, bittersweet tale."
—Laura Morelli, art historian
and *USA Today* bestselling author of *The Stolen Lady*

"A sweeping tale of power, love, and the bonds of family, *Antoinette's Sister* is a compelling coming-of-age story set to the backdrop of one of the most volatile periods in Europe. Giovinazzo has deftly weaved fascinating and rich details through the narrative, and in Maria Carolina Charlotte, created an endearing yet strong protagonist who must learn the demands of a monarch to save her country from ruin. I couldn't put it down!" —Heather Webb, *USA Today* bestselling author of *The Next Ship Home*

"Diana Giovinazzo's *Antoinette's Sister* is a fast-paced, dramatic retelling of the life of Maria Carolina Charlotte, Queen of the

Two Sicilies. Giovinazzo deftly brings to life this fierce and brilliant queen, who uses her prowess to become a savvy leader of Naples while trying desperately to save her beloved sister, Marie Antoinette, from disaster in Revolutionary France. With uprisings, love affairs, and plenty of court intrigue, this juicy historical story is like a rousing Philippa Gregory novel, only set under a warm Italian sun." —Stephanie Storey, bestselling author
of *Oil and Marble* and *Raphael, Painter in Rome*

"*Antoinette's Sister* is a feast of royal fiction, full of court politics, international intrigue, family loyalties, and power struggles. And at the center of it all is a determined and fascinating real-life historical woman. Diana Giovinazzo brings Queen Maria Carolina Charlotte to life, as well as the vibrant portion of Italy that she ruled. This book will absolutely sweep you away."
—Alyssa Palombo, author of *The Spellbook of Katrina Van Tassel*

"Offers an exceptional portrait of 18th-century Austria's Habsburg royal dynasty…This sprawling tale of power, intrigue, and ambition is a winner." —*Publishers Weekly* (Starred Review)

"Philippa Gregory fans will love this story's mix of real history and drama, made personal with the strong and relatable voice of the queen of Naples and Sicily." —*Booklist*

"With a narrative focused on Charlotte and interspersed with letters from her siblings and mother, Giovinazzo's captivating novel highlights the rise and fall of a strong female monarch against the backdrop of the French Revolution and Napoleonic Wars."
—*Library Journal*

"Rich, fascinating, and informative! *Antoinette's Sister* is an alluring, compelling tale…of the struggles, sacrifices, hopes, fears, entangled relationships, love affairs, schemes, and treachery that surrounded one of the most powerful families of the time."

—BookBub

"A worthwhile read, and thanks are owed to Diana Giovinazzo. It may well encourage further exploration on the part of the reader, and perhaps other scholarly and creative work in regard to both Charlotte and the history of her kingdom."

—*New York Journal of Books*

"Charlotte is a compelling character, and *Antoinette's Sister* proves she is worthy to break out of her sister's shadow."

—BookReporter.com

"Delivers meaningful, impactful interactions between characters that leave the reader with a sense of deep fulfillment…Vibrant."

—BookBrowse

"Giovinazzo does what many historical fiction writers set out to do and few actually accomplish. She plucks a relatively obscure character from history and brings her wholly to life. Charlotte is a fascinating, strong-willed woman, and her struggles to cement her place in the Neapolitan court are compelling."

—Manhattan Book Review

THE WOMAN IN RED

"*The Woman in Red* is an epic tale of one woman's fight to take control of her circumstances to create the life of her dreams. Anita Garibaldi is a modern woman in the nineteenth century who led with her heart despite circumstances so dire, most mortals would give up. Her passionate affair with Giuseppe Garibaldi freed her from a provincial life into one of passion, danger and purpose. Ms. Giovinazzo has crafted a spectacular story in this stunning debut." —Adriana Trigiani, *New York Times* bestselling author of *Tony's Wife*

"Anita Garibaldi, one of the greatest unsung heroines in history, comes to passionate life in Diana Giovinazzo's searing debut novel, *The Woman in Red*. Brazilian revolutionary, gaucho, and partner-in-arms to her husband, Giuseppe Garibaldi, Anita is a feminist icon to die for." —Mary Sharratt, author of *Ecstasy* and *Illuminations*

"Diana Giovinazzo establishes herself as a worthy new voice in historical fiction with this irresistible tale of Anita Garibaldi: firebrand, lover, soldier, mother, revolutionary. Garibaldi isn't just fierce, she's ferocious. Her unstoppable energy propels this novel forward through tragedy and triumph, soaring all the way."
—Greer Macallister, bestselling author of *The Magician's Lie* and *Woman 99*

"Anita Garibaldi is exactly the kind of courageous woman whose astonishing story of defiance and dedication—to freedom and to her passions—I've been craving. Told in her bold and unflinching voice, *The Woman in Red* by Diana Giovinazzo brings this brazen, complex woman—and the man she fought beside—vividly to life." —Erin Lindsay McCabe, *USA Today* bestselling author of *I Shall Be Near to You*

"Captivating…Giovinazzo adds realistic details to the fast-paced narrative. The novel's focus on a strong woman who defied the odds to follow her heart will appeal to fans of historical fiction."
—*Publishers Weekly*

"A great swashbuckler...Epic in scope, adventurous in nature, dreamily romantic, and occasionally a nail biter, this is the story of a passionate love affair, a feminist before feminism's time, history as it happened in three countries, triumph, and tragedy."

—*New York Journal of Books*

"Giovinazzo gives the reader a fascinating look at nineteeth-century South America and its culture, where machismo prohibited women from any meaningful role or status in society. It's Anita Garibaldi's fight against those prohibitions that make her such an inspirational character...*The Woman in Red* is a finely crafted, exciting page-turner and is highly recommended for readers interested in learning about strong and empowered women."

—Historical Novel Society

"Giovinazzo deftly brings Anita and her story to life in this sweeping saga...Entertaining and educational, as well as a wonderful way for readers to meet a lesser-known historical figure whose own life story could very well help influence their own by encouraging others to dig deep within to find courage and bravery."

—Ovunque Siamo

ALSO BY DIANA GIOVINAZZO

The Woman in Red

Antoinette's
Sister

DIANA
GIOVINAZZO

GRAND CENTRAL
PUBLISHING

NEW YORK   BOSTON

Copyright © 2022 by Diana Giovinazzo Tierney
Reading group guide copyright © 2022 by Diana Giovinazzo Tierney and Hachette Book Group, Inc.

Cover design by Olga Grlic. Cover photo © Illina Simeonova/Trevillion Images.
Cover copyright © 2022 by Hachette Book Group, Inc.

Grand Central Publishing
Hachette Book Group
1290 Avenue of the Americas, New York, NY 10104
grandcentralpublishing.com
twitter.com/grandcentralpub

Originally published in hardcover and ebook by Grand Central Publishing in January 2022.

First Trade Paperback Edition: November 2022

Grand Central Publishing is a division of Hachette Book Group, Inc. The Grand Central Publishing name and logo is a trademark of Hachette Book Group, Inc.

The publisher is not responsible for websites (or their content) that are not owned by the publisher.

The Hachette Speakers Bureau provides a wide range of authors for speaking events. To find out more, go to www.hachettespeakersbureau.com or call (866) 376-6591.

Library of Congress Cataloging-in-Publication Data
Names: Giovinazzo, Diana, author.
Title: Antoinette's sister / Diana Giovinazzo.
Identifiers: LCCN 2021033006 | ISBN 9781538720127 (hardcover) |
    ISBN 9781538720134 (ebook)
Subjects: LCSH: Maria Carolina, Queen, consort of Ferdinand I, King of the
    Two Sicilies, 1752-1814—Fiction. | Naples (Kingdom)—History—1735-1816—
    Fiction. | LCGFT: Biographical fiction. | Historical fiction. | Novels.
Classification: LCC PS3607.I4686 A58 2022 | DDC 813/.6—dc23
LC record available at https://lccn.loc.gov/2021033006

ISBNs: 978-1-5387-2012-7 (hardcover), 978-1-5387-2013-4 (ebook),
978-1-5387-2014-1 (trade paperback)

Printed in the United States of America

LSC-C

Printing 1, 2022

For Amanda
Some sisters you are born with, while others find you
working at a hat shop … at Disneyland

THE LINEAGE
OF
MARIA THERESA

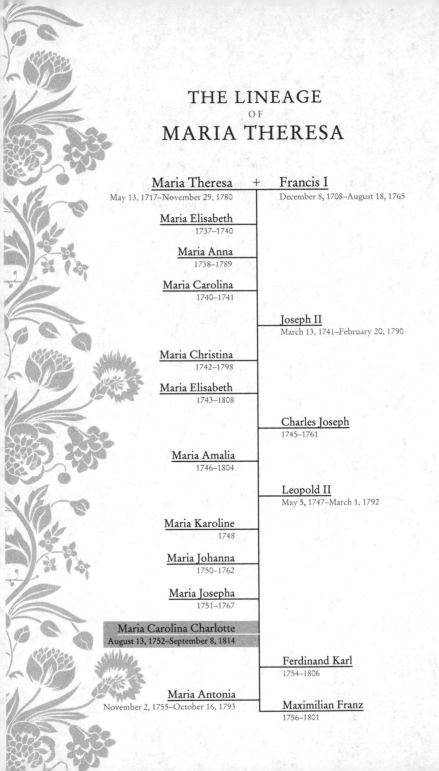

Maria Theresa + **Francis I**
May 13, 1717–November 29, 1780   December 8, 1708–August 18, 1765

Maria Elisabeth
1737–1740

Maria Anna
1738–1789

Maria Carolina
1740–1741

Joseph II
March 13, 1741–February 20, 1790

Maria Christina
1742–1798

Maria Elisabeth
1743–1808

Charles Joseph
1745–1761

Maria Amalia
1746–1804

Leopold II
May 5, 1747–March 1, 1792

Maria Karoline
1748

Maria Johanna
1750–1762

Maria Josepha
1751–1767

Maria Carolina Charlotte
August 13, 1752–September 8, 1814

Ferdinand Karl
1754–1806

Maria Antonia
November 2, 1755–October 16, 1793

Maximilian Franz
1756–1801

THE LINEAGE
OF
MARIA CAROLINA CHARLOTTE

Maria Carolina Charlotte   +   Ferdinand I
January 1752–January 1825

Maria Theresa
June 6, 1772–April 13, 1807

Luisa Maria
July 27, 1773–September 19, 1802

Carlo
January 4, 1775–December 17, 1778

Maria Anna
November 23, 1775–February 22, 1780

Francis I
August 14, 1777–November 8, 1830

Maria Christina
January 17, 1779–March 11, 1849

Gennaro
April 12, 1780–January 1, 1789

Giuseppe
June 18, 1781–February 19, 1783

Maria Amalia
April 26, 1782–March 24, 1886

Unnamed daughter
stillborn, July 19, 1783

Maria Antonia
December 14, 1784–May 21, 1806

Maria Clotilde
February 18, 1786–September 10, 1792

Maria Enrichetta
July 31, 1787–September 20, 1792

Leopold
July 2, 1790–March 10, 1851

Alberto
May 2, 1792–December 25, 1798

Maria Isabella
December 2, 1793–April 23, 1801

Here we are at the end of all things. You who thought you could best me. You are the Icarus, and I am the sun. All these years, you have been my constant tormentor. You took away my sister and my kingdom, but you can never take away my identity, for I am a queen, a Habsburg daughter, and you will forever be known as a usurper.

As you read this, know that the courts of Vienna have ruled in my favor. My husband and I will be restored to our rightful place as king and queen of Naples while you will be left with nothing. Which is more than you deserve.

Yours Faithfully,

Maria Carolina Charlotte

Queen of Naples and Sicily

CHAPTER ONE

NOVEMBER 20, 1765

There were few things as enjoyable as being able to see the unveiling of a suitor's portrait. The event, attended by four of my six sisters, was an opportunity for us to assess what our mother's intentions were. Our mother, Empress Maria Theresa, was not only the ruler of the Austria-Hungary Empire, but was also the absolute ruler of the Habsburg royal family—all eleven of us. No Habsburg child, male or female, was immune to her strict cultivation. We were all expected to be rulers in whichever court the empress mother deemed appropriate and, as such, were savagely pruned by her sharp tongue.

On this day, my younger sister Antoinette and I skipped down the hallways quickly, passing the ornate tapestries depicting the proud double eagles of the Habsburg crest. Large paintings, commissioned by the greatest artists in all the kingdom, celebrated the greatness of the Habsburg dynasty.

"Did you hear about Josepha's new fiancé?" Antoinette said with an evil grin, her blue eyes sparkling with the news she was burning to tell me. The older we got, the more differences I began to see in our looks. At one point, we were considered to be indistinguishable, even though I was three years older. While her hair had maintained its ash-blond coloring, mine had darkened to the color of chestnuts. In every other way, our features were the same, from our blue eyes to our rosebud lips. Day and night, people would tell us; that's what we were. One the counterpart of the other.

"They say that young Prince Ferdinand is just as mad as his older brothers," Antoinette interjected, breaking up my thoughts.

"Where did you hear that?"

"Why, the maids of course. They know all the palace scandal." Her eyes widened with joy. "Now that King Carlos rules Spain, he has to reposition what titles his sons are going to inherit. They say his older brother died of severe melancholy. That's how he got the Spanish throne."

"What makes you think Ferdinand and his brothers are mad?" It was always a great annoyance when my sister heard the best secrets before I did.

"Well, everyone knows the eldest son, Philip, is an imbecile; they can't even include him in court life. They only trot him out on important occasions, and then he is shuffled back to his rooms. The poor prince had to be excluded from the line. They couldn't even consider him as a ruler. Carlos's second son, Carlos the Fourth, is of course destined for the Spanish throne. But Naples, that belongs to Ferdinand." She shrugged. "It's the lesser kingdom anyway, so it's probably for the best. I can't picture Josepha ruling anything more prestigious."

Of all six of my living sisters, Josepha was the one Antoinette and I liked the least. Well, not quite the least: Elisabeth, because of her great beauty, was Mother's favorite and therefore could do no wrong. It was no secret that Mother intended on her getting the best marriage out of all of us. While I, on the other hand, was always being criticized for my behavior.

The title that Mother sought for Josepha was Queen of Naples, not one of the more prestigious titles. The Kingdom of the Two Sicilies took up the southern half of the Italian peninsula. Keeping to itself, the kingdom was seen more as a puppet of Spain than an independent country.

Once, the Holy Roman Empire had held almost all the territories of the Italian peninsula, but, as Mother liked to lament, our grandfather had squandered them away. The Two Sicilies had been ours, and Mother wanted them back in the Habsburg fold, regardless of the cost. This marriage alliance was so important that Mother had attempted to marry our sister Johanna to the young king, but she died before the negotiations got very far. Now, it was Josepha's turn to fulfill Mother's will.

"How terrible this is for her," I lamented. "She has to marry our sister's intended husband."

"Only you would think that." Antoinette laughed. "You refuse to even share a name with a sister who died well before you were born."

I shrugged. "I don't want to be confined to anyone else's fate."

We turned the corner and skidded to a stop on the royal red carpet, just in time to avoid running into the large gold-and-white porcelain vase perched on the pedestal. The butler that stood nearby raised an eyebrow as I grabbed the wobbling antique vase, steadying it on its roost. "Sorry," I mumbled as we scurried toward the small royal parlor. The hallway, white with gold trim, was lined with paintings of former rulers. Pompous men who didn't come close to the empress mother's fortitude. They each stared down at us in judgment. All except one, Francis I, the Holy Roman emperor. Our father.

It'd been only a few months since his death, but his absence could be felt throughout the whole palace. He was the one who had tempered Mother and brought a smile to her face. When he was young, they had called him the "sweet little cavalier." But for all his charm, Mother had almost not been allowed to marry him.

Grandpapa wasn't convinced that the indebted Duke of Lorraine was the best match. Grandpapa had regularly threatened to cancel the whole thing, but Mother had refused to marry anyone unless it was her dear prince. Later our father proved his loyalty to the crown when Prussia betrayed us.

When Grandpapa realized he could find himself with a daughter as an heir to the kingdom, he created the Pragmatic Sanction, a document naming our mother, Maria Theresa, as the next in line for the throne. But the document wasn't official until he had the support of another country. He managed to get the backing he needed from Prussia, but once he died, Prussia invaded, thinking Mother was weak. It was our father who stood by her side, who helped her defend the kingdom. Together, my parents had sought the glory of the Holy Roman Empire, but now that Father was gone, it was up to Mother to keep the legacy alive.

"Charlotte, come along." Antoinette tugged at my arm. "We're going to be late."

"Well, there you are!" Elisabeth said from her perch opposite the door. Like the spoiled child she was, she held out a goblet for the servant girl to refill, never once bothering to acknowledge the lesser creature. "We were beginning to think that you wouldn't make it."

"I was trying to replicate your toilette," I said, "but I found that I just didn't have the number of creams and powders required. How many is it that you use now? Twenty?"

Elisabeth sneered at me in response before taking a long sip and shifting her gaze, with her ice-blue eyes, to Antoinette. Instinctively, I took Antoinette's hand and pulled her into the golden-trimmed armchair with me. She sat partially on my lap as we shared the chair.

The room covered in gold brocade was one of the more familial rooms in the palace. Though too quaint to hold all eleven of the empress mother's children, it was large enough to hold four of her seven daughters. We were spread out on overstuffed blue sofas and matching chairs. Mother had ordered the drapes, in blue as well, to be opened, so that we could better see the portrait of Ferdinand that sat covered in front of the marble fireplace. Near the front of the room, directly in front of the painting, sat Mother with my sister Josepha at her side.

Josepha was only a year older than me, but the difference between us could have been a vast cavern. Josepha tried to model herself after Elisabeth in both attitude and looks. She had little patience, especially for the likes of me, but spent as much time as she could doting on our eldest brother, Joseph, Mother's coruler and heir apparent. Next to Josepha was her governess, the serious Countess Lerchenfeld.

Lerchenfeld was Mother's intermediary in the care and upbringing of all the empress mother's daughters. It was Lerchenfeld's duty to see that we had the best tutors, from music and dance to philosophy, so that the archduchesses would be the envy of the Holy Roman Empire. She also managed the other governesses, like Antoinette's and my own vile warden, Countess von Brandeis.

"Ladies, I believe that now that we are all here, we can begin the viewing," Mother proclaimed with a little wave directing a servant to remove the burgundy cloth draped over the painting. For a moment, we all stared in silence. Shock, really. And then— I couldn't help myself—a burst of laughter erupted from my gut and traveled to Antoinette. Mother snapped her head to us, her hawk eyes fixed on our uncouth behavior. I pressed my face into Antoinette's shoulder, doing all that I could to hide my laughter.

"Well, he's..." The words died on Elisabeth's lips. There was no way to rectify the situation. The young king's beady black eyes stared back at us. They were a little too close together, but they weren't even the worst feature on his face. His nose, that poor bulbous appendage, jutted out from his face like a beak. Only, unlike a bird's beak, it had a rounded bump at its tip that resided just above a pair of exceptionally large lips.

"He is by far the ugliest man I have ever seen!" I exclaimed as my sisters turned to me.

"Charlotte, that is enough. We do not need your commentary," Mother said, not bothering to look at me. "This will be a most fortuitous marriage."

"For him, maybe," Antoinette whispered in my ear. I snorted as everyone's eyes turned back to me.

"According to his tutors, he is of amazing health," Countess Lerchenfeld stated. "He is strong and well loved by his people."

"At least he has that," Antoinette murmured.

"Ladies, I believe we have seen enough. You may leave. I would like to speak with Countess Lerchenfeld alone." My sisters all got up and filed out of the room, but I slipped behind the ornate door. Pressing my ear to the gap between the hinges and the wall, I listened intently to the two women discuss my sister and her future husband.

"Tell me, Countess, how are Josepha's studies progressing?" My mother's commanding voice drifted from the room.

"Quite well. I feel that she is going to make a fine ruler."

"Good. Very good. This gives me comfort. The situation in Naples is far worse than I was led to believe." I could hear my mother set down her goblet. "King Carlos is worried about the mental stability of his sons; it is understandable after the problems he has had with his eldest. But it would appear that he is afraid all three of his sons have the illness."

"Are they indeed ill? More importantly, what of Ferdinand?"

"I don't know." My mother's sigh fell heavy about the room. "According to my ambassador, the regents who have been controlling him have sought to control the country. Their method for doing this has been to keep the young man out of all affairs of state. I am told that the young king spends his days hunting, playing games, and carousing with the common people. He has no sense of duty. No patience for matters of state. And I don't believe he even knows how to read. He may not be ill, but he is certainly a fool. And fools make incompetent rulers."

"What do we do, Your Highness? Is it too late to back out of the agreement?"

"It has always been too late to go back on the agreement. Catherine the Great is waiting for any opportunity to pick at our borders. We can't afford a war with Russia. Spain is the greatest military power on the continent, followed by France. If I can marry my daughters into those Bourbon families, then we stand a chance to secure the stability of the Holy Roman Empire." There was a long silence. "I just wish this didn't feel like I had to sacrifice Josepha."

"What would you have me do?" Lerchenfeld asked.

"Prepare my daughter to rule the country like a proper Habsburg queen. I don't want to do this, but I am a queen before I am a mother."

"Yes, Your Majesty."

I scurried down the hall, burning to tell Antoinette what I heard.

Dear Charlotte,　　　　　　　*March 1765*

Out of all my children, your behavior worries me the most. Don't you see that every punishment I put in front of you is an opportunity to learn from your mistakes?

But instead of learning, you subvert me. I take away your supper, but you employ a small army of maids to bring you cake. (Yes, I know of your secret cake supply.) You say your prayers with the devotion of a housefly.

And, worse yet, you openly call your governess an ogre in public! You are ill-tempered with all your ladies, particularly while they are dressing you. Charlotte, you will never be esteemed, much less loved, by those that you govern if you behave in such a manner.

Furthermore, you have a penchant for idleness, which is dangerous, especially for you. You and your sister play childish tricks. You make improper observations and raise your voice too much.

I am doing my best to raise you properly to be an honorable ruler, but I fear you will be wholly lacking in the virtue necessary to lead a kingdom. If I had shown even an ounce of your irresponsibility, I would never have been able to hold together my realm. If I carried on as you do, I would never have been able to competently lead my empire, let alone protect it from the men who tried to rip it away from me.

I pray that you will see the error of your ways and change before it is too late.

Yours,

Empress Mother

CHAPTER TWO

MAY 1767

A silent assassin called smallpox was sweeping through Vienna and the rest of Austria. This was not the first time that the virus had paid a visit to the Habsburg family. When it initially reached the doorsteps of Schönbrunn Palace, about five years ago, the royal physicians had implored Mother to try the new form of medicine called inoculation. "The process involves taking the virus from a pustule of an already-infected person and introducing it to an otherwise healthy person. The process is showing great promise in the city of Boston in the American colonies," they told her. Meanwhile, Mother's religious advisors disagreed. "To do this would thwart the will of God. Man was not meant to intercede in such an unholy manner," they said.

It wasn't until our brother Joseph insisted that he get inoculated that Mother relented, deciding to allow the older children to get the inoculation if they wanted it. Those three were my brothers Joseph and Leopold and my elder sister Johanna, soon to be married to the king of the Two Sicilies. And while Joseph and

Leopold lived, Johanna did not. She died from the inoculation. After that, Mother took her chances with the virus.

The family was regularly checked for fevers and rashes, but in the end, no one was safe from the devastating virus. Smallpox visited the palace again, finding new hosts among the family that had not yet been touched by its brutal effects. The first of us to come down with the illness this time was Elisabeth. Beautiful, vain Elisabeth, she told the physicians, "Do what you must to save my face, the rest of my body be damned. If I lose my beauty, let me die. I would rather be dead than be deformed." She lived, but her face was horribly disfigured.

After Mother contracted smallpox herself, earlier in the year, she had sequestered Josepha, Amalia, Karl, and Maximilian. None of them had had the virus before, and she wanted to make sure they remained safe. Antoinette and I had had the virus when we were young, but we were placed into quarantine right along with the others. The doctors were concerned that we could get it again if we were exposed.

Life sheltered away from the rest of the family was incredibly dull. Brandeis lectured Antoinette and me from sunrise until supper. The Countess von Ogre thought this a great opportunity to train us as proper archduchesses. Antoinette and I, on the other hand, wanted nothing more than to escape the confines of this sorry excuse for palace life. While Brandeis droned on and on about long-dead relatives that I could not care less about, I kept my eyes fixed on the perfect spring weather that allured me from outside the window. The palace grounds were filled with lush green lawns and flowers of vibrant blues and pinks.

During the long evenings, we sat in the family parlor, which was called the Yellow Room, but in truth, the only yellow thing about the room was the upholstery on the cushioned chairs. Day after day, we stared at the same white walls with the same loops of ivy painted at the very top. There were no balls or concerts. No hunts. Our evenings were spent playing chess, reading, or inventing whatever new form of entertainment would keep us from going mad. That is, all of us but Josepha. While Amalia and Karl created elaborate battles with toy soldiers, Antoinette and I made up new card games. We did what we could to make the best of life in isolation, but Josepha was intent on sulking.

"This is no use!" Josepha exclaimed, slamming her book shut. "I can't read another philosophy book or any more history."

"All this studying will make you a better ruler," Amalia said, looking up from the toy soldiers strewn about before her.

"What's the point? I'm going to die anyway."

All our heads snapped up. "What's that supposed to mean?" I asked.

"I know I am going to die because of the other Maria Josepha," she said with a sigh, as if we were supposed to know this already. "We share the same name, and that means we are going to have the same fate. I know it. She died of the pox, and so will I."

"That is the most ridiculous thing I have ever heard," I said.

"Oh, please!" Josepha's face reddened. "You went to Mother and had us all call you Charlotte because you didn't want to be connected to our dead sister Maria Carolina. And you call me ridiculous?"

"That's different. I didn't want a secondhand name. If I shared the fate of our deceased sister Carolina, I would have died a long time ago." It was a horrid custom, which I despised, that after the death of a child, the next born would be given the same name, as a way to remember the one that had passed. I was the third Maria Carolina. The first had died shortly after her first birthday of severe muscle spasms. The second, born in between Leopold and Johanna, lived barely long enough to be christened.

"You know nothing of these matters. You're just a child," Josepha retorted.

"I know enough not to believe in silly superstitions." Rolling my eyes, I looked at Antoinette. "Come on, let's go to our rooms." She got up and quickly followed me.

The moment we got to our bedroom, Antoinette fell onto her bed. "I swear, if I have to spend one more day with her, I think I will give myself the pox."

"She's like an old lady," I said, coming to join her on the bed. "What if we escaped?"

Antoinette looked at me curiously. "Escape? How?"

"Trust me," I said with a devilish grin.

I learned early that with a well-placed bribe, almost anything can be accomplished. A bit of gold, or even some of the jewelry I no longer had use for, when placed in the right maid's palm, would allow us the freedom my sister and I so craved. It was with this lesson in mind that Antoinette and I managed to have Brandeis occupied while we made our escape.

Our day in the sunshine was more delicious than the ones I was forced to watch from the window under the tutelage of Countess von Ogre. Pleasant winds flowed from the east, pushing out all the clouds and revealing a deep-blue sky. Tufts of wild seedlings floated through the air.

"Josepha thinks she is better than the rest of us because she's marrying a king," I lamented as we made our way to a remote part of the grounds. "Just this morning, she called me an ignorant child! How can I be an ignorant child when she is only a year older than me?"

Antoinette spread a blanket out for us to lie on next to a patch of pink peonies. "Ignore her. Soon she'll be married and living in Naples. Then she'll no longer be our concern."

Antoinette picked a nearby flower and began to twirl it between her fingertips, humming as she did, while a feeling of unease grew in my stomach. Mother was already busy making negotiations for my marriage and my sister's. One of us would be married to the Dauphin of France, and the other to nobility with influence that would benefit Austria. "Antoinette, do you think when we get married that we'll ever see each other again?"

Antoinette let out a little laugh that sounded like bells rising into the air. "That may be the silliest thing I have ever heard. If I am queen, I expect you to be one of the members of my court."

I smiled at the thought. She reached over and took my hand in hers. "Oh, yes, I'll need my older sister next to me. If I become queen, you'll provide counsel and, at the very least, beat the heads of state into submission."

We broke into fits of laughter and spent the rest of the afternoon daydreaming about all the ways we would help our future kingdom and how we would be different from our mother. "I will always tell my children that I am a mother first and a queen second," Antoinette said, suddenly growing serious. "That's the way it should be."

I was about to open my mouth to agree, but a dark cloud drifted toward us. Sitting up on my elbows, I eyed the intruder on our perfect day. "Antoinette, I think it's time to head back." Following my gaze, Antoinette agreed.

Only we weren't quick enough. On our way back to the palace, a downpour let loose. We ran through the pouring rain as thunder rippled through the air. We turned a corner, and I slipped, pulling my sister down with me. Mud splashed up, staining both our dresses. I got up and hoisted Antoinette from the muck. "Quick, through the servants' entrance!"

Normally, that was a safe place to enter without notice, but this time as we rushed through the door, I discovered we were in great danger. The fearsome sight of our mother stood before us. Her large form took up most of the doorframe, blocking our escape to the hallway, and she was furious. Both of our heads snapped down in submission, to look at our mud-covered shoes.

"What were you two thinking?" She scowled at us with her arms crossed in front of her broad bosom. This alone caused Antoinette and me to tremble with fear. She never needed to yell; she needed only to whisper, and men would cower. "Do you know how worried Countess von Brandeis was? How worried I was? Of course you don't, because you are selfish girls who think only of yourselves."

I dared to look into my mother's gray-blue eyes, now as stormy as the world outside, but my gaze withered as she glared at us.

"I probably shouldn't even ask whose idea this was," she growled. "Should I, Charlotte?"

"Mother, I—" At that precise moment, a glob of mud fell from my hair. It bounced off my nose and fell with a splat on the brown stone floor.

Her scowl deepened, and her face became crimson. "You are future queens. One of you will be the queen of France. Charlotte, you are always the source of gossip, and your attitude is appalling. You are the elder sister. You should be setting a pious example for Antoinette. From this day forward, you will be separated from each other."

We began to protest, but she raised her hand.

"Not another word. Antoinette, you will have a private tutor, and Charlotte, you will be placed with Josepha and Amalia. There will be no more secret confidences, no more contact at all whatsoever."

With that, our mother turned on her royal heel and left. Antoinette's grip on my hand tightened. "What are we going to do?"

"We'll pretend to follow her rules, of course," I said. But deep in my heart, I feared that not even my well-placed bribes would get us out of this.

Dearest Sister,   October 15, 1789

Do you remember when we were children and confined
to the palace? You were driven mad from the boredom.
Even then, you were reluctant to be placed in a cage, and
given where I am now, I can understand how you felt.

   Those days, though troubling for you, were some of the
happiest days of my life. When I close my eyes, I can still
see Josepha by the fire, her face bent over her books, and
Amalia and Karl, lost to the war games of toy soldiers.
Back then, most of the family was too busy for us. What
a wonderful childhood. I had you all to myself, from our
games with Brandeis to our endless adventures. Though
the last one ended in disaster. I still laugh at the memory
of mud falling from your head as you attempted to plead
your case to Mother. These are the memories I return to
over and over during these dark times.

   We may not be able to visit again for a long time, but
know that I cherish these memories of when you were
my Charlotte and we were happy.

Your Loving Sister,
Antoinette

CHAPTER THREE

I sat with my family in the church sanctuary as we watched Josepha being married by proxy to Ferdinand of Naples. She made a gorgeous bride, in a gown of ivy green, with blooming pink flowers and a white quilted petticoat. Joseph, our eldest brother, stood in for her bridegroom, looking as benevolent as one of the many statues Mother had commissioned for her private chapel. Proxy weddings were commonplace, particularly amongst the nobility. If a groom could not be present for the wedding, a substitute, or proxy, would stand in his place. This served to protect the nobleman's interest in the marriage. It was a promise, if you will, that the bride would indeed arrive at her destination. If she didn't, then there would be financial compensation for his troubles.

While everyone else's eyes were on Josepha, I watched Antoinette. She was purposely placed on the other side of the church. Even at the family gatherings, Mother was always trying to prove that her will was stronger than ours.

Leaning forward, I coughed, hoping to get Antoinette's attention. Leopold elbowed me, and I returned to watching the ceremony.

"Don't worry. I'll pass a message on to our dear sweet sister, but only if you stop fidgeting." I smiled up at my brother, who made a poor attempt at grinning while he kept his eyes on the bride.

I could always count on Leopold to take pity on me. Outside of Antoinette, he was the one who understood me best. Unfortunately, as he was the Duke of Tuscany, I did not get to see him or his pretty wife, Luisa—the Spanish infanta and Ferdinand's sister— very often. Leopold, at twenty, was always wiser and kinder than the rest of my elder siblings. Luisa's jovial nature brought a balance to his dry wit.

After the ceremony, I had hoped to catch Antoinette's eye, but she was quickly shuffled over to our mother and, therefore, out of my reach.

"I wonder if you would do me the honor of having the two best ladies in all Austria accompany me to luncheon."

"Excuse me?" I looked up into the smiling face of Leopold, who held out an elbow for me. On his other arm was Luisa. "Oh, yes, of course," I said, taking his arm.

"I do miss the gossip of Habsburg court life," Leopold said with a mock sigh. "Life in Florence is lovely and the Tuscan air is great for our disposition, but I would like to be kept abreast of all the comings and goings of my sisters."

I knew what my brother was doing: He was attempting to distract me from my melancholy.

"Why does your sister Elisabeth wear a black veil?" Luisa asked. "Is she in mourning?"

"Only for her looks," I responded. "Smallpox ravaged her face and body, so now on the rare occasion she leaves her apartments, it's always in a veil. It's why she can no longer marry." Elisabeth had been intended for Louis, the Dauphin of France.

"And all those years, she enjoyed mocking our poor sister Anna for her hump," Leopold said. "This new husband of Mimi's," he continued, moving down the line of our siblings, "does he further the great and bountiful Habsburg empire?" Mimi, also known as Maria Christina, was a masterful manipulator. While Elisabeth had been Mother's jewel, Mimi was as dear to Mother as her personal spaniels.

"Well, now that Elisabeth is no longer a favorite of the empress mother," I said, "given that she is no longer of use to the crown due to the loss of her looks, Mimi has managed to achieve something none of the rest of us could. It would appear that our dear sister is going to marry for love."

"Love? Why, that's a novel concept," Leopold teased, after which he received a playful thwack with Luisa's fan. "Ow," he said. "What I'm sure you know is that people in our position do not have the luxury of marrying for love. It is strictly a business transaction."

"Which is overseen and approved of by our dear empress mother," I added. "None of her children breathe without her express permission."

"Precisely." Leopold kissed his wife's temple and said in a lowered voice, "If one is especially lucky, they develop strong affections."

Luisa smiled and squeezed his arm in response.

"It seems her and Prince Albert's marriage prospects greatly improved after Father's death. As you know, Leopold, Father would never allow her to get away with this. But now, Mimi, who always gets what she wants, is free to coerce Mother into letting her marry the husband she wants. And I heard that Mother is *gifting* him with a fortune appropriate to keeping a Habsburg daughter in the life to which she is accustomed."

"Oh, to live in the sunshine of Maria Theresa's acceptance." We came up to the banquet room doors, and Leopold bowed. "Thank you, ladies, for the scintillating conversation."

The luncheon was held in the formal dining room, reserved for dignitaries and other nobility. The room sparkled in the light from the long windows. Around us, scenic paintings of palm trees and lush gardens covered the walls, and red roses burst from the tabletop vases. The early afternoon sun bounced off the crystal goblets and chandeliers, scattering little rainbows across the tables and walls.

Leopold and Luisa sat across the table from me and Amalia. Mother, Joseph, Josepha, and Antoinette sat at the opposite end. Peering down the table, I watched as Mimi talked to Antoinette. She was most likely droning on about her wedding plans. I could tell Antoinette was bored by the way she pushed her food around her plate. If only we could talk to each other.

"After luncheon, we'll be visiting the crypts, as a family," Mother declared to the surprise of us all. Josepha's fork dropped with a loud clatter that echoed in the silence of the room.

"Mother, please," Josepha whispered.

"Please what?"

"I don't want to go to the crypts," she said softly. Tears swam in her green eyes. No one could blame our sister for not wanting to face the one thing that terrified her above all else: death.

"Do not give in to the dramatics. You leave for Naples in the morning. This is your last chance to pay your respects to your father and your sisters." Mother waved her hand in the air, both dismissing Josepha and ordering the next course to be delivered. Next to Mother, Josepha's tears began to fall onto her plate.

Across the table from me, Leopold raised his glass as if to give a toast. I smiled and returned the gesture, for we knew in Austria there was only one way: the empress's.

Later that afternoon, we arrived at the Capuchin Crypt, the resting place for our family since 1618. Anyone who was privileged enough to be born or married into the Habsburg family was buried here. Our procession moved through the rows of sarcophagi lined up, waiting for us to pay our respects. Those who were not of royal lineage had coffins of simple copper with a cross affixed to the top. They often stood next to royal tombs carved of stone, with the ghoulish faces of skulls staring back at us.

Upon viewing the expansion of the crypts, Mother exclaimed, "Well, here we will have a good rest."

The vestibule that would one day house her now held our father, Francis. While everyone was gathered around him, I watched Antoinette at the back of the group, her eyes downcast. Her pale beauty was radiant in the sun that shone through the upper windows, illuminating the crypts around us. As Mother talked about her plans for a grand memorial that would take up the expanse of the room, I slipped around the group and finally caught Antoinette's attention. When she saw me, her countenance lit up and she followed me down the hall to the privacy of the founders' crypt.

In the safety of the room, she embraced me, her bony shoulder poking me just below my shoulder. "I am so happy to see you!" she said.

"Me too. How is Brandeis? I hope she is not too awful."

"No, I can survive her. How are you? Is Josepha incredibly boring?"

"I have Amalia to keep me entertained."

"Hopefully not too much! That's my job."

"Well, you got a new puppy. If you get to have a puppy, the least you can do is allow me Amalia," I said, choking back tears as Antoinette played with the curls in my hair. "We don't have much time. Mother will never keep us separated for long, I promise. We'll find a way to send letters to each other."

"Antoinette!" Countess von Brandeis called.

"I have to go. Send me a letter as soon as you can." She rushed away as I collected myself, wiping tears from my eyes.

I slipped into line between Leopold and Luisa as they exited the crypt. "Funny, I didn't see you with us as we gave our love to our deceased relatives," my brother said.

"Must have been a bit too dark. I swear I was there."

"Uh-huh," he said with a little smile.

Soon, Mother, Josepha, Joseph, and the others emerged from the red brick church. "There. Was that so bad?" Mother asked.

Josepha didn't answer her question. She kissed our mother's cheek and got into her carriage. "Don't worry, Mother. I will take good care of her," Joseph said, kissing Mother as well. "Her spirits will lift once we depart."

We watched as the carriage carried my sister away to prepare for her trip to Naples.

OCTOBER 1767

The news came as a shock to everyone in the family. Josepha fell ill with smallpox just as they were to cross the Alps into the Republic of Venice. She was dead within days. While the court was in mourning for her, Amalia and I were summoned to our mother's presence, along with Countess Lerchenfeld.

We knew that only the most private and urgent news was shared from Mother's private parlor. All but one of the walls were covered in fine blue silk; the exception held a floor-to-ceiling mirror—the only testament to the empress mother's vanity. Along the opposite wall was her large sofa, also a matching shade of blue. I had always assumed that she liked to sit there to admire herself in her most regal dress. But on this day, as Mother sat on the sofa, the light from the gold-and-crystal chandelier scattering bits of light all over, her face was stern.

Amalia and I sat in chairs opposite Mother, waiting for her to begin. She fiddled with her cane for a moment, then said, "While we are most aggrieved over Josepha's passing, we have other matters to attend to."

I shifted in my seat, certain there was no way that this conversation was going to end well. "If Leopold is married to Luisa, why can't that be enough to ensure our bond with Spain?" I said. "Why do we need another marriage?"

"Excellent question, Charlotte," Mother said. "I'm glad to see your mind is not completely wasted away from gossip. The reason is that in order to marry Leopold, Luisa had to renounce all rights to the Spanish throne. She does not have any sway with the king. Whoever marries his son Ferdinand will have the ear of King Carlos and will be able to act in the best interests of Austria. Furthermore, Russia is encroaching on our land to the east, and the English have the largest navy in the world. If we can consolidate the Spanish and French Bourbon lines, we can create a defense stronger than that of England and Russia combined. This marriage is for the good of the Holy Roman Empire."

Mother took a moment to let the information sink in. "Amalia, as you know, I previously presented the idea of your marriage to Ferdinand. At the time, Carlos said no. Apparently being five years older than your husband was unacceptable."

I tilted my gaze toward Amalia. She looked just as terrified as I felt.

"But given the circumstances, I have presented him with the idea again. Only this time, I have also given him the option of you, Charlotte."

"No…"

"Charlotte, you are a year and a half Ferdinand's junior, and you most likely will be a better match in King Carlos's eyes."

I was to be married off to the man that I spent so much time mocking. The man whose nose doubled as a tree branch. This wasn't fair. Why was I destined to live in my sisters' shadows? "Mother, you can't do this to me. I am not ready for this. I'll do anything. I'll join a convent. You have always said that it is an honor to serve our Lord." Panic gripped my chest. "Let me do that. I can be a servant to the Lord and a servant to our family. You can have me placed in the Vatican."

"Charlotte."

"Mother, please, anyone but him. Anyone! What about an old widower? That would be good, right?"

"Charlotte, enough." She drove her cane into the tile. Its resounding clink resonated through the room, bringing all my objections to an abrupt end. "There is nothing decided yet. As you will someday understand, I am a queen before I am a mother. The kingdom needs this alliance, and you have a duty to the crown. I have already sent the letter to the king. It's only a matter of weeks before we have a decision."

Amalia and I sat there in stunned silence. Hot tears burned my eyes, and I began to jostle my leg up and down. I needed to get out. I needed to get away from my mother and her stupid insistence that I had a duty to her crown.

"I will summon you when we have news from the king."

Without a further word, I ran. Tears flowed down my cheeks and into my hair. As I dodged servants moving about their business, the words of my mother rang in my ears.

Finding my way to the doors, I burst outside and let out a guttural cry, which made a flock of birds take flight into the clear blue sky. Collapsing to my knees, I pulled thick fistfuls of grass from the earth, roots and all. I dug my fingers into the damp soil. I wanted to sink into the ground, to become a tree and hide, like in the stories of old.

First I was given someone else's name, and now I was to have someone else's intended husband. As Josepha had known she would die from smallpox, I knew I was destined to wed Ferdinand, king of Naples. Wiping the tears with the back of my hand, most likely smearing mud as I did, I made a promise. If this was going to be my fate, then I would make it my own.

Charlotte,   *May 20, 1770*

They took Mops. Poor sweet little Mops. Lerchenfeld told me that I would be allowed to keep him with me, but she was wrong. They said that I am not allowed a dog, because it would dirty my skirts. They plopped him into the waiting arms of one of the Austrian attendees, as if he were a soiled garment.

I know you hated that little thing, and I suppose if I were you, I would feel the same, particularly if I were replaced by a dog. But, you see, when Mother separated us, I thought my world would end. For days and days, I was of the most melancholy state. All I did was cry. I would not even leave my bed until I was ordered. Then Brandeis brought me a puppy. She set him down on the bed, and as if he could feel my sadness, he wiggled under my arm. His little snub nose snuffled until he found my face and kissed me until all my tears were gone. For the first time in days, I rested peacefully with his warm little body curled at my stomach, his soft snores their own little lullaby.

In order to become Dauphine of France, I had to be stripped of all things Austrian, literally and physically. When I first arrived, they made me go into a tent and remove all my clothing. They then moved me to another tent, where I was inspected and then allowed to put clothing back on, only French clothing instead of Austrian.

Oh, Charlotte, everything is so odd. Mother told me,

as I am sure she told you, that I am to adopt all that is French, but I'm not sure if I can. My heart and soul are Austrian and forever will be.

Your Loving Sister,
Antoinette

CHAPTER FOUR

There was always something captivating about the bees that floated through the royal garden: The way their little bodies would dip down from the pollen that clung to their legs and feet. Their buzzing, which sounded like a foreign language as they made their way through the flowers.

That was what the people in the palace reminded me of as I returned from the outside. I didn't know how I made it back to my bed, but I awoke fully clothed to Antoinette pressing a cool, damp towel to my forehead. Hot tears flowed at the sight of her angelic face. "Antoinette, I don't want to marry him."

"Shh," she said, getting up and sitting on the bed so that she cradled my head in her lap.

She hummed as she petted my hair.

"I hate her," I said. My sister let me grip her skirts with my fists and cry into her thighs. "She only cares about power. We're nothing but her pawns. Every one of us. Even Joseph and Leopold. I'm never going to be like her," I sobbed. "Never."

Antoinette said nothing as she continued to pet my hair and hum a sweet tune. My sobs turned to sniffles, and soon I was asleep again, my sister's song echoing in my ears.

Soft knocking at my bedroom door slowly brought me back to consciousness. Small speckles of dust danced in the orange-red sunlight that stretched across the room, casting odd shadows. Sitting up, I rubbed the sleep from my eyes. "Enter." I yawned.

Lerchenfeld came in, carrying a tray of cold meats and small cakes. The countess was everything that my former governess, Brandeis, was not. Lerchenfeld wore simple dresses in muted colors, and though her graying auburn hair was always pinned up, a wisp of it always fell from her temple. "I thought you might be a bit hungry," she said. She set the tray down and stepped back.

Leveling my gaze at her, I asked the main question that had been turning over in my head. "How bad is it?"

Lerchenfeld blanched. "Your Highness, I don't know what you mean."

"I heard you and Mother talk when you revealed Ferdinand's portrait. I know what she said. That my future husband was not capable of being king."

"Well, we don't know if he is going to be your husband yet."

"Please, don't give me false hope. King Carlos turned down Amalia once before. He will do it again. Tell me about my betrothed."

Lerchenfeld sighed as she took a seat at the foot of my bed. "What you need to understand is that the king does not know how to rule. Your mother raised you and your siblings so that you would become the great leaders of Europe. Think what you may about the empress, but she wants to equip you with every tool possible to succeed."

"And Ferdinand's father, does he not want that for him?"

"Of course King Carlos wants what's best for his sons, but he went about it in a different way than your mother. You see, he was told by his physicians that physical exercise would ward off maladies of the mind. After what happened with his eldest son, he made a point of making sure all his children were physically active. Only with Ferdinand, it seems that his regent took this to an extreme." I began to pick at one of the small cakes while Lerchenfeld continued. "Though Ferdinand is sixteen, he has the mind of a child. He is surrounded by flatterers who insist that there is no one better. They say he is fair, though he has been known to give in to the dramatic."

"What do we do then? How do we prepare for the inevitable?"

"You take your studies more seriously. I will be enlisting the economics tutor that assisted your brothers. Though you are fluent in Italian, we will need to make sure you are well versed in the local dialect."

"The local dialect?"

"Yes, it would appear that, because the king prefers to spend his time with the common people of Naples, he has a tendency to primarily speak in dialect."

"Oh," I said. Fat chunks of chocolate cake broke apart in my fingers as I contemplated what my future was going to be. Mother had never hesitated to tell us her stories about what she went through to take control of her kingdom. Of how the day after her ascension both France and Prussia began to pick at her kingdom like vultures. She had had to learn quickly to defend her territory, because her father did not bother to teach her how to rule like a capable monarch. I supposed that was why she was so tough on us. Now, as I took in the bits of cake attached to my fingertips, I wondered if I would be subjected to the same tests she was.

"Charlotte, I don't say these things to scare you. I say them because your mother and I want you to be prepared. Above all, you have the most important role to carry."

I wiped the cake from my hands. "When do we start my new lessons?"

"Tomorrow." Lerchenfeld gave me a sad little smile. "I think you are far more capable than anyone else realizes, and I will do all that I can to give you the tools to be so."

"Thank you," I whispered. But I didn't feel any better.

* * *

Three agonizing weeks later, I was sitting with Amalia in my mother's lavish personal parlor, waiting for the empress to make her entrance. I stared at the floor-to-ceiling mirror on the opposite wall. The two girls reflected within it sat on the same blue cushioned sofa, with the same gold chandelier dripping with crystal. My face was nearly as pale as the white marbled floor, but I was certain that the girls in the mirror weren't as nervous as we were.

"I hope he chooses you," Amalia said, her soft voice echoing off the mirror.

"What do you mean by that?" I whipped my head in her direction.

"It's just that if you marry King Ferdinand, that will leave me to marry the man that I love."

At twenty-one, she was naïver than I was at fifteen. "Marry for love? What are you thinking? We are Habsburgs. We marry for the will of the empress mother."

"Mimi did it," she said. "Mimi was able to marry the man that she loved. Mother granted her wish."

"Mimi always managed to manipulate Mother into doing whatever she wanted her to, and you are not Mimi."

Color rose up Amalia's neck. "Mother can be made to see reason. August said."

"August?"

"Yes, Charles August. He promised that if I spoke to Mother and then he spoke to her, that we could make our love—"

"Wait." I shook my head, trying to comprehend what she was saying. "You mean Charles August, Duke of Zweibrücken?"

"Yes."

"Amalia, August is only a duke. His influence is his little duchy in Prussia. You are an archduchess, a position far higher than his. There is no way that Mother will allow you to be married to anyone with such little influence, much less in a duchy in Prussia of all places."

"You don't know that."

"I do, and if you had any sense, you would as well."

The expansive oak doors opened, and the empress mother swept into the room, followed by Countess Lerchenfeld. I tried to read their passive faces for any sign of what was to come. Even though I knew, deep down, what was going to happen, I hoped that maybe, just maybe, I would be rescued. That fate would smile down on me.

"We have the king of Spain's decision," Mother stated as she sat on her chair. It was a miniature throne of sorts, trimmed in gold, and it sat in the middle of the room. From here, she dictated her orders for the family. "Charlotte, as I am sure you suspected, you are the bride of choice."

My mother continued to talk, but the ringing in my ears blotted out her words. I was to be married to the king of Naples. There would be no more begging. No dealmaking. This was the future that she had chosen for me. Next to me, Amalia gave a little smile of triumph.

"Charlotte? Do you hear me?" Mother asked.

"Yes, Empress Mother," I mumbled. The next several minutes were filled with instructions that I didn't care about. My mind was focused on one thing, and one thing only. I was going to be queen of Naples.

Dear Charlotte,   *April 1768*

In time, my daughter, I hope that you will see that this marriage is the best thing for you. It is an honor to be able to fulfill your duty to the crown and our Lord. Over the years, I have trained you for this, to be a ruler who is just, who is intelligent, who can lead her people.

I expect regular updates on the events of your court life, no matter how minute the detail, so that I can advise you on how best to manage your household. Also, do keep me updated on all personal matters, so that we may be able to plan your future heirs.

Do not hesitate to write me, to let my years of knowledge as a sovereign be a guide for you.

I know that over the years I have been harsh on you. You and I have not always gotten along, and you have felt that my affections were greater for your siblings. But I would assure you that nothing could be further from the truth. I was hard on you because I knew you were capable of great leadership. You are cunning and witty; when combined, those characteristics can be quite charming. These are also going to be the skills necessary to keep your country stable and prosperous.

I know that by sending you to Sicily you will thrive.

Your Mother,

Maria Theresa

CHAPTER FIVE

April 7, 1768

I stood at the altar in my white-and-gold gown, staring at my brother Leopold. He held my hands as we said our vows. I tried to imagine what it was going to be like with Ferdinand standing in front of me instead of my brother. But here, in front of all these people, I felt like I was standing on the edge of a cliff. As my eyes drifted toward the throng of family and courtiers gathered, I could feel the tender squeeze of my brother's hands. His steady gaze held mine as he recited the lines meant for my bridegroom. When the ceremony was done, he kissed both my cheeks and whispered, "You are stronger than this."

The luncheon took place in the same dining room where we had held Josepha's luncheon, complete with the gold-rimmed dinner plates and the bursting red flowers that matched the red drapes leading to the great dazzling spring world outside. Around me, the hum of polite conversation filled the table, but I stared at my plate, pushing around the roast duck, the tiny bones making dams in the brown sauce, as I contemplated my future. Was I always to be subjected to my sisters' fates? My mother clinked her crystal goblet with a spoon, and I let my thoughts rest among the remains of my food as Mother began to speak.

"I'd like to say a few words in honor of my daughter Charlotte." My grip tightened on my fork, either in preparation for what she was about to say or to stab someone. "Though some may say that she is headstrong and impetuous, I say she is a child who has always known her mind. I remember when, at the tender age of seven, Charlotte came storming into my apartments, followed closely by her governess, declaring that she was not to be known as Carolina anymore. That, henceforth, she would be Charlotte. I knew my daughter would not be one who would allow someone else's will to be forced upon her, and that she would be the one doing the enforcing. The Kingdom of the Two Sicilies will be blessed to have you, Charlotte." Mother took a long, deep breath before she continued. "And Austria will not be the same without you."

Tears swam in her eyes, and I thought the great empress was going to cry. This was shocking for me; Mother never cried. Emotion was a sign of weakness. If she cried, the men around her would point out why she could never effectively rule.

But then she recomposed herself, putting the royal smile back on her face. Raising her glass into the air, she declared, "To my daughter Charlotte, the queen of Naples!"

Later that afternoon, as we left the palace, Antoinette stood by the carriages, waiting for me with tears streaming down her cheeks. "I wanted to say goodbye."

I wrapped my arms around her. Not knowing how long it was going to be until we saw each other again, I wanted to hold her close, to take in the scent of lilac from her hair, the way her bony shoulder always poked into mine when we were pressed together. Pushing Antoinette back, I held her at arm's length, taking her in from her soft blue eyes to the dainty point of her chin. She was my sister, and we would forever be connected, regardless of our distance. "We'll write to each other every single day."

"Are you sure?"

"I'm a queen now. Mother has no more power to keep us apart."
I smiled through my tears.

"I am afraid it is time for us to leave," Leopold said, placing
a hand on each of our shoulders. "I promise, Antoinette, that I
will deliver our dear sister safely to Naples and that she will be in
constant correspondence."

* * *

Safely to Naples.

We rode past gently sloping hills of emerald green, marbled with
swaths of red and pink and white. These hills, like rolling waves,
were my constant companions. Never was there a day when I didn't
get to see the beauty that surrounded me. I had always known that
my mother would marry me to some nobleman, but I had never
thought I would leave Austria. It had never even crossed my mind
that she would send me somewhere so foreign—so distant.

My heart lurched. This was quite possibly the last time I would
ever see my homeland. Would there be such beautiful flowers in
Naples? Would the hills be as green? Would there even be hills?
Our expansive royal carriage was lined with gold satin, with large
windows that I pressed my forehead against, watching as the last
of my country went by.

"We'll stop just before the border and then make an early start
into the Republic of Venice in the morning. I'd like to get to Parma
by the evening," Leopold said from the seat next to me. I nodded,
too mournful to form any words. Out of the corner of my eye, I
saw him share a look of worry with Luisa.

I knew what they were thinking, and I did not blame them. It
wasn't like me to not state an opinion of any kind, but words could
not express my sadness at the thought of leaving home. Instead, I
picked up the small wooden box with my initials burned into the

lid. Holding it close to me, I caressed the smooth, cool wood. This box was all that I had left of my home. A gift from Antoinette, it was the place where I kept all my letters. Within those pages, there was still something left of my sister. Her essence infused within each ink-stained word that she wrote. A sudden pang of grief filled me, and I held the box tighter. I was never going to see my sister again.

"Charlotte," Leopold said, placing a warm reassuring hand on my arm. "You needn't be scared. Luisa and I are right here with you. I won't leave Naples until you have settled. I promise."

"Yes," I said, but his words were of no comfort.

"You're worried about Antoinette, aren't you?" Luisa asked.

"There will be plenty of opportunities for you to see each other when you become queen. How many times have I visited Vienna? I think I see you more now than I did when I lived at the palace." Leopold tried to laugh, but the joke died shortly after the words fell from his lips.

"I was your age when we departed Naples. The idea of living anywhere besides the Palazzo Portici was terrifying," Luisa said. "I stood at the stern and watched until Naples receded, convinced that I would never see home again—or even the Italian peninsula, for that matter."

"But you did find your way back," Leopold said with a grin and a sharp gleam in his eyes.

"Yes, I did," she said, smiling back at him. "And I can go back to visit Naples whenever I like."

At the border of Austria and the Republic of Venice, we stopped to stay at a town house that stood looking over Lake Garda. I stood on Austrian soil, eyeing the glorious Alps, which stretched all the way to the heavens while simultaneously their reflection stretched across the clear blue lake. This place was tranquil, but a darkness overcame me while I stood there taking in the beauty surrounding me. I trembled with fear.

"Lovely, isn't it?" my brother said, coming up beside me. "I often like to stop here when I am journeying home from Vienna."

"It is breathtaking."

"Then why do I feel like I am taking you to your execution?" Leopold said.

I looked around us. Luisa busied herself directing the staff that was carting our trunks into the house. It was only my brother and me standing on the terrace. "Perhaps it feels like you are. Austria wouldn't let Josepha leave. What if it does the same to me?"

"Charlotte, please, superstitions have never suited you. If anyone killed Josepha, it was Mother and not Austria. And don't even say it. As much as Mother likes to think it, she is not Austria. She is only a mortal woman."

"Do you know what it is that I am entering into?" I asked.

Leopold stared out onto the lake, his fingers tapping on the stone railing. "I have been briefed," he finally said. "I am aware that it is not the most…ideal situation."

"Leopold, I don't know if I can do this," I admitted. "We both know I was not the first choice for a bride. Mother offered up three of her daughters before she even gave me a thought. She offered Amalia before she offered me. Amalia! And we both know how much of a dolt she is." Staring down at the rocky cliff below me, I momentarily wondered if a tumble from this height would be so bad. "It's not just the position that frightens me; it's what I am going to live with. The stories I hear about him scare me. I can't do this, Leopold. I can't."

"Maria Carolina Charlotte, that is the first and last time I will ever hear the phrase 'I can't' fall from your lips. Ah, don't protest. I have said it, and it cannot be undone." He smiled. "Charlotte, you have to understand, there is nothing that you of all people cannot do." He moved to face me, taking me by the shoulders. "You were always meant to be a queen."

As I looked into my brother's reassuring face, I did all that I could to try to believe in myself the way he did. But no matter how hard I tried, I couldn't find the faith that he had.

Dear Joseph,   *May 1768*

As you requested, I am sending you an update on our sister Charlotte and the precarious situation she has found herself in. I have tried to reassure her, giving her faith in her abilities, but I don't think that will be enough.

I believe that our sister's disposition and that of our new brother Ferdinand are not compatible. Charlotte is antagonistic when faced with any criticism and has a deep desire to have her way in all things. Her temper is that of a passing storm, quick to form but over fast. Countess Brandeis was too harsh on her, and though the empress mother knows and sees all, I wish Charlotte had spent at least another year under the care of Countess Lerchenfeld.

Within a healthy kingdom with a well-balanced husband, these qualities might have been diluted, but I fear that with this young king, anything that he does will only add kindling to the fire that is our sister. Every account that I have heard and read about this man tells me that he is as self-centered, obnoxious, and as spoiled as our sister.

My words may seem harsh, but I feel that I can speak of her as only a brother can. Charlotte was never intended for this role, and I worry for her. I worry that she may not be up for the task of queenship. That is why I feel that in the coming months you and I should exercise our utmost vigilance. Be prepared to step in should the Kingdom of the Two Sicilies need us. I recognize that this alliance is needed now more than ever, but I feel that our sister needs us more. Should this marriage not prove fruitful, it will not just be Charlotte's kingdom in danger but ours as well.

Your devoted brother,

Leopold

CHAPTER SIX

After we crossed through the Republic of Venice, we eventually made our way to the Duchy of Tuscany, my brother's realm. As with my beloved Austria, the lush green hills dipped and curved like gentle brushstrokes in a painting. But where my Austria's hills held flowers, Tuscany's had grapevines. Rows and rows of neatly organized grapes.

"Our biggest export," Leopold remarked as he watched me stare out the window. "Thanks to the monks, we have been able to cultivate some of the greatest wines in all of Europe."

Sulking in the carriage, I could understand how the grapes felt. Soon I would be as tamed as they were.

The cypress-lined entrance led up to the massive Castello di Magona, with its grandiose square turrets and ivy-covered walls. There was a beauty to this new place, a dignified charm that made me feel at ease. We would spend a week here before moving on to Naples.

Once we were settled, I spent most of my days reading. Leopold, knowing me almost as well as Antoinette did, chose an apartment for me at the southernmost point of the castle, one that had a settee by the window and an ample amount of light. I spent most of my mornings there, leaving the window open to let in the spring breeze, scented with lilac and grass. On those tranquil mornings, I could pretend that my future in Naples was not going to happen. That it was nothing more than a bad dream.

But no matter how hard you try, you can't push away the inevitable.

It should have been no surprise, then, that as I found myself reading next to my window, a maid came by with a note from Luisa, inviting me to a picnic with my young niece and nephew in two days' time. I was thrilled to be able to spend time with her and the children. My niece Maria Theresa Josepha Charlotte—or Little Charlotte, as I preferred to call her—was sixteen months old and carried with her the fair looks that the Habsburgs were known for. My nephew Francis, at three months old, was a stout child with a pleasant disposition.

On the given day, a sunny May afternoon, I sat with my sister-in-law as we shaded ourselves with our parasols. Around us, servants bustled about, setting up our picnic table, which was anything but simple. Meanwhile, the children played on the rug in front of us. We laughed as the nurse tickled Francis's chin with a little yellow flower and he wiggled and cooed.

"Children are such a joy at this age. Don't you think?" Luisa said as Little Charlotte flopped onto her lap with a small flower in her fist.

"They certainly are," I said, smiling down at my niece.

"I'm sure you'll have some before long," my sister-in-law teased.

And just like that, the impending marriage I was trying to forget became real. My future sat before me, staring me in the face, daring me to look it in the eyes.

"Oh, Charlotte, you look as if you've seen a ghost. I didn't mean to frighten you." Luisa reached out and patted my arm. "Don't be nervous. That's why I invited you here today. I wanted to talk to you about my brother."

I looked upon my sister-in-law's face anew. She was not just the wife of my brother; she was also the sister of my husband. But I had never truly taken into consideration how alike they might actually be. The broad, bulbous features of Ferdinand were tamed on her. Her nose sloped straight down but didn't have the bulb at its tip, and those small, dark eyes on her looked alluring.

"I know you have heard things—about my family, and Ferdinand in particular."

My back went rigid. "Yes," I responded cautiously.

"Put your mind at ease. Ferdinand is not mad. But having been granted every luxury, he has become spoiled." She tenderly petted her daughter's hair. "Though we should discuss my younger brother Philip and his illness. You see, Philip has always been special to us. Well, to my siblings and me, that is. At first, our parents were overjoyed at having an heir. There were two girls, me included, before they had him, but it became evident at a young age that there was something not quite right. He wasn't like the rest of the children."

Luisa smiled as Little Charlotte wobbled off into the waiting arms of her nurse. She heaved a deep sigh and continued. "Philip liked gloves, but more than that, he liked the feeling of the gloves, the way it felt when they were slipped onto his hands. He would sit with Ferdinand and me, letting us put gloves on him. Glove after glove—he delighted in us layering them. He had a contagious laugh, billowing out from his belly.

"Charlotte, I tell you this because Ferdinand is fond of Philip. Our parents hid Philip away; the heir to the throne was an imbecile, and they were embarrassed by him. Sometimes I think that Ferdinand wanted him around simply because he despised their hypocrisy. But more than anything, Ferdinand wanted him around because he genuinely cares about our brother. Philip is the

Duke of Calabria, and Ferdinand insists that our brother stay in the Kingdom of the Two Sicilies with him. Which I agree is for the best, given that Ferdinand is truly the only one who can care for our brother."

"Does Philip live in the same palace as Ferdinand?"

"Not quite. Philip lives within a private wing at Palazzo Portici. Philip's every need is met by only the best physicians." She took my cold hand in hers. "When it comes to Ferdinand, what you need to remember is that even though he may be...eccentric, he means well. Do not hold the poor education he received at the hands of his regent, Tanucci, against him."

"Your Grace, luncheon is served," one of the servants said with a bow.

"Wonderful. I am famished." She rose from her chair and held a hand out to me. "Let's enjoy the lovely meal and not talk of these serious matters anymore."

Dearest Charlotte,   *July 1770*

Mother has instructed me that I should consult you on matters of marriage and court life. What a turn of events! When we were young, Mother insisted that we not speak because of our terrible influence on each other, and now it seems you are the best person to give me advice. If I weren't so miserable, I would laugh.

Oh, Charlotte, everything I do in France is wrong. I am watched both day and night; any sense of privacy is a fairy tale. I am forced to dress and prepare for my day in front of an audience. Women stand around and watch, as if it is a play. They see everything, from how I am dressed to the application of my cosmetics. There are some things that a woman should be allowed to keep for herself (like the mouche to cover my lone smallpox scar). There is nothing hidden from their prying eyes.

Oh, how they gossip! They don't even hide it. They sit and watch me only to gather for their war against me, a war that I never even began and have no desire to fight.

Perhaps just as annoying is the fact that I cannot simply be passed a goblet of wine. Anything that is given to me must go through a lesser servant first, unless my lady-in-waiting is present. Then the lesser servant hands the object to my lady, who then gets to hand it to me. A simple glass becomes exceedingly bothersome being passed through so many hands. So much so that I have stopped asking. I never thought I would miss Mother's court, with its formalities, but never were they this elaborate. I miss her practicality, the way she would cut through to the heart of any matter. Mother would never have time for such frivolity.

I am continuously scolded about my behavior. I am reprimanded if I spend time with my few friends. I am scolded if I laugh in public. Twice a day, I am required to visit with "the aunts," as I like to call them. They are my husband's dear and precious aunties, but they seem to think they are my mothers. They are perhaps the worst critics of all. They pick at me the way vultures take to a carcass.

Nothing I ever do is right, and worse yet, all Mother can do is critique me from a distance. I turn to her for support, and all I get in return is a lecture. Doesn't she know how much I have to deal with as a new queen?

Doesn't she care that they treat me so poorly? Why must Mother give her opinion when all I want is for her to take sympathy on me?

How did you do it? How did you expel your enemies? I wish you were here with me. That I could have my determined sister by my side once more, to defend me or, at the very least, to entertain me during these horrific royal toilettes.

Your ever-faithful sister,
Antoinette

CHAPTER SEVEN

May 11, 1768

The gentle countryside of Tuscany gave way to the sharp, jutting hills of Naples. In the distance, I could smell the briny scent of ocean as we made our way to Caserta Palace. My new home. The trembling that racked my body grew more and more violent as the carriage drew me farther into the Kingdom of the Two Sicilies. After what felt like years, we arrived.

The only thing that loomed larger than Caserta was Mount Vesuvius herself. From the outside, my future home was grander and larger than any palace that I had ever seen, including Schön-brunn Palace in Vienna. From the outside, the light-red brick palace was the size of two palaces put together, with large windows that let in the bright sun of the Neapolitan afternoon. "Leopold," I whispered, and before his name had fallen from my lips, his warm hand was on my arm, and I breathed deeply, knowing that I still had my brother here to help me.

As we drove through the gates, I could feel my heart thud, each beat sending waves of anxiety through every limb and crevice of my body. The carriage came to a halt, and for a moment we sat there, Leopold and I, in a heavy silence. "We could turn around," I whispered. "Go back to Tuscany."

"You're braver than that," he responded, giving me a quick nod and stepping out of the carriage. Holding out his hand, he led me out into the blinding light.

Once my eyes adjusted, I was looking upon my husband, King Ferdinand of the Two Sicilies, standing in front of a large entourage of courtiers and servants. His face was the same one that had stared back at me from the portrait: the small black eyes, large lips, and long nose. I dropped into a deep curtsy, as Lerchenfeld had taught me to, but the king looked bored. As if this were a game he had already tired of. Ferdinand's eyes swept up my light-blue traveling gown, coming to rest on my bosom, before he turned to a young man next to him. He whispered something; I knew not what, but I could guess. The young noble giggled as he took me in as well.

A portly man, whose belly hung low over his belt, stepped forward. His thick black eyebrows stood out in contrast to his long gray hair. He bowed politely. "La Sua Maestà, it is our honor to finally be able to meet you in person. Let me, Bernardo Tanucci, your humble servant, be your guide. We thank God that you have safely arrived in Naples."

"Yes, we are quite grateful," Leopold answered on my behalf.

I stared at my husband, not sure what to make of him or what kind of person he would turn out to be. Was he the kindhearted, misunderstood man that his sister said he was, or was he the crazed idiot?

"I think Her Majesty is tired and would like to take some time to retire to her rooms to refresh before this evening's feast," Leopold interjected, making me realize that the men were still talking.

"Of course, of course," Tanucci said, snapping his fingers, which signified that it was time for the staff to begin taking away my trunks. Ferdinand elbowed his friend, and the two disappeared into the palazzo.

How dare he. This man who was to be my husband thought no more of me than a passing cloud. Hearing the carriage door close, I turned to see a maid walking away with my box of letters. "Wait!" I called out. The woman stopped. "That box. Bring it here."

Hesitantly, the maid approached, holding the box out to me. "Thank you." The smooth wood soothed me as I cradled it in my arms. Having the box in my hands felt like I had a piece of my sister with me as we entered the palazzo.

"Caserta was initially built for King Carlos. He ordered that the palace be the envy of Europe and that it be more illustrious than Versailles," Tanucci said as we crossed the threshold. "Vanvitelli, the chief architect, is still in residence."

"Is the castle not finished?" Leopold asked.

"Your Grace, Caserta will only be finished when it is the shining light of architectural elegance," Tanucci responded.

At first, I thought Tanucci's words were bluster, but even as we entered the gallery that wrapped along the entire first floor with its elegant arches, I could see that this palazzo was something special.

Looking beyond the arches, I could see one of the beautiful courtyards, enchanted with sunlight that spilled over a multicolored rose garden. But it was the octagonal vestibule that opened up to the most beautiful staircase I had ever seen that took my breath away. The rich notes of violins floated down from the balcony above us as we began to climb the ornate marble stairs that led to a landing guarded by two stone lions. I stared openmouthed at the facade in front of me, adorned with three statues.

"What do those statues represent?" I asked.

"Oh, those." Tanucci stopped on the stairs, turning back to face me. "Each of them represents the reasons why someone would approach a king. The one on the far left asks for a favor, the one in the middle is for protection, and the one on the far right warns not to be dishonest with His Royal Highness. If you will notice, King Carlos is the Maestà Regia in the center statue."

I tried to get a good look at my father-in-law's face as we moved up the stairs but was shooed along by our delegation. My eyes swept over the rest of the entry. The ceiling was adorned in frescoes more pristine than anything I had seen in Vienna. In each corner was a painting depicting Apollo in one of the four seasons, while in the center was a larger painting, in hues of orange and gold, showing the same god lounging amongst his adoring public.

"The marble that you are walking on came from the ruins of the Romans of antiquity," Tanucci boasted. "Each slab is a reminder of the greatness that our kingdom was built from."

I looked over to my brother, his features impassive, as our entourage moved through the winding hallways of the castle. Along the way, I caught glimpses of more magnificent statues and paintings.

"Caserta shall be better than Versailles when we do eventually finish," Tanucci said. "Though I have it on good authority that we smell better." Even as we moved through the palace, servants and maids bustled all around us. Caserta was a city in and of herself.

When we arrived at the royal family's wing, Tanucci bowed. "At this point, La Sua Maestà, I will be taking my leave of you. I wish to discuss certain matters of state with your brother before the formal wedding."

Leopold came up to me and kissed me on both cheeks. "Charlotte," he said, "take this opportunity to get some rest. When I can, we'll have a light supper in your apartments."

And with that, he and the rest of the men were gone, leaving me alone with my new attendants. The guards opened the grand double doors, and I found myself in a bedroom that was far more luxurious than my room at Schönbrunn Palace.

As Tanucci had proclaimed, Caserta was under construction, forcing the royal family to occupy what were meant to be staterooms, with a promise that our quarters in the east wing would eventually be ready for us. Still, the bedroom and royal toilette had been designed with me in mind. The royal toilette was blue, with gold gilding the walls.

My rooms had alternating panels of rich green silk. From the ceiling, a fresco of angels looked down on me with countless strings of pink flowers in their arms. They surrounded an immense sparkling crystal chandelier trimmed with porcelain flowers of yellow and blue. On the far wall was a large canopy bed in a green silk that matched the wall trimmings. And in the center of the room was a large round stone table.

Setting my box of letters on the table, I could imagine countless mornings of letter writing while I nibbled on pastries. I moved to the windows, which looked out over another gorgeous courtyard filled with blooming flowers and newly planted hedges illuminated by the fading afternoon sun. Behind me, my servants scurried about as they settled me into my new home.

Dismissing all my attendants, I flopped onto the bed. Staring up at the golden canopy draped above me, my thoughts drifted to my new husband. Ferdinand's behavior had been downright rude. Who did he think he was? He may be the king, but I was queen. And not just any queen, but a Habsburg archduchess. I was descended from a long line of rulers who commanded respect.

And that comment to his friend, that slack-jawed buffoon who snickered. No one laughed at me like that. They didn't dare. My husband and his little courtiers would learn that I was not to be mocked. As I drifted off to sleep, I dreamed of all the ways I would make his men pay for their disrespect.

Dear Charlotte,   *May 1768*

I would like to take this opportunity to instruct you on the ways of a proper marriage. These words of wisdom come from my experience with being a queen, a wife, and a mother.

We shall begin with the foolish notion of love. It is an unnecessary emotion when it comes to the marriage bed. As monarchs, the only love that we are called to feel is the love for our crown and country. Should you find yourself in love with your husband, then your role as queen will be easier. However, if you find it impossible to love your husband, you must not let him feel this on any account. A man's ego is fragile, and if he feels that you do not care for him, he cannot rule. Thus, he will make your life unbearable. Remember, you are his counterpart in all things. It is imperative that you act as if you are passionately in love with him. Even if you are not, he must feel it.

From the moment you marry Ferdinand, you will no longer be Austrian; you will be Neapolitan. Do not continuously talk about our country or draw comparison between our customs and theirs. There is good and bad to be found in every country, and I pray, daughter, that you find the good in Naples. Your soul may still be Austrian, but your heart and mind will be Neapolitan.

Your Honorable Mother,

Empress Maria Theresa

CHAPTER EIGHT

MAY 13, 1768

Two days later, I stood in front of the looking glass, scrutinizing my features in my wedding dress. I wasn't fooled by the woman who stared back at me. Underneath all the rouge and the sapphires that held the loops and curls in place, I could see the scared fifteen-year-old girl. The girl who wasn't ready for any of this.

Above me, the angels hid their faces, supposedly out of modesty, but I think they knew how much of an imposter I was. Looking at the wall beyond me, I sneered at the painting. Three nymphs, encircled in gold laurel, held on to each other as they laughed. At least they were happy. Taking slow, controlled breaths, I smoothed out my dress. The same gown that I had worn at my proxy wedding I now wore for my husband.

"Charlotte." Hearing my brother call, I made my way into the other room. Leopold's face broke into a gentle smile. "Dear sister, you look even more lovely than you did at your proxy wedding."

"Leopold, I'm not sure if I can go through with this." My heart thumped in my chest, begging to burst. "Ferdinand is truly awful.

The past two days, I have seen him move about the castle, and he is simply the worst sort of royalty, more so than anything I had ever seen in Vienna. He thinks that he is handsome and clever, but he is neither. I don't know how I can be married to this man."

My brother took both my hands in his. "You have a duty to the crown of Naples and the crown of Austria. That is to be your highest priority, above all. You must be the honorable queen that I know you can be." He kissed my forehead. "I will not be far away and will do all that I can to support you."

Leopold escorted me and my entourage through the palace. The royal cathedral, still under construction, was not suitable for our wedding, which meant that we would be married in the royal theater. The theater, a wedding present for me, was an extravagant scene to behold. Located in the west wing of the palace, the walls were covered in rich gold and topped with a dome that was insurmountable in height. Cherubs, dancing next to the Bourbon coat of arms, smiled down on me. Leopold and I walked down the center aisle underneath an extravagant chandelier that sparkled in the flickering lamplight. I could not bear to look to my right or my left. I didn't want to see the whispers of these new nobles who seemed to have an opinion on everything. On the stage stood Ferdinand and a priest with a simple golden altar, which in comparison to the splendor around me was a bit disappointing.

I whispered my words as I exchanged vows with Ferdinand. It was all I could do not to flinch or make a face as his large lips came toward me at the end of the ceremony.

The banquet room was subdued, the ceiling a compilation of angels who watched as the diners supped and laughed in the late afternoon sun. The paintings on opposite walls depicted my father-in-law, Carlos, on a white steed as he valiantly conquered Naples. As my eyes swept over the men strewn about the painted battle-field, I thought back to my lessons with Countess Lerchenfeld.

Lerchenfeld and I had sat in the parlor, reviewing the history books that lay about the table and sofas. "The kingdoms of Naples and Sicily were traded between the countries of Spain, Savoy, and Austria for the better part of a century," Lerchenfeld had lectured, "but it wasn't until Austria was forced into a war with the Turks that King Philip the Fifth of Spain took his opportunity."

I was eyeing a pair of little birds that swooped in the blue-gray sky in the winter world outside our window.

"And what year was this?" Lerchenfeld asked.

I jumped at the question. "1717?"

"1718. It would be nice, Charlotte, if you paid more attention to your studies and less to the birds." Her eyebrow rose as she looked down at me. "Now please explain to me what happened."

I picked at a string on my skirt. "King Philip invaded the island of Sardinia, deposing King Vittorio. He pleaded, with any country who would listen, to restore him to his throne. If they did, he would give them part of his territory."

"Very good." She patted my leg. "You *were* listening. Your grandfather came to the rescue and defeated the Spanish. In return, King Vittorio gave him the island of Sicily. Since your grandfather also controlled the southern half of the peninsula, also known as Sicily, the kingdom became known as the Kingdom of the Two Sicilies, with 'the king of Naples' being the official royal title."

"But we no longer control the Two Sicilies."

"That is right. You see, your soon-to-be father-in-law, Carlos, marched into Naples and took it from your grandfather. According-ing to your mother, this was one of her father's biggest failures. It is on your shoulders to bring the Kingdom of the Two Sicilies back under Austrian influence."

My memories came to an abrupt end when one of my husband's courtiers made a loud congratulatory toast from down the table. "Careful, La Sua Maestà. Before you know it, she'll have you on a leash."

"So long as it is encrusted with jewels," Ferdinand yelled to them as bits of food flew out of his mouth. "If I am to be a kept man, I shall do it with a flourish."

Brooding, I stabbed at my food. I didn't have any appetite for the quail in a rich red wine sauce. All I wanted to do was retire to my rooms and hide.

"Maria Carolina," another one of the courtiers said, approaching us. "We were deeply saddened to hear about the death of your sister Josepha."

"Yes. It was terrible," Ferdinand added. "I wasn't allowed to go hunting for two whole days. It was an utter bore."

"I am sorry that my sister's death was such an imposition to you." I took a long swig of wine to keep myself from saying something I shouldn't.

"Not to worry. Playing funeral cheered me right up," my husband said matter-of-factly.

Choking on my wine, I managed to spit out, "You *played* funeral?"

The courtier suddenly went white and stepped away as Ferdinand began to tell me the details of his game. "We found a young page who looked quite feminine, especially once we put him in a lady's dress. That was my idea, by the way. Stole it from one of the women at court. Then we got a coffin and adorned it with flowers. You would have loved it; we chose only the supplest roses."

My fist tightened around my goblet, but Ferdinand, not understanding that anything was amiss, kept talking. "The best part was that we dripped melted chocolate on his face so it would look like smallpox. I wish I could take credit for that, but, alas, a king must give credit where credit is due. We walked all around the castle in our own funeral procession. Afterward, we went to my inn in town and had a great laugh. I even made the page stay in the dress."

I could feel a flush climbing up my neck as my husband continued to explain in great detail how he had had the page boy prance around pretending he was a princess, pox marks and all.

Scanning the room, I wanted to scream. These people were celebrating a hollow prince.

Having courtiers fawning over the royal family was nothing new. They worshipped Mother because of her strength, Joseph for his wisdom. But these people were different; I could feel their falseness. It emanated from them in waves as they fawned over Ferdinand, building him up. And he fed off it, sucking their bones clean, like the bits of quail that clung to his lips and chin.

And I was supposed to consummate my marriage tonight.

The thought made my stomach churn. Mother had said that I had to make him believe that I loved him. That from this moment on, I had to be completely devoted to the Bourbon crown. Chugging down another goblet of wine, I prepared for what I needed to do: have sex with my husband. Ferdinand belched, and I motioned for a servant to bring me more wine. It was going to be a long night.

As the feast began to wind down, with only a few drunken guests left who slurred their congratulations, I made my way to my rooms. I trembled from fear as my ladies removed my dress and prepared me for the evening. Fighting the urge to cry or vomit, I wished I still had Antoinette by my side. With a small smile, I remembered when she had promised that I would be a regular in her court. We were such children, making promises that we could not possibly keep.

I steadied myself. There was no use in dwelling on the past. In the other room, my husband was waiting for me, and I had a duty to the crown to see through. Taking three deep breaths, I stepped through the doorway into my bedroom. My husband stood by the bed, ready for me in all ways. Without saying a word, I lay on the bed and waited for Ferdinand. I knew what to expect; Lerchenfeld had been frank and did not add flowery words about what would happen. Going to bed with my husband was my job as queen and consort. There was no romance to my duty.

Ferdinand smelled of fresh soap and cologne. He also proved to be fairly attentive, as he caressed and moved softly during our time together, luring me to a pleasure that I didn't expect. His breath hot against my neck began to come in rapid grunts as his thrusts became more forceful. He then paused, letting a great gasp rattle his body.

He rolled off me and patted my arm. And that was it. Within moments, my new husband was softly snoring by my side. Lying on my back, I stared up into the gathered green silk of my canopy. I was now the queen, not only in title but in act. How I felt, I could not say, because I didn't understand it myself. I was now what many considered to be a woman, but I didn't feel any differently than I had before the act.

Still, there was something changed. Not physical—no, it was more of a change within my heart. I felt empowered. Perhaps this was what it felt like to be a woman, to go through this rite of passage and come out on the other side a survivor and, what's more, not hating the act.

I looked over at my new husband with his soft snores. I still didn't like him, but if this was the work that I was to do for the sake of the Habsburg crown, then perhaps it wouldn't be too bad.

Leaning on one elbow, I watched Ferdinand as he slept. He looked like a child, one hand tucked under his pillow, his other draped across his chest. The words of my mother echoed in my head: *Your husband may not be handsome, but at least he doesn't stink.* And frankly, my mother was right. Ferdinand never even had a shadow of a beard. Even his fingernails were clean. I yawned and slipped back down into my pillow, thinking about this new Charlotte and what opportunities she promised.

It wasn't until the wee hours of the morning that I heard Ferdinand stir by my side. Sitting up in bed, I watched as he began to dress.

"Where are you going?"

"Hunting, of course."

"Hunting?" I looked around the darkened room. "What time is it?" I could barely make out his form as he stood against the soft reddish-gold light that seeped between the drapes.

He smiled in the darkness. "It is quite late for me already, and to not hunt on a beautiful day like today would be an utter sin."

And with that, Ferdinand left me in the darkened room so that he could go out hunting. Now that I was already awake, I wrapped myself in my robe and sat down to write letters. One to Mother, letting her know that her daughter had faithfully accomplished her duty, and one to Antoinette, letting her know the details of my wedding.

June 1768

Adjusting to life at court was another matter entirely. Trailing behind Ferdinand, everywhere he went, were his hunting dogs. Not three or four, as Mother would have by her side. My husband liked to have all fifteen of his hunting beasts following him around. His shaggy hounds barked and tumbled over each other as they raced down the royal hallways, defecating wherever they saw fit. The dogs I could get used to; a decent maid could help solve most of the messes. What was more troubling was that the court lacked entertainment.

The nobility gossiped and carried on with their follies amongst themselves, but overall, the court was boring. Outside of Ferdinand's games and his times at the inn or with one of his pets, there was nothing to distract, let alone anything resembling *culture*. Plays—proper plays, not put on by my husband—were rare. Even the walls of the palace were bare. They had not invited any artists to come and decorate beyond the frescoes that had been commissioned by King Carlos. It was as if the court had given up on doing anything without the influence of Spain.

It was hard not to miss Vienna; it wasn't simply the shimmering palace and art that I missed. It was the gaping absences of my sisters. Sadly, I had grown accustomed to not having Antoinette, but the others, even Amalia, who was preparing for her marriage to the Duke of Parma, would have been a welcome presence. There is something about sisters that goes beyond the connection that you have with any other living soul. Sisters were bonded in a shared womanhood. I could never recapture what I had in Vienna, but I could seek out a bond with my ladies or, at the very least, find some ways to entertain myself.

It was a sunny afternoon when my ladies and I stood in the reception hall outside the royal throne room. Neapolitan women dressed in the fashions of the Spanish court, with high necklines and hemlines that fell below their ankles. Their dress was far more conservative than anything we wore in Vienna, which tried to compete with the French styles.

"I think a piece by Handel would be quite appropriate," I said to the small group of women gathered around me. "He was always a favorite of my mother's, and…"

The rest of the words died as my ladies began to lift their skirts and screech so loudly that I swear glass cracked. Soon women were running, pushing through the double doors as an army of furry little creatures scurried to safety. I looked through the melee to find my husband crouching down next to a wire cage, a rat in hand, laughing at the chaos.

"You!" I yelled, storming toward him. "What is the meaning of this?"

Ferdinand looked up at me, tears streaming from his eyes. "Did you see the way they ran? All over a few rats!"

I got down so that I could meet his gaze. "They ran because you are a spoiled, selfish child." I grabbed the rat from his hands, holding it tightly as it struggled against my grip. "If you do anything like this again, neither you nor your rats will be laughing. Do you hear me?"

Ferdinand took the rat back from me. "Do not hurt Lord Prospero."

"Lord Prospero?" I asked in confusion.

"Yes." Ferdinand clambered up from the floor. "That is the name of my favorite pet rat." He stormed from the hall, and I followed, taking large steps to keep up with his strides.

"I know that you feel you can do whatever you want," I said, "but what you did to my ladies was rude."

"Rude?" Ferdinand turned to me. "I was only having a little fun. I'm allowed to do that, because I am king."

"Fun? This is inappropriate behavior for a court, much less a king."

We had reached the door to his rooms. "Well, maybe I don't want to be king!" he exclaimed, attempting to slam the door in my face.

I thrust half my body inside before he could close it. Ferdinand had always come to my rooms, and now I knew why. Though he was always clean and presentable, his bedroom was anything but. Ducks, a whole flock of them, wandered everywhere. Feathers floated through the air as the birds hopped down from his unmade bed. One waddled around his blue marbled table picking at crumbs. Covering my face with my sleeve, I tried not to gag at the smell.

"What is this?"

"This is my kingdom," he said, shoving Lord Prospero into a cage. "That is Signor Waddles," he said, pointing to the duck on the table. "He is rather bossy. That there is the Marquis di Torta Limone. I gave him that title because he is quite fond of the lemon cakes from the kitchen."

"I don't care about your ducks."

"Well, if you are going to talk to the Marquis di Torta Limone like that then you can just see your way out."

Ferdinand turned from me and began to feed an old cake to one of the birds. Steeling myself, I strode to the windows and threw each one open. Fresh spring air rushed into the room as I proceeded to move about, much to Ferdinand's protests, shooing the ducks out the windows.

"What is the meaning of this?" Ferdinand exclaimed, trying to close the windows.

Blocking his way, I pushed him back. "I will not have this. Not in my court."

"This is not your court. It's mine. Just like this kingdom. Everything is mine, not yours."

"Then act like it!" I bellowed. "You only want to be a king when it suits you. When you can have your fun with none of the burden. Being a leader does not work like that. The people of Naples are counting on you. It is time you behave like the man they expect you to be and not a child."

"What would you have me do, oh wise queen?"

"My ladies, they will not be the victims of your games anymore. If I see another rat loose within the castle, I will sic your dogs on it."

"They would never."

"They are dogs. They act as their nature dictates, which is more than I can say for you," I spit. "Furthermore, you'll have this room cleaned...daily. You are a king, and you will not only act like one but live like one."

"And what if I don't give in to these demands?"

"I can take my staff and move to another castle. I don't have to stay here. While you are staying here like a cuckold, I will move to Portici, without you." When he didn't flinch, I continued. "I'm sure my mother would be interested in a letter from me detailing your games. The empress of Austria would most certainly give a full report to your father on what has happened."

Ferdinand's face fell. "You wouldn't."

I stepped closer to him and sneered, "I would." Striding to the door, I called over my shoulder, "Clean up this mess!" And I slammed the door.

Charlotte,   *June 1768*

It troubles me that the household staff that attends you does not do so to our specifications. I shall be sending you a team of attendants to care for you and to train the rest of your staff. It is important to be a shining example to your people to live a righteous life, both within the soul and within the home.

I would recommend that the ladies that you surround yourself with be of the most pious disposition. Do not lend yourself to coquettishness nor allow it to be tolerated amongst your inner circle. Keep them occupied with noble pursuits, for you shall be judged against the weakest of your ladies.

Concerning the matters of your husband, I understand especially in this situation how hard it can be to find some commonality. I recommend that you show an interest in the things that he likes to do. I have heard that Ferdinand is quite fond of hunting, so use that to your advantage. Share that interest with him. Even if you do not like it, make an effort to do so. Once you and he can share mutual interests, can you make a friendship. For really, that is the basis needed for you two to rule effectively as equals.

Gain his trust. It is critical that during this time you find common ground with your husband. You must become his most trusted advisor in all things, not only for the sake of the Two Sicilies, but for Austria.

Yours,

Empress Mother

CHAPTER NINE

MAY 27, 1768

At first, Ferdinand tested me, to see if I would pick up everything and move to another castle without him. In the morning, I walked into the family parlor and found Ferdinand sitting at my chess table with the Marquis di Torta Limone. He gave me the briefest acknowledgment from the other side of the room as he fed little pieces of *sfogliatella* to the vermin. I turned on my heel and ordered the nearest maid to begin packing my things. By the time the carriages were loaded, the Marquis di Torta Limone was enjoying his new life in the barn and I had a new diamond bobble around my neck as an apology.

But now that things were quiet, I was at a loss as to what to do with myself. In the weeks after our argument, Ferdinand was out with his games, either hunting or visiting his inn—I had lost track of which one it was that entertained him each time. Without him, the other nobles grew bored and disappeared from the palace.

Morning light seeped in through the windows as I wandered by myself, my footsteps leaving haunting echoes in the empty rooms. Soon my attention turned to the grounds of Caserta, with her gently sloping pathway leading to a waterfall in the distance. I summoned my lady Sabina, the Marchesa di San Marco, and we set off for a stroll. Sabina was tall and stately, her black hair always swept up into the most fashionable of styles. Even the wisps of hair that blew into her face from the light westerly wind were elegant.

"Have you lived at Caserta for long?" I asked her.

"Yes," she said. "My husband and I came here shortly after we were married. My family hails from Apulia, but given that my husband is a longtime friend of Ferdinand's, we just had to come here." She took my arm as we continued to walk along. "I, too, was disheartened when I first arrived. These western shores have nothing on the ocean off the coast of Bari, but you will soon see that Caserta—and Naples, especially—will steal your heart. You just have to surrender to all that is *bella Napoli*."

I patted her arm. "I shall yield to your wisdom."

It was truly a lovely day, and I could feel my spirits lift with every step I took. Perhaps Sabina was right: I just needed to let myself get swept up in the beauty of my new country. Birds sang in the nearby trees, and I didn't feel so trapped by the palazzo. I stepped closer to the edge of the lawn to get a better look at one of the pools below me. That was when I was startled by movement at the edge.

"La Sua Maestà, I am dreadfully sorry." The young man climbed the steps and gave a deep bow. He was tall, with thick wavy brown hair. "I am Carlo Vanvitelli. My father and I are the architects working on the palace and the gardens."

"No offense taken," I said. "I was just admiring these pools. Though they look a bit…" I searched for the right word so as not to offend the palace architect.

"Unfinished?" He smiled, revealing charming dimples. "Yes. My father, Luigi, has given everything to finish this palace and its grounds." Carlo took a deep breath, his eyes sweeping over the expansive lawns. "And it would appear that I will be completing his legacy. My father and I are the reason why you were married in a theater and not the chapel, and for that, I must offer my humblest apologies. There have been several delays, which is bound to happen when you set about to make a work of art the size of this. But since you are here in the garden, may I give you a tour?"

"My lady Sabina and I would be delighted."

"There is the aqueduct, which we have just completed," Carlo said as we began to move up the garden. "The water flows through at the far end and then to each individual pool." I stood enraptured by Carlo as he explained his plans for the garden. "We plan on making statues and fountains finer than anything you will find in Rome. My father was the apprentice to Nicola Salvi himself and had a hand in creating the Trevi Fountain."

"You are quite proud of your father."

"Yes, he is a great man. It was quite a coup when King Carlos lured him from Rome and the pope. But this palazzo, it was his opportunity to build something all his own. Something that would last for centuries, long after the Vanvitelli name has faded from history."

In the few moments I had been speaking with him, I could picture it. All of it. The fountains that glittered in the sunlight. The opulent statues that dotted the landscape. Even going further, the cathedral that rivaled those in Rome. This place was special, and I wanted to share in the Vanvitelli vision. "You mentioned that there were some delays?"

"Yes. We have not had an adequate amount of funding. Excuse me, La Sua Maestà, I apologize for speaking so candidly. *Mi dispiace*, but it just feels as if Caserta is being neglected. I don't know what is happening, but what was once an endless stream of funding is now a slow trickle. Still, I should not feel too bad about it. At least we are still getting some funding. Other projects within the city are not so lucky."

"What do you mean?"

"I believe I have said too much. Please excuse me."

* * *

For the rest of the day, my curiosity about what Carlo meant filled my head. I wanted to know why construction had stopped and was determined to talk with Ferdinand about it. The problem was that the only time I had alone with him was when he visited my rooms, which did not leave much time for discussion.

Though we rarely had a meal alone, I decided I would broach the subject during supper. At our table, Ferdinand and I sat at the center. To my right sat Sabina, while on the other side of Ferdinand sat his regent, Tanucci.

When Ferdinand was apart from Tanucci, he was reasonable and, if I dared to say it, enjoyable to be around. But the moment Tanucci appeared, whispering in my husband's ear, Ferdinand changed; his hunger for the cruel malice he found humorous took over. Tanucci hung over my husband's shoulders, barely allowing him to think for himself. He was always there to bring him back to his way of thinking: the correct way, the Spanish way. Any original ideas about governing Naples were brushed aside, leaving Tanucci and his men to control everything. The men Tanucci surrounded himself with worshipped every word that fell from his greasy lips, and they sat in a place of privilege above all other courtiers, me included.

"Charlotte, how was your day?" Ferdinand asked. His eyes swept the dining room as he sipped his wine.

"I had a wonderful walk through the garden."

"Did you now?" He smiled at something in the distance.

"Yes. I understand there are many projects that have yet to be finished."

"Why do you want to worry yourself over that?" Tanucci leaned forward. "Matters of state are too troubling for a pretty face such as yours."

"Though I appreciate your compliment," I responded through gritted teeth, "I still would like to know about the status of architectural projects within my palazzo."

Tanucci waved a hand in dismissal of me and started up a

conversation with Ferdinand about his latest hunting adventure. I set my fork down and declared, "I'm no longer hungry. I'll be retiring to my rooms."

"Would you like me to visit your rooms tonight?" Ferdinand whispered in my ear.

"No, I am not feeling well," I said. And with that, I stood up and left the hall, leaving the men in my wake.

Unable to concentrate on my book, I stared up at my canopy and decided that I would find a way to talk with my husband alone. But how? He was always with his obnoxious friends or being followed around by the rancid Tanucci.

When Sabina arrived at my doors the next morning, we set off to find my husband. We eventually made our way to my husband's office, where we were greeted by an elderly man, who appeared to be his secretary.

The small room within the stateroom section of the palace was lined with books. A lone window allowed light to pour in over the old man's desk. Upon seeing us, his round face was in a state of complete shock. Quickly he dropped his quill and rose to his feet, bowing so deeply that his forehead touched the top of the desk. "La Sua Maestà," he said, "to what do I owe the pleasure?"

"I'd like you to set aside some time for the king and me alone. I'd like to have a proper meeting."

"Yes, La Sua Maestà. When would you like?"

"This afternoon?" I ventured.

"Oh, I am sorry. The king is hunting today."

"Very well then. Tomorrow?"

"Tomorrow he is unavailable. He is playing fishmonger in the morning."

"Fishmonger?" I looked in confusion from the secretary to Sabina, standing by the door. "What is this game, fishmonger?"

"Well, fishmonger," the secretary blustered, "is someone who sells fish."

"Yes, I know what a fishmonger is!" I exclaimed, feeling my patience ebb. "But how does my husband make a game of it?"

"The king goes to the markets early in the morning and buys all the fishermen's catches." The secretary gulped. "He then gives the fish away to the people, and in turn, the people pretend to pay him."

I was at a loss for words. "What about in the afternoon?"

"He always plays chess with the elderly men of the city, in the park in the afternoons."

Taking in a steadying breath, I asked, "What of the day after that?"

The secretary consulted his schedule. "La Sua Maestà will be away for the weekend...playing innkeeper."

"I am the queen! When can I have an audience with my own husband?"

The secretary fumbled with the pages before him. Finally looking up at me, he said, "Tuesday." I was relenting, but he added, "Two weeks hence."

Rage started to fill me, but Sabina quickly took me by the elbow. "La Sua Maestà, I think I have a better idea."

"And what would that be?" I snapped.

"Let's meet the king halfway. At one of his games. We'll pay him a visit tomorrow morning while he plays this fishmonger game of his."

The next morning, Sabina and I set out for the fish market. A large crowd gathered as seagulls swooped under the overcast sky and the waves crashed into the rocks below. In the distance, I could hear Ferdinand's voice above the fray.

"Fresh fish! Come and get your fresh fish!"

I stepped forward, the people around me took notice and bowed, making room for me to approach. I watched as my husband, dressed in the clothing of a common man, complete with a cap on his black hair, helped an old woman. She wore the uniform of a widow, from the little black scarf on her gray head to the old, scuffed shoes on her feet.

"Signora, if you are not sure which fish to choose, might I recommend the swordfish? It is quite hearty, and perfect with a bit of lemon."

The woman shook her head, and some of the gray hairs slipped from the knot at the nape of her neck. "That is too much for me. I live by myself, and it would go to waste."

"Ah, I see. Quite the dilemma." His eyes swept over the table, trying to help her decide. "Quite the dilemma," he repeated. Ferdinand didn't try to rush the woman or force her to make any decisions she was not ready for. There was a gentleness about my husband that I had never seen before. For all his games and immaturity, he was kind. Perhaps it was as Luisa said: There was something more to him than the boyhood foolishness that Ferdinand exhibited.

"Might I make a suggestion?" I asked.

A large smile broke across Ferdinand's face as he called out, "*Regina mia!*" As he proceeded to bow, he said, "I would be honored if you would grace us with your opinion, given that I am but a lowly fishmonger, lucky to be a peasant in your kingdom."

I couldn't help but return his smile and feel a bit of the fun that he was having. "I think the lady might like the perch. They aren't too large, and perhaps she may be able to salt-cure it. Make it last longer."

"*Che bellissima!* Yes, signora, I think the queen is right. The perch would be an excellent choice."

The old woman thought a moment and then nodded her consent. Ferdinand carefully wrapped the fish in paper and handed it to the woman. She pretended to pay him and then went on her way. Ferdinand roguishly leaned against one of the poles as he turned his attention to me. There was something almost charming about him there amongst the fish souring in the morning sun. "And, regina mia, what fish can I get for you today?"

I made a show of trying to decide which fish to get. I cocked my head, an attractive affect that I knew to always produce a favorable response. "I have it on good authority that the king has a penchant for fried mussels."

"Well, then you should buy the whole lot." He leaned against the pole. "Is there anything the queen would like to purchase for herself?"

"Yes, I am quite fond of *mazzancolle*. I should like to purchase as many as you wish to part with."

"*Sì*, La Sua Maestà."

"And would you be so kind as to have someone deliver it to the palazzo for me?"

"I shall deliver to the queen whatever her heart desires. I am but your humble servant," he said with a bow.

Arm in arm, I walked with Sabina back to Caserta. "That was strangely entertaining," I said.

"It was, wasn't it? Perhaps we should watch more of his games."

"The people seem to love him. Perhaps I could use that to my benefit."

"How so?" Sabina asked.

"The common person, whether they are from Naples or any other country, doesn't know what they want. But they know what they see. If they can see my husband as their savior, they are more likely to support the monarchy." I smiled at the thought. "He can have the heart of the people while I seek the heart of the nobility."

Charlotte,   *June 20, 1770*

Mother advised me on the ways of marriage, that I am to do all that I can to make my husband love me and that if

I cannot, then I must find some commonality. But what if I cannot make him love me or if he doesn't take an interest? She never talked about what happens then.

That first night, when the attendants left Louis and me, we sat in the quiet of the room, listening to the clock on the mantel as the seconds ticked away. I tried to start a few conversations with him, but they quickly died. After an hour of torture, he patted my hand, rolled over, and went to sleep. To think that Lerchenfeld went to such pains to make sure I understood what I was supposed to do!

Ever since our wedding night, I have gone out of my way to find something that I can connect with him on. I was so relieved when it was suggested that we go on a hunt. You know how much I like to hunt. But when I arrived at the hunt, he sputtered a little and quickly got on a horse and rode away! He won't even look at me. It is as if I repel him.

It would not bother me if we continued in this matter. I could be perfectly happy being left to my own devices, but there is so much pressure on me to provide an heir. The court gossips about my husband, and I assume you know whom they blame. When did things change for you and Ferdinand? Was there something that you did that helped?

Your Sister,
Antoinette

CHAPTER TEN

June 1, 1768

The golden afternoon sun streamed down across the two-tone brown tile floor as my ladies and I gathered to sing "Thine Be the Glory." We had secured an empty room near the theater, overlooking one of the inner gardens.

"Let's start from the beginning, ladies," I said.

> Thine be the glory,
> Risen, conqu'ring Son;
> Endless is the victory,
> Thou o'er death hast won;
> Angels in bright raiment
> Rolled the stone away,
> Kept the folded grave-clothes
> Where Thy body lay.

I heard the soft click of the door behind me. Looking over my shoulder, I could see Ferdinand standing by the door. He waved for us to continue singing, and so we did. That is, until we heard him sing. As he belted out the chorus, his voice, sharp and proud, rose above all the others. It didn't matter that he couldn't carry a tune; the joy that he felt while singing was evident in his features.

After the song was over, he looked about the room. "That was wonderful," he said. "Shall we do it again?"

"We have been practicing for well over an hour," I responded. "I believe my ladies need to rest."

"Oh, well, I suppose that is understandable." His smile fell. "But would it be possible for me to sing with you at your performance, for the court?"

"It would be our honor," I said.

His smile returned, and the ladies begin to file out of the room, leaving me an opportunity, at last, to be alone with Ferdinand. "La Sua Maestà," I said, "it is a lovely afternoon. Would you be so kind as to take a turn about the garden with me?"

For a moment, he opened and closed his mouth, then said, "Yes, I think that would be most lovely."

He held out an elbow, and we left for the garden.

The sun was bright, and I was thankful for the shade of my parasol as we walked down the path. For a while, we were silent, and I searched my mind for something to say. "It's lovely, isn't it?"

"Yes," he said, looking over the pools.

"I spoke with Carlo Vanvitelli."

"The architect?"

"Yes. He shared his beautiful vision for this place. This garden, in particular, with its majestic fountains and statues. It would be a place for us to hold the finest balls in all of Europe. Under your reign, we could build something that lasts for generations."

Ferdinand looked out over the lawns, taking his time as he watched the tufts of flower seeds that dipped and swirled around us. "I want to make my father proud, but more importantly, I want to make the people happy. They have so little, and I have all this!"

He opened his arms wide, to indicate the grounds of Caserta. "The people are all so…true."

"True?"

"Yes. They don't pretend to be anything that they are not. And the wigs, they don't wear those. I know it is fashion, but I find it disturbing when a person covers up any part of their head. It is as if they are hiding their true self."

"No masquerades. Duly noted." I smiled, and Ferdinand chuckled softly next to me. "I find it noble that you want to make the lives of your people better. Is that why you play fishmonger?"

He shrugged. "I play fishmonger because I like to believe that I could be a good fisherman. Either that or an innkeeper."

"But what you do for our subjects is quite noble. The people appreciate it. I can see it in their faces."

He shrugged in dismissal. "The people who come to the fish market, that's the only time they eat for a whole week. A week! It's not fair."

"There are things you can do, *we* could do, to help the people."

"The people," he whispered as we began to walk again. "Yesterday, when I was playing chess in the park with my friend Giorgio, he told me about the years he spent as a clockmaker. Imagine that: your whole life spent building clocks. The ticking alone would drive me mad. But he liked it. He said that it was a comfort to him. He keeps a clock in his bedroom; you know, the ticking helps him sleep." He looked out over the lawns again.

"I simply like to be around the people, listening to their stories. If I make their lives better, then so be it. I'm not one to pass judgment, but I want to give them things that they need or that would make their lives just a little more pleasant. Like a base wage so they never have to go hungry. I could create a whole new city and call it Ferdinandanapoli.

"It's a nice thought." His eyes glowed with enthusiasm. "Tanucci said we could never do it. But it would be good to take care of the friends I play chess with. Giorgio's wife died three years ago. He's been on his own since. I wanted to move him into Caserta, but Giorgio refused. He says he couldn't manage the stairs. Palaces have too many stairs, after all. Plus he has a nice arrangement with the widow next door. Living with me would ruin that."

I couldn't tell if my husband was insane or simply a misunderstood savant. It was clear he had a heart for the people, and they, in turn, loved their Re Nasone, King Big Nose. But what of the nobility? There was no way that we would be able to accomplish anything if they were not on our side. If we were going to find a way to rule Naples, I had to find a way to win the nobles' devotion. "Tell me," I said, "what other games do you enjoy?"

"Hunting," Ferdinand answered right away.

"There is nothing more thrilling than chasing down prey," I said. "It is perhaps the most basic of human instincts, yet it allows us to remain civilized."

"You like to hunt?"

"Yes, I do. It was one of my favorite activities with my sister Antoinette. The empress mother even had special riding outfits made for us."

"Is that so? Well, the court and I will be hunting again next week. Perhaps you should come with us."

"I would like that very much," I said as we made our way back to the castle. The truth was, I hated hunting. The killing of innocent beasts. The horses. It was not the kind of activity that I readily took part in. It was true, however, that Antoinette loved it so much so that Mother had to practically give a royal proclamation to force her to change out of her riding costume. Antoinette was always begging our brothers to take her on their outings, and she did have a special outfit made just for her.

But there were larger issues at stake than my dislike of hunting. I needed to make a positive impression with the Neapolitan nobility, and I needed to make a stronger connection with my husband. It was as Mother had said—*find common ground*—and it appeared that the only way for me to do that was to go hunting with my husband and the court.

* * *

On the given day, I arrived at the palace stables, ready in my hunting costume made of the deepest green with a gold trim. The collar of my coat was open, revealing exquisite white lace ruffles, which were mirrored around the cuffs. On my head, I wore a black tricorne, trimmed in a gold lace to match my riding costume. It was tilted ever so slightly to the right, to show off my best features. I found my way to two of the most popular nobles at court, who were deep in conversation as they waited for their horses.

"Regina mia, you look quite dashing today," Signor Branciforte said with a flourish and a bow. Nicolo Branciforte was a regional governor and a favorite of Ferdinand's. "But I wonder, how will we ever be able to pay attention to the hunt when we have such beauty to distract us?"

I smiled at his charm, but before I could say anything, the other nobleman, the black-haired council member who had been aloof since my arrival, clasped Branciforte's shoulder. "Come now, Nicolo, don't tell us that all this time you have been so distracted by beauty that you haven't been able to shoot a single animal."

"I'll have you know, Medici, that just two weeks ago I shot a stag," Branciforte quipped.

"Yes, but did anyone see you do it?" Medici responded. "I have it on good authority that any deed, however small, does not count unless it is witnessed by those who would seek to amplify your ego."

"If Signor Branciforte says that he shot a stag," I said, addressing the men, "then I believe it is up to us to take him at his word, for what is a nobleman but a man of unflinching honor, regardless of the beast's size."

"Tell me, La Sua Maestà," Medici asked as our horses were being led out. "Have you ever fired a weapon before?"

I mounted my horse and looked down at the young nobleman with the dark eyes. "I am a lady, signor. You should know I have a great many weapons in my arsenal."

The Medici name was one of the oldest and most prestigious names on the whole peninsula. This particular Medici, named Luigi, was of the Ottaviano branch. His great-grandfather broke away from the Florence Medicis in order start his own *comune* east of Naples. Though they were separated, they still kept their ties with the Florence line. I had watched him as the rest of the nobility vied for an opportunity to speak with him. I knew that I needed to make him an ally.

We rode out into the lush green forest of Naples. The golden morning sun shone brightly through the gaps in the tree canopy. Our company moved through the moss-covered trees, Ferdinand at the front and I a short distance behind. It was while we were moving through the forest that I saw it. Standing on a hill, looking down at us as we rode by. A lone two-toned gray wolf. Stopping my horse, I made eye contact with the majestic beast. Everything fell away; it was solely the wolf and me. Two equals in a lonely world, each with our own hunt. A cloud passed overhead, and he was gone.

A horn blasted, breaking the quiet of the forest. Solidly at the center of the pack, I kept up with the men as we galloped through rippling streams and jumped over fallen trees. The company came to a stop just in time for me to see Ferdinand raising his gun and shooting a wild boar. He missed its head, but his shot hit the beast's shoulder. The boar stopped and took a few steps back, then charged—directly at me.

The nobles were scrambling to get off their horses to save me, but with my gun at the ready, I raised it and shot the beast right between the eyes. My heart pounded like hooves as I watched it fall. The shocked expressions of the men mirrored my own as I lowered my gun.

That night, as we supped on wild boar with the court, Tanucci patted my husband's shoulder. "I would like to congratulate you on such an excellent catch. It was delicious."

"Actually, my good man, the credit for the kill must go to my queen. The boar came right for her, and she raised her gun and shot it, right between the eyes. She is an excellent marksman."

Daintily, I dabbed the corners of my mouth with my napkin and looked up into the surprised face of Signor Tanucci. "Yes, I have a knack for taking down a threat." I held Tanucci's glare until he broke away. I slipped another sumptuous piece of boar in my mouth and chewed slowly, with the flavor of victory filling my mouth.

My Dear Sister,   *January 1777*

Mother is on one of her battle charges again. I foolishly thought that once I was married and away from Vienna, I would be able to escape her sharp tongue. I should have known we could never get far enough away from her reach.

This time, Mother's tirade is about my "spirit of dissipation," as she so lovingly refers to it. Our Austrian ambassador reports regularly on my behavior to Mother. Does your ambassador do the same? It is quite bothersome, don't you agree?

But I digress. I shall not spend this letter complaining

about my ambassador when it is Mother who has received the vast majority of my ire, and I hers.

Versailles feels more like a prison of mirrors than a palace, and it was only when I was able to ride out on a hunting excursion that I felt free. On more than one occasion, I even challenged Philippe, Duc de Chartres, to a horse race. This began a friendly rivalry, but I looked forward to that freedom more and more each time. According to Mother, it is no way for a queen to behave, especially if my husband is not present, but Louis is never there. He is either sad, for reasons that he cannot express, or he is in a drunken stupor somewhere in the palace. Mother, of course, will hear none of this. For I am the queen and must lead by adopting her pious nature.

Speaking of piety, the foul Austrian ambassador has written to her about my gambling. You tell me I must ingratiate myself to the nobility, that I must have their hearts in order to succeed, while Mother writes pages and pages of letters imploring me to go to church more. That is how I will win over my rivals, she says. Clearly Mother has forgotten what it was like to be around the French. Gambling at the royal salon is how the nobility amuses themselves. It is how they communicate. I have tried to explain this to her, but it makes no difference. That woman seeks to take away anything that gives me joy.

Your Loving Sister,
Antoinette

CHAPTER ELEVEN

JUNE 1, 1768

I was in the midst of writing a letter to my mother, thanking her for the maids that she had sent me, when Sabina came to my rooms. She sat at my table, pushing my breakfast tray to the side. "There is a matter I wish to discuss with you."

I set my quill down, folding my hands in front of me. "Go on."

"There was a custom that was once practiced when Queen Amalia was here. The people would present their daughters who were of age to the queen. She in turn would gift them with twenty thousand ducats for the girls' dowries. It has been suggested that we reinstate this practice."

"Would the treasury be able to afford this?" Immediately my mind went to Tanucci and the iron fist he had over the government, along with its finances.

"The money comes from the city, which in turn comes from the nobles. They are the ones requesting that we do this. It is a way for them to show their favor for the common people of Naples. The dowry fund is filled by them every year. If it is unused…"

She raised her empty palms, as if in surrender. "It is no secret that the nobility is not fond of Tanucci's financial advantages."

"If I do this, I simultaneously anger Tanucci and make a good impression on the nobility?"

"Yes, and because you have the backing of the nobility, there would be no way to stop you."

"Then, Sabina, what are you waiting for? Make the arrangements."

"Arrangements are already being made. We only needed your permission. We plan to hold the event on June tenth. There will be a ball in your honor featuring all the young women before gifting them each with their dowry."

"It sounds like this has been planned for a while."

Sabina gave her most devilish smile, the one that made her red lips curl up only at the corners. "Ever since your safe arrival in Naples."

* * *

The grand vestibule, located at the center of the palace, with floor-to-ceiling windows, felt magical as the moonlight streamed into the octagonal room. Tiny candles lit up the entire space, giving the effect of a thousand twinkling stars that gleamed against the polished red marble pillars. Looking up, I couldn't help but marvel at the ceiling, each section containing a perfect geometric pattern of squares and roses. On the floor, girls from all over the city twirled and swayed, their brightly colored dresses looking like a garden full of flowers. Each of them—the daughters of merchants, tradesmen, and paupers—knew that by being here tonight they could have the potential to make a good marriage.

Sipping my wine, I delighted in the success of the evening as the violins cut through the chatter with a delicate melody. The Marquis di Domenico gave a deep bow and said, "La Sua Maestà, we would like to say what an honor it is to have you here with us. If I may be so bold, you bring an air of sophistication that this court has so desperately needed."

My eyes drifted to my husband, who was talking with a few tradesmen that had accompanied their daughters to the ball. "Thank you. I am glad to be of service to the court."

"Tell me, is it true that the child prodigy Wolfgang Amadeus Mozart played for your court?" the marchesa, a petite woman with a round and hopeful face, asked. Her large green eyes sparkled with curiosity.

"Yes," I said, remembering our visit with the young child, whose talent was far superior to his six years. "The empress mother had both him and his sister come and play for the court." My audience's eyes widened with anticipation, eager to hear more. "Though he is a gifted musician, my sister and I thought of him more as a playmate."

"As a playmate?" they both questioned.

"Yes, after Wolfgang and Nannerl performed, Antoinette and I played chase with them through the Hall of Mirrors. Wolfgang was quite in love with my sister. He declared he would marry her one day, even going to my mother to request her hand."

They gasped. "What did she do?"

"She patted him on the head and apologized, because the arch-duchess was already intended for another."

"Would you be able to have him come to Caserta? For a perfor-mance?" the marchesa asked, hungrily gobbling up any tidbit I offered.

"I could certainly write to Wolfgang and make a request. I'm sure he would enjoy a reunion with one of his fondest childhood friends."

It was the perfect opportunity to bring up a salon. All of the most fashionable courts in Europe had one. My mother's court hosted the most talented artists and scientists, who all clamored to have an invitation to one of her salons. With the proper planning, the Neapolitan court could rival France or Vienna.

"I was considering hosting a salon," I said, "a place where artists and influential people of Naples can gather. Would you both honor me by being my first guests?"

"Name the date, and we shall be there," the marquis said with another bow.

A trumpet rang out, signaling that it was time for the girls to be presented. Taking Ferdinand's arm, I allowed him to escort me to our throne room. Bathed in moonlight from the arched windows all along the south side, it was perhaps more lavish than any room at Schönbrunn Palace. Though the walls were ornately gilded and Bourbon crests spread throughout, it was the ceiling where Vanvitelli's innovation truly shone. In the center was the most magnificent painting. Rich with hues of red and blue and green, it depicted the very first stone at the palace as it was laid by King Carlos III.

With all this opulence, our thrones were the least significant things about the room. The modest chairs had matching lions on each side, and above them was the golden statue of an angel, her hand gracing the lion of the house of Bourbon. In her arms were tablets to symbolize the justice of the crown.

I sat with the king as, one by one, Naples's eligible daughters were put forth. They each curtsied, and I gladly handed them their bag of ducats.

I reveled in the triumph of this moment. With one fell swoop, I had managed to make a good impression on the nobility, further distance Tanucci from his hold over our kingdom, and bring joy to these young women. The money would allow these girls to make not only prosperous marriages but hopefully happy ones. For it was the stark reality that a woman's fate rose and fell on her ability to make a good marriage.

Dearest Sister,   *November 1770*

I long for your advice now more than ever, and you are the only one I trust in such matters. My husband's grandfather, Louis the Well-Beloved, as the people like to call him, flaunts his mistress in court. The audacity astounds me. There are some things even a king should not do. Worse yet, the people seem to respect her. I cannot understand this, as Madame du Barry is the most ignorant woman I have ever met.

Men, particularly those of the noble class, will have their women, but the French not only accept this—they openly celebrate it. A mistress to the king of France is treated as if it is a cabinet office to aspire to!

My Louis's grandfather has always had a woman by his side. First, there was the tragic Madame du Pompadour, who thought she could influence the kingdom, but she was nothing more than a pawn in our mother's games. Now, there is the arrogant, narcissistic mistress Madame du Barry.

She sought to befriend me, but I don't want to be seen with the likes of her. My Louis and others at court don't like her either, but she expects me to embrace her as a sister. I would much rather spend an evening with Mimi than to spend even a minute with that vile, opportunistic woman.

Do you remember when we were small and Mother took us to the summer palace during the spring? Under normal circumstances, this would not be odd, but Mother brought us there in the dead of night, and I know why. The servants pulled us from our beds to ride for the palace because Father had taken another lover. I remember dozing on your shoulder the whole way. The floral citrus scent of the bergamot perfume that you used at the time still comforts me. There had never been a day when Mother's emotions were not in line, hidden behind a mask of royal duty—until that night.

You and I were so excited to go to the summer palace early, without our other siblings. Those meadows of our childhood and the hot summer days spent by the lake were true happiness. But whether it was excitement for the adventures to come or a foreboding, I simply could not sleep at home that night. You snored. Yes, dear sister, no matter your objections, you snore. Growing restless, I slipped out of our bedroom in search of the kitchens, but in doing so, I found myself in the shadows of our parents' room.

The pleas, the awful screeching pleas, that Mother emitted burst from the room. "I chose you! I could have given in to my father, but you were the only one for me. Why can I not be enough for you?"

I never heard his response to her. It was always too soft. How odd is it that long after a person's death, there is always one thing that we can remember, like a smell, a curve of the cheek. With Father, I will always remember his voice. The louder Mother got, the softer he became. Father's voice would lower, each word carefully chosen, the consonants becoming crisper. I couldn't hear what Father said, but the shattering of glass rang through the night.

Eventually Father gave in and the woman was set aside, but it was never for long. This vicious cycle was one that he and Mother would play out over and over again.

The aunts tried to encourage me to take pity on the woman. Our father may have had his dalliances, but at least he had the decency not to flaunt his women at court in front of our mother.

Your sister,
Antoinette

CHAPTER TWELVE

June 19, 1768

"Don't worry. They will be here."

I paced back and forth as Sabina sat in her chair, sipping wine. Granted, we were early, but I still felt anxious. I had taken over the large parlor. The room was lined with cream marble columns and gray stone carved with the most intricate designs, all leading to the fresco on the ceiling of the apostles rising to heaven on great white fluffy clouds. Four card tables had been set up and chairs arranged for personal gatherings underneath the great golden chandeliers. Even though the objective was for the nobility to be seen and socialize, there had to be proper amusements, along with food and wine. All I needed now was for people to come.

"Sit down and have some wine," Sabina said.

"I don't want any wine," I snapped.

"Well, sit down anyway. You are making me nervous, and I don't like being nervous. It gives me wrinkles," Sabina said, patting the skin under her chin. "I make a point of never being nervous. It is terrible for the constitution." She sighed. "Truly, Charlotte, come and sit. When people come, which they will, they will want to see you relaxed and not so"—she waved her hand in my direction—"this."

"Very well." I flopped into the chair next to her. Shortly thereafter, the guards opened the doors and the nobles streamed in—everyone from the Domenicos to the Medicis. Standing to greet my guests, I said, "Tonight is not a night to stand on pretext and ceremony. Please, enjoy yourselves, as we are the best of Naples."

To my right, a scientist was enthusiastically discussing our volcano with a nobleman who looked to be just as eager. To my left, people sat around whist tables; the sounds of their cards slapping down were intermixed with laughter. Sipping my wine, I took pleasure in my accomplishment.

A short man with thick eyebrows and a long, angular nose approached me. "La Sua Maestà, I am Ferdinando Galiani."

"Oh, Galiani, what a pleasure it is to meet you! I just read your treatise on the value of money."

"You've read my work?"

"Yes, and I found it most fascinating when you spoke of the relationship between the supply of money and the price of goods. One thing that left me curious, though, was that there may be an equalization between money and goods. What conditions do you think would be necessary for this to happen?"

"I am deeply honored that you would find my writing fascinating, for even my mother has a terrible habit of dozing every time I try to recite a passage. Please tell me you read my book to help you sleep."

"No, surely, I read it during the light of day, and not once did I yawn." I returned his broad smile. "Tell me, why are you not the head of our treasury?"

"La Sua Maestà, I shall grow stout on the richness of your flattery. Alas, the university has a firm hold on me, and the treasury has other…governors who prefer not to share their grip." He drained his glass of wine. "If you will excuse me, I find that I am sorely lacking in the way of spirits." Galiani gave another bow and left to find a servant.

My time with the nobles reminded me of trying to help Antoinette with her needlepoint. She and I would spend hours trying to get the embroidery just right. According to von Brandeis, it was a worthy occupation for a lady. However, no matter what Antoinette did, every time she turned her work over there was a giant knot in the back, the strands of blues, pinks, and greens blended together in a rainbow.

"I can't do this!" she protested once, passing the hoop and cloth to me.

"You have to have patience," I said as I began unraveling her mess. With the tips of my fingers, I pulled the strings, one thread of color at a time. When one became too tight, I pulled on another, loosening them until the knot gave way.

Antoinette stood over my shoulder, her head resting on the back of the winged chair. "Move that blue thread there," she said, poking her finger in the middle of the knot.

She laughed as I swatted her hand away. "You should be more careful with your sewing."

She shrugged. "That's why I have you."

"There is going to come a day when I won't be here. Then you'll have to clean up your own messes," I said, handing her needlepoint back to her.

"Oh, Sister, I'll always have you," she said, giving me a quick peck on the cheek.

That same method of disentanglement and patience was going to need to be applied here. Strand by strand, I had to unravel the mess Tanucci had made of our government. The nobility was the first step. If I could get their support, then I could have anyone I wanted on the council—assuming I had a son of course.

"Charlotte!" I turned to see Sabina sitting at a card table with the Marchesa di Domenico and another woman I had yet to meet.

"I saved you a spot at our whist table," Sabina called over to me. I took a seat across from the marchesa, making her my partner. Sabina sat next to me and introduced me to her partner, a woman by the name of Giuliana.

As Sabina dealt the cards, the marchesa asked, "Where is the king this evening? It is not like him to miss a party."

I waved a hand in dismissal. "He is away for the weekend at his farm." In truth, I didn't want Ferdinand here. Though I had recently seen an improvement in my husband's behavior, I couldn't trust him with a larger group, one that was so important for our future.

Giuliana shot a look at Sabina, who in turn pressed her lips together in a thin, tight line. "Oh, look," Sabina said. "The trump suit is hearts."

I sipped my wine as I watched the cards being slapped down on the table. Initially, Sabina and Giuliana led the game, collecting the most tricks. Sabina started the next round, leading with a spade.

"It doesn't make you upset that the king has left for his farm so soon after your marriage?" Giuliana asked, placing a jack of hearts on the table, her intention to steal the hand.

"No. Why should it? The king has his games, and I have mine." I slapped the king of hearts down, taking the trick for myself. I started the next round with the jack of clubs.

"Well, I would think that trysts like these would be concerning. I mean, one cannot simply let a dog roam loose." She gently set a queen of hearts down.

I shrugged. "Why should I care how far the dog roams? If properly trained, he will always come back. A good dog knows where his meals come from." I slapped the ace of hearts on the table and looked to the marchesa. "If I am not mistaken, I do believe we won."

"It would appear we have," the marchesa responded with a wry grin.

"In that case, we should get some celebratory chocolate."

Arm in arm, I strode away with the marchesa, not letting myself think about what my husband may or may not be doing on his little farm. He could have his farm, but I had my own court to oversee.

The door opened on the other side of the room, and Tanucci strode in looking as if something foul had been affixed to his upper lip.

"Go fetch the chocolate. I'll be there in the minute," I said to the marchesa before I made my way to the door. "Signor Tanucci, it is an honor to have you pay a visit to our little gathering."

"Little?" he said, looking over my head at all the people gathered around enjoying themselves. "It would appear that every nobleman in Naples is in attendance."

"Oh, yes, I was quite surprised to find so many people interested in my salon. The people of Naples are hungry for real culture."

Tanucci's frown deepened. He opened and closed his mouth like a fish, but then Signor Medici walked up, a glass of wine in hand.

"Tanucci!" Medici exclaimed, greeting him. "You are a bit late for all the revelry."

"My secretary seems to have lost my invitation."

"How tragic," I interjected, but if the men heard me, they paid me no mind.

"The queen has put together quite the *festa*, hasn't she?" Medici said.

Tanucci pursed his lips and reluctantly agreed. "If you'll excuse me, there is someone I would like to speak to." He walked away from us, his cane clicking in time with his heavy gait.

"And there goes the once-great Bernardo Tanucci, a relic of a bygone era when men like him were revered. But now, he is nothing more than an old man riddled with gout, trying to hold on to his last threads of power." Medici gulped at this wine. "We were all disappointed when King Carlos selected a northerner as our secretary of state."

"Why, Signor Medici, you do paint a very grim picture." I

regarded him; he was a stern man, but I couldn't tell if he was someone I could trust. He didn't seem to be fond of anyone.

Medici drained the deep-purple wine from his glass. "That man, La Sua Maestà, is the reason why Naples is nothing more than a city-state of Spain and not a country in and of itself." Medici lowered his voice and leaned in toward me. "If you did intend to not invite him, you have just drawn a distinct battle line. For if there is one thing that Tanucci hates more than threats to his power, its women who don't know their place."

Medici gave a little wink and went to find more wine. The lively banter floated through the air, mixing with the shimmering lights of the chandeliers. I stood by the doors and watched Tanucci as he took a seat at a card table. His gaze constantly moved about the room. And though tonight was a victory, the battle was far from over. I had one goal and one goal only. To get rid of Tanucci.

My Blessed Daughter,   *December 1771*

There are few things in this world that could make me prouder than the news that you are with child. Children are gifts from God. They give us a legacy and fulfill our duty as pious rulers. Keep me updated with every development of my future grandchild, the future ruler of Naples.

Regarding your bouts of morning illness, I found that a tea made of ginger helped. Also, keep away from spicy foods. The women in our family have a tendency toward strong indigestion during our pregnancies. The last thing you want is for this child to keep you from your duties as a queen.

This brings me to the matter of your marriage contract. Per the agreement, you are to attain a council seat upon the birth of an heir. And this is not to be an ornamental position; no, you are to be a full member, with voting privileges. It is critical that you are not kept from your position. We do not want what happened to your husband to happen to your son. You must oversee his education and his kingdom, for what good is a proper education if he doesn't have a kingdom to rule?

Your Mother,

Maria Theresa

CHAPTER THIRTEEN

June 7, 1772

Staring down into the bassinet, I watched as my daughter, robust and pink, squirmed in her bed of fluffy white blankets.

I have a daughter.

It was difficult to find my motherly affection amid the disappointment raging against the guilt. I had not produced an heir.

Reaching out, I took her little hand in mine. Her grip on my finger was sure and strong. Lightly, I ran a thumb over her tiny fingers, memorizing every crescent line of her knuckles, the wonder of her nails. Every feature, so foreign and yet so familiar. She was my child. Mine.

I wanted so much to simply love my daughter. To love her without any sense of duty. Without any sense that she needed to be something more than what she was. Gathering her in my arms, I held her out so that I could get a better look at her. "I'm sorry. I am so very sorry that you could not have been a boy. It's the men of this world who get everything. They are the ones who get to rule and determine their fates, while women, like you and me, are left with the consequences of their actions."

The child's blue eyes looked all around her. She was an attentive little thing. Perhaps that would help her get far in life. "But I promise that I will not leave you wanting for anything," I said. "Men may have the advantage because of their sex, but I will ensure that you will be able to meet any challenge. You will have only the best tutors and governesses, equal to the best princes in all of Europe."

A soft knock interrupted us. Ferdinand entered. "I wanted to pay a visit to the two most beautiful women in all of Naples and Sicily," he said, quietly approaching us. "Is she asleep? Can I hold her?"

"Of course," I said, handing our daughter over to him. A large smile slowly spread across his face as he stared into our daughter's eyes.

"I'm sorry," I blurted, then immediately regretted having broken the spell that my husband was under.

"For what?" Ferdinand looked bewildered by my admission.

"I didn't give you a son." When he still looked confused, I added, "An heir."

He thought for a moment as he continued to hold our daughter. "These rules—who can be king, who can't be—are as useful as who can hop on one foot and who can't." Ferdinand looked back down at our daughter. "You know of my brother Philip, yes?"

Aside from the one time that Luisa had brought him up to me, I had not heard the hidden Duke of Calabria's name mentioned openly within the walls of Caserta. Still, I was able to discern from others that there were certain aspects of his features that were different from those of his siblings: His green, almond-shaped eyes were slanted upward, with tiny spots discoloring the irises. He was short in stature and not athletic like his brothers. But this was the first time that my husband had mentioned him.

He moved to the window so that the warm late spring sun could shine on him and our daughter. "My brother always made me laugh. Not at him, mind you," he said, turning back to me. "But he had this joy about him that could not be rivaled. It wasn't enough for my parents that they had removed him from the line of succession; they completely removed him from court. We were not allowed to see him except on special occasions and under strict observation. And we were never, ever to speak of him in mixed company."

Ferdinand bounced our daughter gently in his arms. "He was their heir, and they treated him like something to be ashamed of."

I thought back to the stories my mother had told me. She wasn't supposed to be the heir to the throne either. After my grandfather's death, the very countries who had sworn they would support our mother in her newfound role as queen invaded Austria. They had assumed that she was weak and that they could pilfer her territory. She and her young family were forced to flee to Bavaria for safety and then to rally her troops and take her kingdom back.

Perhaps if I were to have only daughters, I thought, I could do the same. My child could eventually become the queen of the Two Sicilies. The one failing that Mother always complained about was that her father, even though he knew she could become empress, didn't train her in the same way he would have trained a prince. "I had plenty of dance lessons," she would say, "but I never got any instruction on how to rule a government." Watching Ferdinand wiggle his long fingers in our daughter's face, I vowed that my daughter would never have the disadvantages that my mother had.

Ferdinand handed the baby back to me. "I am happy with our child. A child, regardless of their sex, is a gift to be treasured."

Passing the baby to her nurse, I asked him the question that had been weighing on me about Philip. "The reason you keep your brother here, in the city, is it because of your parents?"

"They don't deserve Philip." His eyes met mine, and I could see a stone-cold anger. Any anger that I had seen from my husband before was a flash, an instant reaction to his pleasure being taken away from him, but this was something new. "Our daughter will not be treated any different from her future brothers. I will promise you that," he said. "But we have yet to choose a name for the child."

"A name. Yes, that would be important." I looked at my baby, now fast asleep. There was only one name that even come close to making her the type of woman I wanted her to be. "Maria Theresa," I said, meeting my husband's gaze. "For my mother, the bravest woman I know."

"Maria Theresa," he repeated. "A fine name."

As we stood there watching our daughter, I couldn't help but think of my mother. Though she was a constant cause of my aggravation when I was a child, next to Antoinette she was the one person I wanted most in the world. It was her that I craved, her voice that I missed now. I wished she were here to help me navigate this new role, not just as a queen but as a mother.

Dear Sister,   *May 1773*

The most disturbing rumors have come to my attention, and I feel compelled to visit in order to investigate them. Is it true that your husband has a menagerie within the palace walls? Another instance reported is that your husband has struck you on more than one occasion. If this is the case, you must inform me at once. We cannot allow behavior like that to continue, particularly with your latest pregnancy. What if the child is an heir? We cannot have him damaged because of your husband's anger.

Mother is also concerned about the actions you and

your husband took a few months past. According to those who report to her, you, Ferdinand, and your attendants paraded through the streets of Naples yelling and carrying on as if you were savages. And there is another reported instance when you and Ferdinand got into a screaming match in front of the whole palace, over a muff. (Truly, dear sister, are you that spoiled that you would cause a scene over a simple piece of clothing?)

Charlotte, I of all people can understand the need to rebel against the constraints of the Habsburg legacy, but one must always be aware of the consequences of those actions and how they are perceived by others. One night of frivolity is not worth a lifetime of disrespect from your subjects.

I shall be making my own assessment of your life at court and will be reporting to Mother all of my findings.

Your Faithful Brother,

Leopold

P.S. You should know that Mother has taken to calling you and Ferdinand the Royal Brats.

CHAPTER FOURTEEN

July 25, 1773

The court was in a flurry, preparing for the arrival of Leopold, from feasts to hunts. I wanted to show my brother that Naples was a happy place and that the rumors were untrue. On the day Leopold arrived, Ferdinand and I stood with a retinue of attendants, including Tanucci, who stood on the other side of my husband. I shifted my weight from one foot to the other, growing increasingly uncomfortable in the Neapolitan heat and in my pregnancy.

As soon as it was safe for my husband to return to my bed after Theresa was born, I had found myself pregnant again. Rubbing my protruding belly, I hoped that this child would be a boy. But as quickly as the hope rose, I buried it. I swore I would be pleased with another daughter, should that be the case, even though we all knew that once I had a son I would be able to take a seat on the council and finally challenge Tanucci's hold on the kingdom.

But all thoughts of affairs of state and how they pertained to my future child evaporated as my brother exited his carriage. "Dearest sister." He kissed both my cheeks and then gave a curt nod to my husband. "Ferdinand," Leopold said, practically in a growl. My husband's eyes flashed as he gave a curt nod in return.

The rumors about the Royal Brats had reached my father-in-law, Carlos. He was unhappy with our behavior and the allegations that his son was treating me poorly, and he made sure Ferdinand knew it.

The day my husband received the letter from his father, he fell into a fit of rage, destroying not only his rooms but mine. "What does this mean that I beat you?"

"I don't know," I said, trying to take the letter from his hand, but he pulled his arm back, keeping it from me.

"It says here that I kicked you and on more than one occasion I slapped you." He let the letter from his father fall to the floor as he spied my treasured box. I lunged for it, but he pushed me aside. "These letters that you write to everyone"—he pulled my letters from the box, throwing them all over the floor—"your mother, your brothers, your sister…do they slander me as well?"

"No!" I cried as tears ran down my face. "I swear to you these rumors do not come from me. You need to trust me."

"Trust you? What reason do you give me to trust you?" He threw the box to the ground, and I watched in horror as it bounced along the tiled floor. "Charlotte, you need to decide where your loyalties lie. Is it with me or with your Habsburg mother?"

When I took too long to answer, he said, "That's what I thought." He stormed from the room, leaving me in the wake of his anger.

Getting down on my hands and knees, I tenderly picked up my box, noting a giant scar in the shining wood: a crack that stretched diagonally from one corner to the next, cutting through my initials, *MCC*. I traced it, the roughness cutting into the pad of my finger. Oh, how I missed Antoinette. She had a softness about her that contradicted my harshness like no other.

I closed my eyes and tried to imagine her crouching beside me, surveying the damage left by my husband. *Well, it's no use leaving this here,* she would say. She'd hum as we cleaned up the mess, another one of her wordless tunes that as a child would annoy me but that now, I would give anything to hear again. Reaching out as far as my large belly would allow, I scooped up all my letters. One by one, I placed them in order by sender. Antoinette's first, of course. A small hum escaped my lips as I worked.

I had never seen my mother as interfering when it came to my life here in Naples. Though she was always criticizing my manners, telling me how to conduct myself, I had looked at her lessons as sage advice. But the rumors she was spreading felt like a betrayal. My husband had never hit me in anger. Of course he had a temper. Who didn't? But for it to be inflated to this level was unthinkable.

In the weeks since our argument, Ferdinand and I had not spoken and he spent extra time away at his inn. Now as I watched my brother speaking with Tanucci, I knew I had to put a stop to this.

At the dinner table, my brother and husband sat across from each other, locked in a silent war. Ferdinand stabbed at his food, so hard that I winced over the damage it was doing to my plates. Leopold took small bites, his eyes never leaving my husband's face. Tanucci, ever present, blathered on, boasting about how great Caserta was: The salons were as robust as the ones in Paris. The artists that were now flocking here were the best in all of Europe.

Never once did he mention that I was the one who had started the salons. It was my effort to hire female artists, authors, and poets seeking to find a patron that led Catherine Read—the same Scottish woman who had painted the royal family in England—to come to Naples. It was a small coup on my part, given that she was much loved by the English queen Charlotte.

Leopold, for his part, was a quiet tempest. He was not one to lash out in bursts, as Ferdinand did. No, Leopold calculated. He gathered up all the evidence and then struck, never missing his intended target. This was a lesson I had learned all too well. After an exceptional argument with Brandeis when I was a child, I had been sent to my rooms without supper. Later that evening, Leopold knocked on my door, a plate of cold meats in hand.

"I have brought you a peace offering."

"No cakes?"

"The condemned do not have the luxury of being able to choose."

"Very well," I said, taking the plate from him. "But only if you play chess with me." I knew he could not resist his favorite game. It was the reason I kept it in my personal parlor.

"You drive a hard bargain." He winked and sat at the table.

I nibbled on my food as we began to play. Pieces moved in quick succession. At eleven years old, I had been Leopold's opponent for half my life, ever since I took a keen interest when he would play with our older brother, Joseph, on our family evenings. I moved my king, and within seconds Leopold moved his queen. "Checkmate."

"You win all the time," I whined. "Can't you let me win at least once?"

"Now, where would be the fun in that?" He was already moving to reset the board. "Chess is a lot like life. Once you have the ability to master the game, you will have the ability to master life."

"Is that so?" I answered skeptically.

"Yes, your first lesson is that you must always anticipate your opponent. Gather as much information as you can and use it against them. For example, I know you always like to lead with your king. That leaves him exposed."

"And the second lesson?"

He held up the queen in response. "You neglect your queen. Never, ever neglect her. She is the most important piece in the game."

I thought about those lessons now as Leopold quietly let the men at the table talk. No one knew strategy like my brother did.

"I have arranged a sailing venture for tomorrow morning," Tanucci interjected, oblivious to the tension in the room.

"It would be lovely to spend the day sailing with my sister," Leopold responded, pushing the food around his plate.

"Oh, Charlotte won't be joining us," Tanucci said. "The doctor has said she is not to have any excitement." He shoved a heaping fork of pasta into his mouth and continued to talk with his mouth full. "Too much excitement will keep her from having a boy."

Leopold's head darted from Tanucci to me.

"It's all right, Brother," I said, ignoring Tanucci. "Spend some time with your brother-in-law. We'll have the whole of tomorrow afternoon."

Leopold set his fork down. "What kind of medical advice are you getting?" he asked me.

"You don't approve of our physician's advice?" Ferdinand growled from his seat. "What a surprise." He sipped at his wine. "A Habsburg not approving of a Bourbon."

"I was simply asking a question," Leopold said.

"Of course you were." Ferdinand picked up the jug of wine and left the room.

"Well, tomorrow will be quite entertaining," I said.

Dearest Sister,   *April 25, 1777*

I wish I could visit with you, but instead, I am paid a visit from our brother Joseph. He was sent on Mother's behalf to assist with my marital problems. Charlotte, you know of my problems with my husband, and I do not wish to discuss these delicate matters with any of our brothers, much less Joseph. He is the last person who should be giving marriage advice.

Joseph claims that his marriage to his "beloved Josepha" was one of deep love and mutual admiration, but it would appear that our eldest brother has a revisionist approach to his past or, worse yet, he is oblivious to the ways of women. While Joseph was blissfully married, Josepha was miserable. Do you remember? She used to walk around the palace sniffling—that was, until her friendship with Mimi.

I don't know when things changed, but I remember they were always together. Their friendship, though, was unusually close, don't you think? There was one time when I spied them alone in one of the parlors we used only when the family was entertaining. There was something intimate in the way Josepha brushed a wisp of hair from Mimi's face. It was so gentle, her fingertips grazing Mimi's cheek as if she were a fine porcelain doll that she didn't want to ruin. And Mimi, her eyes were locked on Josepha's.

Mimi always seemed to act as if the rest of us were a personal affront to her, because we took away Mother's attention and resources. But when it came to Josepha, Mimi seemed to soften.

With all my complaining, I still have to admit it is wonderful to finally have a family visit. I am so far from everyone, especially you, that Versailles feels as if it could be a part of the Americas! Mother has promised to come as far as Flanders, but it never happens.

Yesterday, Joseph and I went for a walk in the royal menagerie. He is quite fascinated with our elephant; perhaps we should get him his own for his birthday?

He asked about my relationship with Louis. I fully

expected him to scold me for not trying hard enough, but he listened. He didn't berate me or tell me that it was all my fault. He simply listened. Once I finished complaining, he asked about my makeup. "This rouge that they make you wear," he said, "you could use a little more! Go on, put it under your eyes and the nose as well. You can look like one of the Furies if you try!"

It was the first time I had laughed in weeks. Please send me a letter as soon as you can. I miss you more than you will ever know.

Your Sister,
Antoinette

CHAPTER FIFTEEN

The cool summer morning grew into a pleasantly warm afternoon. While my brother was sailing with Ferdinand, my ladies and I sat in the shade of Caserta's great lawns. Stroking my large stomach, I watched the warm breeze play in the leaves in the trees that bordered the pathway and flowed down to the pools, rippling water across the surface. The roar of the waterfall, only a few yards away, echoed through the garden. While we picnicked, I was able to keep an eye on the staff as they prepared the grounds for tomorrow night's festivities. They hurried about the base of the waterfall, setting the tables and lanterns. For a moment, I could almost forget the pressures of being a queen. Little Theresa was enjoying being held by her nursemaid, who pointed out little flowers, much to my daughter's delight.

Everything was blissful, until my brother purposefully stomped up the lawn toward me. He stood before me, in freshly laundered clothing, his hair still wet and a look of sheer anger splattered across his face.

"What are you doing?" I said. "You're going to catch a cold."

"I need to talk with you about your husband." Leopold forced the words out through clenched teeth.

"Yes, yes, of course." I picked up my parasol and bid my ladies to stay where they were so that I could walk and speak with my brother in private. "Is something the matter?"

"Everything is the matter!" Leopold burst out. He looked over his shoulder at my ladies watching us and then collected himself. "During our sailing venture, the boat capsized."

I gasped. "Ferdinand, did he get hurt? And you, are you hurt?"

"Everyone is safe." Leopold took one more look behind him before whispering, "Your husband, though, behaved most abhorrently."

"He wasn't the one who capsized the boat, was he?"

"No, that was an accident. When we fell in the water, your husband panicked, splashing and carrying on as if we were all going to die. When our companion vessel arrived, he started shouting for them to save him first, the rest be damned. And I was in the water with him!" Leopold shook his head as we continued up the great lawn. "I simply do not understand his state of mind. Before the ship capsized, he was jovial—and even, dare I say it, mature. The moment the boat capsized, it was as if he were a different person. When we were safely aboard the other ship, he continued to bark the most ridiculous orders and abused anyone who came near him. Is he always like this?"

"He has his moments. I find that when he is around civilized people such as us, he tends to pick up on their behaviors. Was Tanucci on the boat with you?"

"No, he was on the boat that rescued us, but I watched him with the king. What hold does that man have over your husband? When we were brought on board, Tanucci treated him like a child. Believe me, if Mother ever caught one of our tutors treating me or Joseph like that, she would have surely had them exiled from Austria."

I pulled my brother into the little grotto that was being built for me with the help of Signor Vanvitelli. The stone hideaway was cool and far from the prying ears of the court. Ivy flowed through the opening in the roof, where the sun illuminated the newly laid tile, imported from the recently discovered location of Pompeii. Vanvitelli and I decided to leave patches unfinished so that it would look more like pathways of the ancient city. When this place was finished, it would be my sanctuary, reminiscent of the Roman ruins, complete with old statues.

"If anything, Tanucci enables him," I told my brother. "When he is around, my husband's whole demeanor deteriorates to that of a child." I took a seat on a bench, stretching my aching back. "You will soon see that the one who runs this country is Tanucci. He gives in to every demand of Spain and squanders everything else. My people struggle for food while he slurps the marrow clean of Naples's bones."

"This is why you must have a trusted regent. The corruption is astounding." Leopold's face softened. "How is the baby?"

"Strong," I said, wincing as my soon-to-be-born child proceeded to kick at my insides.

"Good," he said, with his hands on his hips. "And the rumors?"

I sighed. "Do we need to discuss them?"

"I need to know if my favorite sister is safe."

"Of course I'm safe. These rumblings from Mother are unfounded."

"He has never hit you?"

"No." I winced as a sharp pain radiated across my lower back.

"The ambassador said that he was slapping women, yourself included."

"We were playing a game. Ferdinand was blindfolded, and he had to find us, and when he did, he slapped our bottoms."

"Hitting your ladies? And you? Charlotte, you are a Habsburg. Don't you understand the responsibility that comes with that?"

"I have been reminded of it since the day I was born." I

slammed the top of my closed parasol down into the stone, the act reminding me of my mother. My fist closed around the handle, and I braced myself against the wave of memories of her reminding me and my sisters of our duty to the Habsburg crown. And what did this sense of duty get me? I was not equipped for the world I was thrust into. "Leopold, you have no idea what I have to deal with. I want to help my people. I want to civilize the court. But there is only so much I can do in my present circumstances. Do you know how guilty I feel about not wanting a daughter when you know as well as I do that our mother ruled Austria better than any man that came before her?" My voice caught. "I dread having another daughter because of that damned clause."

"What clause?"

"I can't get a seat on the governing council until I have a son. An heir to the throne. And it's killing me that, every day, I am stuck here unable to do anything because my kind is continuously underestimated." I stretched again, still trying to ease my aching back.

Leopold's anger faded. "You know I never truly believed that Ferdinand abused you."

I raised my eyebrows in response.

"You are far too stubborn for any of that. I imagine you'd lick your wounds for a spell and then rain fire down on the city. If not the whole country."

I let out a small laugh. "I can assure you: My husband has not caused me to rain hellfire upon the city yet. His council on the other hand..." The words trailed off as I struggled slightly to get up. Leopold reached his arms out, and I gladly used them to brace myself as I moved to an upright position. "Let's not talk about this anymore," I said. "We should go inside. Luisa will murder me if you fall ill."

July 27, 1773

We held our banquet in front of the Fountain of Diana and Actaeon, at the base of the Great Waterfall. The statues, newly finished, depicted the story of Actaeon spying on Diana in the midst of her bath. As punishment, the goddess turned the hunter into a stag so that his dogs would rip him apart. While the palace of Versailles was adorned with paintings and statues of Apollo, I could think of no better goddess to be a patron to our palace than Diana. She, too, would not allow a man to get the best of her.

The Great Waterfall, fed from the Carolino Aqueduct, flowed into all the pools that lined the long walkway that led to Caserta. Looking down from the fountain, I marveled at the garden, illuminated by thousands of small candles, it was so beautiful that it put the heavens above to shame.

Leopold and Ferdinand found a tentative truce in their war. Leopold gained a fresh understanding of my life in Caserta, while my husband recovered from his momentary lapse of insanity. I was feeling relieved by the general pleasantness of the evening.

Ferdinand rose, goblet in hand. "It has been a great pleasure having Leopold at Caserta. He brings with him all the charm of my Habsburg in-laws. To my brother!" he exclaimed, raising his goblet into the air.

Smiling at Leopold, I thought that finally we were a court that could be respected. That was until the next proclamation fell from my husband's lips: "Because we have such an honored guest in our presence, we will have a royal sack race!"

Leopold nearly spit out his wine. The nobles clapped in excitement.

"Ferdinand, do you think this is appropriate?" I said. I had hoped that this evening would allow us to show my brother how sophisticated we were, but, alas, I was wrong.

Ferdinand gave me a quizzical look before hurrying around the table and gathering up the burlap sacks, each one embroidered with the royal *B*. He held a sack out for my brother, but Leopold waved him off. "I shall stay by the queen, to keep her company while you race."

Ferdinand shrugged and turned back to his audience. "We shall have three groups. The winners of each race shall battle for the grand prize." A footman walked out, carrying a pouch on a royal cushion. Ferdinand reached his hand in and pulled out a fistful of ducats. "To the winner go the spoils!"

I stayed with my brother by the tables, watching the chaos unfold. Ladies attempted to stuff their voluminous skirts into the burlap sacks. The indigestion that had been plaguing me all day returned, making my chest burn from the acid that rose from my stomach. "Are all my pregnancies going to be such torture?" I grumbled, ripping a piece of bread. "This child better be an angel when he comes out, because I swear he has already given me enough trouble to last a lifetime."

"When is the baby due?" my brother asked.

"Not for another five weeks," I groaned through a mouthful of bread. Acid tried to creep up my throat, and the only thing I could think of was to shove more bread in my mouth to neutralize it.

"Luisa is always most uncomfortable at this stage."

"Bless her," I said, rubbing at my stomach.

"You can take a break, you know. Childbirth is quite taxing."

"Being able to make any changes in this country relies on my having a boy. Once that happens, then I can rest. Anyway," I said, giving my brother a playful nudge, "this is only my second child, and you have six. I will not be outdone."

As we laughed, Signor Viventor, the royal physician, stumbled toward us. I could smell the ripe scent of old alcohol wafting from him. "La Sua Maestà." He attempted to give a little bow but stumbled again, catching himself on the arm of my chair.

Protectively, Leopold set the doctor right, though the physician swayed a bit. "I am glad to see that you are in fine health. Though I wish you would take more of my advice." He hiccupped.

"What advice is that?" Leopold asked, looking from the doctor to me.

"Why, rest of course," the doctor said, leveling a bleary-eyed stare at my brother. "It is not a prudent thing to let a woman out of bed once she has become with child. They are too fragile, you know."

I rolled my eyes.

"Do you have any suggestions for indigestion?" Leopold dared to ask.

"Leeches." Signor Viventor hiccupped again. "There is nothing that can substitute for a good application of leeches." Suddenly his attention turned to the distance. "If you'll excuse me, I have matters of state to attend to. Don't worry. The head of your military is on his way!" Signor Viventor called out as he pranced toward the people gathered with the burlap sacks.

Leopold's brows crinkled with confusion.

"Yes, you have just met the head of our military," I said.

"But I thought he was a physician."

"He is. He is both, physician and head of our military."

"Does he have any military experience?"

"About as much as much as his medical experience. His idea of problem-solving is to apply leeches to everything. Have an upset stomach? Apply leeches. Uprising in Palermo? The practical application of leeches to the rebels will do the trick."

"But how? Why?"

"For one, Viventor married into the right family. Then he won the favor of my dear husband."

"But he made him the head of your military?"

"He amuses the king, and he who amuses the king is useful to Tanucci."

"Regina mia!" Ferdinand called out from the foray. "Come and bless our competition."

"You see, Brother, I am the queen of fools," I said, pushing myself up from the chair with minimal difficulty. "*Il mio re,*" I said, lumbering up to my husband's side. "I don't need to bless this race, for the only champion I care about is you." I pulled a yellow handkerchief from my bosom, arguably his favorite feature of mine, and waved it. "A favor for my champion! May he win the royal sack race as well as he has won my heart."

Ferdinand took the scarf from me and raised it in the air.

The show was over, and I slipped back away from the crowd as a dizzy spell threatened to overtake me. Leopold was quickly by my side. "What can I do?"

"Get me a real doctor." Bracing myself against another wave of dizziness mixed with nausea, I said, "And pray that I have a son."

Summoning a few of my ladies, I made my way back to the castle, but soon after I got to my rooms, I felt my waters break.

Two hours later, my second daughter, Luisa Maria was born.

My Dearest Sister,   *January 15, 1775*

How wonderful that you are with child again! How I wish I could be with you to see your children. Tell me, do your daughters look like you or me? I do not mean to be vain, but I do hope that they are a reflection of us. Of the way we used to be.

I know I am sounding melancholy again. It is a habit that Mother says I need to break, but I can't help it. I miss the way our lives used to be.

The nobility hates me, which wouldn't be so bad if it were not for the fact that my husband is cold. I wish I could have a family even half the size of yours. Maybe then I could feel love again. How could I have come to a country and be so hated when all I did was marry the man I was ordered to?

Please write to me as soon as you can. I live for your letters. Those moments when I can read about your life are an escape from the dreary confines of my sad, lonely world.

With all my love,
Your Antoinette

CHAPTER SIXTEEN

I had my son.

Carlo Tito Francesco Giuseppe, Duke of Calabria, heir to the Kingdom of the Two Sicilies.

A strong and healthy child, his wails pierced the night air, as if he, too, was celebrating our joint triumph. Holding him in my arms for the first time, I felt the weight of not just him but of all that I must now accomplish.

Once, Countess Lerchenfeld told me that it wasn't just the Romans who had occupied Sicily. Great Arab dynasties ruled the land as far back as 832. They had universities filled with great mathematicians and scientists at the forefront of innovation. Irrigation systems were built that brought water to land that even the Romans had given up on. And silk, the finest silk in all of Europe, so rich that it rivaled that of the Orient, was brought to Sicily. Even after the arrival of the Normans, we were a bastion of science and progress, building castles as grand as anything you could find within the Holy Roman Empire.

Now, after centuries of changing monarchies and waves of

plague, the country was in ruins and our treasures were ravaged. Naples and Sicily were nothing more than city-states at the mercy of Spain. Any requests made by King Carlos were fulfilled by Tanucci, regardless of the needs of our people.

As I sat up in bed, holding my son in my arms, I knew that I would finally have my opportunity to take over the country. With my influence, we wouldn't be a reflection of Spain or Austria. "You, my darling boy, have made me a very happy woman," I said, kissing my son's forehead.

A week later, feeling my strength return, I made my way to the council chambers. Before Carlo was born, I would sneak into the long room when the council was not in session, my fingers trailing along the grain of the shiny lacquered table, imagining what it would be like to sit amongst the men, to be able to rule the Two Sicilies. At the far end of the room, behind the seat designated for the king, tiny particles of dust were dancing in the light that tumbled in from the open window. Slowly I moved to the head of the table, reveling in my long shadow as it stretched out before me. Sitting in the place meant for the king was…exhilarating. I could see in my mind's eye all the nobility and heads of state looking to me for guidance.

Now, I would make Naples and Sicily a glorious country once more. As I walked through the door of the council chambers, proud of my achievement, I was greeted by looks of shock from men that sat around the table. At the head, where Ferdinand should have been sitting, was Tanucci. He had stopped midsentence, his jaw agape.

"La Sua Maestà, what brings you here today?" Tanucci stammered.

"I'm here to take my place on the council."

The other men openly laughed. I could feel my heart pound and heat rise up my neck. I was not going to be laughed at, especially by the likes of them. Storming forward, I grabbed an empty chair from the corner and slammed it down in the one small opening between the two men closest to me. Looking around the table, I could see Signor Viventor, Signor Medici, and many other nobles, still looking surprised by my presence, but one person was missing. "Where is Ferdinand?" I asked.

Tanucci chuckled and wiped a small tear from the corner of his eye. "He doesn't like to be bothered with matters of state. He is out hunting."

"Oh, well," I said, trying to regain my position, "I'm here now, so we can continue our meeting."

"*Mi scusi*, we don't mean to be disrespectful," Tanucci began, "but wouldn't you feel better planning court amusements with your ladies? Or planning the castle's garden? You needn't trouble yourself with such bothersome affairs as these."

"Per the marriage contract that was negotiated between my mother and King Carlos, I am here to fulfill my duty as regent to the prince of the Two Sicilies." I folded my hands on the table before me and stared into Tanucci's soulless brown eyes at the opposite end, the place meant for the king. I gave a small smile of triumph when he was the first to break his stare.

"Surely, we don't need a regent yet. The prince is but a babe," Tanucci said.

"It is never too early to properly train a future king," I countered.

"I don't remember any discussion with King Carlos over this."

"Maybe he didn't confide in you as much as you thought. I read the marriage contract myself."

"Then you must be mistaken," he retorted.

"No. I don't believe so. My mother and I discussed this; it was well planned out long before I arrived in Naples. Signor Tanucci, are you saying that the empress of the Holy Roman Empire is a liar?" I exaggerated the shock in my voice for effect as I reminded him and the rest of the council who my mother was. I knew her influence was the biggest card I could play in this argument, and I wasn't afraid to use it.

The attention of the men sitting at the table volleyed between Tanucci and me. As their heads turned back to Tanucci, he began to sputter. "No, no, I would never make such an assertion."

"Then you are willing to create an international incident," I said.

"International incident?" Tanucci said, trying to catch up.

"You see, by not allowing me to sit here on the council, you'll be in violation of the marriage contract." I looked about the table. "Tell me, which one of you is the treasurer?"

A mouse of a man slowly raised his hand. "I-I am." He sniffled a little as his eyes darted about the room.

"Would the treasury be able to refund my dowry to the Holy Roman Empire?"

"Refund your dowry?" Tanucci questioned, his voice rising to a pitch of a mezzo-soprano. "What is the meaning of this?"

"Mi scusi, signore, but I asked a question of your treasurer." This is what my mother had trained me for. I gestured toward the treasurer. "Signor, please continue. Would the treasury be able to pay my dowry back in full?"

"No," he said. He was so quiet that I almost didn't hear him.

"So the money that was sent here from my mother has already been spent. Is it possible to get a full accounting of the funds?"

"The council does not have time for these games," Tanucci roared.

"If you violate my marriage contract, the Kingdom of the Two Sicilies will owe the Holy Roman Empire the entirety of my dowry. Also, because you cannot pay interest on the funds or pay them back, for that matter, my children, all three of them, would become property of the Holy Roman Empire."

"The royal family cannot be given away," Tanucci insisted.

"Oh, but they can. If you read the fine print of the contract, you will see that Maria Theresa and her coruler—Joseph, my brother— *can* take possession of me and my children. You can try to fight me on this, but I guarantee you my family's armies far outweigh those of Naples and Sicily. That is not even considering the armies of my brothers in Tuscany and Milan or my brother-in-law's men in Parma. May I also remind the council that my dear sister is the queen of France. I am sure their army would like an excuse to invade."

"You would purposely ruin this country because you can't get your way?" Tanucci said.

"Well, my mother must refer to Ferdinand and me as the Royal Brats for a reason."

"La Sua Maestà," one of the other men said, "if you did this, you would not only bankrupt the country but would never be allowed to remarry. You would spend the rest of your days in a convent."

I shrugged. "The convents in Austria are quite lovely. I don't need to remarry. My life will be very full raising the future king of Naples under the influence of Austria."

These men were loyal to Spain, and Spain only. To them, the thought of the Habsburgs taking over would be tantamount to a bloodless invasion.

"I believe it would be prudent to let the queen stay here," Medici began. "Tanucci, you can follow up on the contract terms before the next session."

"Very well, she can remain here for now, as an observer," Tanucci grumbled, and he restarted the meeting.

Medici made eye contact with me and gave me a little nod of approval before turning his attention back to matters of state.

Leaving the council chambers at the end of the meeting, I pulled the treasurer aside. "I meant what I said. I expect a full accounting of the country's finances."

The look of fear that crossed his face gave me immense joy for the rest of the day.

* * *

The following week, I arrived at the council chambers, my personal diary in hand, ready to take notes, when I nearly ran into Ferdinand sulking by the door. "What are you doing here?" I asked.

"Tanucci informed me that I must come to every council meeting from now on. Apparently I am supposed to act the part of king." He fiddled with a coin in his hand. "Now you're here, so this meeting won't be dull."

As we entered the room, Tanucci beckoned Ferdinand toward him. There were a few minutes of comical confusion about exactly where the men would sit. Tanucci and Ferdinand both went for the same seat at the head of the table and then tried to acquiesce to the other at the same time. Eventually Tanucci took the coveted seat, with Ferdinand to the right, his long legs stretching out before him as he slumped in the chair.

"We have received word that there is another uprising in Palermo," Medici began. "Signor Viventor, can we send two thousand soldiers to the city to keep things under control?"

Signor Viventor's body swayed as he made a gesture of dismissal with his hand; he was drunk again. "Uprising or Barbary raids, they are all the same. What can we do?" he said while unsuccessfully squelching a burp. "The people of Sicily are like children. They'll tire out from their tantrum, and the world will go on. Sending troops would be a waste of time. I should know—I'm a doctor."

"Who is the viceroy?" I asked. "Have we elicited an opinion from him on these matters?"

"Why would Giovanni Fogliani Sforza give us any opinions? He isn't in Palermo," one of the men said with a small chuckle, as if I should have known this already. Meanwhile, Ferdinand let out a large and obnoxious yawn.

"Well, where is he then?"

"I believe he is hunting," one of the men said. "I'm not sure where, though."

"Oh, Giovanni is always one of my favorite hunting companions," Ferdinand said, cheering up. "Let's see, it's January so he is most likely at his estate outside of Salerno. Unless he has gone to his family's home in Milan."

"Does he ever go to Palermo?"

"Usually in September, but it can vary," Ferdinand responded.

I choked on my shock. "If he is the viceroy for Sicily, shouldn't he be living in Sicily? How can he govern?"

"Govern?" Tanucci said, scoffing. "We don't expect him to govern. All the edicts for Sicily are sent there directly from Naples. Further, the Sicilian nobility like to have him out of the way. We need to keep them happy, after all."

"No wonder our people are revolting. How can we effectively manage our people if there is not a proper government in place?" I said. "I make a motion that we remove Signor Fogliani immediately and replace him with someone in Sicily."

The table around me erupted with counterarguments:

"Fogliani has been in his position for years. He bought his title with his family's hard-earned money. How can we take it away?"

"You must understand we have a way of doing things here in Naples. You don't understand because you are from Vienna."

"How can it be too much to ask for a viceroy to be where he belongs?" I said. I thought about the way the Holy Roman Empire was organized. Yes, Vienna was the seat of the central government, but there were electors that acted as an intermediary for the empress.

The men looked at me as if I were daft before one of them spoke up. "By being within the Two Sicilies, he is still in Sicily, just not the Sicily that you imagine."

"But why isn't he on the island?"

"Who wants to be on the island of Sicily anyway?" someone said, and the men around me chuckled.

I was growing frustrated. Talking with these men made me feel like I was speaking in circles. But I had to be like my mother. Not once did she break to surrender when she was told no. If she had become agitated or openly cried, her enemies would have pounced. Slowing my breathing, I did my best to channel her, to imagine what my mother would have said if she were standing beside me. "The people need to see that they have a government that cares. That we are not some nameless entity ruling from a city that most of them will never visit. We need a clear and decisive presence."

"La regina is being logical," Medici said, cutting through the chatter. "We *should* install a viceroy from Sicily. Perhaps with his oversight, we could put an end to the Sicilian foolishness once and for all."

Reluctantly, the others agreed with Medici's logic. While the men voted for a new viceroy, I watched Medici. I couldn't tell if he was friend or foe, but for now, I would accept him as an ally. I needed him and his influence if I was ever going to get Tanucci and his followers out of Naples.

"Well, I shall be on my way," Ferdinand said, getting up from his chair.

"You're leaving?" Tanucci said. "The meeting's only just begun."

Ferdinand shrugged. "Work with my wife," he said. "She knows everything anyway." And with that, he strode out of the room and the rest of the men turned to face me.

I smiled graciously. "Let's move on to our next subject, shall we?"

Charlotte,   *December 20, 1777*

I need your most prudent and earnest advice. Joseph has asked for my assistance in getting the French government involved in his acquisition of southern Bavaria. I don't have the mind for political games as you do, and your wisdom in these matters would be greatly appreciated. Joseph seeks to invade southern Bavaria, but he expects me to persuade France to help.

France has become close with those Americans—that is the name that the people of the American colonies have begun to call themselves. Their ambassador, a man named Benjamin Franklin, has created quite the stir. In lieu of wearing a wig, he wears a fur cap. The people are most enamored with him; his image appears on almost everything, from snuffboxes to hats. We couldn't help but have him at Versailles so that he could explain to us his invention called electricity. He has charmed the nobility, which has worked to his advantage, since he has been asking for money from anyone who will listen, and he was able to convince our foreign minister, Charles Gravier, to recognize this United States of America as a legitimate country.

While these men argue over the Bavarian territory, the Americans are struggling for their freedom, and by supporting them, we could deal a fatal blow to our arch-enemy, England.

I can either side with our family in another pointless war, led by our brother, or side with the nobility, for once earning their respect. Please let me know your council as soon as you get this letter.

Yours,
Antoinette

CHAPTER SEVENTEEN

The winter sun crept through the window of the family parlor at Palazzo Portici, where we often spent our winters. The light fire that was crackling in the fireplace gave the room a comfortable warmth as I sipped the hot chocolate that sat by my side. My new personal librarian, Eleonora Fonseca Pimentel, was proving her worth after procuring for me the most interesting book, recently translated to French, called *Gulliver's Travels*. Eleonora was a woman who had impressed me with her wit and intelligence. I had decided I had to find her a place in my court. Gulliver was just about to meet the emperor of Lilliput when Ferdinand came sulking into the parlor.

"Weren't you out hunting?" I asked as Ferdinand came to sit next to me. He stretched out on the sofa, his head resting on my lap while his legs dangled over the side.

"Yes, but it was doomed." He pouted, making a pillow for his head with my skirts. "Just as I fired at an amazing buck, a servant moved, snapping a twig. The beast ran, and I missed."

"Did you at least give chase?"

An annoyed face looked up at me. "What kind of man do you take me for?" he huffed. "It would have looked so beautiful above this mantel." He reached out an arm, indicating the fireplace before us.

Thinking he was going to settle in with me, I began delving into Gulliver's adventures again while stroking his black hair.

"What is your book about?" Ferdinand said, his eyes half-closed.

"It's about a man who goes on a journey to strange worlds."

"Does he come to Naples?"

"No," I said with a little chuckle. "He doesn't travel anywhere in the realm of the Two Sicilies."

"Bah," he said, turning so that he could look up at me. "What is the point of reading it then, if he doesn't at least go to Sicily?"

Reluctantly, I set the book down and kissed my husband's forehead. "There are plenty of other places to visit." Ferdinand started to play with the bows of my stomacher. "Eleonora told me he also visits a land of giants," I said.

Ferdinand sat up on one elbow and kissed my collarbone. "Is that a fact?" he said, his lips moving up my neck. I had just recovered from birthing Carlo and had yet to welcome my husband back into my bed. But that made no difference to him. Within moments, he was on top of me, his hands searching under my skirts. "I believe there *are* interesting places to explore," Ferdinand whispered in my ear.

It wasn't long after that when I began to crave colatura di alici with extra chili, something that I had craved with all three of my pregnancies.

Four weeks later, my fears were confirmed when my courses did not begin. I was pregnant again.

November 1775

"La Sua Maestà, please wait!" The young physician my brother Leopold had sent to me hurried to catch up with me and my lady Sabina. "This is not healthy for you or the baby."

I came to an abrupt halt, nearly causing Sabina to run into me. This man, practically a child with his floppy brown curls and lanky frame, was supposed to be the physician who would see to my health and deliver my next baby. He was meant to ease my frustrations, but I wanted to murder him. "So help me, Domenico, if you tell me to rest one more time, I will send you to the dungeons."

He looked scared, but then he planted his feet, as if steadying himself against my wrath. "Your pregnancy is only at thirty weeks. You have to be careful. This pregnancy is complicated."

"Every pregnancy is complicated," I spit. "This is my fourth child. I think at this point one can call me an expert."

"But this one is more complicated than most. I worry for not only the child's health but yours." Domenico turned to Sabina. "Please tell her," he pleaded.

"Regina mia," Sabina said, "you have had multiple incidents where you have nearly lost this child. Perhaps it is time to listen to the physician."

I felt like I was explaining myself to a group of children. This child had been nothing but problems from the moment he was conceived. The more I had embedded myself in the council, the more the men there resisted my presence—especially as my pregnancy progressed. My only ally was Medici, but I still couldn't rely on him. The man was still aloof and seemed to give his opinions only when it benefited him. Meanwhile, Tanucci had a whole army of nobles on his side, chief of which was the Spanish ambassador. I didn't know what he was telling my father-in-law, but I was sure that he was the one responsible for the rumors surrounding the parentage of my baby.

This pregnancy was a burden. I needed to make changes for the sake of Naples, and I couldn't do it from my confinement. There was so much to do. Why didn't anyone understand that? The thought alone made me even more irritable. Everyone, my unborn child included, was standing in my way. "Right now, the council is moving to vote on the usage of my country's funds for the betterment of Spain," I said. "Spain!"

"If you don't remain on bed rest, you could die. Don't you realize how dangerous this is?" Domenico implored.

"Don't you dare talk to me about danger. Every time I give birth to a child, I know very well that I might not walk away from the ordeal. Tell me, when was the last time you gave life and faced death at the same time?"

When Domenico didn't answer, I turned and stormed toward the council chambers.

Throwing open the doors, I was pleasantly surprised by the shock sprawled on their faces. "La Sua Maestà, what are you doing here?" Tanucci began. "This is no place for a woman in your condition."

"This is exactly where I should be." The wild eyebrows of the Spanish ambassador seemed to take on a life of their own as he stared at me with contempt.

"Please," the ambassador begged. "Spain has been nothing but an ally to Naples. We are as much your family as Austria."

"Except that my family does not have its fingers in my treasurer's pocket every time I turn around."

"Surely, that is not an accurate description," the Spanish ambassador countered.

"You seek to steal thousands of ducats from my treasury, and you dare to call us family."

"How dare you insinuate that the king of Spain is a thief. We only seek funds to reinforce our borders. A safe Spain is a safe Naples."

"A safe Naples? Currently there are Barbary pirates sailing up and down our coast, raiding at will," I said to the ambassador, then turned to my secretary of state. "Tanucci, you yourself have devised a multicountry coalition of ships to protect us from the pirate threat. It is a good idea, but it will require several thousands of ducats from us alone. We will need cannons, guns, even frigates. Still, I want to implement your plan. I don't understand why you are now opposed to it."

Tanucci examined his fingers, refusing to meet my eyes.

"Why use so many ships when we can have the same effect with a coastal flotilla," Viventor said. "All those ships, they are so costly. Do we need so many guns? Give the money to the Spaniards. We have relied on them for years, and we should continue to rely on them now."

"I would suggest going back to medicine," I said to my former physician, "but you were terrible at that as well." Though he no longer oversaw my well-being or my family's, I still couldn't get him off the council, since he remained head of the military.

"Spain is only doing what is best for Naples and Sicily," another member, with eyebrows that fell over the rim of his glasses, tried to reason. "This is the way it has always been done, even when Carlo was the king of the Two Sicilies. I don't see any reason to change it."

My glare moved back to the ambassador. He crossed his arms and looked at me smugly.

But there was one thing they were forgetting: Never underestimate the queen.

"How convenient that when Spain wants something, we are all too quick to hearken to her call," I said, "but the moment that we need assistance, she isn't there to help. The ambassador is living proof. Our people need us to come to their aid, and all this council wants to do is latch itself to a king across the Mediterranean. And you have the audacity to complain about the Habsburgs."

"Would you have us rely on your Habsburg family?" Tanucci questioned.

"At least my family has followed through with its promises."

"Or do you mean sheltered your indiscretions?" the ambassador retorted.

An awkward hush fell over the room. I wanted to reach out and rake my nails across his face. But then I remembered my mother. Bracing against the table, I clenched my teeth, then spoke. "These indiscretions, as you so like to call them, are nothing more than rumors perpetuated by my enemies at court." My eyes met the ambassador's. "I can assure you they are false. And while you all sit here and make assumptions about who sired my child, our people are suffering." I looked at all the men, then continued. "Right now, as I speak, there is open warfare in the English colonies. Is that what you want? Is it? England couldn't control her people, and if you don't act now to protect our coast, that will be us." A sudden pain ripped through my abdomen, causing me to tighten my grip on the table, my knuckles white against the pressure. I could feel a wetness spread between my thighs. "For the love of God, choose Naples," I said.

"La Sua Maestà," Medici whispered, "are you—"

"Just take the vote." I could not hold myself up much longer, nor could I appear weak.

"Very well." Medici did as I asked, and one by one, the majority cast their votes for Naples.

Tanucci and his followers pushed their way from the room. But just before he left, Tanucci stopped beside me. "You foolish child," he said, "you don't know what you have done."

I met his glare with my head held high. "I have done far more for Naples than you could ever dream of."

Tanucci swept from the room. The ambassador paused briefly to size me up. I smiled through my pain, and he gave me a look of disgust.

"Sabina," I said, reaching for my lady, "escort me to my chambers."

"Sì, *madonna*," she said, clasping my elbow.

We moved through the halls, freshly decorated with paintings from the artists that I had lured here from Paris, and people greeted us as we passed. Feeling the wetness grow, I feigned my pleasantries, periodically stopping to wince as my contractions grew. As soon as we made it to a private room, I reached up my skirts, praying my hand would come back clean.

But it did not.

My hand was covered in blood. "Quick, get Domenico," I yelled. "Now!"

As Sabina leaped from the room, barking orders to the people around me, I stood there shaking. Staring at my hand, all I could think was, *I killed my child.* The pain of what I had done stabbed through my gut. While I had been so focused on Naples, I had neglected the well-being of my child.

"I killed him," I whispered, holding my bloody hand out to Sabina as she rushed back to me. "I killed my baby."

It was no secret how I felt about this child. How I thought he was an imposition. My knees buckled as I choked back a sob. The icy tendrils of guilt wrapped around my heart, gripping it, spreading pain throughout my chest. Gold sparks popped along the edges of my vision. Domenico rushed into the room just before my world went black.

Charlotte,   *July 15, 1789*

The gossip these French people utter when they think I am not listening is of the vilest nature. The people need to focus their anger somewhere, and if I am to be their target, then so be it, but, Charlotte, they are coming after my children.

They say that I am of the lewdest character and that all of my children are bastards. There was even a cartoon. I do not want to repeat it, but for the sake of your understanding of this situation, I must share. In the drawing, I am cradling my son, with Louis standing next to us wearing the horns of a cuckold. Underneath the photo, it says, "Be careful not to open your eyes to the secret of his birth."

And it is not just my people; the Spanish embassy has gotten involved! They passed around a pamphlet with a drawing of the dauphin, asking, "Who the Devil produced him?"

What did I do to these people to make them hate me so? I have taken to hiding at the Hameau de la Reine. I cannot take these vicious attacks against me and my family. At least when I am at Hameau, I am protected from the slings of their bows and arrows.

Your Sister,

Antoinette

CHAPTER EIGHTEEN

Slowly I awoke and took in my surroundings. Someone had combed out my hair and changed my sheets. A small fire crackled in the fireplace as sunlight slowly faded into a soft glow in the room around me. To my right sat Ferdinand, our tiny baby, barely bigger than his palms, resting in his hands.

"Look at you," he was saying, with eyes full of love. "You are the tiniest baby I have ever seen. By royal decree, we shall call you Principessa Polpettina." There was movement as a little fist rose in the air while the child let out a yawn. My heart pounded in my chest. My child was alive. "Oh, you agree. Very good," he said, still talking to the baby.

"I think our child deserves a more regal name than Little Meatball."

"Ah! Mama is awake!" Ferdinand rose from the chair, bringing the tiny girl with him. "Regina mia, meet your daughter, Maria Anna." He set the baby in my arms. "Normally, you get to introduce our children to me. But this time, it's my turn. I like this change." He kissed my forehead.

I looked my daughter over. She was indeed small. Smaller than any child I had ever seen. Tears fell from my eyes. I could see from the look on my husband's face that he thought they were tears of joy, but it was fear. She was early, and I feared she would not last the winter. This was all my fault. If I had only listened to Domenico.

"I trust you heard the rumors?"

"Which rumors?" Ferdinand said, reaching a finger out for our daughter's hand.

"The ones where they say the child isn't yours."

He was quiet for a moment. "Don't you think she has my nose?"

"Ferdinand, I am trying to have a serious discussion with you. Someone is spreading vile rumors about me. Stories like these could topple a whole monarchy."

"Yes, but her nose. Look at it. It is quite large, don't you think? Even on a face so tiny. Perhaps she will grow into it." He cocked his head to the side. "Yes, I do say she inherited my nose. She got your eyes, but I am certain she has my nose. All my children do."

Ferdinand kissed my forehead again and rose. "I shall leave my ladies to get some rest." He walked to the door and stopped. "Oh, you might be interested in hearing that I had the Spanish ambassador sent away."

"You did?"

"Well, almost. He is packing up his things under the dutiful eye of our soldiers. It came to my attention that he was causing too much stress on you and our children, and, we can't have that."

"Ferdinand, can I say something?"

"Of course, regina mia. I always enjoy your insight."

"Husband, I need a break from having children." The words tumbling from my mouth felt like a weight had been taken from me. "I don't care if you explode—I simply cannot have another child."

Ferdinand dipped his head in acknowledgment. "You have earned your rest," he said.

And with that, my husband left the room.

Holding my daughter in my arms, I looked into Maria Anna's clear blue eyes. "It is true," I said. "You do have your father's nose. I'll tell you a secret, little one: After all these years, I kind of like it."

Dear Sister,   *May 21, 1776*

I am glad that Domenico Cirillo has been helpful in your pregnancies and that he does not regularly expound upon the benefits of leeches. Do not let Domenico's youthful looks fool you. He trained at the finest universities in London and Paris, and as a native Neapolitan, he should help bring you a fresh perspective on your new homeland. I hope you find it refreshing that he cares more for the sciences than he does for military matters. Beyond being a brilliant physician, he has a love for botany; perhaps you and he can discuss your garden. Be sure to ask him about his time in the salons with Voltaire. I promise you will find them exceedingly entertaining.

Concerning your other request, I promise that I was not ignoring you. Finding you a replacement for the head of your military has been one of my most difficult decisions. Do I send you an upstart general eager to make a name for himself, or do I send you the man whose advice I rely on more than any other's, including our mother's? I chose the latter, dear sister. Perhaps it is my sentimentality or simply because I want to see you succeed. Like all those games of chess we played when we were young. Every failure was a lesson until, finally, you bested me. Truly, I was just as happy for your win as you were.

Now that you have a country of your own, I want to see you succeed. Perhaps the Kingdom of the Two Sicilies will become a better country than the Duchy of Tuscany. There is only one way for that to happen, and it has everything to do with the man standing before you right now.

Sir John Acton is one of my most trusted military advisors. Please know that parting with him is a great sacrifice. His bravery and knowledge of military endeavors are second to none. However, should Mother hear about his true nation of origin, she would be most aggrieved. While Prussia and Russia are her rivals, England is composed of heathens.

I entrust him to your care because I know the Kingdom of the Two Sicilies is in greater need than Tuscany. Listen to everything he says. Keep him close. Learn from him. He is a great asset, and I pray that he improves upon the safety and sanity of your kingdom.

Your Brother,

Leopold

CHAPTER NINETEEN

May 28, 1776

I folded the letter and took in the man standing before me. His light brown hair, graying at the temples. The brown eyes that crinkled ever so slightly at the corners. His features, though serious weren't off-putting, he felt approachable. Sir John Acton stood before me dressed in the crisp uniform of a Tuscan naval officer.

"What experience do you have with pirates?" I said.

"I have not had any experience with pirates directly," he responded, "at least not the ones that have been plaguing your coast. However, I have developed a lightweight sailing ship that is fast and effective. During the Spanish invasion of Algiers, my fleet successfully protected the Spanish armada while they retreated."

"Retreated? You are here, being interviewed to be the head of my navy and you are conceited enough to admit that you failed."

"I am a naval officer who believes in being honest with his commander, for it is in our mistakes that we learn the greatest lessons. The invasion of Algiers was a failure even before it began."

"How so?"

"The Algerians knew of our arrival, and though the Spanish

commander, Admiral O'Reilly, gave specific instructions to land on the west side, the Spanish armada landed on the east side. The cannons became mired in the sand, and it was a massacre. We barely made it out with our lives." Acton stood straighter. "It is a mistake I never intend to make again."

I tapped my brother's letter against my desk. I had since begun to create an office for myself within the state department wing. As was the way of things at Caserta, my office was still being furnished. But I had my desk, plain and unassuming, which was perfect for me because it was perpetually covered in paper and ink.

"Your accent, it's English. I thought you were from Besançon?"

"My parents were English—Jacobites, to be more specific—who died tragically. I was raised by my uncle in Besançon. He was a noted French officer and encouraged me to follow suit."

I lurched at the mention of Jacobites, a group of people who opposed the ruling party of England. They insisted on another man as ruler. Opposition such as that scared me. In this case, it had fostered open rebellion. One that had come to a bloody end at Culloden. These were ideals that I did not need in my kingdom. Especially now. "Will the Jacobite principles you were raised with influence your work?"

"Your brother Leopold can assure you I am a loyal servant to the crown. I was loyal to Tuscany, and I will be just as loyal to the Two Sicilies."

"What has my brother told you about our current situation?"

"Everything. I received a full briefing before accepting the position. He wanted me to be fully aware of the situation I was being placed in."

"And?"

"And I feel that I can be of service. That with Naples and Sicily we have a blank canvas to form a navy that is second to none. Once you have your borders secure, we can focus on enriching the lives of the people."

"Well, consider the position yours. I am glad to have you on the council with me. We will also hold a salon in your honor."

"A salon? I don't believe that is necessary."

"One thing you will need to learn, Signor Acton, is that in Naples, a salon is always necessary."

* * *

"I do have to say he has a certain…air about him," Sabina said, watching Acton from over the rim of her goblet.

"I do not know what you mean," I said, trying to deflect as my eyes followed him. He had an ease about him as he made his way around the room, socializing with nobility and artists alike.

"No, truly, a man like him is worldly."

"Sir Acton is twenty years older than me."

"That simply means he knows things. He's…experienced." Sabina laughed at me as I blushed. "Oh, please, don't act so innocent. No one would blame you if you and he became *friendly*."

I gasped. "Sabina! I've already suffered through one rumored affair. I don't need another."

"Look at Signora Romano," she said, pointing to the heavily painted woman currently flirting with the elderly Barone Polizzi, who seemed to be just as taken with her. "She ended a three-year affair with the wealthy Signor Filanga, who found himself a much-younger woman."

"What does her husband think of this?"

Sabina shrugged. "What does he care? He's having an affair with his page."

She tutted at my shocked expression. "We marry for position, for wealth, but we have affairs for love. We finally get to enjoy ourselves."

"Yes, but I get criticized at a standard that is far above them. I am a queen, a woman in power. There is no sin too small for me to get reprimanded for."

She gave a sly little grin as Acton approached. "All I ask is that you simply remember what I said." Sabina winked and walked away.

"Your Majesty, I have to admit I am truly honored by the festivities. But there are some concerns that I have regarding the current state of our military."

"Besides the fact that there is no money, and our sailors don't know the difference between a mast and a sail?"

"Yes, they are severely undertrained. I'd like to implement a strict training regimen." As Acton continued to talk, I couldn't help but think of Sabina's words. Acton was handsome—that was true—but I could not have feelings for him. He was minister of the military, and therefore we could be nothing more than colleagues.

"I would like to know what you think," Acton was suddenly saying.

"What I think?"

"About recruiting officers from Austria, and perhaps from the northern Italian territories."

"Yes, yes, of course. Bring in whomever you need, but no one from Spain." My eyes moved about the room before falling on Tanucci, who was talking animatedly with a few noblemen that he had cornered. "The Kingdom of the Two Sicilies needs to break away from the yoke of Spain, at all costs. Is that clear?"

"Perfectly." He nodded.

"What are your thoughts about the rebellion in the Americas?" I asked.

"I believe that the English made many critical mistakes in the management of their colonies and the people have a right to be upset, but to openly incite violence against one's government is not appropriate."

"Do you believe that we will face the same problem here, in Naples?"

"Under the right management, no, I don't believe so. People inherently want to be governed, but the moment the government fails to make them feel safe they will rebel." He gave a small, sweet smile. "I have some books I could share with you on the philosophy of a group called Freemasons, if you like."

"So long as I am not fated to become Francesca da Rimini because of it," I quipped, though I did not expect him to understand my reference to Dante and the doomed lovers.

"I would never dare to think myself worthy of being your Paolo."

"You've read Dante?" I was so used to having Eleonora as the only one I could talk to about books that Acton startled me.

"Who hasn't? *The Divine Comedy* is an integral part of literature. Though I prefer *The Aeneid*."

"I'm sorry, but I have to disagree with you. *The Aeneid* is a horrid book."

"Madame, I think I can no longer be in your service." He tried to hide his smile as he gave his mock resignation. "How can you not enjoy *The Aeneid*? There is so much adventure, the battle of Troy. How can you not be thrilled by what happened at Troy!"

"Because of the destruction of Carthage and its queen." I took a sip of my wine, my heart pounding with excitement. It was thrilling to be able to talk with someone who understood my love for literature. "The other books in *The Aeneid* are all well and good, but I simply cannot stomach book four. It ruins all twelve of them."

"I would think that a woman who enjoys the story of Paolo and Francesca would enjoy the story of Aeneas and Dido." Acton's eyes brightened, and I felt a rush of joy, knowing he enjoyed this too.

"Easy," I countered. "Paolo gave Francesca books. Aeneas only gave Dido empty promises."

"Yes, but both Paolo and Francesca died because of it. Her husband found them together, and he ran them both through with a sword."

"Well, at least they died together. Aeneas left Dido, and she killed herself, completely abandoning her kingdom."

"He didn't *just* abandon her. He founded Rome."

"That doesn't matter. Dido was Carthage's queen. She was responsible for the well-being of her people. At some point, we must understand that there are greater loves in this world than those of the flesh. Look at Beatrice and Dante: He loved her more than anything, but his love was so pure that it transcended the physical."

"Why, Your Majesty, I do believe that you are a romantic."

"I am, though I recognize that love does have its limits. I simply..." The words died away as Ferdinand strode through the doors of the salon. He hardly ever came to the salons, usually instead taking the opportunity to play innkeeper or dairy farmer. I tried to look pleased upon my husband's entry, but I could not help feeling like Francesca the moment she is caught by her husband with Paolo.

"Ferdinand, what brings you here?" I said. "Weren't you supposed to be at your inn?"

"And miss the great war hero from Tuscany? I would never." He took a swig of his wine and glared at me. "You have been extolling him to anyone who would listen. I had to meet the man who has entranced my wife." Ferdinand's jaw clenched as he looked Acton up and down. Acton gave a curt little nod in response. "Well, I hope you live up to such high expectations. If you will excuse me, there is a spot being held for me at the whist table."

I watched my husband as I stood next to Acton in awkward, stunned silence. Ferdinand rarely took an interest in me beyond his nightly visits, and I was suspicious. My husband didn't show emotions like this, and I couldn't help but wonder what ideas had been planted in his head and by whom. I glanced at Acton next to me. He, too, was watching my husband as he sat down at the whist table.

Dear Sister,   *January 1779*

The philosophy books you sent me are most interesting. Though I cannot speak for your Freemasons, as you call them, I do have to say that I am quite taken by the philosophies of a Jean-Jacques Rousseau. Have you heard of him? You were always more of a reader than I was. That is why I have included a copy of "The Social Contract" for you.

Reading his books, I have concluded that the best thing to do is to show the world what a great mother I can be. Rousseau says that women are the ultimate nurturers and intended caregivers. He even says that women should nurse their own children, regardless of their station. I have taken to doing that with my daughter, much to Mother's wrath. She has sent me countless letters filled with her fury about my most recent actions. But she doesn't under-stand; she has never been under such scrutiny. She has never had her motherhood questioned as I have.

I wish things could be different. Mother always spoke of our position as being a divine right, that God chose us to be stewards of the people and that as such, we need to be responsible. But I can't help but doubt those divine intentions. When I escape to my farm, I feel at home. I can play with my daughter and animals and simply be at peace. If that feels so right, then why does life at Versailles feel like such a nightmare?

Yours,
Antoinette

CHAPTER TWENTY

I was his Francesca. He brought me books. The writers spoke poetry that sang of free ideas, of the relationship of science to art, of government's responsibility to its people. I wanted to know more and couldn't wait to find Acton to discuss these principles and how Naples could use the ideas of these men to our advantage. I had the opportunity to build something, a country that could be respected. Naples would be a beacon of innovation.

When Acton arrived at my office, I couldn't help but pepper him with questions. "These men, they say that we can have equality among the masses. How can that be the case when we have a nobility?"

"Perhaps being a part of the nobility can be something that could be attained," Acton said with a smile, setting his maps down on the table.

"What about reforms? We can develop laws that can bring about equality between our citizens."

"Certainly," he said, laying out his notes for the meeting.

"And what of the navy? Can we apply these principles to our military?"

"How fast did you read all those books?"

I shrugged. "A week. I like to read."

Acton's chuckle broke from his throat, making his Adam's apple quickly bob. "I will have to make a point to find you more books."

"It would be a welcome respite for my librarian. I have been sending poor Eleonora all over Naples for new literature."

"We can certainly grant poor Eleonora a reprieve." His eyes softened as he looked down, his long lashes sweeping low. I felt drawn to him, much more than I wanted to be. More than I should be. It was enough to stand with him. To have him near me, his scent of light tobacco and citrus. Unlike my husband, he was someone who read for pleasure. There was always a new book in his hand. It was refreshing to have someone who talked to me like an intellectual and not about hunts or little games.

Acton cleared his throat. "I am sure these men will be honored that you are reading their work."

"You know them?"

"Well, many of them. When we were pushed out of France, many of us came to the peninsula but have yet to call a place home."

"You were pushed out of France?"

"Yes, the Freemasons are not what one would call welcome in that county. Those who stay are forced into hiding. Many have gone to England, but with the war, they are not finding England the most welcoming of homes."

"Bring them here," I insisted. The words felt right. "These Freemasons of yours, they encourage science and art as well as philosophy. We could use them in Naples. We will welcome them. Make it a priority."

He gave me a little bow. "I shall send word to my friends."

* * *

Now that the children were getting older, I insisted on having quiet dinners with Theresa and Luisa. Away from the interference of courtiers, we sat in the private dining room, surrounded by red silks and crystal chandeliers that sparkled in the twilight. At four and almost three, they were already training to be young royals.

Ferdinand, a loving father, enjoyed the time with his daughters. While we sat at the table, he would regale them with tales of the people he would meet on the street. The girls would giggle as he told them of fishermen battling giant fish, or about the old woman who mistook him for a beggar when he bought a turkey from her. If the girls were good, which in Ferdinand's opinion was always, he would give them a ducat before sending them to bed.

On this evening, there was something different. He came into the room and kissed each of the girls on the head before sitting down at the head of the table.

"I sent a letter to the Swiss painter Angelica Kauffman," I said. "She has been doing such lovely paintings in England that I could not help but invite her to Naples to paint the family. I imagine Queen Charlotte of England will be upset that I stole another one of her artists, but it isn't fair they she gets all the nice portraits, don't you think?"

"This man...Sir Acton, as they call him," Ferdinand said, ignoring my question and moving aside as the servants brought us our first course of antipasti, "do we like him?"

"Yes, we do," I said.

"Hmm." He stabbed a chunk of salami. "He has a rather weak chin, don't you think?"

"I have never noticed," I said. The girls' attention moved between me and their father.

"Perhaps that is a fault of yours," he said, twisting the fork around.

"I would rather we not play this game," I said, gulping down my wine. "Especially not in front of the children," I tried to whisper.

"I like games," Luisa offered, sitting up straighter as the servant replaced her antipasto plate with another, a small bowl of mushroom-and-truffle risotto.

"Shh," Theresa whispered. "This is not that type of game."

"Oh, but, Theresa, it *is* that type of game," Ferdinand responded, swirling his fork around his bowl. "You see, Mama has been spending time with a new friend."

"Ferdinand, we don't have to do this now. Not in front of the girls."

"No, they should know," Ferdinand insisted. "Mama has spent a lot of time with someone who is not Papa."

I looked at my husband's face. His lips shone with olive oil. "You have never held an interest in my activities."

"Perhaps it's time I do." He wiped the food from his face. "I'll also be visiting your rooms tonight."

My chest clenched. Ferdinand seldom gave orders, but, in these matters, I didn't have much of a choice. Of all my freedoms as queen, I did not have a right in this. "Very well. If you must."

He threw his napkin to the table. "Apparently I do."

I continued to gulp my wine, motioning for the servant to bring more. It wasn't so much that my husband was making his marital claim; it was that when he did, there was a good chance that a child would not be far behind.

Theresa and Luisa sat at the table with their jaws gaping open. "Don't gawk," I scolded, setting my goblet down. "We will finish our dinner in a civilized manner and then be on our way. There is no point in dwelling on Papa's outburst."

Charlotte,   *July 18, 1775*

The recent rebellion in the American colonies is most troubling. You cannot let their idea of self-government seep into the minds of people in your country. Once it does, it will embed itself and rot your people's hearts. Truly, this rebellion can be traced back to the Glorious Revolution and King James II. If he had only held on to his country and had not run away to France the moment the Prince of Orange made a play for the country. It is as the theorist Jacques-Bénigne Bossuet said: A king's person is sacred. It was God who anointed David as the rightful king and made it so that Solomon would follow his father. Because of this, it is a sacrilege to go against a monarch. If you allow your people to go against the monarchy, they go against God himself.

When my father died, I did not even wait a full day to summon the privy council. With your father to my left and the imperial crest of the Habsburgs behind me, I looked over the heads of the men who had served my father so faithfully but had despised me, dismissing me as a flippant child. Though I was heavily pregnant and wanted desperately to rest my swollen feet, I stood there on the steps to the throne—the very steps my father and his father before him had climbed—because like them, I was anointed by God. It was there that I proclaimed my right as the divine monarch of Austria and that I would not let any man, woman, or beast intrude on that.

You are not only a shepherd to Naples but the queen, appointed by God himself. You have a duty to lead your people toward a path of righteousness. Tending to your flock, you must see to their physical and spiritual needs. For it is the wise shepherd who uses both love and the rod.

Your Mother,
Maria Theresa

CHAPTER TWENTY-ONE

SEPTEMBER 1776

This country was no longer the strange place that I had feared when I was fifteen. Now, at the age of twenty-four, I found that this city seeped into my very being. Naples, my beautiful Naples was a part of me, and I a part of her. I loved everything about her—from the sharp brine of the ocean, fresh and new in the early morning, to the heady, sweet scent of seafood fried in olive oil filling the streets, from the vendors who hawked *cuoppo napoletano* to the passersby. But life in the Kingdom of the Two Sicilies was not simple. We were regularly exposed to elements that sought to kill us. Mount Vesuvius, that great queen, rose far above the rest of us, a reminder that life could be taken away in one great eruption, just as had been done in Pompeii.

If the volcano didn't kill us, the food shortages certainly would. We were able to get wheat for pasta from the large farmlands to the south, and with the help of subsidized mills, we were able to provide dried pasta. This both helped the people and kept the rat infestations under control. But it was not enough; it never was.

In between us and the great farmlands of Basilicata and Calabria were great swaths of land we called wastelands. Lands where nothing could be grown or cultivated, space that even the Romans had given up on. The wastelands were a problem that we needed to conquer if there was ever to be stability in the country. It wasn't just that our people needed crops; we needed commodities that could be easily traded. Mining for brimstone was a messy business, and dangerous. Men descended into the depths of hell itself, naked, because any clothing worn would burn in the soul-crushing humidity. Brimstone could not be the future of the Kingdom of the Two Sicilies.

Turning from my papers, I watched as the rain bounced off the large windows, forming great pools of mud in the courtyard below. The contrast of the dark clouds that rolled over the grounds made the trees look like bright emeralds. When my physician, Domenico Cirillo wasn't tending to the family, he could often be found out among those trees. He had a passion for horticulture. If anyone would have an idea on how to get something to grow in the wastelands, he would be the one.

Domenico's office was one of the largest rooms in the palazzo. In addition to the office, there was a laboratory and a small living space, which I think he kept as extra storage for books. Through the opened doorway, I could see that there were stacks of books piled on top of tables and near the foot of the bed. Stepping into his office was like walking into a small jungle. Plants hung from the top of bookshelves and tumbled down over every inch of the shelves. The walls were covered with framed exotic insects, some I recognized as butterflies or beetles. Others were far stranger, their colors standing out against the overwhelming green. I half expected an animal to crawl out of one of the crevices.

His back to me, Domenico flipped the pages of a large book while what looked to be an orchid sat like the pieces of a puzzle on his desk.

"If you have brought my lunch, Maria, set it on the table. I promise I'll eat it before it gets cold this time."

"Well, I certainly hope so. It would be a shame if you died from hunger. I can only imagine the scandal."

Startled, Domenico whipped around to face me. The magnifying goggles resting on his nose made him look like an insect. "La Sua Maestà, it is an honor. What brings you here? Is everything well?" He pulled the goggles off and threw them on the table. His face turned slightly pink from embarrassment.

"Yes, yes, of course." Though it was raining outside, the room felt warm and bright. "As I understand it, your hobby is botany. Is that correct?"

"Well, it is a bit more than that, I'm afraid. I did manage to get a degree in it. There is much to be found in the study of plants that can be applied to the well-being of humanity…" Domenico's voice trailed off when he saw my amused face. "Sorry."

"I have a project for you. Something for you to focus your studies on when you are not tending to my family. Are you familiar with our wastelands?"

"Yes! They've been considered fallow for some time, but it's quite fascinating. The ash from the volcano, called tephra, is made up of little bits of glass. It is not just bad for plants, but for animals as well. And you're not asking for an explanation, are you?"

"No." I smiled. "But can you make something grow there?"

"Make something grow?" Domenico puffed out his cheeks as he thought for a moment before letting the air out in a huff. "The tephra within the soil is simply volcanic glass. The English ambassador, Lord Hamilton, has recently suggested that when you add water to the tephra, the volcanic glass turns into a mixture of clay. We were just talking about it a few days ago. There is a French chemist, an Antoine-Laurent Lavoisier, who proposed a new element that he calls *oxygène*. Perhaps Hamilton and I can use this element as a means to study this new theory…And I am talking too much again, aren't I?"

I smiled graciously. "I would like you to oversee this personally. Ask our English ambassador if he would like to assist you."

"Sì, La Sua Maestà." He looked like one of my children after I granted them a sweet.

"If anyone can grow vegetation within the wastelands, it would be you," I said. "With your help, we could create a crop that could feed hundreds of people."

"So, not only do you want me to grow something in a place where nothing ever grows, you want me to make sure that it is edible."

"Yes, exactly."

"With all due respect, you may be madder than your husband."

"Sometimes I think the same thing."

"I'll have to do a thorough examination of the soil, of course, and base the possible plants off that."

I cleared my throat, bringing Domenico back to focus on the situation at hand.

"Yes," he said. "I will bring you my findings as soon as possible."

Leaving his office, I made my way to the council chambers. The council itself was already changing with the presence of Sir Acton. Between him and Medici, I was able to tip the balance of power to my favor. The men that Tanucci held as his allies had slowly begun to fade away. Viventor, no longer able to hold control over our military or to be of use as the official royal physician, decided to retire to an estate just outside Sorrento. Others began to grow frustrated with my forcefulness and began their retirements as well. Now out of the original seven council members that Tanucci held, he only had two in addition to himself: one, a priest who was the bane of my existence, the other, a Prince di Paolo. What he was the prince of, I didn't know.

There were more titles of nobility in Naples than in all of

Austria. The titles were handed out often and almost randomly, at Ferdinand's whim. He also loved to share the title of prince, especially when he was young. There were more princes in Naples than there were dukes or barons.

As was typically the case, I was one of the first to arrive for the council meeting. Medici was next, followed closely by Acton. Naturally, Tanucci and his loyal men were the last to enter.

"I have a trade proposal that I would like to bring to everyone's attention," Acton said.

"Let me guess," Tanucci groaned. "You want to make a trade alliance with Austria, because we all know the sun rises and sets on the Austrian Empire."

"I would like to trade with the English."

"The English!" Tanucci exclaimed. "They are the archnemesis of Spain, Austria, and France! If we trade with England, we will alienate our allies, the queen's mother included."

"Then perhaps our allies should have done more to help our economy," I responded, my patience already beginning to slip from my grasp. The more often Tanucci let out one of his obnoxious outbursts, the more I wanted to throw a book at him. A very heavy book. "We have a glut of brimstone in our mines outside Palermo. Selling it to the English could help boost our economy. We could finish some of these projects that the Spanish king conveniently left half-done."

"As you all know," Acton interjected, "the English are in dire need of our raw materials. They are willing to pay us handsomely for our brimstone. The only problem is that our ports are not big enough—particularly here in Naples."

"So now you want us to spend money on expanding our ports? That's about as useful as throwing it into the sea," one of the advisors quipped.

"I'd like to throw you into the sea," I mumbled.

Acton cleared his throat in an attempt not to laugh.

"I propose that we use the port outside Brindisi," I said. "It's close enough to Sicily and we can provide safe passage against the Barbary pirates. The offer that we have received from England is substantial."

"Yes," Acton began. "They are in desperate need of supplies in their war with the Americas."

"Now we are getting involved in another country's conflict?" Tanucci yelled.

"No, it would simply mean that we are taking advantage of an opportunity," Acton retorted. "But it is true that we are undermining our long-standing alliance with France, Austria, and Spain. I know la regina is too young to remember the Seven Years' War and the atrocities that the English committed. France will consider this a personal slight."

"Is France going to build our universities?" I asked.

"*Mi scusi.*" The little priest with thick glasses and a long straight nose leaned out so that he could be seen by everyone at the table. He was a favorite of Tanucci's, and I dreaded the words that were going to come out of his mouth. His bony, liver-spotted hand was raised in the air. "Before we move forward with finishing any universities, we must get permission from Rome."

"Why Rome?" I questioned.

"Because all places of learning must be approved by the pope himself. Anything not sanctioned by him cannot be built."

"I will not have some man, from another region, telling me what I can and cannot build in my own country."

"But he is not a man," the little priest interjected. "He is God's emissary."

"And I am the anointed ruler of this country. I am the one who is tasked by God to do what is right for Naples. We need hospitals and universities. My kingdom has needs, and I will see to it that they are fulfilled, regardless of what the Papal States have to say. Let the pope take care of Rome. I shall worry about Naples. We will move forward with Signor Acton's plan."

I turned to Acton and said in a lowered voice, "We'll go to my office after this and draw up the edict. I'll have Ferdinand sign it this evening."

"Very well," Acton said, shuffling some papers in front of him and making a point not to look in my direction.

"You can't do this!" Tanucci continued to argue.

"In case you have forgotten, Signor Tanucci, I am the queen of the Two Sicilies. I am the one descended from King David"—I rose from the council table—"not you."

Charlotte,   *November 24, 1773*

You have always been the wise one in matters of the heart, and I hope you will advise me now. Since arriving in Paris, I have become the talk of the city. The people love us. Neither Louis nor I can walk in private anymore. The crowds press in, wanting their opportunity to see the new young rulers. They chant for us and get so much joy from just a simple wave. The people are so frenzied whenever they see us that Louis and I were relieved to be invited to a masquerade ball at the opera house. Donning a gown of the softest blue with flowers embroidered in gold, I determined that for that evening, I would not be Antoinette, the Dauphine of France, but rather, Josephine, the daughter of a merchant from Lyon.

All was according to plan. That was until he arrived: Count Axel von Fersen.

Oh, Sister, he was beautiful! He was standing in the midst of the crowd, under the glittering gold chandeliers, which reflected the moonlight that streamed in from the large windows, and it was like looking upon an angel. As he lifted his goblet to his plump, pouty lips, he watched me in turn. My breath caught as he moved forward. Before long, we were wrapped in a conversation away from the crowd. Conversing with him was as natural as talking with you. When he asked for my name, I told him it was Josephine. I was a merchant's daughter who was available to flirt and was open to what the future held. The party swirled around us, but I cared only about the count.

The spell was broken when a woman recognized me. She squealed and dropped into a deep curtsy. It took Fersen a few moments to understand, but then he kissed my hand and thanked me for the pleasant conversation. The masquerade was ending, and as much as I didn't want to, I had to let go. I have all the jewels in France, but the one that was most precious to me was lost as he fell back into the crowd that had gathered around me.

Oh, listen to me going on. I am being foolish, aren't I? None of this matters. I will never see the count again; he is returning to Sweden. But I find myself rubbing the place on my knuckles where I can still feel the imprint of his kiss.

Your beloved yet foolish sister,
Antoinette

CHAPTER TWENTY-TWO

MARCH 1777

Acton was walking with me from the council chambers to my office. "I've found another book for you, though I am sure you have already read it," he said. To my delight, he handed me a thread-worn *La Vita Nuova*, written in the original Tuscan dialect. I carefully opened it and took in the faint scent of vanilla and aging paper. The book, a series of poems about Beatrice, the unattainable love of Dante's life, represented cherished time with my sister. "I love this book," I said. "Wherever did you get it?"

"There is a bookshop just outside the city center. They have the oldest texts."

"It's beautiful," I said as my fingers grazed the back cover. "'*Ballad, I wish you'd find where Love has gone, that you and he would seek my lady out.*' When I was younger, I thought this was one of the most romantic books I had ever read. I even read passages to Antoinette. She, however, did not agree."

One corner of his mouth lifted. "When people think about Dante, they think of *The Divine Comedy* and overlook his early poetry. The medieval poets always *named* their loves, but Dante focused on the act of love itself. *La Vita Nuova* is all about the act of falling in love."

As we approached the doorway to my office, Acton stepped aside so that I could enter first. What was it about him that made me feel like I was a foolish girl? Trembling slightly, I walked into the room quickly. Perhaps if I wasn't so close to him, if I didn't feel the heat from his body, these feelings would fade, like the rain that had poured all morning but then evaporated with the afternoon sun.

My thoughts trailed off as I found myself staring at his lips. Acton brushed my cheek with this thumb, and I could feel myself being pulled toward him. He leaned toward me, and his lips parted and touched mine. The kiss was tender and exploratory at first, but the passion soon grew, and I found myself thirsting for more as his tongue searched my mouth. His fingers entangled themselves in my curls as we bumped into the desk.

All of a sudden, something started jostling from within the armoire, causing it to shake. The doors burst open, and Ferdinand came rolling out.

"I knew it!" he proclaimed, clambering to his feet. "I knew the two of you were, were"—he wagged his finger in our direction—"lovers!"

"Ferdinand!" I exclaimed. "What is the meaning of this?"

"Tanucci warned me. He told me that this one here"—he wagged his finger again at Acton—"was an Austrian spy sent here to usurp my rightful place as king."

Acton, red-faced, took a step back. "I shall take my leave. Your Majesties..." Acton bowed, his fists clenched at his sides.

I watched as he turned on his heel and left the room, the door slamming behind him. "You," I said, turning back to Ferdinand. "How could you?"

"How could I? You have been carrying on with that man under my very nose."

"There is plenty that goes on under your nose. It's rather large, and you are rather oblivious."

"I have given you everything, Charlotte. Everything."

"I know all about the wench you keep at the inn you so like to frequent." The color drained from his face as I continued. "The fair-haired, buxom beauty you are keen on. There are no secrets you can ever keep from me, Ferdinand."

"She is nothing."

"Of course she is not," I said. "I know all about the women you keep at your disposal. I don't care about them, because they are not a threat to me. Now I have found someone who interests me, who can talk with me like an adult, and you want to take him away? You have your women; let me have this."

"I can't have a mistress who might upset the balance of government, but you can choose a lover who can make decisions on my behalf?"

"When have you ever cared about any decision made in this country? The only thing you care about is your games."

"I am the king! I can kill you both and have your bodies thrown out the windows of the palace."

"Go ahead and try," I sneered. If I was to be the Francesca in this little play, I was going to die fighting.

"Why him?" Ferdinand asked, his voice raw with emotion

"Because Acton is the only competent man in this whole kingdom." The words hung between us. I wanted Acton because he was clever and refined. He was everything I expected a king to be, and I knew he was everything my husband was not.

Ferdinand closed the gap between us, and his mouth engulfed mine. He raised my skirt, finding the area between my legs. Grasping me by the thighs, he lifted me so that I was on top of the desk. He was rough and forceful, but I liked it. It disturbed me how much I liked it.

But as quickly as it had begun, it was over. Panting, I held my husband by the neck, his lips pressed to my ear. "Get rid of Acton," Ferdinand growled. He glared at me before pulling himself away.

As I sat on the desk, Ferdinand strode out the door, readjusting himself as he went.

There, in the aftermath of our lovemaking and the argument, I knew, beyond a shadow of a doubt, there was one thing I would not do: I would not get rid of Acton.

My Dear Charlotte,   *January 10, 1780*

I have the most wonderful news to share with you. Count Fersen, my angel from the masquerade, has returned! After he left for Sweden, I didn't expect to see him again, letting him live for eternity in my fantasies. When I saw him again, the years that had passed didn't matter; we were still the young courtiers at the opera.

I swear to you, Charlotte, this time I could not let him go. I made sure he got an invitation to every dinner party, every ball, and every hunt, so that I could steal moments alone with him. I know that it could never be, but, dear sister, did you ever wish for someone so badly that you risked everything? Even if it just meant sitting across a dinner table from him.

But I fear that I may lose him forever. Fersen is already threatening to leave again. He is talking of joining the war for American independence. It is his choice to leave, and I trust that he will return, as he did before. But to be certain, I have used my influence with the famed Rochambeau and secured Fersen a position as the general's aide-de-camp.

Your Sister,
Antoinette

CHAPTER TWENTY-THREE

May 1777

Sitting in the garden at Palazzo Portici, I listened as the ocean breezes jostled the fronds of the palm trees above, making them sound like bits of paper shaking in the wind. I could make out the upper dome of Mount Vesuvius high above the trees. Years before my father-in-law stepped foot here, she razed Portici to the ground. Carlos was in the middle of restoring the palace when he got the idea to build Caserta and to keep Portici until the new palace was finished.

Rubbing my hand over my growing stomach, I thought about how my newest child, my fifth, had come to be and the subsequent chain of events that followed.

After my husband gave me his ultimatum, I cleaned myself and found my way to Acton's chambers. His study was what I had pictured a naval officer's room to be, with books neatly shelved in an order that was surprisingly pleasing to the eye. Acton slowly spun the globe that was on his desk, his finger tracing the lateral lines that encircled it. When I cleared my throat, he looked up at me. "Your Majesty, I am sorry, I took liberties when I shouldn't have."

"Pack your things."

His shoulders slumped as he started to speak, but his breath hitched. Swallowing, he started again. "I understand, and I shall not ask for a recommendation."

"We leave for Palazzo Portici in two days, together," I said. "Be ready."

"Yes, Your Majesty," Acton said, a small smile returning to his face.

I decided I would give Ferdinand what he wanted, but at a cost.

The first time I swore to leave Caserta, it was only a threat, but there were other times when I packed my things and left for Portici. Each time, I would stay there until Ferdinand came to find me with a trinket of contrition. Once, my husband had angered me to the point of leaving a theater performance where he had had a bit too much wine. It was the story that Leopold had referred to when he was sent to Naples to investigate us on our mother's behalf. That evening, as Ferdinand and I jostled along, he started to become obsessed with the muff I was wearing.

"That's quite odd," Ferdinand said, staring at my arms. "That thing you are holding: What is it called again?"

When he was this drunk, he thought every word he said was witty gold. Often, he would laugh at his own jokes when I didn't join in his merriment.

Ferdinand continued to whine, so I mumbled, "It's a muff."

"Muff. It's a silly word when you think about it. Muff," he said. "Muff." He let the words languish in the air as he emphasized every consonant, his upper teeth biting into his lower lip as the sound of the f slipped out like a muted snake. "Muff. Can I hold it?"

"No," I said, clutching it closer to my body. "It was a gift from my sister Antoinette." She had sent it to me for the Christmas holiday, with a sprig of lilac in the middle so that it smelled faintly of her. I couldn't even look at him. I stared out the carriage window, watching the black water that lapped against the rocks along the road.

"Please, let me see it. I only want to pet it." Ferdinand swayed with the carriage as we rolled down the cobblestones. "I bet it's soft, like a kitten."

"No."

"Please?"

"No," I said. "Now leave it alone. Stop acting like a child," I muttered.

"I'm not a child. I'm the king!"

Ferdinand grabbed the muff. We struggled in the carriage, and I kicked at him, my fingernails snagging in the silk lining.

"Ferdinand, no!" I pleaded, but it was no use. My grip slipped, and the muff wound up in his hands.

"You see, this isn't so bad," he said, stroking it like a cat in his arms. "It's such a soft little kitten."

"There, you've had your fun, Ferdinand. Now give it back."

"I think Kitty wants to take a swim."

"Ferdinand, no!" I cried, but it was too late. With one swift motion, he threw my muff out of the carriage.

"Be free, little kitty!"

I let out a scream that sounded like a strangled cat as my fingernails found my husband's face. My nails dragged across his cheek before he pushed me back into my seat by my wrists. "I hate you," I said. "You are selfish and vain. I resent ever having to marry you."

When we arrived at Caserta, I had my maids put all my things into trunks. Portici was on the other side of Naples, and as far as I could escape from my husband. I stayed there for a month, wallowing in my anger. That was until he showed up with a brand-new muff for me and a delightful necklace, made of rubies, that rested on my collarbone.

"I'm sorry," he said. Tears rolled down his cheeks as he begged for forgiveness. "I was a terrible husband. I have not been the same without you, and neither has Caserta. I need you. Please, Charlotte, please come home." Ferdinand fell to his knees, wrapping his arms around my knees. His forehead pressed again my stomach.

"I suppose I can come back," I said, letting my fingers dig into the soft mink fur of the muff. It wasn't the one from Antoinette, unfortunately—that could never be replaced—but at least this one had come with a necklace. I thought Antoinette would approve of the trade. She was always fond of jewels.

That was the first of many trips away from my husband. I no longer made threats. I simply took my household and left for the palace. Eventually Ferdinand would return, and there was a part of me that missed him.

I had expected Ferdinand to come running to me sooner this time. Normally, he would wait no more than a week, maybe two, before he came back to me. But it had been months since I had left.

Sitting there, under the shade of the palms, I realized that I had not only grown fond of my husband's antics but that there was a part of me that loved them. I loved him. The way he cared about his people and furiously loved his children. When he was away from the court, he was charming and a pleasure to be around. Our people lovingly called him Re Nasone, and I had to admit, the people of Naples were not the only ones fond of that large nose.

Then there was Acton. He and I discussed literature and philosophy. He challenged me, to do better and to lead the Two Sicilies under the principles of Enlightenment. Being with him made me feel intelligent and capable. I was not a petulant woman to be tolerated, but a colleague to be respected. I treasured my talks with him and wanted more. Without the interference of the court, we were able to share stolen kisses within the walls of Portici. Was it possible to be drawn to two men at once for different reasons?

"Mama!" I heard my children cry as they came careening around the corner and straight into my outstretched arms. Little Theresa was almost five, while Luisa, always wanting to be like her older sister, was not far behind, at almost four. The two girls were the first to greet me, followed by Carlo and Anna, who came racing around the corner. Carlo tripped, but I was able to quickly catch him before disaster struck. I held them out so I could inspect their dirt-covered clothing.

"You look like little street urchins," I said, wiping the dirt from their faces. "Where have you been?"

"We saw Pompeii!" Theresa exclaimed as Luisa nodded fervently beside her. "And we got to dig for bones!"

The children's governess came up behind them, only slightly out of breath from having to keep up with them. "The children were allowed to dig for pottery. While we studied the city's history."

Theresa held out a shard for me to see. "For you, Mama."

"Oh, how precious. I will cherish it forever," I said, kissing her proud little face. Pompeii, recently discovered during my father-in-law's reign, was ripe for exploration.

"I'm going to save mine and give it to Papa," Luisa said. "If that's all right."

"Of course, my darling. Perhaps Frau Huber will help you write a letter to him."

Luisa nodded and placed her pottery shard back in her pocket. She and her father shared a special bond.

"Frau Huber, take the children to wash up before our supper."

"Yes, Your Highness." She bowed and whisked the children away.

I hired only the best governesses from Austria for my young children. If they were to be the future rulers of Europe, then I could not allow the same mistakes that King Carlos had made with my husband.

Charlotte,   *September 18, 1776*

As you know, Amalia and I did not part amicably when she left for Parma. For a time, she kept a correspondence with me, but that has stopped as well. I sent Mimi to visit Amalia on my behalf, but she reported that your sister is behaving in the crudest manner.

Amalia has usurped her husband in the most obnoxious way. She has made a complete mess of Parma, expelling every prime minister the duchy ever had. Mimi reports that she has even begun to dress as a man!

We must act as a unifying force and excommunicate her from the family. Do not respond to her letters, and if she comes to Naples, turn her away immediately. Amalia must learn that this behavior is not acceptable.

Your Mother

CHAPTER TWENTY-FOUR

JUNE 1777

Sitting under the garland-trimmed peach walls, I thought back to when I first arrived in Naples. Everyone had thought it was odd that I sipped coffee. The locals, wrapped in their superstitions, believed the brew to bring on *il mal occhio*. For years, the Neapolitan maids would leave chili peppers under my teacups to ward off the potential misfortune. Thankfully, the people soon came around to it and I no longer had to tolerate chilis under my cups.

"Domenico has sent a report about finding vegetation for the wastelands," Acton said, interrupting my memories.

"Oh, I have been looking forward to this." I set my cup down and tried to take the report from him.

"Patience, my dear queen, patience." Acton laughed, pulling it back. "You are not the only one who can bestow favors." He cleared his throat and held the papers out in front of him. "Domenico says that, after a thorough analysis of the soil, they found that after years of deposits from the ash, the ground has developed a strong layer of glass particles. However, after some testing, they found that the glass becomes unstable when exposed to water." Acton's eyes scanned the page. "I didn't know how much Domenico liked to talk until I read one of his letters…Ah, here we are. The point is that soil in this ash deposit is not very deep, so something with a shallow but sturdy root system would be ideal. Anything with a deeper root system would perish."

"Enough about the soil. Tell me what he is going to plant."

"Domenico proposes that we plant olives."

"Olives?"

"Yes, Your Majesty, olives."

"Olives," I repeated, leaning back in my chair and thinking this over. "Why olives?"

"He says that their roots are shallow, and they can prosper in both a well-irrigated environment and during a drought," Acton said, lifting an espresso cup to his lips.

"Utilizing olives in the wastelands can create more trade."

"Which means more money for Naples."

"Well done, Domenico. Write to him immediately and tell him that we approve." I kissed the palm of his hand. "I like this idea of good news. Please tell me more."

"At your will, my queen." He winked.

Just then, a servant appeared. "La Sua Maestà, there is a man here to see you. He says you and he have a long history, and he comes with an important message."

My back went rigid, and my eyes darted to Acton. I thought for sure this was another of my husband's games.

"We'll see him, here."

"Sì, La Sua Maestà."

The servant reappeared with a young man of medium height. His shoulders were slender, and he held a tricorne in his hands in front of him, his fingers gripping the edge. He had blond hair, tied at the nape of his neck, and wore the clothes of a gentleman. There was something familiar about his face, and for a moment I thought it was one of Leopold's younger sons with his eyes and the Habsburg nose. In a rush of recognition, I ventured, "Amalia?"

She grinned broadly as she bowed. "At your service."

I looked to Acton, whose jaw sat agape. "My sister and I will take a turn about the royal zoo."

As we walked through the gates of the zoo, I kept glancing at my sister, trying to get used to this new look she had adopted.

"I can assure you I am the same Amalia."

I chuckled. "Perhaps a bit more rebellious than before."

My sister smiled. "There is perhaps a bit of that."

We stopped and watched as a mother Barbary macaque picked lice from her infant. The sweet little monkeys were acquired from explorers in the Atlas Mountains and were always a favorite of mine and the children. But Amalia's smile faded as she looked at the mother monkey with her child.

"Mother wishes she were able to drown me in the river, like the runt of the litter that I am." She wiped a tear that had fallen from her eye as the baby monkey climbed up its mother's back. "I have taken the same actions as you. Done for Parma what you are doing for Naples. My husband had no interest in ruling his duchy and was quite content to let it descend into chaos while he sequestered himself in an abbey to pray. Meanwhile, the position of prime minister went to men from outside our duchy. Man after man sought to use my territory for his own gain—the French, the Spanish. You would think that Mother would be proud, that she could for once look at me and say, 'That is my daughter, Amalia, and I am proud.' She's just angry that I expelled her Austrian, the fat idiot that he was." Her face flushed, and her fists clenched. "I did everything she wanted. Everything. I gave up my Charles August for her, my one love. But, no, to her I am considered the Royal Brat."

"Well, I hate to inform you, but I had the title first."

"At least she forgave you."

"Sometimes I question her forgiveness," I said. "But what exactly did you do?" There had to be more to our mother's anger. Something had to have made her react so harshly.

"I took over Parma." She grinned. "It was quite the coup, I might add. My husband is the foulest of creatures and has no interest in being a ruler."

"I don't know—I may have bested you in that. My husband likes to rip the wigs off of any visiting dignitaries."

"My husband doesn't like to bathe."

"No…"

"Oh, yes, I had to have a discussion with the priest, telling him that I would not allow my husband to touch me until he utilized the thorough application of soap. Only when the priest and he spoke did he agree to bathe."

"Why?"

"Because my husband had dreams of being a monk. And through his devotion to God, he has vowed to denounce all his earthly privileges, which includes bathing. He spends every waking moment in the chapel praying. The only reason why I have children is because the priests advised him that it was his godly duty to procreate." She gave me a smirk. "Want to trade?"

"Not for all the gold in the world." Amalia and I laughed. "But your coup," I said, "how did you manage it?" I bumped my sister with my shoulder.

"When I got there, I was advised to take orders from a Monsieur Guillaume du Tillot. He was minister of the state, and while my husband was busy pretending to be a monk, du Tillot ran the duchy. He was nothing more than a puppet for France, and he had the audacity to give me orders. After what Mother put me through,

I will never take orders again." She shook her head. "Tillot thought he could order me about like he did my husband, but I was able to find proof that he was pocketing money from the royal coffers. So I had him fired."

"You did?" My spirits rose. If she could get rid of her problematic minister, I could too.

"It was a hard struggle, and I thought that there might be a civil war. But, in the end, I was able to find someone new. First, it was a Spanish minister, but he bothered me too. It felt like I had traded France for Spain. So I dismissed him as well and hired a prime minister from within Parma who was respected by the locals. That is the key, find a replacement who is respectable to everyone— except Mother, of course."

"And your husband, what does he think of all this?"

Amalia shrugged. "So long as he can spend all of his time at the abbey, he doesn't care. There is no hiding the fact that Parma controls herself."

I wrapped my arm through hers. "Sister, I am truly happy for you. But I still have a question: Why the men's clothing?"

"Why not? I like it." We continued walking, then paused at the elephants chewing their morning hay. "I wear men's clothes because for the first time in my life I feel like I am myself. I never felt comfortable in the dresses Mother made us wear. When I wear a suit like this, I know I am not beholden to anyone. Mimi doesn't understand, and told Mother I had gone mad."

"What does Mimi know? Mimi only cares about Mimi. The rest of us are more of a nuisance."

"I still think about it," Amalia said as we moved on to the lions. Our one male lion looked up as we approached. He let out a massive yawn that showed his fangs before flopping his large head back down. "Mimi was able to get away with marrying her choice, but the rest of us were forced to abide Mother's will."

The fresh smell of hay and cat drifted through the air as we watched the lions lolling on their backs, soaking in the morning sun. "I can't pretend to know our mother's thoughts," I said, "but she still remembers the Austria that once was. Austria before our grandfather made a mess of things." I thought of the Two Sicilies. Would I act so differently if I were in my mother's place?

"But at what risk?" Amalia turned to face me. "I can't help but feel as if you, I, and Antoinette are nothing more than cattle, just dressed up in fancier clothes."

"Amalia, you're being a bit dramatic, don't you think?"

"Charlotte, you of all people should see the damage Mother has done to Antoinette. The French hate her; they would kill her if they could. Mother made an alliance with a country that despises all things Austrian, our sister included."

"Don't lecture me about our sister," I snapped at Amalia. "I get her letters. I know her anguish. And there is not a day that goes by when I don't resent our mother for what she did to all of us, especially to Antoinette, but there is nothing that we can do. We can't dwell on the past."

"Maybe for you. I had a chance for happiness. Now I need a papal order to make my husband wash." Amalia turned from me, a shaking hand wiping away another tear.

I took a steadying breath. Amalia was not the only one who worried over Antoinette. The situation in France was getting worse, and I feared Antoinette would get caught in the middle. I could hardly ride into Paris and rescue her. Not that Antoinette would let me. Though I was only in Naples, it felt like I was across the sea.

But I could do something to help the sister who was in front of me. I put a hand on her back. "Please, Amalia, let's not fight." Amalia faced me again, and I wiped a smudge from her cheek. "I want to enjoy our visit and hear all about my beautiful nieces and nephew."

⚜

La Mia Regina,   *July 15, 1777*

I would like to give you a status report on the olive horticulture project. Were you aware that the English ambassador, Sir William Hamilton is a volcanologist? He and I have determined that the Sessana variety of olives is not only drought-resistant, but the roots are shallow enough to not be affected by the tephra. Thankfully, it can produce a very flavorful oil, which, as you know, is important when it comes to exportation.

The king has taken a keen interest in science. Though he has been quite busy with the council, sitting in with us during our meetings and asking questions, particularly about the volcano.

La Sua Maestà, I hate to add to the court gossip, but I am concerned about the king. While we were out surveying the saplings, the king asked me the strangest questions, wanting to know the negative impacts that this could have on the economy, particularly in regard to the merchants importing oils.

In the months that you have been away, the cultivation of the Neapolitan olive has been first and foremost on his mind, but now, like the wind, his mind has changed, and he claims that he must think of others over our experiments. I trust you will know what to do about these new opinions of his.

Your Humble Servant,

Domenico Cirillo

CHAPTER TWENTY-FIVE

I read Domenico's letter twice, leaving my morning espresso to sit cold on the table before me. My husband didn't know anything about economics. He normally paid attention only to the things that truly piqued his interest. Economics was not one of those things.

Acton entered the morning room and kissed my head. "What news do you have from Caserta?" He put a biscuit in his mouth but paused midchew. "Is something amiss?"

"My husband has become concerned with trade." I motioned for a servant to bring me a fresh espresso as Acton took the letter from me.

"And with the Papal States, for that matter," he said as he skimmed it. "He has never once shown an interest in trade."

"Can you have your people look into this? I want to know how Tanucci is managing to influence my husband this time."

"Are you sure it's him?"

"He thought he saw a weakness, but with your help, it will be his undoing."

"I will do my best," Acton responded.

"You always do." I grabbed his hand. "You are the one person in Naples that I can always depend on."

His thumb caressed my hand. "I would hate for you to lose faith in me."

"Not for all the gold in Naples," I said, beaming back at him.

* * *

"No, it's my turn to be the empress!" my daughter Luisa yelled, chasing after her sister Theresa.

"No, I was named after Grandmama. I should be the one to play her," Theresa declared with all the authority of an eldest child at the age of five.

"It was the children's idea to put on a play for you," their governess said. "They are quite taken with their aunt and have recently been learning of your mother's part in the War of Succession."

"Mother's greatest victory," my sister remarked. "Next to having Antoinette become the queen of France, of course."

"Or Mimi simply breathing."

Amalia laughed. "Oh, to live up to Mimi's glory."

I chuckled while kissing my daughter Anna's head. In the shadows of the palm trees, the older girls put on their play, while Carlo swatted at a bush with a stick that I believe he intended to be a sword.

Anna was the only one of my children not to join in the revelry. She rested her head on my shoulder as her fingers played with the lace of my collar. Of my children, she was the most fragile. I didn't have to worry about Theresa and Luisa harboring hatred for Anna as my sisters and I did over Mimi. The girls treated her like another one of their dolls, and for that, I was thankful.

Anna coughed into my neck, and my heart tore. With every burst that escaped from her little pink lips, I was racked with guilt all over again, reminding me that my ambition—my desire to take control of the council—had nearly cost my daughter her life.

Another cough escaped Anna's lips.

Kissing her little forehead, I swayed with her ever so slightly. Our mother had expressed her ambitions through her children—more specifically, her daughters. Each of us an extension of her, we were to rule Europe at any cost, unless we failed her by allowing our looks to be spoiled by the pox. Watching my children, I made a silent plea to God that I would not make the same mistakes as my mother.

"Your Majesty."

I turned to see Acton standing behind us.

"May I have a word with you?" His eyes glanced at Amalia and the governess. "In private."

"Yes, of course." I passed my daughter to her governess and followed him away from the garden to the great patio that overlooked the ocean. "I assume you have heard from your people?"

Acton's lips were pressed together, and his face was drained of color.

"Acton, what is it? You're starting to worry me. What did you find out?"

"The king has a mistress."

"Oh, that." I waved a hand in dismissal. "I know all about his women. Tell me, is it the innkeeper woman? Oh, or the farm girl that brings eggplant to the market? I had to endure eggplant for a whole week while they were carrying on behind the cobbler's shop. Let me say, I was quite happy when that ended; one could only eat so much eggplant without turning purple."

"Charlotte, it's a noblewoman."

My ears began pounding. Someone in my court had taken up with my husband. They had betrayed me. Whoever this woman was, by influencing my husband, she was trying to undo all the work I had done. "Who?"

Acton shifted his weight from one foot to the other, his eyes trained on the ground.

"Who is my husband carrying on an affair with?" I demanded.

"Sabina."

"Sabina? My Sabina, the Marchesa di San Marco?"

"The very one."

I found my way to the waist-high stone columns that looked out to the ocean. The laughter of the children in the garden below drifted toward us in the warm ocean breeze. Sabina. I had trusted her. She was my friend, and she had turned on me.

Closing my eyes, I tried to gain control over my rapid breathing. Tanucci thought he could get rid of me. All these years that he controlled my husband had led to him thinking that he was as one of us, an ordained monarch. I tried to channel my mother, but all I could see was anger.

"Charlotte"—Acton's baritone soothed my troubled world— "what would you have me do?"

"Prepare my things. I'll leave for Caserta in two days' time. And do not announce my arrival ahead of time. I want to keep an element of surprise."

"And me?" I could hear the strain in Acton's voice, even though I still couldn't look him in the eye.

"You'll stay here, until I send for you."

"Very well."

I turned on my heels and left to make my preparations, my skirts swishing behind me. I was going to do exactly what my sister Amalia did. Mount Vesuvius had nothing on the wrath I was going to rain down on Caserta.

CHAPTER TWENTY-SIX

JULY 1777

I took exceptional pleasure in watching the footmen stumble over each other as they scurried to serve the children and me as we disembarked from our carriages.

"Tell me, where is the king?" I asked, climbing the great marble staircase.

"La Sua Maestà is in a council meeting," the butler responded, trying to stay ahead of me, taking two stairs to my one.

I slipped off my carriage gloves and cloak, throwing them in his direction. "*Perfetto*."

Arriving at the council chambers, I threw the doors open. "Hello," I said. "Did you miss me?"

The faces of shock that stared back at me were delicious. Tanucci's jaw fell so far that I could have sworn it hit the ground. Around the table were people I had not appointed to the council, men I had never met. The little priest seemed to shrink at the sight of me.

And my husband, that great buffoon, sat up and grinned as if this were one of his games.

I pulled up a chair and plopped down. "It would appear that we have new council members. Please, let's go around the room and introduce ourselves and tell me who appointed you."

"La Sua Maestà, this isn't necessary," Tanucci began.

"Know your place," I snapped. "You seem to have forgotten that you are not the crowned monarch of this country. You have a position on this council based on our will. Everyone who is not an anointed ruler of the Kingdom of the Two Sicilies can be replaced at my leisure. And that, absolutely, includes you, Signor Tanucci." The color drained from Tanucci's face. "Now, as I was saying, who are these people that usurped our valid council members in their absence?"

"We were appointed by the king," one of them stammered.

"Were you now?" I said.

"It was him!" my husband barked, shooting up from his chair. "It was Tanucci. He coerced me!"

"Ferdinand, my dear husband, please leave. This is no place for children." My husband approached me, attempting to give me a peck on the temple, but I placed a hand on his chest, stopping him. "I will deal with you later."

With his head hung low, Ferdinand left the room.

Rising from my chair, I addressed the group of men before me. "In fact, I call this meeting adjourned. Each of your positions will be reviewed, and if I deem that you are worthy enough to sit on this council, you will be asked to return. If not, well, then, I hope you have a pleasant retirement."

"You can't do that!" Tanucci exclaimed, standing up so fast that his chair flew back in a heavy clamor.

"Did I accidentally speak in German? I said you are all dismissed."

"No! The king is the one who dismisses the council, not you."

"I am the regent to the prince, and as such, I will not see the Kingdom of the Two Sicilies fail," I said, looking pointedly at

Tanucci. "For too long, you have had your fingers in this country's business, and where has it gotten us? Your ability to meddle in our affairs has come to an end." I glared at all the men still staring at me. "Now go! Leave, or I will have the army escort you out!"

The men still sat there, unsure of what to do, as Tanucci and I glared at each other, waiting for the other to break first. "Guards!" I called.

The head of the royal guard burst through the door. "Sì, La Sua Maestà?"

"See to it that each and every one of these men are escorted from Caserta."

With the guard standing by, the men quietly stood up and filed out of the room. Tanucci, the last in line, walked up to me. "This isn't over."

"Like with everything else, Tanucci, you are so very wrong."

Under the eyes of the guard, he stalked out of the room, grumbling as he went. With the council back under my control, I moved on to my next point of order. Sabina.

* * *

It was fitting that my final moments with Sabina would be in the place where I felt I had had the most victory, the salon. Card tables sat empty of patrons as I waited for her. Shadows danced about the cream-colored walls from the light of the dimmed crystal chandeliers. The faces of the angels looking down on me now seemed to take a more sinister form, their vengeance mirroring my own. The only sound in the room was from the chessboard as the soft scrape of the pieces echoed as I moved them about.

Holding the queen piece in my hand, I remembered my mother's reactions to our father's frequent acts of betrayal. All pretense of being a queen had left her as she begged our father to give up whatever woman he was spending his days with. Like her, I craved loyalty, not just from my subjects but from the people who believed they were close enough to call themselves my friends. But I would not let that thirst for loyalty deprive me of my duty to Naples.

So long as my husband's liaisons didn't pose a threat to my power, I didn't care what he did. This time was different. Sabina was mine. The thought that she could violate my trust in such a way made me want to destroy her. Having her murdered would be too easy. I needed to set an example; Sabina's betrayal was a dangerous precedent.

"You wanted to see me, Charlotte," Sabina said upon entering.

"That would be Regina Maria Carolina," I said, not looking up from the chessboard as I reset it. It took all my strength not to throw the pieces at her.

"Sì, La Sua Maestà." She dipped low into a formal curtsy. Glancing up, I could see her hands tremble as she gripped her dress.

"Tell me, Sabina, do you play chess?"

"No," she replied. "I never learned to play."

"That's a shame. It has always been my favorite. My brothers taught me when I was young. Many a life lesson can be taught moving these little figures around. Like what to do when a trusted ally has betrayed you." I motioned to the seat opposite me. "Please, sit."

Sabina sat in the chair, wrapping her arms around herself.

"How did you enjoy being queen?" I asked.

"Cha— I mean, La Sua Maestà, I didn't—"

"Don't play the coquette with me. Tell me, did you strut about Caserta the moment I left, or did you wait a few days out of respect?" I waved my hand in the air. "Oh, don't bother answering. We both know you have no respect for anyone, yourself included."

"No," she blurted. "It was all Tanucci."

"Tanucci. Every day with this Tanucci business. I'm getting

tired of hearing his name." My fingers wrapped around the stone bishop, as I decided whether or not I should lob it at her head. "When I first arrived here, you called me naïve, but you decided to align yourself with a bloated, antiquated old man."

I threw the bishop. Admittedly, I was aiming for her head, but I missed, the figure clinking somewhere in the distance. "Your loyalty was supposed be to be to me!" I said.

"This wasn't the way it was supposed to happen," Sabina whimpered.

"Enlighten me, how was it supposed to happen? Were you going to take my place? Have an affair with my husband and undo all the progress I have made in my country?"

Sabina's lower lip quivered. "Tanucci needed a woman who was able to sway the king. Ferdinand did remark that I was pleasing."

"Oh, that I understand. We all know my husband is a spoiled man. He sees a pleasant form and will go after it like a dog. What I want to know is why? Why did *you* do this to me?"

She paused, looking me in the eyes for the first time. "Because I missed the way things used to be. When your time was spent with parties, doing what a queen is supposed to do. You are not meant to meddle in the affairs of men. Tanucci feels that you were taking the country in the wrong direction. He and his allies are not happy with your alliances. They want their Naples back."

"They want their Naples back!" My hand swept across the chess table, sending the rest of the pieces scattering all over the floor. "What you, Tanucci, and every other usurper who dares to defy me must understand is that this is *my* Naples. She is mine! I am her queen, and I demand loyalty from all of my people."

As the orange-red sunlight slipped in through the open windows, I could see beyond the carefully placed plaster that sculpted Sabina's face. The must of rotting flowers that made up her perfume. It all worked together to hide the truth, that there was nothing to Sabina. For all the cosmetics in the world, she was nothing more than a pawn. A pawn for the men who had designs on my country. I decided to pass my sentence. There was nothing more that I wanted from her.

"You will be exiled from the Kingdom of the Two Sicilies," I said, rising from the table. "You will be sent to Spain, and you will never set foot on this peninsula again."

"The whole peninsula? You can't control all the regions."

"Can't I? You forget who my family is. If you so much as breathe Italian air, I will kill you."

"But what of my husband? My children?" For the first time in all the years that I had known her, she was showing concern for her family.

"They may do what they wish. But they will never show their face in my court ever again. You have two days to pack your things and board a boat."

"That's not enough time," Sabina pleaded.

"Then I suggest you get going now." I walked out the door, leaving her alone in the empty salon.

CHAPTER TWENTY-SEVEN

July 1777

Now that I had sent Tanucci and his allies away, I had one last problem: my husband. Slipping into the family parlor, I found him sitting in an armchair by the fire, his favorite dog draped across his lap. The large head of the hound rested across his knees as Ferdinand stroked its head while he stared into the fire.

"I went to the nursery this afternoon and spent some time with the children," he said, not looking up at me. "I missed them. Carlo and Anna grew so much over the last few months. When you are young, time feels so slow. But now, I'll never get used to our children growing so quickly."

"Perhaps if you were not such a buffoon, you wouldn't miss your family for months at a time."

Ferdinand nodded as he continued to pet the dog. "Tanucci?"

"Retired."

"That's probably for the best. Sabina?"

"Exiled to Spain."

"Huh, I expected an execution."

"I thought about having her drawn and quartered, but it's simply too messy."

"You could make her walk the plank in shark-infested waters."
Ferdinand played with his dog's ears, smiling slightly.

"I guess I was feeling benevolent."

"And the baby? How is he?"

I put my hand to my stomach. "Strong."

Ferdinand nodded. "Are you staying?"

"I suppose I should. You can't be trusted with the crown when
I am away."

"I trusted Tanucci," he said. "After my father found out he was
to be the king of Spain, it was Tanucci who cared for me. It was
Tanucci who pleaded with my father to let Philip stay with me.
My father was going to take Philip to Spain. He didn't care that
my brother needed stability. A change like that would have been
devastating." Ferdinand looked up at me for the first time. His
eyes were rimmed with red. "Tanucci was a father to me, better
than the one I had."

I sat down in the armchair opposite him. "But he took advantage
of you. If he truly took your interests to heart, he would have
fought for Naples as he fought for Philip. Think about the olive
trees and what they can do for our people."

"I like Domenico and his olive trees. Your plan, to create
employment for my—*our* people, it's going to help so many."

"And Tanucci, what did he tell you?"

"It wasn't only Tanucci feeding me the lies."

"No?" Suddenly I was confused. Who else was manipulating
my husband?

Ferdinand fidgeted. "My father. He said that you were a terrible
influence. That things would be better for the country if you
were no longer allowed to be on the council, that you should be
pushed back to your duties as a consort. He was also the one
that was telling me of your supposed affair with Acton. Tanucci
and Sabina confirmed it," he said. "But then I started working
with Domenico—his science is fascinating. And I realized that

everything you have done for the Kingdom of the Two Sicilies has been to help us. I've also talked to the people. The old men I play chess with love you. The women, they have meat to put in their stews now. That's because of you."

I moved around to face him. "It's not just me."

"Acton," Ferdinand whispered.

"Yes. Acton."

"Do you love him?"

"Yes." Tears stung at my eyes. "You have to accept him. I need him just as much as I need you."

"Sabina told me you and he were together, and the way I saw the two of you look at each other." Ferdinand gulped. "The baby."

"It's yours."

"Good," he said.

"I will stay, but only if you agree to let me name Acton as my prime minister."

"Your prime minister?" Ferdinand began to protest, but then his face softened. "Fine. But I don't have to like him."

"I don't expect you to. You also have to let me take full control of the whole council. I only need you to show up when it's time to sign the decrees."

"Very well."

Ferdinand got up from his chair, his dog at his heels. He gently caressed my arms. "Will we ever be back to what we were?"

"No," I said to Ferdinand's frowning face. "We will never go back to what we once were because we must be adults now. The both of us. You are no longer governed by a regent."

Ferdinand leaned down to kiss me, but I turned my head so that his lips hit my cheek. "Right," he said, biting his lower lip and stepping back. "That will take a while as well, yes?"

I nodded. He still needed to prove his unquestionable loyalty to me.

* * *

Two days later, Ferdinand and I stood at the upper window and watched Tanucci and Sabina take their leave in carriages piled with trunks.

"It's going to be especially hot this afternoon," I said, watching with the drapes pulled back. The hot Mediterranean sun beat down on the courtyard.

"Perhaps we can walk with the children to your grotto and have a picnic lunch in the shade," Ferdinand said, standing beside me.

"Oh, that sounds lovely," I said, looking back at my husband. A warm smile broke out across his face.

Tanucci made his way outside.

"Where is he going again?"

"He has a home out in the country. A small villa where he can grow grapes, make wine."

"He'll finally be the king of his own kingdom."

Tanucci suddenly straightened up and looked back at us. I gave him a little wave, and even from this distance, I could see his face flush red.

Soon after, Sabina scurried out of the palazzo, her husband following shortly thereafter. Their two sons, lanky young men, slowly trudged toward the carriages.

Taking Ferdinand by the hand, I pulled him away from the window. "Come, let's gather the children." I felt a renewed vigor now that Tanucci was gone. Acton was on his way here from Portici, and the council was mine. The throne of Naples and Sicily was mine.

I could now understand how utterly content Amalia was when she expelled her enemies from Parma. And as for my mother, I only hoped that she would be proud over this new turn of events.

Our troubles were far from over. My father-in-law and Spain would not be happy, but I could worry about that tomorrow.

Today, I was going to celebrate my victory with my family.

My Dearest Charlotte,   *July 15, 1780*

I am writing to inform you that your uncle Charles of Lorraine has passed. He was the last of my childhood friends. When we were young, he always followed your father and me around, joining in our revelry. When they told me the news of his passing, my first thought was that the good Lord doesn't under any circumstances want to call me to Himself yet. And that makes me sad.

Time crashes into me, the days all blur into one, and I can feel the life being pulled from me. At my age, I need help and consolation, for I am losing everything I love, one after another. I am crushed by it all.

To make matters worse, your insufferable brother Joseph has not ceased in his travels. Not only does he plan on meeting with that woman from Russia in the name of a peace treaty, but he seeks to go to England. He just returned, and now he wants to go across the channel to meet with those Protestants. The English are almost all deists and freethinkers. A confrontation with these people should shake your faith in everything held sacred by good Catholics. But at least I have my Italian colonies, the regions held by you, Leopold in Tuscany, Karl in Milan and even Amalia in Parma. You four are my shining lights of Europe.

Though I am incredibly proud of my Italian colonies, you, my dear daughter, are the one who has made me the proudest. When you were proposed for marriage to Ferdinand, I feared for the outcome. By now, I am sure that is not a secret; we all feared your volatile nature.

But in truth, my daughter, of all my children, you are the most like me. From the moment you were born, you not only had my looks; you had my spirit.

You are determined, cunning, and have a well of strength that will see you through your hardships for decades to come. Charlotte, you are my daughter, and I am endlessly proud of you.

My hands have swollen from the gout and the sickness of my bones, which ache beyond measure even now as I write this letter. I doubt I will be able to write often, but please do keep me updated with all the news of your court.

Your mother,

Empress Maria Theresa

CHAPTER
TWENTY-EIGHT

The summer heat was starting to give way to the gentle warmth of autumn as we moved the court to Portici for the festivities. A low fire crackled in the marble fireplace as the children lounged on top of each other on the carpet, enraptured by Ferdinand's animated history lesson on the upcoming Feast of San Gennaro.

"A long time ago, when the Romans still ruled Sicily, there was a bishop by the name of Gennaro. He and the other Christians were persecuted by the Romans."

"Mama," Luisa asked, looking back at me. She was lying on her stomach, while Anna was flopped over her back. "What does 'persecuted' mean?"

"It means to treat someone poorly because of their religion." I was on the sofa, rocking our newest child, Francis, in my arms.

"Oh," she said, turning back around to face her father.

"Well," Ferdinand began again. "One of Gennaro's friends was captured, and being the good man that he was, he went there to try to intercede on his behalf, only he was arrested too!"

The children gasped. They heard the story every year on the eve of the feast, but it still never failed to entertain them.

"Tell them about the lions!" Theresa exclaimed while Anna wiggled into her lap, her doll clutched in one little fist.

"I will get to that, my darling," Ferdinand said. "Don't ruin it for the younger ones."

Theresa blushed slightly, but I knew the story was more for Theresa and Luisa. Anna was preoccupied with her doll, while Carlo, on the other end of the carpet, was more interested in touching his toes and waving his bum in the air. He came close to me, and I playfully patted it. Carlo jumped up in a fit of giggles, grabbing his rear and then crawled up onto the sofa to snuggle with his brother and me.

"As I was saying," Ferdinand continued, "the good bishop was captured and was sentenced to death. The Romans threw him into the middle of their colosseum so that he could be eaten by lions!"

At that, Carlo sat up and roared.

"Yes, my son, the lions went after him just like that!" Ferdinand added. "But the bishop thought quickly and blessed the lions. And you know what those mean old lions did?"

"What, Papa?" the girls asked in unison.

"They bowed. The ferocious lions refused to eat him!"

"But he wasn't saved, was he?" Theresa said.

"No, little one, he wasn't. The next day, they beheaded both him and his friend, but a woman, knowing Gennaro was special, took some of his blood. Now it is here in Naples."

"But not all of the blood is here, though," Theresa said.

"I am surprised you remembered that. Out of the original two vials of blood, Naples is missing half a vial. Your *nonno*, King Carlos, took the blood with him back to Spain so that he could always keep a part of Naples with him."

"That's not all he took," I grumbled. Ferdinand gave me a

knowing smirk. He knew my current feelings for his father, which were not pleasant. He had sent letters to us complaining about our treatment of Tanucci and our overreliance on Austria.

"What's going to happen to the blood tomorrow?" Luisa asked.

"I don't know, *cuore mio*. We will have to wait and see when we get to the church. If the blood has liquefied, then we are guaranteed prosperity."

"But what if it doesn't turn to liquid?" Theresa asked. "What happens then?"

"Then we have to pay heed, because San Gennaro is trying to warn us about terrible things to come."

"But don't worry. If that happens, it will only last a year," I said.

"Oh no," Ferdinand said very gravely. "If it stays solid, the bad luck could last for several years."

"Thanks," I said to my husband. "Now you will give the children bad dreams."

"No, they won't have bad dreams," Ferdinand said, gathering the girls in his arms. "Because my daughters are good girls. They'll say their prayers tonight, and tomorrow God will reward us all by liquefying the blood."

Just then, the governess came in to collect the children for bed.

"I hope you're right," I said, handing a now-sleeping Francis over.

Ferdinand gave me a broad smile. "Have faith, regina mia."

* * *

The next morning, the family led a royal procession to the Monastero di Santa Chiara. As we proceeded, we had the children pass out coins to the thankful people of Naples.

Walking up to the Gothic church, I felt as if I was just one cog in a steady stream of people who came before me. This monastery, which had been a part of the Naples landscape since the fourteenth century, now welcomed me and my family. Kings and queens for centuries had taken part in this holy rite and, with the Grace of God, my family would continue to be a part of that for generations.

At the center of the monastery was the seal of the Anjou royal family. It wasn't so much the men of that family but the women who inspired me. When King Robert of Naples did not have a legitimate heir to the throne, he named his granddaughter Joanna as his heir. Going a step further, he completely ruled out her husband, Andrew, a prince from Hungary. If Joanna didn't live, Andrew would be excluded from the line. And if they didn't produce an heir, the crown would go to Joanna's sister.

Taking our seats at the front of the church, I thought about Joanna the queen who came so close to greatness, but the men pulled it away. Four hundred years passed, and history had yet to change.

Andrew was murdered, and the Hungarian government blamed Joanna, so they did what any warmongering nation would do, they invaded. They overthrew the whole Anjou line, turning the kingdom over to an Angevin ruler. I had my opportunity to do what Joanna could not.

* * *

The priests solemnly entered in their own processional, the precious vials of blood in the lead priest's hands. I watched their faces as they moved past, hoping for some clue as to what the outcome was. But not a single one of them gave any indication of the results.

Next to me, Ferdinand tensed. "It has to be liquid," he whispered. He closed his eyes as his lips moved in a silent prayer.

"The blood is solid this year," the priest announced.

With a faint choking sound, Ferdinand stormed out of the chapel, to everyone's shock. I passed the baby to Theresa and ran out the door. The bright midday sunlight momentarily blinded me. But, regaining my eyesight, I saw the form of my husband pacing back and forth in the pathway, next to pillars painted in brightly colored florals. The tips of the leaves on the long, thin trees had begun to fade to yellow.

"Ferdinand, what has gotten into you?"

"It can't happen like this. This wasn't supposed to happen. I said my prayers, I did everything right."

"Stop. The blood has solidified before, right? This certainly can't be the first time."

"But this is the first time I cared." Tears swam in his eyes. "This is the first time I had faith."

"Oh, Ferdinand, it doesn't happen like that." I approached him gently. "You can't control these things."

Ferdinand kicked at the hedges in response. "You don't understand. The bad luck from the solidified blood could last years, Charlotte. Years!"

"Listen to me." I grabbed him by the elbows and pulled him to face me, my head barely reaching his shoulders. "These omens don't mean anything. There is nothing we can't overcome."

He hugged me, resting his head on top of mine. As we stood there, I couldn't help but feel Joanna's spirit in the rustling leaves, soaked into the stone that encompassed us. Naples was mine, and I was not going to let anyone take her from me.

Charlotte,   *October 20, 1777*

What Spain is trying to do is unjust, but please, dear sister, this is not the time to lose your temper.

It's most likely pointless that I am telling you this,

because you probably already know, but your husband wrote to me. I am pleasantly surprised to see that your husband has in fact changed. I can tell from his letter. He wanted my advice on governing. All along, you have said that under the proper guidance, he would flourish. I will admit I had my doubts, but you were right: Ferdinand has grown.

I have taken the liberty of sending a message to our brother Joseph, making him aware of the plot. Rest assured that all of Austria, Tuscany, Parma, and Milan will rally to your side. We are Habsburgs, and above all else, we are loyal to the Habsburg crown, no matter what country it resides in.

Just, please, for the love of God, do not lose your temper.

Leopold

CHAPTER TWENTY-NINE

The ambassador from Spain, Signor Las Casas, though he was an improvement on the last, was still an insufferable man. He spoke so highly of Madrid and its wondrous architecture that Ferdinand and I made a game of it. Every time we heard him talk of Spain, we put a finger to our nose. The one who lost had to pay the winner a ducat. I was quite pleased, as by the end of the week I was able to purchase the loveliest cameo.

Naples was not to Las Casas's liking, which was not surprising. Most of the people who moved here from Spain were unhappy. If they weren't complaining about our reforms they were complaining about our food, or the unfinished buildings, or even the people.

One early October afternoon, Ferdinand sat at my desk signing the edicts that I handed him. It was a part of our daily schedule; he would sit and sign edicts after his mornings with our citizens. After this, he would play with the children before venturing into the gardens to visit with Sir Hamilton and Domenico to discuss the status of our olive trees.

"What's this one for?" he said, looking at the document I had placed in front of him.

"The royal archives. The scholars will finish recording the history of the Two Sicilies."

"Oh." His brow wrinkled. "And this is a good thing?"

"Yes, it was a project that had begun two regimes ago but was never finished."

"Right," he said, and signed.

There was a knock on the door, followed by Las Casas. He bowed deeply. "Thank you for taking the time to meet with me."

"Yes, but please be prompt," Ferdinand said. "My children and I have plans to lay siege to Paris."

I chuckled at the ambassador's confusion. "I hope this one will be better than the last," I said.

"As do I," Ferdinand responded. "The children have gained their mother's propensity for fighting."

"Pardon me," Las Casas interrupted. "It has come to my attention that a person you hold in your midst is a traitor."

"Who?" I demanded.

"Sir John Acton."

"That's preposterous!" I yelled.

"We have it on good authority that he is sending secret letters to our adversaries."

"The only adversary I am aware of is the one standing in front of me," I said, leveling a glare at the old man.

"Where is the proof?" Ferdinand asked, much to the shock of both me and the ambassador.

"What do you mean, proof?" Las Casas said.

"Proof." A confused Ferdinand looked from the ambassador to me. "You know, when you want evidence to convict someone of something." Ferdinand turned back to me and said quietly, "That is what 'proof' means, isn't it?"

"Yes, dear," I said.

"Oh, good. I have been doing a bit of reading with the children. It's quite entertaining."

"Excuse me," Las Casas interjected.

"Ah, yes," Ferdinand said, puffing out his chest. "Proof. Do you have it?"

"Well, I…," Las Casas stammered.

"You either have proof or you don't." Ferdinand looked back up at me. "I don't understand what the confusion is."

"We have a letter!" Las Casas said. "I simply can't produce it at the moment."

"Very well. When you have proof, bring it here. Now run along. I have kingly things to do. Regina mia, do you have any more of those decrees that you would like me to sign?"

I handed more paperwork over to my husband as the ambassador slunk out the door.

"You defended Acton."

He shrugged. "I like him more than Las Casas. Acton's not always going on about…Where is he from again?" Ferdinand scratched his name on the edict and motioned for another.

"Tuscany, most recently."

"You see? He doesn't share boring details like that, though frankly, if someone isn't from the Two Sicilies, I really don't care." He looked over the papers. "Am I free to go?"

"Yes."

He kissed the top of my head before leaving the room. Sitting back against my chair, I thought about Acton and his return to court. Since his arrival in August, the tensions around the palace were exceptionally high. My decision to name Acton as my prime minister was not helpful, but then again, most of the Neapolitans did not like that I was bringing in an outsider to begin with. And the Spaniards? They simply did not like me out of principal.

But I didn't care. Somewhere in Madrid, my father-in-law, King Carlos, was regretting making a deal with the Habsburgs for this marriage. The thought alone brought me endless joy.

However, these complications were beginning to wear on Acton. He was regularly cross, and this new turn of events was not helpful. When we met in my office, Acton was especially gruff, dropping his books onto the table.

"I take it you have heard of the accusations," I said, watching the color in his face rise.

"How could anyone consider me to be disloyal to the crown that I am serving?" He pushed his fists into the table.

"I can assure you this will amount to nothing."

"How do you know?" He closed his eyes and pinched the upper bridge of his nose. "From the moment I stepped foot in this country, it has been one peril after another. First, your husband wants my head, and now the king of Spain and those loyal to him insult my integrity. It's too much."

"Do you want to quit?" I was afraid of what his answer might be. His devotion was tantamount to my success. As in chess, the queen was made all the more powerful by having her rook on the board. Acton was my rook.

"Most days, yes." He released the bridge of his nose and looked at me. "And then other days, when you and I... It doesn't matter, though, does it?"

"Of course it does."

"Why, Charlotte? Why should it matter? A man can only take so much abuse."

"It matters because I need you."

"There are many men, if not on this peninsula, then in Europe, who could easily take my place."

Taking his hand in mine, I held it against my cheek. His rough thumb traced the edge of my cheekbone. "No. There is no other."

Acton pressed his forehead to mine. "I wish that were true."

His breath hitched, and I continued. "You are a sailor. You know storms pass."

"And what of Spain?" he asked.

"Spain can go to hell."

He gave a small smile. "They are going to cause a lot of trouble for us."

"Let them." My hands slipped to his chest. "Naples and everything within it is mine."

November 1777

"You plan on having me deposed!" I hollered, throwing the book at the ambassador. Unfortunately, I missed, and it hit the bookshelf with a clatter, its pages fluttering as it fell to the floor.

We stood in the council chambers: the Spanish ambassador and his men, Acton, the king, and me. Las Casas, the small man that he was, felt that he had to have an army behind him just so that he could share my father-in-law's plans with me. If I hadn't been so angry, I would have been flattered.

"Spain feels that you are no longer capable of running the Kingdom of the Two Sicilies."

"And you think you'd do better." I reached for another book to throw, but Acton moved it before I could lob it at the ambassador.

"Spain would not rule the country itself. We would install an already established heir."

"Who do you plan on placing on my throne?"

"Ferdinand's throne," Las Casas corrected.

"My throne," I insisted, slamming my fist on the table.

"Your son," Las Casas said, raising his chin.

"Carlo? He's two years old."

"We'll have regents in place."

"Spanish regents, I presume? Because they have done wonders for this family." I looked sideways at Ferdinand. "I'm sorry."

He shrugged. "You make a good point."

"What I want to know is what is going to happen if the bloodline ends," Acton interjected.

"You are all right with this?" I questioned.

"Did I say that I was all right with this?" Acton quipped. "What I am saying is that if Spain has plans of putting a two-year-old child on the throne, they are clearly not thinking in the long term."

"If Carlo does not survive to maturity, we would place Francis on the throne," Las Casas said.

"Oh, that makes even more sense." I hugged myself as I began to pace. "Francis is still an infant. My father-in-law would rather put an infant on the throne than let a woman rule."

"What happens to the line of succession if both Carlo and Francis do not reach maturity?" Acton asked. "As the queen said, they are both still quite young."

"The queen can have another," Las Casas asserted.

"That makes me feel better. I'm going to be a bitch only meant for whelping pups." I threw my hands up in the air in frustration. "Don't you men worry. If one child dies, my husband will simply continue birthing children from me until I dry up."

"Would you put one of my brother's children on the throne if both my sons die?" Ferdinand asked. He clenched his fists. "I never liked my brother. He was always the spoiled one. I don't want his children ruling the Two Sicilies."

"We do not intend on removing your family," Las Casas said. "We are appealing to the sensibilities of both of you."

"You threatened us!" I was able to get my hands on a book out of Acton's reach, and I threw it. This time, it found its mark, the ambassador's arm.

"You see!" Las Casas protested, holding his arm. "The queen has bouts of passion that make her incapable of ruling. Her relationship with Acton alone is putting this kingdom in peril. Not to mention the matters of the letters that she sends all over Europe."

"Oh, yes, those letters you keep going on about." I spread my hands out before me. "Where are these deeply incriminating letters?"

"The king of Spain has them."

"How convenient." I crossed my arms and went back to my sulking. "My brothers will love to hear all about this. You know Joseph has had some success in Bavaria," I said, suddenly turning to Acton.

"You can't keep involving Austria in this country's affairs!" Las Casas objected.

"You involve Spain."

"That, that right there is one of our problems!" Las Casas yelled. "Ferdinand, you used to come to us for advice. Spain and France have always been this country's greatest allies, but ever since this woman came into power, she has been nothing more than an extension of the Habsburgs' thirst for power. We tried to have the queen removed from the council, but now this is our only option."

"Go ahead, bring your armies," I said. "Bring all of Spain down on us. I don't care. You will never take the Two Sicilies from me. I swear to the God above I will burn your whole country down before your ships even reach the shore."

Las Casas and his men stormed from the room.

Acton looked at me. "This is far from over."

"I know," I said, suddenly feeling cold. This must have been how Joanna felt when Hungary was preparing to invade Naples. I had to be brave. Unlike Joanna, I was going to fight for my country until my dying breath.

Charlotte,   *March 5, 1778*

I wish this could be under better circumstances. That the good news that I have to share could be celebrated without the sour tang of sorrow. First, the most pressing matter that you want to know: the status of your throne. Joseph and I have been able to make Spain see reason. Carlos understands that your heirs, Carlo and Francis, are far too young to assume the responsibilities of the crown. That if they were to die before they reached maturity, the throne of Naples and Sicily would be in great peril.

It would appear, dear sister, that no one wants to take a risk on an unstable Naples and Sicily.

Take care, little sister, and know that you and your family are in my and Luisa's prayers.

Your Loving Brother,

Leopold

CHAPTER THIRTY

FEBRUARY 10, 1778

During the months that followed, Las Casas continued to argue his case for my sons to bypass me and Ferdinand. Letters went back and forth between Joseph and King Carlos, each threatening war, while Leopold did all that he could to be the peacemaker.

While men argued my fate, I was left to try to create some sort of normalcy. Slipping into the royal nursery, I watched as my children created grand worlds out of their imaginations as fat cherubs holding wreaths gaily danced about on the ceiling above. My daughters played with dolls in their elaborate dollhouse while Carlo, barely three, was engrossed in stabbing whatever my daughters discarded. Watching the twinkle in his eye, I could tell it would be only a matter of moments before he charged, breaking up my daughters' games.

They were too young.

Spain wanted Carlo on the throne of the Kingdom of the Two Sicilies. I was no fool. Whoever controlled the prince controlled the kingdom. The fate that awaited my son, should Las Casas have his way, was the fate that befell my husband. Any sway that I had over the Kingdom of the Two Sicilies would most surely be dissolved. All the progress would be wasted as Spain took control once again.

Carlo came running over to me, falling onto my lap. He smelled of powder and just a tinge of sweat from his games. I petted his blond curls and wondered how anyone could consider placing my son above me. The burning in my stomach startled me. I was his mother, and yet I resented him simply because Spain had suggested he usurp me. He was only a child, yet his life was more valuable than my own, simply because of his sex.

He buried his face into my knees before taking off at another run. I had to find a way to stop Spain.

* * *

While I focused on an invasion from Spain, another enemy was spreading through the Kingdom of the Two Sicilies. It quietly entered homes and killed whole families before making its way to Caserta.

I was in the middle of hearing my morning mass when the governess slipped into my private chapel. She dropped to her knees beside me and crossed herself before urgently whispering, "Your Majesty, I need to speak with you. There is something wrong with Anna."

"What happened?"

"Anna woke up with a fever and is complaining of a headache. She says it hurts to sit up."

"Oh, it sounds like simply another one of her illnesses. Keep her comfortable, and I will visit this afternoon."

"No, Your Majesty, this feels different," Frau Huber said. "I have been around a lot of children. I can spot a childhood illness; this, I don't want to draw conclusions, but I think you should call for the physician."

"Yes, I'll get the physician, and we'll be there shortly."

Within minutes, Domenico was in Anna's room. There had been no expense spared for the children's rooms, especially Anna's. Adorned in purple and gold, one corner was filled with dolls. There was the redheaded doll with the curly hair that she had gotten during her last cold. Another with hair the color of corn silk. That one was for the bloody noses she kept getting last winter. The list went on and on. And each rosy-cheeked porcelain face staring back at me was a reminder of my guilt.

Because she was born so close to Carlo, we were raising them as twins, in much the same way Antoinette and I had been raised. Anna was half the size of her brother, with skin so pale that any offending bruise was a glaring rebuke of my ability to be her mother. Her bones were made of china, delicate, and she was small in my arms. Every hug, every tumble, brought on its own anxiety. Theresa and Amalia were on strict orders not to exhaust their sister too much, and, thankfully, they listened, treating her as their personal doll.

"I took the liberty of separating the children. Just to be safe," Frau Huber said. "Carlo is quite distraught. Theresa and Luisa are with him now."

"I'll see to him after this," I said as I watched Domenico prod my tiny child. She sniffled in Frau Huber's arms, and the jutting ridge of her spine caused my stomach to sink with despair. I wanted to be holding my daughter, comforting her, but it was not allowed until Domenico finished his preliminary examination. My poor child, in the two years that she had been on this earth, had spent more time with a doctor than a child should.

Domenico lifted up one arm and immediately looked up at Frau Huber. I couldn't see his face, but I could see the look of knowing concern on hers. Immediately he stopped his examination and scrubbed his hands in the washbasin as Frau Huber settled my daughter back down.

"I'd like to speak to you outside," he whispered. The moment we walked out the door, Domenico gave me his grave news. "It's smallpox. There is a pustule under her arm. It's only a matter of time before more come."

Smallpox. The illness that had taken half my family in Austria had now set its eyes on my children here in Naples. This illness was just another reminder of my inadequacies. "My sister and I were this age when we had the pox. Certainly, it won't be that bad," I said out loud, trying to comfort myself more than anything.

"I'm afraid that's too hard to say, La Sua Maestà." The worry that creased the physician's face ran deep. "This illness can hit children hard, particularly children of her constitution."

I gulped. *Children of her constitution.* Another slap in the face.

"Charlotte," Domenico said, using my name for the first time. "For the sake of the royal family, you need to inoculate everyone."

"No. The children are strong enough for this to pass, just as it did for my sister Antoinette and me."

"No." Domenico, not much older than myself, stood in front of me, his fists balled at his sides. "Regardless of their strength, they can still die. Let me do the work you charged me with. Let me inoculate your family."

"Inoculations are too dangerous," I said. "I watched my sister Johanna die. Whole swaths of my family are dead, and fortunes changed, because my family put faith in inoculations. No, I will not risk my family."

"Then you have to leave," Domenico said.

"Leave Caserta? Are you mad?"

"If you won't inoculate the children, then you have to leave. These are your only options, and don't think I won't challenge you, regina mia. You may be the center of the country, but I am the one who is responsible for your well-being."

Storming away from Domenico, I went to find my children. They were all huddled together on Theresa's bed. Carlo sniffled into a pillow as my eldest rubbed his back, in the same manner I usually did for them when they weren't feeling well. Luisa sat at the end of the bed, watching them.

"Where's Anna?" Luisa asked upon seeing me.

"She is in her room with the doctor," I said, getting on the bed and pulling Carlo into my arms.

"Anna," he whimpered in his sleep.

"I know," I said. I took over rubbing his back as he continued to whimper.

"Is Anna sick?" Theresa asked from her corner of the bed.

"Yes, my darling, Anna is very sick. We will have to stay away from her until she gets better."

The girls nodded as I stroked Carlo's hair.

One of my first memories was when Antoinette and I were children and we were stricken with smallpox together. Though we were sick, we felt like we had all that we wanted. For two weeks, it was her and me creating imaginary castles under our blankets in the large bed that we shared. We were given every luxury two young girls could think of, from toys to food; even my dreaded lessons were canceled. In the end, Antoinette had two marks, one on her face and another on her arm. I had just the one, on my upper arm.

From the moment Anna was born, she and Carlo had never been apart. Siblings raised so closely were never meant to be separated. And yet wasn't I doing the same thing that my mother did to Antoinette and me? Keeping my children apart to protect them?

As I ran my hands through Carlo's blond curls, I hoped that this separation would end soon, because I wasn't sure how much more of this Carlo could take.

February 23, 1778

I am a queen before I am a mother.

Orange-gold light streamed in through the Gothic windows, spilling over the remains of my daughter Anna. The royal mourners were long since gone, and I was left sitting alone with the heavy, all-encompassing silence. It wrapped around me and settled by my side, gripping me, as I waited for Anna's casket to be interred in our family vault under the floor. The cloister, devoid of all noise except for birds chirping somewhere in the distance, comforted me as I sat vigil. Wrapping my black shawl around me tighter, I tried to ward away the penetrating cold that lingered among the stone pillars, but it was no use. The frigid silence numbed me to my core.

How did my mother do it? How did she lose so many children yet still manage to carry on? The great Empress Maria Theresa of Austria gave birth to sixteen children but lost six of them to disease before they even reached adulthood. Did it become easier over time? I couldn't imagine that. One thinks that they can never get over the pain of childbirth. But this was a pain far worse.

My soul ached. If I were any other woman, I could let myself break down. I could sink into my bed and not get up for weeks, even months. No one would blame me. They'd say, "Poor Charlotte, the death of her daughter broke her. Such a shame."

But I could not break.

Looking back at the great iron doors, I shivered. When I stepped outside again, I would have to be Maria Carolina Charlotte, queen of Naples and Sicily. This grief would be nothing more than a scar, hidden behind vain cosmetics. I hung my head and said a prayer as I let myself linger in Santa Chiara's embrace. Naples could wait, just this once, while I sat with my daughter.

Charlotte,   June 5, 1789

He's dead, Charlotte. My son is dead. Louis-Joseph had been sick, so I took him from Versailles to my estate. I thought he would be safe. I thought that I could protect him. If there is one thing that I should be able to do in this life, it is protect my children. Apparently I can't even do that.

This grief, I don't know how I can get past it. It is an open black pit that will never be filled. How can I go on? How can I move past this and put on a brave face for the court? Any amount of weakness that the court perceives will just be used to further attack my character. Can't I just stay at the Hameau de la Reine forever?

Your sister,
Antoinette

CHAPTER THIRTY-ONE

February 28, 1778

Was it sympathy that allowed Ferdinand back into my bed? Or was it the fact that we were the only ones who felt the rawness of the loss of our daughter?

My husband, for all his faults and immaturity, was a good father. He spent his afternoons with the children, where his chief concern was how much he could get them to laugh. It was their innocence that he loved, their ability to always be honest.

Upon my return to Portici, I found Ferdinand in our family parlor. The walls, once seeping with the joy of family, were now devoid of mirth. The haunting light of the fireplace spread along the walls and over the darkened chandelier. I thought back to our last visit, when the children were enthused about the Feast of San Gennaro and sat in rapture of their father's stories.

Now Ferdinand sat in an armchair, watching the fire as the flames pranced along the dying logs and stroking the head of his favorite hound. The shaggy brown hound sighed as he nestled against Ferdinand's knees.

Silently I placed a hand on my husband's shoulder. Reaching up, he grabbed my fingers in his.

"Did you see to Anna's interment?"

"Yes."

"Good."

"I should make sure the other children are settled," I said. Thank goodness Francis was too young to know what was happening.

"I already tended to that. I also made sure they got extra sweets. Not that they ate them. Especially Carlo. Please, sit," he said, motioning to the chair across from him. "Neither of us should be alone after burying our child."

"I'm not surprised about the children. Growing up, we always felt the sting of the loss of a sibling." I smoothed out my skirts as I sat in the chair opposite my husband. "When you are young, you think you'll have your brothers and sisters by your side until you grow old. When your parents are gone, they are your last connection with your family, your history. But when a sibling dies, especially if it is when you are a child, you feel the sting more acutely. You don't just lose a sibling; you lose a shared sense of history."

We sat by the fire, letting the crackles and pops soothe us: Ferdinand with his chin resting on his hand, I with my fingers twisted in the black lace of my dress, and the giant dog snoring on the carpet.

"I should go back to my rooms," I said while rising.

The dog stretched and let out a satisfying yawn that I couldn't help but catch. Suddenly the events of the day had settled around me, and I felt tired and ready to sleep. Ferdinand rose as well. "Please, stay." Taking both my hands in his, he pressed them to his lips.

Our eyes locked. In moments, Ferdinand's mouth was on mine, his hands knotting in my hair. Connected to each other and still fumbling with our clothing, we sank to the carpet, coming together in our shared grief. There, in front of the fireplace, I needed him. The one soul who felt the raw, agonizing pain as much as I did. His broken heart pounded in his chest. I pulled him to me, comforted as his strong arms held me closer still.

Afterward, we lay on the rug, my head in the crook of his arm as his fingers played in my hair. "We were a good match, weren't we?" he said.

"I think we still are." My fingers traced his ribs until I found a spot that tickled him. He grabbed my hand and pressed a kiss into my palm before holding it against his heart.

"The way you love Naples," he said, "I thought I was the only one who loved her like that. We shared a vision."

"I still have that vision."

He rested his arm behind his head and stared at the fresco above us, the angels frolicking in the moonlight. "If we still share a joint vision for our country, do you think that we will find a way back to what we had before? I would like to visit your rooms again, if you will let me."

I stroked his cheek. If he wanted to, he could force me. There was no court, no council, that could stop him. But here, in the aftermath of that mutual expression of grief, I didn't want to let go. I wanted the companionship that only he could afford. Closing my eyes, I felt my hot breath against his neck. "Yes."

December 1, 1778

Every room within the walls of Caserta was decorated for the Christmas feasts. A grand manger scene had been erected in the ballroom, each doll hand-carved by a local artisan. Every fireplace held a *ceppo*, which burned from the start of the Christmas season to Epiphany, when La Befana visited the children. And on the mantels, bookshelves, and every other corner imaginable a bauble of some sort was displayed.

But in our personal parlor, the spirit of Christmas was nowhere to be found.

"We have no choice but to leave the city," Acton said, addressing Ferdinand and me. He was made even more sure of himself with Domenico by his side.

"I will not be forced out of my own home! Especially not when my child is sick."

Since Anna's death, Carlo had not been the same. He barely ate. His days were spent crying and sulking in his room. Not even Ferdinand could get him to release even a little of his sorrow. And now, Carlo was sick. Smallpox had resurfaced in Naples, and this time it threatened to take my son.

"These last few months have been awful on you, I know," Acton said, lowering his voice. I knew this trick; he thought that he could treat me like a wild beast, that I could be soothed by the tone of his words. He should have known better. "You've lost a child, and Carlo has not been the same."

"I'll not leave him," I insisted.

"La Sua Maestà, listen to me," Domenico begged. "Smallpox has ravaged Naples. We cannot risk your life—"

"I had smallpox when I was five."

"But your unborn child hasn't," Domenico retorted.

My hands went reflexively to my stomach. I was thirty weeks pregnant. With Ferdinand visiting my apartments, it had been only a matter of time before I was with child again.

Domenico continued to plead his case with me. "There is so much about this illness that we still don't know. We don't know if your immunity will be passed on to the child, and if you give birth while the virus is in the area, we don't how it will affect him."

"What about inoculation for me?"

Domenico shook his head. "It's too dangerous. There is a chance it could still give you the virus. And with your being pregnant, it's too great of a risk. Right now, the best option you have is for you to leave."

"No, I won't hear of it!" I yelled. "I left Anna, and I have regretted it ever since."

"Then inoculate the children!" Domenico yelled back at me. "If you didn't adhere to this foolish fear of inoculating your children, we wouldn't have to do this."

"Think of Francis," Acton pleaded. "He is just over a year old. If Carlo dies, Francis will be the heir presumptive. You have to think of your healthy son in addition to the kingdom."

Tears were swimming in my eyes as I looked into Acton's dark-blue ones. "This isn't fair. I want to stay with my son."

"But you can't," Acton said softly. "I know how much this weighs on you, but you have to do what is right for Naples and Sicily."

"Acton, it seems that I am always doing what is right for Naples and Sicily, all at the expense of my own family. Is there any other way?"

"I wish there were," he said.

"We'll leave Naples," Ferdinand said, cutting through the argument. He was leaning against the window, not taking his eyes off the garden below him.

"Very well," Acton said, bowing to Ferdinand.

I glared at Acton, but he came close to me and said, "This is for the best. You'll soon come to see this as well." He placed a gentle hand on my arm before making his exit.

"Philip has smallpox," Ferdinand said, turning back to the window. I put a hand on his shoulder, but he shrugged it away. "You aren't the only one who has to choose between family and Naples."

"Oh, Ferdinand, I'm sorry."

"The decision isn't yours to make anymore. We'll do what's necessary for our family." Kissing my cheek, Ferdinand left me alone in the parlor, the remains of the *ceppo* crumbling in the fire.

The next day, we retreated to the country, far from the reach of the disease. And Christmas? None of us felt like celebrating the feasts. First, we received news that Ferdinand's brother had died, and then, not even a week later, we received word that Carlo, too, had passed.

The letter slipped from my hands as it fell to the floor. My son was dead, and I couldn't even be there to bury him. His death, just like Anna's, was my cross to bear. I hadn't listened to Domenico. I thought I knew best, and now he was gone.

"At least he is with his sister," Ferdinand said, getting up from the breakfast table. "As if that is any consolation." He threw his napkin on the table. "I'll be out hunting."

January 1779

After the spread of smallpox subsided, we returned to Caserta, just in time for me to give birth to another daughter, Christina. But there was no celebration. Her birth was overshadowed by the grief we all felt at the loss of Carlo.

As I sat in her nursery one starless evening, shortly after her birth, I wondered if she, too, would be sacrificed on behalf of the Two Sicilies. If there were ever to be a sacrifice big enough to satisfy the kingdom.

⚜

Dear Charlotte,   *December 5, 1780*

It is with great sadness that I must report that our dear mother has departed from this world. As you were aware, she has been sick for quite a while, but about a month ago she went hunting with Mimi and her husband. At first, I protested, but Mother simply said she would not be confined until the good Lord had deemed it appropriate.

As Mother hobbled off to the carriage, Mimi promised to look after her. But she didn't. They took an open carriage and got caught in a storm. Soon after, Mother came down with pneumonia. Rest assured, Charlotte, Mother fought for every breath until the very end. We tried to encourage her to take the potions prescribed by the physician, but she turned them all away, insisting that she didn't want to be taken by surprise.

I was the only one allowed to sit vigil after she banished Mimi and Elisabeth from her presence for fear of them seeing her as weak. The weather was poor, with a fine drizzle settling over Schönbrunn. My eyes were half-closed when I heard her murmur, "This weather is bad for so long a journey."

Rushing to her side, I tried to push up her pillows, but she waved me away, telling me not to fret, for it was a good enough day to die.

With that, the woman who we thought would live forever let out her last breath. All of Austria mourns for our empress, Maria Theresa Walburga Amalia Christina. I may have waged many a battle with her, but I have never been her enemy.

Amid all this sadness, as I prepare to take full control of the Holy Roman Empire, I want you to know that Austria will continue to be a valuable ally to the Kingdom of the Two Sicilies.

Your brother,

Joseph
Emperor of Austria

CHAPTER THIRTY-TWO

December 10, 1780

I clasped my hand over my mouth to stifle the scream in my throat. At the age of twenty-eight, I felt like an orphan. Running to my letter box, now overflowing from years of correspondence, I pulled out my mother's letters. Reading each one in order, I let my fingers trace the slanted loops and bends that were her handwriting. Now more than ever, I craved her.

A world without Maria Theresa made me shiver with fear. Without her, I could feel a shadow over Caserta, the same shadow that I felt sure was passing over all of Europe, leaving her children a little worse because of it. There was no room for detraction or rebellion. Mother didn't allow it. Even the smallest edicts given by the empress were to be followed without question. There was no ruler who could even come close to Her Majesty.

Joseph had given me his assurance that he would stand with Naples and Sicily in any emergency, but I couldn't help but worry how far he would go to protect us. Mother had brought up the use of troops only when it was absolutely necessary. But Joseph? He would send a whole army for the sake of one protest.

Of all of us, Joseph was the one who fought with Mother the most, but now that she was gone, he was going to take advantage of his newfound freedom. With Joseph, there could be a firm resolution to the growing unease in France, but the other territories would most certainly suffer.

His age was another matter of contention. After the tragic death of his wife and daughter, he had refused any mention of another marriage. He was nearly forty with no intention of marrying or bearing any more children. His successor was to be Leopold. Which meant that the title of Duke of Tuscany would be left for one of Leopold's children. I would have to make sure he considered one of my daughters for his son when they were of age.

I searched through my mother's letters, hoping that any advice she had left for me could be savored, like the crumbs left over after a cake.

Mother had forced her will on all of us, but now as I held a hand to my growing stomach, thinking of my latest pregnancy, still early in its term, I could understand. Not only did Empress Maria Theresa need to grow her dominion, but she needed to secure her children's roles in the world. Soon I would be placed in the same position.

My mother had given birth to sixteen children, while this child growing inside me would be my eighth, and my greatest worry was that my children would be established enough to survive in this ever-changing environment.

When Antoinette was first married to Louis in France, she was loved. Now the people had turned on her, and I feared the worst. I could not let my children fall victim to the same treachery. They needed to be given opportunities that would both support them and the well-being of the Two Sicilies.

Just like my mother had given me.

It was a realization that I didn't like. My mother had controlled who I married and why. At the time, I hated that she decided to send me to Naples, but now, as I was faced with similar decisions, I could understand why. Everything was for the glory of the Two Sicilies. We were the anointed royalty; this was our burden.

I wiped the tears from my face when there was a knock on the door. "Come in," I ventured.

Acton entered. "You weren't at our meeting. Is everything all right?"

"No," I said, breathing a heavy sigh as I attempted to keep a wave of fresh tears at bay. "The court will be entering into a period of mourning."

"Why?" Acton's brow creased with worry.

"The empress of Austria has died," I said, putting the box of letters away. "Give me a few moments, and I will accompany you to council. You can update me on events as we walk."

"Are you sure? Wouldn't you want to cancel the meeting, at least for today?"

"No," I said. "It is not what my mother would have wanted."

"Very well," he said, waiting for me outside my rooms.

Taking a moment, I went to my looking glass to smooth my hair. I paused. I could see so much of my mother in the woman in the mirror. From her blue eyes to her oval face, whether I liked it or not, I was my mother's daughter.

Dear Charlotte,   *August 1, 1786*

I was recently paid a visit by the precious Mimi. I truly believe that she visited me simply out of jealousy. Why would that woman do anything for anyone within the family?

After Joseph's first visit, he and I forged a friendship

that I never expected. Our brother, without the shadow of the empress, is funny and kind. He has a dry wit that I do think you would appreciate. His visits have become pleasant occasions. I only wish I had been able to know him better when we were children. It is Mimi's jealousy over my relationship with Joseph that prompted her to grace us with her presence.

Mimi found our French customs to be pompous and the food too rich, and at every opportunity, she compared Versailles to life in Vienna. Mimi complained so much that the nobility here began to openly comment on how arrogant the Austrians were, myself included.

I spirited her and her husband away from the public eye to my estate in the county. Of course, she did not like that either. She complained about being brought to a hovel instead of staying at a nice palace. The whole time she bragged about how much our mother loved her and what a great tragedy it was that she had died.

For the rest of my days, I will never understand why a woman who has been given so much could be so rotten in her very heart.

One day, while we were enjoying a sun-filled afternoon by the river, Mimi decided to turn her attention to Marie Thérèse. She said it was a shame that so many of the Habsburg looks were not passed on to my daughter, that the French features were not apropos for a girl so lanky, and that she was far too forward. Mimi complained that a child should not even be allowed in the presence of adults. As if she would know what is proper for children, given that she has none of her own.

I am constantly criticized by my court, the people, and even foreign counties; I could not let Mimi abuse my daughter. Without wasting another moment, I insisted that she leave the Hameau de la Reine in the morning, even if I had to have the armed guards escort her.

Charlotte, I truly never want to see that woman again. Any resentment I felt toward her as a child has been amplified threefold. I wish I had a friend, a true friend, at court with me. You are so far away, and I miss you more than you could ever know.

Your Sister,
Antoinette

CHAPTER
THIRTY-THREE

APRIL 18, 1785

I stood at the back of the salon, watching as the guests walked in and took their positions at card tables. Since the end of the war in the Americas, there were more former English generals and nobility calling Naples their home. Many were disillusioned from the events that had transpired; others just wanted someplace new to call home.

Sir William Hamilton, recently returned from England, walked into the room, greeting many of his compatriots. The longtime English ambassador was the childhood friend of King George III's. The two were so close, in fact, that Hamilton called him his foster brother. However, I was surprised to see him alone, given the rumors. "Acton, I thought he brought a woman back from England with him?"

"He did, but she is his mistress."

"Oh," I said, watching as Hamilton took a spot at the card table. That explained why she hadn't made an appearance at court. "I am happy he has found a new companion. It was such a shame when Catherine died. I did so enjoy her; she played a beautiful

ANTOINETTE'S SISTER   223

pianoforte. Even Mozart found it to be moving. Tell me, what do you know about this mistress?"

"Her name is Emma Lyon. She was a notorious socialite in London, a favorite model of many of their popular artists. Prior to this, she was attached to Charles Greville, Hamilton's nephew. The fact that she ran away with Hamilton was quite the scandal."

"And they live as man and wife now?"

"No, not entirely," Acton said. "He lives in the upper apartment in his home, and she is in the lower. From what I understand, she has her own life, and he doesn't interfere."

"Then how is she his mistress?"

Acton winked. "I'm a bachelor. How am I supposed to know these things?"

I laughed and placed a hand on his arm. "Tell Sir Hamilton to come here. I am curious about him and this new friend of his."

In a short time, Acton presented Hamilton to me, who bowed in turn.

"I understand you have been working with Domenico on our olive tree initiative," I said to him.

"Yes, the effect of the volcanic particles within the soil is quite fascinating. It has been an honor to be able to work with him and the king on this matter."

"I am so glad that you are enjoying your position here in Naples. I imagine it is quite hard to study volcanoes in England."

Hamilton chuckled. "Yes, we are known more for our seafaring than we are for our volcanic activity."

"Tell me, how are your countrymen finding Naples?"

"It has the most healing air after the loss of the colonies."

"It's the southern air," I said. "Tell me, does your friend Emma find this as well?"

Hamilton sputtered a little as his eyes darted from mine to Acton's. "Yes," he finally said. "She has been finding it quite soothing. She also has a love for the antiquities and has been taken with your Herculaneum and Pompeii."

"She would certainly love my garden then. It's a shame you can't bring her here so that I can meet her."

Hamilton pulled at his collar. "Yes, that is a shame."

"Perhaps I can go to your home then."

"I-I simply don't know about that," Hamilton stammered. "Our apartments are so small."

I shrugged. "Then it will be a small party. Not every fete needs to be a grand affair."

* * *

Three weeks later, Ferdinand and I were in a carriage bound for Sir Hamilton's home.

"I should hope we can talk more about volcanoes while we are there," Ferdinand said with a grin. "Hamilton and Domenico have the most fascinating conversations. I can't understand half of it, but it is still quite enjoyable. Did you know that Vesuvius isn't the volcano that destroyed Pompeii? It was Mount Somma. Vesuvius is only the inner crater."

Under the influence of Domenico and Hamilton, my husband became obsessed with geology, often retelling facts that he had already shared, but because he was so excited, I humored him. It was better that he be interested in this than in something more meddlesome.

"Tell me again, why we are going to Hamilton's home?" Ferdinand asked as we rolled through the darkened Neapolitan streets. The happy chatter of townspeople going about their evening entertainments, intermixed with the ruckus of parties already under way, cut through the night.

"Because I thought it would be nice to have a party away from the palace for once."

"Does this have anything to do with Hamilton's new mistress?"

"No, of course not."

"You are a terrible liar," Ferdinand said. "You want to know who this woman is, just in case she is a threat."

"She'd only be a threat if you slept with her."

Ferdinand shrugged with one shoulder. "The night's young." I kicked at his shin, and he laughed. "I'm simply saying that this woman is all everyone can talk about. The famous model and socialite from London. You want to see what the fuss is about, because for once people are talking about someone other than you. Oh, don't look at me like that, regina mia, your reasons are nothing to be ashamed of. If I had any competition, I'd want to know all about them as well."

I huffed and looked out the window. As much as I hated to admit it, Ferdinand was right. This woman was the talk of Naples. This scandalous model who had sought the richest men in society was now attached to my English ambassador. She was known for being a model for painters in some of the most scandalous positions. I pictured a little blond thing covered in rouge. I was sure they could smell her perfume halfway to Sicily. I worried what kind of trouble she could cause should Hamilton make her his spouse.

Greeting us at the door of the large two-story town house was a petite brunette with large green eyes, a perfect button nose, and small Cupid's bow lips. Immediately she dropped into a deep curtsy, her loose pink gown flowing around her; it looked more like a dressing gown than it did a formal dress. I was immediately taken aback by her.

"Your Majesty, it is an honor to have you in our home," she said in halting Italian.

"It is a pleasure to meet you as well."

"Please, follow me to our dining room." Her long, dainty fingers shook as she tried to usher us into the home with all the grace of an English duchess. We walked through a narrow hallway that opened to a large parlor, filled with paintings of ancient Pompeii, except for the pianoforte in the corner, where a lone vase filled with bright flowers stood, and a miniature portrait of Catherine, Hamilton's wife. The wall to my right was covered in swooping soft-pink drapes with opposing Roman columns.

Ferdinand grinned and leaned toward me. "I think she likes you."

We were seated at the center of the table in the dining room, with Emma to my right and another ex–English soldier to my left. Across from me were Ferdinand and Hamilton. The rest of the table was filled with Englishmen newly arrived here in Naples. The dining room was similar to the parlor, with its walls covered in paintings.

"Sir Hamilton, I see you have become quite taken with not only our volcanoes but also our artifacts," I said as a servant set a plate in front of me.

"Yes, every day we are finding new clues as to how these people died and the historic ramifications of a volcano of this size. We can use these findings to prevent such damages in other parts of the world," he said, his face lighting up at the opportunity to talk about his passion. "Truly when it comes down to it, if the wind had blown in the other direction, Naples would have been the one to be covered in ash."

"This city is so beautiful that I can hardly imagine," Emma said. "But then again, if it had, I would be collecting antiques from Naples instead of from Pompeii!" she continued, to polite chuckles from the table.

"You have an interest in collecting antiques from Pompeii?" I switched to French, hoping that she was more comfortable in that language.

"I do. I am in love with the Kingdom of the Two Sicilies. I have only been here for six months, but I could spend a lifetime exploring your amazing realm," Emma said enthusiastically in perfect French.

Hamilton coughed, and Emma quickly changed the subject. "I have the most fantastic bit of entertainment planned for us later. It is a game that William—I mean, Sir Hamilton and I quite enjoy." This time, it was Hamilton's turn to blush.

"I have to admit, I was quite anxious for your visit," Emma said to me softly as conversations broke out around us. "You are such a stunning woman, and the way you have taken charge of the country is inspiring."

As I felt the attention of Emma on me, I could understand how so many people were keen on this English girl. Though she was young, she had a worldliness about her, but at the same time, she had genuine naïveté, which seemed to act as protection from the dangers that lurked within the shadows of her smile.

After dinner, we moved to the parlor for our entertainment. As we sat on couches and settees, Emma took her place between the columns. That was when I realized that it was meant to be a stage. Servants passed around espresso and biscotti as Emma began to talk.

"Now what is going to happen is that I am going to strike a pose, and you, my lovely audience, will guess what the statue is. I'll choose an easy one to get us all started."

Emma placed one hand at her breast and a second over her vagina. Cocking her head, she made the most serene face. I could see how she had become a favorite of painters.

"*Venus!*" an English officer with a thick mustache called out.

"Correct!" Emma exclaimed. "Now this one is my favorite, but it's harder." Emma reached her left hand behind her head and stretched her right hand toward the sky. She arched her head back and focused on her extended hand. She also extended one very long leg, which slipped through the slit in her dress.

"*The Dancing Faun!*" Sir Hamilton called out.

"Yes!" Emma clapped with glee.

"I heard she normally does this in the nude," Ferdinand whispered in my ear, "but this is good too."

Her joy and innocence were contagious, and for the rest of the evening, we laughed and played her game. As Ferdinand said our goodbyes, I grabbed Hamilton by the elbow and whispered, "I want to see this woman at court. I suggest you marry her so that I can have her as one of my ladies." I patted his arm as we left the home.

Two months later, we received notice from Hamilton that he and Emma were returning to London for their wedding.

Smiling, I had my secretary send them a present and an invitation for Emma to join Sir Hamilton at court when they returned.

My Dearest Sister,   *April 10, 1789*

I have fallen again into the German melancholy. You know the state of which I speak, for our family has become ill with it on many an occasion. Mother had it in the end, as did Josepha before her death. This feeling, every morning it wakes with me—this sinking unexplainable dread. It tells me that the day will not bear anything good. I shake for reasons I don't know. So many mornings, I wish that I could stay within the folds of my blankets and never leave.

But I can't because, my husband is frozen in fear and indecision. Though Mother is gone, I feel her presence with me even now. Her impatience, pushing me forward, reminding me that I am a queen above all else. It was why I chose to brave the crowds that jeered and spit at our annual procession from Versailles to Notre-Dame.

Accompanied by the American Gouverneur Morris, I wanted to ensure that these Americans would grow to be our allies. I donned a dress of silver that shimmered in the sunlight, a perfect mirror to the king's gold. In my hair, I wore the Sancy diamond, surrounded by the Mirror of Portugal diamonds. At the tip of my bodice, I wore the de Guise diamond. I refuse to wear a necklace ever again, not after that horrid affaire du collier. I was determined to be the vision of a queen, a queen appointed by God. Even if the people hated me, they would see that I was their blessed royal.

It seemed to go well; the people even cheered for me. Not as much as it was for the king, but it was still enough to quell the trembling within my stomach. Still, I should have known it wouldn't last for long. While we sat in the cathedral, the bishop took the opportunity to preach on the sin of greed and how the royal family embraced this deadly sin.

As I dared look at the faces of the enraptured congregation, my heart fell.

And Louis? He slept.

I hid behind the carefully crafted facade of being a queen until I could sink back into my bed and pretend, just for a little bit, that we were back in Schönbrunn.

Your Sister,
Antoinette

CHAPTER THIRTY-FOUR

We heard the rumblings about France all the way in Naples.

It started with whispers. People couldn't feed themselves. The price of grain became more expensive than gold. The nobility refused to pay taxes, putting the burden to fund the country on the common man. Revolts broke out. All the while, the abuse of my sister grew louder.

It was an overcast morning when I sat with Acton, reviewing the slander against Antoinette and the deteriorating situation.

"What news do you have of Paris?" I asked as Acton sat with me at the table.

"The treasury is empty."

I sipped at my espresso. "That's something we were already aware of. They have been spending at a record pace, and the war that they funded in America certainly didn't help."

"The treasury suspended payments on the government's debts."

Setting my cup down with a loud clink, I looked to Acton in shock. "They are refusing to pay their debts? Can they do that?"

"Certainly. But it won't make anyone happy. And, mark my

words, it will cause more trouble. Loménie de Brienne, the finance minister, resigned. Jacques Necker will be returning."

"Necker?" I broke a biscotto in half, bits of almond scattering across the plate. "My sister told me she hates him."

"He is the only one who can potentially help the country, though, at this point, I am not sure how they will be able to rectify this situation."

Pushing the bits of almond around, I asked the question that had been on my mind. "And the pamphlets?"

Acton sat back and crossed his arms. "They've gotten worse."

"Was your contact in the court able to get any?"

"You don't want to see them."

"I believe I am capable of being my own judge."

"Charlotte, what is the point?"

"I need to know what they are saying."

"They are vile."

"They are about my sister!"

With a resounding huff, he pulled a few out of his book, slapping the offending papers down on the table in between us. Staring up at me was a depiction of my sister—my little sister who I loved more than life itself—with her skirts raised and her genitalia displayed for the world to see. A snickering man was preparing for his turn with her. The pamphlet underneath wasn't much different, only this one had a dog licking at her nether regions. I pushed them away.

My sister Amalia was right. This was all our mother's doing—not caring about the welfare of her daughters, only the glory of Austria. Mother wasn't here anymore, but her daughters had to survive in the web she created.

"I told you," Acton said. "Does seeing that change anything?"

"No, but it tells me about my enemy."

"We aren't going to war with France."

"Of course not," I said, folding my hands in front of me. "But if anything happens to Antoinette, France will be made to suffer for it. These men are intimidated by any woman who exercises any liberty. From the moment my sister came into that country, they have hated her. Whether it was because she held opinions or because she was Austrian, they wanted her gone by any means possible."

"If Necker has his way, he'll be able to get the nobles to loan the state enough money to operate at least for a little bit."

"And if they don't?"

"Then we prepare for a diplomatic crisis."

* * *

My nervousness over my sister's well-being bled from me into every facet of my life at Caserta. The end of summer fetes in the gardens that we normally enjoyed were canceled. In the family parlor, I sulked over the latest literature that was being distributed about Antoinette.

"Luisa and I have made arrangements for us to visit the San Francesco Convent," Theresa said from the chess table, where she and her sister sat quietly around the board.

"Tomorrow," Luisa added.

"No, I have too much work to do," I said, trying to dismiss them.

"Mother," Theresa said, turning in her chair to look at me directly. "You have been working so hard that we are afraid you'll end up in an early grave." My daughter, newly sixteen, had all the confidence of an adult and the same stubbornness I had at her age.

"I agree," Luisa began. "You always enjoy going on a tour of the convents. Particularly with Sorella Martina of the San Francesco Convent."

"Very well," I said, relenting, and the girls clapped in unison. "And make sure you invite my new lady, Emma, with us."

"Already done," Theresa said with a grin as she turned back to the chessboard.

The next day, our carriage bumped along the cobblestone roads toward the convent. Sitting next to me was Emma, pleased to be on this excursion with me and my daughters. The girls chattered as I watched my city roll by. The city I helped build.

When my father-in-law ruled the Two Sicilies, there were the Jesuits, an order of priests who were dedicated to science and health in addition to the soul. They had taken a special vow to the pope, but it came to light that these men, these stewards of men's souls, were banking without the pope's permission. They kept more for themselves than what they were giving to the church, at least that was what the pope said. As a result, the pope not only expelled them from Rome but encouraged Spain, France, Austria, and the Two Sicilies to do the same. King Carlos did as he was told, and for decades the buildings that once housed the Jesuits sat fallow. Until I became queen. The state took over the buildings, and they became the universities and hospitals that my people now enjoyed.

This convent we were going to had been confiscated from the priests and gifted to the sisters. In keeping with the tradition that my mother had, we utilized it as a haven for women to study science, literature, and philosophy. There were no priests or cardinals or male officials allowed. It was a place for women of both the noble and merchant classes to flourish without being molested by the men in their lives.

Built into the mountain, the convent had four stories, each one with a roof of green foliage that served as their gardens. Though the facade looked simple, the inside was filled with statues of the Virgin Mary and freshly painted walls displaying beautiful artwork, most of which was painted by the nuns themselves.

We were greeted by Sorella Martina and her retinue of nuns. The abbess's thick lips broke into a wide smile that cut across her long face at the sight of us. "La Sua Maestà, we are so pleased to have you pay us a visit on this fine day."

"I hope we do not put you in any indisposition."

"For our *patrone*? Never." She smiled again.

She led us to blue-tiled stairs that went up to a balcony over-looking the bay, with Mount Vesuvius in the distance. The bright Mediterranean sun cast slivers of light through the awning that covered us as ocean breezes caressed us and the fruit trees on the terraces nearby rustled. Theresa and Luisa stood at the edge, marveling at the city below us, a city now bursting with pride and commerce, while Emma and I took our place on green settees.

"We have prepared a small luncheon for you," Sorella Martina said.

"Oh, we have already eaten. We couldn't bother you for more food."

"Nonsense," she scolded. "What is a gathering of friends if there is no food? Even our Lord broke bread with his brethren."

With that, trays of sliced turkey and vegetables and fruit were laid out on the small table in front of us. Even though I wasn't hungry I didn't want to be rude, so I took a slice of turkey, or at least what I thought was turkey. The meat wasn't meat at all; it was made of ice. Breaking off a piece, I put it in my mouth, letting it melt around my tongue. "Is . . . is that apricot?"

"Yes!" the abbess said, clapping with delight. "Try the lettuce. It's divine!"

Emma took a piece. "Why that's lime! How refreshing."

"Yes, our cook has been perfecting our flavored ices and ex-pressing her gift for creativity through her food."

"Please give her my compliments." I took another bite of the iced turkey. "And the nuns, how are they?"

"Happy," she said. "Our order has never been so prosperous. We are not only able to help our women but also the women in the surrounding neighborhood. We feed the hungry and use local skilled labor to make improvements on the building. This monastery takes excellent care of us, and in turn we will do all that we can to take care of her. And we never would have been able to do it without our beloved regina."

I smiled as I broke up the apricot ice with my spoon.

"But I see that something is troubling you." Sorella Martina raised her eyebrows as she regarded me. "Shall I venture a guess as to what the reason is?"

"My sister," I said quietly, not looking up at her large green eyes.

"I have heard the whispers and the rumors. I don't believe them, of course. Having personally met you I cannot believe that someone so important to you would be so wanton."

"Thank you," I said as a wave of relief washed over me.

Sorella Martina looked out over the Neapolitan harbor. "During times like these, I can't help but think of the story of Ruth. How she refused to leave her sister, even though the world around her withered. Ruth said, 'For wherever you go, I will go; wherever you live, I will live. Your people are my people.'" The abbess's eyes swam with tears. "Even during the times of the Bible, we find that the devotion of women, of sisters, is a bond that is sacred, that can never truly be broken. Your devotion to your sister, your willingness to fight for her, is honorable. But, remember, she is not your only sister. Those of us here in Naples are your sisters as well. As you seek the safety for one sister, do not forget your sisters here."

Charlotte,   *October 16, 1789*

I do not know what account has reached you in Naples, but I will share with you the events that transpired on that fateful day of October 5th. Please do not worry, I and my family are safe. We just had a bit of a fright.

The women of Paris rose up against us! Filling the courtyard, they spilled out beyond the palace fences. And their chants! To my dying day, they will haunt me. They didn't just wish for me to no longer be the queen; they wanted me dead.

We spent the night debating what course of action would be best. Some thought we should quash the uprising with the army, while others pressed upon the king to listen to the demonstrators' demands. Louis eventually chose an opinion and heard the grievances of a group of women. Since they wanted my head, I decided that it was best for me to not be there, but I passed them on my way to escape. I wanted to hate them, these creatures who sought my blood, but instead, I pitied them. Those poor, wretched souls, covered in filth; their gaunt eyes were more sad than angry.

Foolishly, we thought that was it, that the crowd would disperse. They had had their say, but it wasn't enough. Not for the French. They are never satisfied, and I am always the villain in their narrative.

But it wasn't until early the next morning that I realized the depths of the women's wrath. My attendants were dressing me when we heard the commotion. It was Madame Auguié who first heard yells that were coming not from outside the palace, as they had been all night long, but from inside Versailles. She ran to the antechamber to see what was happening, but a guard stopped her. "Save the queen, madame," he said. "They are coming to assassinate her!"

As my women and I fled for our safety, the only thought that crossed my mind was how ashamed our mother would be of me. Mother would never flee for her life. Her presence alone would force these people into submission. Like a frightened little girl, I took shelter in Louis's chambers while yet again we decided what to do next. How horrible.

It was after all the chaos was over that we learned that the Duc d'Orléans had been in the crowd. The king's cousin was there, dressed as one of the women. I swear to you, Sister, he may not be my executioner, but he will be the cause of my death. He has always hated me, and he had his eyes on the crown long before my arrival. So much of our present troubles are a result of his meddling. The family and I will be taking residence in Tuileries Palace under the protection of the citizens. I am happy my husband has finally made a decision, but I am concerned about this constitution they want to make him sign. If he signs this document, he would sign away all control, giving his power to the National Assembly. The monarchy would become nothing but a figurehead.

Your sister,
Antoinette

CHAPTER THIRTY-FIVE

OCTOBER 20, 1789

"They have my sister," I said, pacing back and forth in the council chambers. Though it was late October, the first bite of winter was already starting to show in the air. "Will someone close one of those things," I snapped, waving my hand in the direction of the offending windows.

"Regina mia, this is no time to slip into hysterics," Medici said.

I shot a look at him. He was one of the few council members brave enough to still look me in the eye.

"All I'm saying," he continued, "is that this is not something to be overly concerned with. She and her family are under the protection of the citizens. They won't come to any harm; the National Assembly has given its word."

"The word of a traitor can never be trusted," I spit. "A captured king is a dead king. He and everyone in his bloodline can be wiped out with a single command. My sister and her children are in grave danger."

"Charlotte," Acton said, speaking up, "Medici does have a point.

We need to think this through rationally. We simply can't invade France to rescue the royal family."

"Why else do we have a military?" I said.

"To protect our interests and not wage war with someone stronger than us," Medici retorted.

"There has to be a way to protect Antoinette's family," I pleaded. "We can't let them sit at the mercy of a mob."

"They'll never let the king go," Sir Hamilton said, leaning forward. "He is too valuable."

"They especially won't let them go to Austria. If Louis goes there, they will only anticipate his return with an army," Acton responded.

"We can bring them here," I said. "We are a neutral country. France can't have a problem with them coming here, and Medici said it himself: We don't have a strong army. We are the best option to save the family."

"That is a possibility," Acton said, rubbing at his chin. "I can write to our ambassador there, seeing if he can mediate. I'll emphasize the sisterly connection."

"And our coalition. Any news?" I asked. My brothers and I had formed a union of Milan, Tuscany, Austria, and the Two Sicilies, even though my country still held a peace treaty with France. Leopold had been silent, and my concern was growing by the day. It annoyed me to no end that my brothers Leopold and Joseph had been keeping their own counsel on the matter and leaving me out. They knew as well as I did that I was just as capable as they were within the political arena.

"I received word from Leopold this morning," Acton said.

I opened my mouth to scold him for not informing me earlier, but he continued to talk. I, however, made a mental note to write to my brother and tell him how cross I was.

"Joseph was able to enlist Prussia and Sweden to commit to going to war with France."

"And what of Spain?" I asked.

"They have as of yet to make a decision," Acton responded, his eyes darting to the Spanish ambassador.

"Of course they haven't," I said, flopping into a chair. "Those cowards, they haven't had a decent leader since my father-in-law died." I turned to the new ambassador, a young whelp of a thing. His position at this point was mostly onlooker, since Carlos IV and his court had long since given up on influencing the Two Sicilies in any meaningful way. "Be sure to pass my sentiments to your master. Feel free to use my exact words."

At the other end of the table, I saw Acton try to hide the smile that played at his lips. "England has yet to commit as well," he said. He gave a little cough before looking to Hamilton.

"And why is that?" I asked, also turning to the English ambassador.

"England has been aloof," Hamilton said. "They say King George is reluctant to get involved in another conflict so soon after the war in the colonies."

"At least they have a valid excuse, unlike my brother-in-law," I said. I turned to the Spanish ambassador again and began to speak, but he cut me off.

"I know, I know. I'll pass your sentiments on to Carlos."

I smiled devilishly. "He at least had the good sense to send me an ambassador who takes directions." My eyes scanned the room. The men looked tired, and, at least on Medici's part, frustrated. "We have nothing more to discuss today. You are all dismissed," I said, waving them away.

"We will get your sister," Acton said, placing a warm, calloused hand on my shoulder. With the other men gone, the two of us were left to our confidences. Leaning into him, I could feel the steady rhythm of his breath as his chest rose and fell, the thump of his heartbeat increasing with my touch.

"Antoinette was never meant for this," I said.

"Antoinette is a Habsburg archduchess. You need to give her more credit."

"No," I said. Rising from the chair, I turned to face him. "Mother took great care when it came to tending to her children, but we were not all raised equally. Mother had her favorites, and by the time my sister and I came along, there wasn't much in the way of a thorough education. When I was younger, I was as spoiled as my husband."

Acton arched an eyebrow, and I couldn't help but laugh at little. "I was young and clearly grew out of it. And when it comes to Maximilian, my youngest brother, we all know how well he turned out, with his gluttony and foolishness. We needn't mention the embarrassment he caused when he went to Versailles."

"But Antoinette has more sense than Maximilian."

"Yes, though she is better suited for the role of a private mother than that of a public queen. Antoinette is too gentle. No." I pressed my fingertips to my lips as I tried to swallow down the tears and anger that clawed up my throat. "I blame our mother for this whole mess. The great empress was too concerned with her political alliances to be concerned with what was best for her children. If she truly meant for my sister to be a queen, she should have been harder on her, on the both of us. Mother wouldn't have cared that Amalia wanted to marry a penniless prince from Prussia and not some lunatic duke. She consistently doted on Mimi and Elisabeth, and look where that got us. Elisabeth is a deformed spinster now, living in a convent, and Mimi, a spoiled duchess who makes all those around her miserable."

Whether I liked it or not, all my animosity for my long-dead mother came rushing out. "Do you think I wanted this?" I said. "That I wanted to be the one who ruled the kingdom while my husband got to go hunting and play games? Maybe I wanted to be the wife who got to be frivolous. Spending my days pampering myself and my children. I love my mother, but her legacy of ambition will haunt her daughters."

Acton pulled me toward him and let me rest in his embrace, the beating of his heart putting my mind at peace.

My Dear Sister,   *March 1, 1790*

I have written and rewritten this letter multiple times. This is perhaps the oddest letter that I have ever had to write, for I have the duty of sharing both pleasant and tragic news.

First, I would like to share that our dear brother Joseph has joined Mother in the hereafter. For all the arguing he did with our mother, in the end he felt like he couldn't live up to her legacy, admitting to me that he felt like a complete and total failure. He even asked that his epitaph read "Here lies Joseph II, who failed in all he undertook." Even in death, our brother still found a way to loathe himself.

And though I am sad about this news, I also feel honored that I am now going to be the Holy Roman emperor. As you read this, I will be on my way to Vienna to take the throne, as our mother once did and her father before her. Please know that I will never waver in support of you and the Two Sicilies.

It is also with great sadness that I must report that my dear daughter-in-law Elisabeth of Württemberg, has died in childbirth. It is a double tragedy for our family, for we have lost a daughter and an heir. My son Francis is in need of a new wife, and I would like to propose a marriage to your daughter Theresa.

My son Ferdinand Joseph shall be the Duke of Tuscany, and he will also be in want of a wife. Perhaps we can also arrange to match Joseph with Luisa. She is only a year younger than Theresa and would make an excellent choice.

Leopold

CHAPTER THIRTY-SIX

MARCH 1, 1790

I knew that this time would come, when I would have to make matches for my children. Theresa, now seventeen, and Luisa, now sixteen, would make wonderful wives. It was my duty as queen and mother to not only protect my daughters but to do what I needed to make sure they made advantageous matches. Not just for their sake, but for the sake of the Two Sicilies. In the warm afternoon of an early spring day, my family gathered in the hidden space beyond my cove that I called my English garden. Filled with exotic plants, I had spent years cultivating it with the help of a botanist, Sir John Andrew Graefer. It had quickly become my favorite space in all of Caserta.

Under the shade of the holly trees, I held my hand against my stomach, as my fourteenth child patiently grew inside me. There were two things you could always count on: that a Neapolitan would never fail to give you their opinion, and that I would wind up with child whenever my husband visited my rooms.

Next to me, Theresa watched the younger children as they enjoyed the day. Antonia, five, sat in the grass making bright-yellow flower crowns that they placed on Clotilde and Enrichetta, who giggled and cooed in response.

A reader's paradise was positioned under a nearby cluster of trees: Rugs topped with great fluffy pillows and a stack of books sat by my children's side. In the center was a low table, where Francis and Luisa picked at a bowl of fruit with their attention focused on their books.

I had had to bribe Francis to join us here this afternoon. At twelve years old, he was incredibly driven, something I liked to think I had had a hand in. His tutor, Herr Keller, a recommendation from my mother, came straight from Austria. Herr Keller was the opposite of Tanucci. A slight man, he had more interest in reading than ruling.

When Keller first arrived, I peppered him with several questions.

"My son is going to be the future king of the Two Sicilies. How do you feel about that?"

"I feel that it is a great honor to teach him," Keller said, pushing his glasses up his nose. His fingers ran through his brown hair, which was started to thin at the edge of his forehead.

"What subjects would you teach my son?"

"I would make sure he is well versed in economics, history, and philosophy." Keller's hands shook slightly as they clasped each other. "It is important that he has a well-rounded base in order to properly rule the country."

"Languages?"

"Your mother informed me that the boy already speaks Italian and French. Are there other languages you would like him to learn?"

"German, for one, and Spanish would be nice. I don't trust the Spaniards at court, and I want to make sure he knows what they are saying behind his back."

Keller bowed his head, and I could see a small bald spot forming. "Yes, Your Majesty."

"And physical exercise? What are your thoughts on that?"

"A king's health is important," he had said, "but I do believe in Aristotle's rule that everything is done in moderation."

A loud splash and a torrent of giggles brought my attention to the shore of the large pond. My daughters Christina and Amalia cheered as blossoming water lilies bobbed violently in the waves. Meanwhile, Ferdinand lifted a large rock into the air.

"What are you ruffians doing to my water lilies?" I called.

"Papa was trying to catch a frog!" Amalia called back to me.

"With a rock?"

"One must neutralize the enemy in order to catch them," Ferdinand said.

Fantastic, just what I needed, my husband teaching my eight-year-old and my eleven-year-old military theory. I was constantly on edge that Ferdinand would pass his bad habits on to our children. "Whatever you do, please don't destroy my water lilies," I yelled to them.

Then I turned to my eldest, still sitting next to me. "Remind me again, dear daughter, why I had the whole family here in my garden."

"Because you wanted to show it off?" Theresa responded as she watched her sisters play with their father.

"You know me so well."

"I am your daughter after all."

"Yes, that you are." I reached out and patted her hand. "In fact, there is something that I would like to discuss with you."

She turned her sweet face toward me. "What is it, Mama?"

"I received a marriage proposal, from your cousin Francis, Uncle Leopold's son."

"When will the wedding be?"

"I'm sorry?" I said in disbelief. I had expected her to put up more of a fuss, as I did when I was her age.

"Mother, I am not naïve enough to think that I have any say in this. You and I both know that marrying me to the heir of Austria is the opportunity you have been waiting for. I simply want to know when it will happen."

"I'll have our ambassador to Austria negotiate a contract with Leopold."

Theresa nodded and then turned back toward the pond.

"Papa!" Luisa called. "Come look at my book. The author is talking about our volcano. You have to read this."

Ferdinand rushed over to Luisa to share the book with her, and they broke into a discussion about the new minerals found outside the last eruption zone. I watched as the two of them fell into their own little world. Soon, I would be informing Luisa of her own marriage proposal, but I wanted to give her one last day to enjoy the family.

As my children ran and played around me, I tried to see them for who they eventually would be. They might not all be heirs to the throne, but they would each play their role for the sake of the Two Sicilies. I would find places for my daughters in the best royal families in support of the monarchy. If Francis had no heirs, it would be up to my daughters, unless this child was a boy. It wasn't just through the military force that I had to secure rule; it was through a solid bloodline. Holding my hand to my stomach, I had high hopes for this new child and what he could be.

Charlotte,   *May 15, 1790*

I am very pleased with the contracts that we have been able to negotiate with your ambassador. It feels only natural that a Maria Theresa be on the throne in Austria.

Joseph is very pleased to remain in Tuscany and has

been quite interested in visiting Naples. I believe he and Luisa will share an interest in studying volcanology as well as literature. I hope Luisa has inherited your love of chess. Joseph is quite proficient.

When it comes to our sister, please remain calm. We must be shrewd in how we approach this. I am still working on securing our coalition, but you have to remember: You are not the only one who is devoted to Antoinette. We all want to secure her safety, but we cannot immediately wage a war. The situation is far more complicated than you can imagine.

As in our chess matches, which you always rushed through, you must take your time and develop your strategy. When you arrive for the wedding, we will discuss an idea that may just work to save our dear sister. Until then, please stop your letter-writing campaign. Every monarch in Europe has received at least ten letters from you and at least three additional letters from Acton. I have it on good authority that Frederick William runs from your letters every time his page brings them to him. Though I do have to say that I am impressed with your ability to make the king of Prussia run in fear.

Your Faithful Brother,

Leopold

CHAPTER THIRTY-SEVEN

August 1790

I crumpled another of Leopold's letters and threw it across the room. The people of France were in open revolt against the monarchy. When Spain threatened to take my throne away from me, Joseph and Leopold had leaped at the opportunity to defend me, Joseph going so far as preparing the Austrian armies for war. It angered me that they weren't doing the same for Antoinette.

The situation is far more complicated. A sorry excuse, in my opinion. Leopold was too afraid to start a war with France, leaving the Habsburg daughters to be sacrificed yet again. Mother may have been dead for ten years, but her daughters were still suffering because of her decisions.

"Your Majesty, is everything all right?" My new lady, Emma, had slipped into my office.

"Yes," I said, massaging the bridge of my nose. "But the world would be a much better place if people did what I wanted them to." I smiled, looking up at Emma. She had been exposed to so much in her twenty-five years that it was easy to forget how young she was.

Shortly after her marriage to Sir Hamilton, I had invited her to the palazzo for a walk in my newly created English garden.

We exited the stone cove and made our way down the steps, lined with broken columns, to the edge of the small lake. Emma let out a little giggle as a butterfly danced around her. "Naples never ceases to surprise me," she said. "I am so glad that William brought me here." She spoke in impeccable French.

"You've mentioned that before," I said. "From what I understand, it was quite a scandal."

She blushed slightly. "I believe William, more than anything, took pity on me." She looked out over the lake, where a frog jumped from one of my lily pads, disturbing the tranquil water. "Life in England wasn't the most pleasant. William said that Naples would be good for my disposition."

"Were you sick?"

Emma looked back at me, her smile fading. "There are some illnesses that are of the soul." She shrugged, and her sadness seemed to vanish "I know what everyone thought about William and me. And there is our vast age difference. But William is kind. So much kinder than any other man I have known. Did you know that he and I lived in separate apartments until we were married?" Her smile returned as we continued to walk along the path lined with pearls of blooming purple flowers. "There is something to be said for unobtrusive men. Do you know that in the evenings we like to sip sherry and read? I never knew I could take pleasure in such simplicity."

It was on that day that I decided to take her on as my lady.

Now, she found me in my office, trying to focus on my letters, a bowl of fresh fruits and cheese sitting uneaten in front of me.

"What's the latest update?" Emma said, snatching an apricot from the bowl before flopping into one of the armchairs opposite my desk. She let one leg daintily drape over the arm of the chair. To anyone else, she might have looked disrespectful, but to me, she looked more like one of the muses in my garden. "Are they going to form the coalition?"

"No. They are all cowards," I huffed. "Has your husband heard anything definitive from King George?"

"No," she said, her small pink lips forming a pout. "William is quite upset about it. This is our home, after all, and France, well, they need to be put in their place after what they've done in the colonies, but the king's sickness has caused a delay in England's ability to function properly." She took a bite of the apricot in her fingers. "I'm going to miss you when you are away. I wish I could go with you."

"I know," I said. As uneasy as I was to leave Naples, I still needed to go to Austria. In addition to Theresa's wedding, I needed to speak with my brother in person. "But I need you here. Someone has to give me the full and complete news about what is happening while I am away."

Emma gave me a mock salute.

"Do you know where the rest of the family is?"

"Joseph and Luisa are in the family parlor playing chess, again." She sucked at the last of the fruit. "Someone should tell them that there are better things to do with their time now that they are married, other than playing chess."

"Oh, dear Emma, marriage is chess."

Having Joseph at Caserta felt like having Leopold with me again. Not only did he look like my brother, but he also had his temperament. Slow to speak, he observed the room, before giving his opinion. On more than one occasion, I found him and Luisa sitting and playing chess, lost in their own confidences. Watching them together, I knew she would do well in Tuscany.

My thoughts turned toward my eldest daughter, Theresa. Ferdinand and I would be accompanying her to Vienna and staying there to help her settle into her new role. As much as I was going to miss her, I had to trust that I have done enough to prepare her for her life as queen. Though she was going to be returning to Austria, I was not going to leave her unprepared. I made sure she had the same contract as I did, whereupon birthing an heir she would get voting privileges on the council. My daughter was not going to be a passive member of her new government.

Before we left, I wanted to make sure to visit Francis. Now a young man of thirteen, he took the task of heir apparent very seriously. Walking into his room, I found him at his desk, reading from a massive tome. "Ciao, Mama," he said, without looking up at me, as he flipped another page.

I ran my fingers through his thick black curls. "We are preparing for our trip to Vienna. I wanted to check on you and make sure that you came down to see your sister off on her journey."

"I will be sure to wave goodbye when the time comes," he said, writing something down on a nearby paper.

"It's a beautiful day, and as much as I love to see you study, it would be good for you to take a rest."

He slapped his quill down, ink splattering across the page, and turned to me. "Mother, please, I am busy."

"Francis, your sister is going to Austria. I expect you to say goodbye."

"She's not going to America. Theresa will only be in Austria. I'm sure I'll see her again."

I started to protest, but he stopped me.

"I need to be prepared," he said, "just in case you and Father are deposed."

"We will not be deposed."

"It's happening to Zia Antoinette. I know how upset you are, how you are begging anyone who will listen to come to her aid. I can't let what is happening in France happen here. I have to be a good ruler. You and my tutor Herr Keller have stressed to me every single day the importance of the job that I am destined to take.

That I can't let myself get led astray like Father. Please, Mother, just let me study." He turned back to his book, dismissing me.

I kissed the top of his head. "You will make a fine king," I whispered as he used his sleeve to wipe his nose.

For the first time, my children had to consider what their fates could be if I failed. I leaned my head against the doorframe.

I would not fail my children. I would not fail Naples.

Charlotte,   *September 1, 1790*

I will forever be in your debt for directing your ambassador to negotiate my and my daughter's release. Think me foolish, if you must, but I cannot leave my son. Even if it costs me my freedom.

This wasn't my first opportunity to escape. Every morning, my husband goes riding. No guards. No attendants. Just Louis and the woods. I thought if I could slip away with the children, we could meet him there and then we could escape. We could rendezvous with my dear Fersen and he would escort us to Austria. I fantasized about crossing the Austrian border into the waiting arms of the homeland.

But that dream could not be.

I was in the drawing room, watching the soothing summer rain when one of my husband's aunts came in. The fragile, elderly woman eased into a chair and started talking about all the things she misses at Versailles. Then she said the most heartbreaking thing of all. She pointed out that she and her sister were all that was left of Louis's parent's generation. His poor sweet mother would be beside herself if she had lived to see this.

The elderly aunt's words pierced my heart, for that's when I knew if we were to escape, it had to be all of us. We could not leave France without my husband's family. I would never be able to live with myself if he could not have his family by his side. How could I hug you in joy when he would be cloaked in sadness?

Charlotte, please do not be cross with me. I cannot be like our mother. I cannot forego the thoughts and feelings of others to get my way. There has to be another way. I trust that when you are with Leopold in Vienna, the two of you will think of a way to bring me home. You were always the clever one.

Antoinette

CHAPTER THIRTY-EIGHT

September 1790

I could barely contain my elation as we crossed the border into Austria. The rolling hills and fields of my home country were just as I had left them. Filled with the lush multicolored flowers and greenery that haunted my dreams.

"Do you see those flowers there?" I said, pointing to a field of bright-yellow plants. "Antoinette and I used to make flower crowns just like that. We tried putting them on our dog, but he kept shaking them off." I smiled over the memory. "We attempted to use a ribbon to secure it, but we got yelled at by Countess von Ogre."

"Countess von Ogre?" Theresa asked.

"It's what I called my governess."

"Your poor governess," Theresa said.

"Your poor mother," I responded. "She was far too controlling. She is why I made sure you had exceptional governesses."

Ferdinand kept watching the window. "Naples is prettier."

"Austria and Naples are both beautiful, in their own ways," I replied.

"It doesn't have the sea and a volcano. Austria is boring."

"Just wait," I said, turning back to the window. "You will find Austria to be quite wonderful."

A few days later, we arrived at Schönbrunn Palace, with its great gardens bursting with unfurling ribbons of red and pink flowers. The massive yellow brick building stood tall against the rich foliage. As we exited the carriage, I took my daughter by the arm. "Welcome home."

The three of us together walked forward to greet my brother and his family. Theresa tensed slightly as her gaze fell on her soon-to-be husband, Francis.

When it came to Leopold's sons, they all looked like a variation of him. Francis had his father's thin nose and Cupid's bow lips, with a long face and a prominent chin. The boy, for he was only twenty-two years old, compared to my thirty-eight years, was clearly shy. Upon first look at my daughter, Francis cast his eyes down, peeking at Theresa through his long blond lashes.

"Brother!" I exclaimed, letting my daughter go so that I could embrace Leopold. "It has been far too long."

He kissed me on both cheeks. "Yes, I have not had the pleasure of visiting Naples in quite a while."

His wife, Luisa, stepped forward. "Please, step aside, husband," she said with a laugh. "I would like to greet my sister-in-law and brother. How is my husband's namesake?" Luisa asked, about my latest child.

"Leopold is doing well. At twelve weeks old, he is a robust child."

"With my nose and lungs," Ferdinand said with a smile. "I swear they can hear him all the way to Palermo!" He wrapped his older sister in his arms.

Leopold took me by the arm. "I remember there was a day when you had fewer children than we did. Now you've caught up with us!"

Together we walked up the great stone steps leading to the

small gallery. The golden eagle statues still stood sentry over the archways leading to the Great Gallery, with mirrors reflecting the fading summer sun. Ghosts of my childhood appeared before me like actors in a play: Antoinette and I in curls and ribbons, racing through the rooms, doing all that we could to avoid our governess. Antoinette tripping, sliding to a stop along the shiny parquet floors. Me, doubling back and falling to my knees next to her.

She wrapped her hands around her shin.

The ghost of me slowly pried her cold hands away. Beads of blood seeped from the open skin. I tore at the lace of my dress.

"But, Charlotte, you will get in trouble."

Shrugging, I wrapped the lace around her leg. "A bit of inconvenience is worth it if it means you are no longer hurt." I pulled her back to her feet. "Come, let's play in mirrors before the ogre finds us."

As the two girls ran from my sight, the image of Mother in all her regal glory strode forward: Her head held high as she prepared to make her entrance. Her immense figure taking up most of the doorway. Her bosom rising from her corset, tightened enough to give her a waist. Gemstones glittering in the light of the crystal chandeliers.

"Charlotte, you've gone white. Do you need a moment to rest?" Leopold asked.

"No, I was just remembering…," I said, letting my voice trail off as we moved from one room to the next.

Images came forth of our family all together before we were slowly parceled out like bits of land. "I didn't expect this," I said, trying to find the words to describe what was going through my heart.

"The memories?" Leopold asked.

"It's been twenty-two years since I have been home." My voice caught. "And Mother—"

"I know," Leopold said, patting my hand. "It's still hard for me to get used to her not being here. I expect her to come storming through a door at any moment."

My eyes began to swim with tears.

"Oh, Charlotte, I am so sorry, I didn't mean to upset you." Leopold stopped our group to look at me.

"Mama?" Theresa asked, moving toward me.

"I'm all right," I said, turning from her as I wiped away the tears that spilled down my cheeks.

"Would you like to go somewhere to lie down?" Leopold whispered.

"I want to go to Mother's study," I said. Mother spent hours in her office, conducting the affairs of the country as though she were in front of an orchestra. However, she was always available whenever her children needed her, even if it was a daughter who wanted to stand before her declaring she would henceforth not be known as Carolina but as Charlotte.

"Very well," Leopold said quietly. He turned to the rest of the group. "Luisa, why don't you take Ferdinand and Theresa to get settled. Charlotte and I have to take care of something."

The family broke off from Leopold and me as we made our way to Mother's study. Her room may have been small, but its impact was felt throughout the country. Leopold opened the door and allowed me to step through. My fingers followed the curve of the wood inlay of pumpkins, whose blue vines, adorned with blossoms, snaked up the wall to the ceiling. I let my fingertip trace the frames of the sketchings, each one in the blue and yellow-white that matched the walls. They depicted lovely picnic scenes, which Mother most surely didn't have time to enjoy. They called this the Porcelain Room, but unlike porcelain, this room was inhabited by a woman whose will would not break.

I made my way to the far side of the room, where her desk sat, the same yellow-white as the rest of the room, next to a window overlooking the grounds below. Outside, birds chirped, and the leaves were turning from yellow to orange to brown.

I placed my hand on top of the desk, my palm caressing the smooth surface. Hot tears pricked my eyes anew when I realized that all her papers were gone.

She was gone.

Closing my eyes, I tried to conjure her: The fragrant rose perfume that trailed behind her wherever she went, filling the room so all we could breathe was her. The gravity of her, the way she pulled us all in. I wanted to see my mother again. Not the one from her portraits, no, the real Maria Theresa. The way her double chin wobbled when she laughed. Her eyes, the subtle way they would squint as she considered the facts of a story. Her warmth. Her hands were always warm. God, how I would take so much pride in her placing a warm thick hand upon my head. To hear her say one more time, *I am proud.*

"Joseph slowly had all her papers moved to his study," Leopold said from the doorway, breaking the silence. "He couldn't do it all at once, of course. Even in her final years, she insisted on working, on being the queen."

"You mean you don't use the Porcelain Room as your study?" I said with a smirk.

"Oh, no, I wouldn't dare," Leopold said. "I may be her heir, but I could never take her place."

"I wonder what she would have to say about this French Revolution."

Leopold let out a short burst of laughter. "She would go charging into Paris with all of Europe behind her."

"Then why aren't we doing that now?" I asked, turning from the desk to my brother.

"Charlotte, you just got here. I thought you wanted to come to Mother's room to have a moment with her memory, not to harass me about our sister."

"Yes, but you said it yourself, our mother would be storming into Paris right now. She would make every other country come to heel under her will. You certainly have one thing right, Brother: You are not Mother."

"For the love of all that is holy, Charlotte, do you hear yourself? You speak as if fetching Antoinette is as simple as riding into France and throwing her on the back of a hay wagon. You expect me to move mountains, but I am just a man."

"You are the emperor!" I shouted. "You have the power to save our sister—wield it!"

"It's not that simple," Leopold retorted.

"Yes, you said that bit already. You 'can't move mountains.'" I could feel my face flush with anger. "While *you* are walking around the palace of the Holy Roman Empire, *I* am the one doing the work. Boulder by boulder. Me. No one else. I'm the only one willing to risk everything to save Antoinette." I pushed past him through the doorway, but he caught me by the arm.

"What would you have me do?" Leopold said through gritted teeth. "Would you have me gather all the forces of Austria and Prussia and invade France? Then what? Make them a part of our country?"

"If that's what it takes, then so be it." I ripped my arm from his grasp.

"Right. Well, while I am in France, saving our beloved sister, Russia will move in."

"Mother was the one who competed with Catherine, not you."

"Mother competed with Catherine because Catherine has been waiting for an opportunity to take our land ever since she assumed the throne. She never told you that Catherine the Great, as the Russians like to call her, keeps tiptoeing over our borders. Every year, her kingdom gets that much closer to Austria. If I go into Paris with our whole army, which I would need to defeat France, Catherine will invade. Mark my words." Leopold stepped closer to me. "And while that is happening, I have Bohemia trying to reignite Joseph's pet war, and Germany threatening to create a constitution all their own just like those bloody Americans across the Atlantic." Leopold rubbed at his forehead with the heel of his hand. "Joseph left me with a mess. I want to save Antoinette, but I can't do it at the expense of Austria."

Pity mixed with guilt washed over me. All the while I had been thinking about my sister, and I didn't stop to think about the enormous task that Leopold had before him. "I'm sorry," I whispered.

Leopold looked up at the ceiling, heaving a large sigh. "I'm sorry too. Let's just get through the wedding, and we'll find a way to save Antoinette. I promise."

I nodded, but I couldn't let it go. Leopold was the one who taught me that it all came down to the queen, and I knew I had to be the one to save my sister.

Charlotte,   *September 15, 1790*

Right now, you are in the midst of wedding feasts, and more than ever I want to be with you. Please give my love to Maximilian, Karl, Leopold, and, I suppose, Mimi. What a lovely thought: the children of Maria Theresa reunited at Schönbrunn. When I sleep, I often dream of our time there, those happy, carefree days. Before all the anger. Before the world barged in and stole whatever shards of happiness we had. We were protected there at Schönbrunn, weren't we? It wasn't until we left that it all went wrong.

My dearest sister, I wish all the happiness in the world for your children. May they only know joy and laughter. May they have the sunshine upon their faces and may the clouds never settle over them for long. But, above all else, may they know that they have an aunt who loves them. Even though we have never met. Even though they are in another country. I want them to know that they are mine, just as much as they are yours, and until my dying day, I will love them.

Your loving sister,
Antoinette

CHAPTER THIRTY-NINE

On the morning of Theresa's wedding to Francis, I attended my daughter's toilette as she stared at herself in the mirror, my mother's tiara upon her head. My daughter wore a flowing pale-blue gown. A gown my mother would have approved of.

"You are far more beautiful than I could have ever imagined."

"Thank you," Theresa said, her voice shaking.

"Before we go out there to meet your father, I want to give you some advice that my mother gave to me." I placed my hand on her cheek. "In all that you do, in all that you say, you will be an Austrian. Be loyal to your new country, and above all else, even if you don't like him, make your husband believe that you love him more than the Christ himself. Men's egos are weak." Moving my hand to her heart, I said, "But here, and in your soul, remember, you will always, always be a Sicilian. Don't let anyone take that from you. Do you understand?"

"Yes, Mama," she said, with the first smile she had given me all morning.

"Good girl," I said, kissing both her cheeks. "Now, let's find your father."

Ferdinand had tears swimming in his eyes when he took his daughter's arm and escorted us to the cathedral. The same cathedral where I was married by proxy. As Theresa said her vows before the congregation, every pew was full of guests: ambassadors, nobility, and family. Across the aisle in the front row, sat Karl and his wife. Now the Archduke of Austria-Este, Karl spent much of his time in Milan.

Behind them was Prince Albert of Saxony and his wife, my sister Mimi, the Duke and Duchess of Teschen. Mimi's long, thin face had scarcely changed in all these years. I wondered if she had adopted Elisabeth's penchant for creams and potions. She had all the looks of a Habsburg without any of the effects of age. I hated that Mimi was the one that was here and not Antoinette.

But my daughter, in her duty to the crown of the Two Sicilies, stood tall. This marriage would help to align our country with the most powerful country in Europe. Our safety and interest would be protected with this union. Unlike me, she didn't mumble her vows. She was the true portrait of a Habsburg queen, with the looks of Antoinette and my cunning.

Once everyone gave their toasts wishing the couple nothing but happiness and prosperity, the children of Empress Maria Theresa gathered to make plans in Leopold's study.

The modest mustard-yellow room was nothing like my mother's office. Leopold stood there with my brother Karl and a man I did not recognize. He had a kind face with a strong chin. His brown eyes scrutinized me as I walked through the door.

"Sister!" Karl exclaimed, rushing over and kissing me on both cheeks. "With all the festivities, I haven't been able to greet you properly."

I held him out so that I could look at him. As Antoinette was said to be my twin, Karl was Leopold's. They had the same thin nose, the same high forehead, and the same Habsburg blue eyes. The eyes shared by Antoinette. "Look at you!" I exclaimed. "You're an old man!"

"Old man?" He laughed. "I am only thirty-six, two years younger than you. So that makes you my—"

"I beg you not to finish that sentence." I laughed, giving him another hug.

"Charlotte, I'd like to introduce you to Count Mercy," Leopold interrupted. "He has been assisting us with Antoinette's situation."

Count Mercy continued to stare at me. "You will have to excuse me, Your Majesty. You look just like her."

"I'm sorry?"

"Your sister." His eyes watered with tears. "I feel like I am looking at her right now."

I took his hand in mine. "I am sure you and I will be dear friends, just as you and she are."

The doorway opened, and Mimi sauntered into the room. Instantly, my happiness drained as her smug face looked me up and down. "Little Sister, it has been far too long."

"For you, perhaps."

"Albert and I have thought about visiting Naples ourselves, but the heat is just not good for my disposition."

"Yes," I responded, "it would be a pity for the Neapolitan sun to melt the ice you call a heart."

"Charlotte," Leopold said in warning as Mimi moved to greet Karl.

"Why is she here?" I protested.

"You forget, Little Sister, that Antoinette is not the only Habsburg daughter," Mimi said, suddenly turning to me.

"I'm surprised you even remember her name; you certainly don't remember Amalia's."

"Don't act like you are the only one who cares."

"You shed fake tears for the much-maligned queen of France, when everyone knows the only person you care about is yourself," I said. "You managed to marry a prince who is only the sixth son of a king, not even close to the line of succession. He has never earned anything for himself, not even his title. The fact that Mother paid so much attention to you was her only flaw."

Mimi's face went from red to crimson within a matter of minutes.

"Charlotte, would you please!" Leopold said. "We have an opportunity to rescue our sister. You can argue some other time when Antoinette is safe. Count Mercy, could you explain the latest developments for us?"

"Antoinette and her close confidant Count Fersen have devised a plan. They are going to escape Tuileries with a heavy carriage and make their way to Montmédy," Mercy began.

"A heavy carriage?" Karl questioned. "Wouldn't it be better if they used a light carriage?"

"That is what Fersen and I suggested, but Antoinette insisted that she and her family leave together."

Naturally, Antoinette would insist that. She could never save herself; there had to be a whole entourage.

"This is ludicrous!" I said. "How are they going to inconspicuously travel?"

"They plan on changing horses at various points."

"Yes, because that is going to help. Surely the French will only be looking for a set of six horses and not one large carriage," I huffed, and put my hands on my hips. "What can I do to help?"

"We need money," Mercy said. "Funds to help build the carriage and make sure they are established when they safely arrive."

"This plan is foolish, and it's never going to work," I said. "But I will give Fersen whatever he needs. He can clean out my treasury, for all I care."

"If you don't agree with the plan," Mercy said, "why are you going to give him money?"

"Because a bit of inconvenience is worth it if I can save Antoinette."

* * *

When I was young, I found Amalia to be annoying. Though she was older than me, she was naïve, and behaved like one of my younger siblings. Now I wished for her to be here almost as much as Antoinette. As we left my brother's office, I asked Leopold if he had heard any news from Amalia since she sent her regrets. "Just that her son's health has not improved."

"She is only using that as an excuse," I said as we made our way across the threshold of the family parlor, where the rest of the guests had gathered. "Her son fell and hit his head well over a year ago. If she was so concerned about his epilepsy, she could have brought him with her."

"We don't know how strong these fits are. I doubt her son would have been able to make the journey."

"Her animosity toward our family has transcended even Mother's death. I have it on good authority that she didn't even send condolences to Joseph."

"Amalia, like the rest of the empress's daughters, is stubborn," my brother said. "Perhaps you and Ferdinand should visit her in Parma on your way back to Naples."

"I wonder what it is about the Italian colonies that creates the oddest queens?" Mimi said just as Leopold and I entered the parlor.

The room stilled as every eye turned from my sister to me.

"You live there," she continued. "Perhaps you could enlighten us. Is it all the garlic, or perhaps it is something within the soil? I know your husband has not stopped talking about his precious volcano since he got here."

Out of the corner of my eye, I could see Ferdinand's face flush.

"Don't engage her," Leopold whispered in my ear, but his words meant nothing, for I was already simmering with rage.

"What would you know about being a queen?" I sneered. "You are only a duchess."

"Archduchess," Mimi said. "Mother made sure I was able to retain my title."

"Of course she did." As the eyes of the room volleyed between her and me, I said, "It was quite a feat how you managed to manipulate our mother to do your bidding. It's a shame that everyone else isn't fooled by your putrid stench."

Leopold gave a large clap. "Let's have some music, yes?"

Immediately the quartet started to play and, with a motion of my brother's hand, footmen started refilling Champagne glasses. When everyone's attention was elsewhere, Leopold grabbed me by the elbow and pulled me into a corner. "Please don't engage Mimi. She will leave here within the week. I will see to it personally."

"I'm sorry. I simply cannot stomach her."

"I have procured a small palace for her and her husband as a gift. She'll be far away from us, but until then please try to keep the peace. I only have time to worry about one sister. I don't need two more trying to kill each other. Do you understand?"

"Yes, dear brother," I said, relenting.

"Good. Now if you will excuse me, I will be taking my leave. I have a letter to write to the ambassador and other affairs of state to attend to."

"You know, even God rested after creating the world."

"God never ruled the Holy Roman Empire." Leopold slipped from the room as the revelry continued.

As I moved to stand next to Ferdinand, I watched Mimi as she and her husband stood by themselves. All the other guests were going out of their way to avoid interacting with them. Taking a glass of Champagne from a footman, I savored my small victory.

My Most Beloved Sister,   *November 15, 1791*

Your words of assurance about Leopold have eased my soul. Though I am still concerned that he won't be diligent in quelling the unrest in France, I will trust your judgment; you know him better than I do. I only hope that he can act soon. The madness that has plagued France has spread to our Haitian territory. Before long, everywhere under French domain will revolt.

I agree with the Haitians' cause, Mother was never fond of slavery, and Joseph made a point of officially abolishing serfdom ten years ago. But who am I to speak out? Especially now, when everyone hates me. Louis does nothing to ease my concerns. He wavers on everything, leaving me to make the final decisions for the monarchy. Which is pointless, because the advisors don't like my involvement in politics. "It is not a woman's place," they tell me. As if they know where a woman's place is.

If there is anything good to come out of this, it is that the Americans have a new secretary of the treasury, named Alexander Hamilton. It is under him that the country has started paying France back for the debt they incurred during their revolution. When I had the opportunity to look over the treasury report, I found that they had taken millions from us. They are the reason we are bankrupt. What a steep price to pay for us to get revenge on England.

Your sister,
Antoinette

CHAPTER FORTY

Three months after the wedding, the Two Sicilies officially contributed to fund Antoinette's attempted escape. In addition to the fees for the specially made carriages, the family needed funds to survive after the escape. If I could have exchanged all the money in my treasury to keep her safe, I would have. Antoinette was precious to me.

It was with this newfound hope that I made my way to Leopold's office. However, my heart fell upon entry. My brother and Count Mercy were deep in conversation. Leopold's brows were creased with anger. Mercy was whispering to him in hushed, hurried tones.

"Good morning, gentlemen. I hope you have some news on my sister."

"Well, we have some news," Leopold said, rubbing at his temple with the heel of his hand.

"The alliance is officially collapsing," Mercy said.

"What do you mean collapsing?" I asked, looking back and forth between the two men. A familiar feeling of dread settled into my chest, making it hard to breathe.

"The various countries have determined that they want something in exchange for the possibility of putting the lives of their soldiers on the line."

"What are they asking?"

"Well, the king of Sardinia wants Geneva, which is controlled by France. Spain would like to get its historical lands of Navarre back. And Prussia is demanding to reclaim Alsace."

"They are worse than children," I muttered.

"Everyone wants something; it's the way of the world," Leopold said. "We can find a way around this. We don't need to work with them."

"We'll give it to them," I said.

"Those lands are not ours to give." Count Mercy said. "If we keep chopping off slices of France, she'll have nothing left to rule."

"Better a life with no country than no life at all."

"Charlotte"—Leopold rubbed at his temples—"either be productive or leave."

Leopold was growing thinner. The shadows under his eyes had deepened. "Very well," I said, settling down to listen to the rest of the meeting. It was evident the stress of running Austria was getting to him. No one was able to do it as diligently as Mother had. I felt pity for Leopold. This was a burden far too heavy for him to carry.

* * *

The winter sun shone over the frozen grounds as I took a walk by myself. The satisfying crunch of snow greeted me as I stepped out the palace doors. I pulled my cloak in closer, inhaling the sharp, cold winter air. I always loved the smell of new snow; the clean freshness stung my nostrils. And the stillness. After the first snowfall, there was always a stillness, as if the world were collectively taking a breath.

I had naïvely thought that staying at Schönbrunn Palace would be as special as it was when I was a child. But to live with one's ghosts is a torture in and of itself. One that, as I was coming to learn, was of my own device. At first, I was happy to be here, but with each passing memory, I felt the sting of the absence of my mother and sister more and more.

Even as ice crystals hung from branches like tiny chandeliers, I knew it would never be the same. As much as I wanted it to, I could feel something else that pulled at my heart.

I longed for Naples.

I longed for Vesuvius, that great volcano rising up, overlooking the city that stretches out before her like a worshipper in invocation to her goddess. The crescent moon of the bay, with water bluer than the sky on a cloudless day. Oh, my beautiful Naples. I missed her more than I could ever have imagined.

It turned out I was not the only one who missed home. Ferdinand was careful not to appear disgruntled in front of Theresa as she settled into her new life as the wife of the heir apparent of Austria. But behind closed doors, in the palace apartment we shared, Ferdinand let me know exactly what he thought.

When I returned from my walk, I found Ferdinand sitting in front of a roaring fire, with thick fur blankets draped across his lap. As soon as I slipped through the door, he began to complain. "I swear I will never get used to this place," he grumbled. "It's always cold. Why is it so cold?"

"It simply is," I said, pouring brandy for us from a side table.

"If I die from this cold, I am blaming you," he said, fussing with his blanket. "I will come back as a ghost, and I will haunt you."

I handed him the brown liquor and took a seat opposite him. "I lived in weather this cold for almost sixteen years. If I survived, so can you."

"And the court is boring. There are no games to play, and I only have my sister and our daughter to talk to. There are not enough Neapolitans."

"You could learn French or German."

"Bah," Ferdinand protested. "Why dirty my tongue with another language?" He took a swig of brandy. "Schönbrunn is no Caserta. We have more grandeur. Look at the Christmas decorations. There is only one Nativity scene. One. At Caserta, we have hundreds throughout the palace. How can you celebrate the Christ child with only one Nativity scene?"

"I have to admit, I do miss my gardens."

"How much longer are we staying here?"

"I want to make sure Antoinette gets home safely."

"Charlotte, it's been three months, I cannot stay here forever."

"I know, but I want to be close when Antoinette escapes France." Tears pricked my eyes. "I know you want to go home, but I need to see my sister."

Ferdinand was quiet for a long moment. "I could never dream of being parted from Philip—that's why he stayed in Naples with me. We can remain here a while longer to make sure she returns safely." He reached out and clasped my hand. "But we still have a duty to Naples."

⚜

Queen Maria Carolina,   *May 20, 1791*

With great sadness, I must report to you that a tragedy has befallen the region of Calabria. At five in the morning, yesterday an earthquake struck. Whole villages have been reduced to rubble.

The council has taken the liberty of sending the military to see to the cleanup of the villages. I have also instructed the navy to take food and other necessities to the people. However, I am going to need your authorization to send additional funds to assist in the restoration efforts.

I apologize for pulling you away from your family. I know how important it is to be able to see Antoinette. Please know if there were any other way, I would choose it, but the Two Sicilies needs you.

I need you.

Yours,

Sir John Acton

CHAPTER FORTY-ONE

May 20, 1791

With each passing day, my anxiety over Antoinette's well-being grew, leading me to spend my early mornings, before the rest of the palace rose, saying my prayers at the palace chapel. At Caserta, mornings were spent at mass, a habit, instilled in me by my mother, that continued well into my adulthood. But here at Schönbrunn, I relished the quiet mornings that allowed me to reflect on my prayers. Prayers imploring whatever saint was listening for the safety of my sister.

The clinking of my rosary beads as they passed over my fingers echoed throughout the sanctuary while I stared at the painting of Joseph and Mary's wedding. The gold that was on display throughout the palace had also seeped through the chapel, touching the statues of saints and angels, forever imploring God on behalf of the great Habsburg family.

I tried to say a Hail Mary, but only the name of my sister crossed my lips as the beads sounded an invocation all their own.

It felt like Antoinette was slipping away from me. From the day she was born, we were destined to be separated. But wasn't that the way of sisters? We are born of the same parents, we share the same secrets, the same confidences, and then we are ripped apart to live separate lives. If there was anything I knew to be true, it was that sisters are our counterparts, the mirrors reflecting who we are meant to be.

Antoinette was always my reflection. She brought out the good in me. My sister was the gentle one, while I was always coarse. All these years, I had cursed our mother for placing Antoinette in France when I should have been cursing Josepha. If Josepha had not died, she would be the queen of the Two Sicilies and I would be the queen of France. I would have taken control of France the way I took control of Naples. These riots and treasury problems would not have happened. Nor would I have devoted so much money on a rebellion that would not directly benefit my kingdom.

The beads of my rosary continued to clink in the silent chapel, reminding me that I could not change what had happened. Josepha was dead. Antoinette was fighting for her life in France, and I was here, powerless, playing with a useless bracelet.

* * *

As I opened the door to our apartments, I found Ferdinand and Theresa together, crying.

"What happened? Is it Antoinette? Is she injured?" I dropped my book and rushed to Theresa's side.

"There was an earthquake in Calabria," Ferdinand said.

I gasped.

"The Marchesa Giuliana died," Ferdinand said, tears spilling down his cheeks. My hand flew to my chest. She and her husband were regular visitors to Caserta, and the marquis had been a childhood friend of Ferdinand's. She was kind to me, especially during my early years in Naples. They had recently left to go back to Calabria to spend more time with their children. "The marquis pulled her out of their burning house. But their daughter was trapped inside. Giuliana heard the screams and broke away from Filippo. She bounded into the house, followed by Filippo, and, and…"

Ferdinand's voice caught as he fell into the sofa, weeping.

"The house collapsed, and they were lost," Theresa finished for her father before thrusting a letter at me. "Acton wrote to you privately." Opening the letter, I scanned the words, feeling the dread in my chest grow.

"We need to return to Naples," Ferdinand insisted, wiping the tears from his face.

"You may go," I said, "but I am staying here."

"What do you mean you're staying here?" Ferdinand asked, his eyes growing large.

"I am staying here and waiting for Antoinette."

"Our people need you," Ferdinand said. "I need you."

"I can't leave. Not until Antoinette escapes France."

"I know Antoinette means everything to you, but our country means more," Ferdinand pleaded.

"I want to stay here, just a bit longer. Please."

"You have to come back with me. We have been here long enough; our people need us."

"Antoinette needs us! Do not make me choose between my sister and my country!"

"You are the queen," Ferdinand said.

And there it was: The reminder that I didn't have a choice to make. That above all else—before being a daughter, a sister, a mother, and a wife—I had to be the queen. It defined me. Engulfed me.

"Very well," I said, hanging my head in defeat.

"Mama," Theresa said, "I'll sit in on the meetings with Uncle Leopold. I can report to you everything they say. I'll let you know the moment Zia Antoinette escapes."

I placed a hand on her soft cheek. "You are a wonderful daughter."

Several days later, I stood at the door to the carriage, looking over Schönbrunn Palace, my childhood home forever altered. With tears in my eyes, I got into the carriage and left for Naples once again, this time with my husband by my side.

June 26, 1791

As we stepped out of the carriage, we were greeted by Acton. I smiled brightly. "It is a pleasure to see you." I took his hands in mine. "I missed you."

Acton held my hands tightly. "We need to go somewhere to talk, in private."

"What's happened? Was there another earthquake?"

"No," he said quietly.

"Oh God, is it Antoinette?" I began to shake.

"It's best to go somewhere private," Acton said.

"No, tell me now," I insisted. "I want to know."

Ferdinand came up behind me. "Acton, what is going on?"

"The escape failed," Acton said. "Your sister and her family were taken into custody."

I grabbed on to Acton's arm, trying to keep from collapsing. An arrested monarch was a dead monarch. Antoinette's life was in peril, now more than ever.

By order of the King and Queen of the Two
Sicilies, Ferdinand and Maria Carolina Charlotte

The French language shall henceforth be banned from use within the walls of the Royal Palace of Caserta. Likewise, it shall not be in use within any official state-sanctioned event, nor within the domain of this country. Any violators shall be fined 500 ducats per incident.

CHAPTER FORTY-TWO

JUNE 1791

Emma sat in the parlor with me as we made our plans to get even with France. "There are definitely going to be consequences on the government level," I said, pacing back and forth, "but we must not allow them to have any leeway within the Two Sicilies."

Emma was sitting at my desk, paper and quill in hand. "We can stop all trade with France," she said. "I am sure that will be helpful."

I waved a hand in dismissal. "We've done that."

"When I was a little girl there, my mother insisted on my always being clean and properly dressed. Which wasn't normal for the street that I greet up on, my mother being a washerwoman after all. The other children liked to make fun of me for dressing so nicely, and once they pretended to speak another language and not understand me. What if we do that with the French?"

"I love it!" I exclaimed. "I do not want to hear the language of the foul people who choose to crucify my sister. We'll ban all things French here at Caserta. Take down all the French art from the walls, put it into storage. We'll take it even further: We'll exile all the French artists."

"Are you sure?"

"Yes!" I said. "We'll write them letters, say something to the effect of 'Though we are thankful for your years of service to the Kingdom of the Two Sicilies, we no longer wish to have any artist or intellectual in our court that is of French origin.' We'll erase all things French from the Two Sicilies." I flopped down and took a big swig of wine. This was going to be endlessly entertaining.

* * *

I was feeling confident about my decision until I sat down with Acton.

"We need to review your proposed changes. I have heard whispers of following France into revolution."

"Whispers? From whom?"

"From the people. They are getting ideas. We need to take measures that will temper these urges."

"France couldn't do that, and look where that got them. Our aldermen, where are their loyalties?"

"The aldermen are elected representatives of the people, so naturally their allegiance is going to be with the people. It might be best if we replace them with police magistrates controlled by the state."

"Make it happen."

"Very well, madame." He pushed my proposed order to ban all things French to me on the table. "Is this truly how you wish to proceed?"

"Yes," I said, pushing it back to him. "We are in a fight with France."

"Prussia is the one that has taken it upon themselves to invade France, not the Two Sicilies."

"Well, I do think we should invade. Our navy is much better than it was before."

Acton placed his hands to his mouth, breathing in deeply. Lowering them again, he spoke very slowly. "Charlotte, I fully understand how angry you are. I truly do. But we must be calculating in our attacks. Our navy may be strong, but it is not *that* strong. And you are systematically oppressing the French people living here."

"Oppressing?" I said, feeling my temperature rise. "Look at what they are doing to my sister. How they treat their women and, Lord help me, their abhorrent treatment of the slaves in their territories. Bah!" I rose from the table and began pacing back and forth in the room. "If waging a cultural war with the French makes them feel oppressed, then so be it. The French blame everyone but themselves for their problems. Everything is my sister's fault. Meanwhile, their nobles are prancing around Paris dripping in jewels."

"Will you at least meet with the ambassador?"

"No."

"You have not spoken with him since you returned."

"And I don't plan on speaking with him again, ever."

"Charlotte, you are the most insufferable woman I have ever met."

"Then it is a good thing I am not your wife."

"That was not meant to be an endearment." He got up from the table. "I'll enforce this, but be prepared to go to war."

"We have to make sure France knows that their behavior is not without consequences. Have our ambassador reaffirm that while we are expelling all the French nationals from court, we will remain neutral."

"Neutral? Since when you have ever remained neutral on anything?"

"Since it means the Kingdom of the Two Sicilies will survive this crisis. We will not remain complacent in our defense against France and everything she represents."

"If you are not careful, France will invade." Acton grabbed me by the shoulders and leveled a steady gaze at me. "We could lose everything."

"France will be more interested in fighting with Austria than with us. Sicily is more like an annoying fly to them."

"Yes, but even an annoying fly gets squished at times." Acton pulled me into his arms, letting me rest against him without judgment.

⚜

Dearest Mother,   *March 2, 1792*

I am burdened with informing you that Leopold has died unexpectedly.

Leopold had been incredibly strained, with the situation in France and the growing restlessness in Austria. Luisa and I thought it would be nice to have a family picnic to distract him. Everything was lovely, and Leopold looked like he was enjoying himself. He even suggested that he and Luisa go for a stroll, like they used to do when they were young. Watching Leopold and Luisa as they walked away, I blissfully hoped that could be me and Francis one day.

That was when I heard it: the most chilling sound to be uttered from someone's lips. I swear to you, Mother, I will never forget the sound of complete and total sorrow as it rang out through the garden.

It was only later that we learned what happened. They were walking, but as they turned a corner, Leopold's legs gave out. Luisa tried to hold him up, but he simply crumbled, like a doll. Leopold's face was not that of peace and serenity, as one would hope when they are about to meet their Maker. He was confused and clutching at his chest before he finally died.

Mama, I fear Luisa will not make it much longer. She has taken to bed and will not eat. I try to coax her, but even getting the slightest bit of broth to cross her lips is akin to a small miracle.

Please know I shall be offering prayers for Leopold on your behalf at mass tomorrow.

Your Loving Daughter,

Theresa

CHAPTER FORTY-THREE

MARCH 16, 1792

The letter from my daughter floated to the floor as my hands began to shake uncontrollably. I couldn't imagine a world without my brother. He had always been my advisor, my friend. The one who took pity on me when I crossed Mother. He was my first chess partner. And now he was gone.

Two men inherited Mother's throne. And two men died within years of taking her crown. If I were like the old women of Naples, I would believe that my mother had placed a curse on the throne. But I knew better. My mother was such a force that no one man could fulfill her duties.

The threat of rain hung in the gray skies over Caserta, reflecting my mood as I paced back and forth in the palace library. The situation in France was quickly deteriorating. Riots were regularly breaking out. War was the only way to save my sister. If Prussia's invasion worked, we could rescue Antoinette and put to bed this ridiculous rebellion. If not, I had to have faith that the new Holy Roman emperor—Leopold's son Francis—would be just as much of a champion for me and Antoinette as his father was.

The baby kicked inside my stomach. Child number fifteen.

I thought I was this expert chess player. That I could move my pieces wherever I wanted on the board and I wouldn't get bested. But sitting here, looking at the letter, that horrible ink-stained message, it felt like I had lost my knight and I was sure that my bishop would be next.

Later that evening, we were in the family parlor, dressed in black to show that we were all in mourning. Ferdinand sat in the armchair across from me as I held my young son, Leopold, in my arms. Our family was much smaller now. Francis sat at the chess table with Christina, my daughter being sorely outmatched. Amalia softly played a happy tune on the harpsichord in the corner. Enrichetta and Clotilde played with their dolls on the rug at their father's feet, while Antonia sat on the sofa flipping through the pages of a book.

My sons Giuseppe and Gennaro had been taken from us by smallpox; even with the inoculations, they were both killed by the virus. Each death, whether it be a sibling or a child, was as painful as the first; they made me want to hold on to my family even tighter.

I was looking over the children when Ferdinand decided to speak up. "What is the news in France?"

"According to Acton," I said, "there were a number of German and Prussian soldiers working as mercenaries within the French army."

"Were?" Francis questioned, abandoning his chess match to come sit next to Antonia on the sofa.

"Yes, were. They abandoned the French military and joined with the Prussian army."

"Well, good for them!" Ferdinand exclaimed. "You see this is the problem with the French: They had the opportunity to change things with Louis, make a stable, more sensible government. What are they even rebelling against now? I've lost track."

"It's always been the one reason," I said. "The middle and lower classes are burdened with the taxes while the nobility, the upper echelon of society, has been able to get away without paying anything."

Ferdinand shook his head. "This is why I want to create Ferdinan-danapoli. I want to create a society where everyone gets a basic income. It is all the government's fault that their people can't eat. Why else should we have a government if not to take care of the people."

"We are moving in that direction," I said, smoothing Leopold's hair, "but proper social change takes time. It can't happen all at once. Look at the United States. They had that big revolution, and it was only a few years ago that they ratified their constitution. Change, proper change, takes time."

"At least they have George Washington," Ferdinand said. "I have been reading the most fascinating things about him. He is a strong leader. That's what France needs. A strong leader like in the United States." He shook a finger at Francis. "Steady leadership. That's what your people will admire. People like your George Washington. Like your mother."

"Thank you," I said, acknowledging my husband's kindness.

"Charlotte," Ferdinand said, "have we given a gift to the president of United States—that is what they are calling him, right? A president and not a king?"

"That's right. But, no, not as of yet."

"Well, we should send his family some gifts from us. A gesture of goodwill."

"I heard he has his own farm," I said.

"Oh, well, I know the perfect gift. I'll give him some of my donkeys, from my farm."

"But, Papa," Clotilde said, "you won't give away all your donkeys, will you?"

"Of course not, principessa," Ferdinand said. "I'll only be giving him the ones that speak English."

Charlotte,   *September 1770*

I had the most haunting dream last night; well, it was more of a memory mixed with a dream. I dreamed about that time Wolfgang and Nannerl visited us.

Do you remember that? The dream started with Nannerl's harp performance. The very performance moved me to tears. Watching her, I realized I wanted to be someone who brought beauty to the world. The dream then moved to that evening when we were playing in the Hall of Mirrors.

We were running down the red carpet, our curls trailing behind us in our reflections as the chandeliers illuminated us. Our laughter echoed down the hall. Then, all of a sudden, it was only Wolfgang and me. Everywhere I turned, I saw Wolfgang standing there, calling to me. "Run away with me," he kept saying.

"I'm coming with you!" I yelled, and each time I reached out to him I found nothing but glass. Soon I was surrounded by glass mirrors and the voice of Wolfgang asking me to run away with him. Dropping to my knees, I cried fat tears as Wolfgang continued to call for me.

Poor Wolfgang. I still remember when he proudly strode up to Mother, declaring that he would marry me. His face grew so red when Mother laughed at him.

But what Mother didn't know was that I would have left with him without giving a second thought.

Yours Always,
Antoinette

CHAPTER FORTY-FOUR

July 1792

"They have arrested both the king and the queen but insist on this trial, this mockery." I set the latest correspondence from the ambassador down on my desk.

Acton rubbed at his temple. "They need to make sure the people know why they are deposing the monarchy."

"It's a show, is what it is!" I exclaimed. "A crucifixion. From the moment my sister stepped foot in that country, they have sought her blood. They never accepted her." I held my hand to my mouth as I swallowed down the bile. "Mark my words, Acton: There is no saving Antoinette. Not now."

"You can't give up hope. They'll most likely let her live in a convent with her daughter."

"If she wouldn't separate her family for a carriage ride from Paris to Montmédy, life in a convent without her son is not an option."

"She may not have a choice." His years as my prime minister had taken their toll, the gray hairs that peppered his temples had spread, and his hairline was receding. The wrinkles around his eyes had grown more pronounced. But his clear brown eyes still focused on me. He was still the handsome man who brought me books. "Trust your son-in-law and Prussia. In the meantime, the new French government has sent an ambassador to replace the last one."

"It doesn't matter," I said, shuffling the papers in front of me. "I do not recognize their country without its monarchy. This 'new France,' as they are calling it, does not get any representation here in Naples."

"At some point, you are going to have to acknowledge the man."

"No, I won't."

"Yes, you will. The last ambassador, Signor Cacault, was furious by the time he left. He was never invited to any salons nor would you even acknowledge him. If he'd had his way, France would have invaded the Two Sicilies just because you offended him. Luckily for us, France is too distracted with Prussia to care. The new ambassador, Armand Louis de Mackau, is a radical."

"He's French. Aren't they all radicals?"

"Baron Mackau's reputation precedes him. Though he may be a moderate member of the revolutionary party, he is still a firm believer in the revolution and its principles. By Neapolitan standards, he is a radical."

"I don't like these revolutionaries," I said. "Their very principles are an affront to everything that we stand for. There is no respect for authority. They think they are progressing society forward, but they are doing just the opposite."

"Right now, France's attention is focused on Prussia to the northeast, but that could all change." Acton closed his books and eyed me. "Mackau will be at court. Will you acknowledge him for me?"

I would give Acton the world if he asked for it. "Very well," I said, giving in. "But only if he follows my rules."

Acton's smile fell. "I will be sure he is made aware."

* * *

A week later, Ferdinand and I sat in the throne room of Caserta. Orange light flowed through the open windows, making the gold-trimmed room shine. Nobles presented themselves one after another, paying their respects, hoping for favors to be bestowed on them.

"Cittadino Armand Louis de Mackau and Signora Mackau," the attendant proclaimed to the room.

This Mackau had a strange face; it was as if it all came to a sharp angle at his nose. Mackau wore a large powdered wig and a burgundy silk suit, a far more elaborate outfit than any costume worn by the ladies of my court. "*Votre Majesté*," he said.

The woman next to him, his wife, was much more pleasant to look at. She had a soft, round face, but her lip slightly turned up while her green eyes moved about the room. Her blond wig was piled high with curls and flowers. From the corner of my eye, I could see Ferdinand growing disturbed by the sight of them.

"It is our pleasure to be guests in your court," Mackau said in French.

"What is he saying?" Ferdinand said to me.

"I don't know." I shrugged.

"But you speak French," my husband said.

"Not anymore."

"Oh," he said. Then he whispered, "That's something you can simply forget?"

"Yes, darling."

"Oh, very well," Ferdinand said. "It's for the best, I suppose. They are wearing wigs. I don't like them. Or their language," he added, leaning back into his throne and motioning for the ambassadors to continue.

"We have come here on behalf of France to ensure our mutual admiration and friendship."

"Stop, stop, stop," Ferdinand said. "Do you speak Italian?"

The Mackaus looked at each other and then looked back to him. "We were told that the queen speaks French." They looked to me. "*Parlez-vous français?*"

I shrugged. "I simply do not understand what they are saying."

"Do. You. Speak. Italian?" Ferdinand asked, overenunciating. "*Italiano.*"

The ambassador's face flushed scarlet. Out of the corner of my eye, I could see Acton dropping his head into the palm of his hand.

"It is of no use," Ferdinand said. "They don't understand a word we are saying."

"It is a pity France is unable to send us their best," I said. "What kind of government sends an official that doesn't speak the language of their host country?"

The court laughed at my joke as the Mackaus rushed around the throne room.

"A rude one. That's who," Ferdinand said. "You see, this is what I was telling the children the other night. France needs strong leadership."

"You are quite right, my dear," I said, waving the French away in dismissal.

With a small smile, I watched as they were ushered from my presence.

Less than a week later, we were standing in the lobby of Caserta's theater. Naples rivaled Venice in the production and demand for opera. It was thanks in part to my childhood friend Wolfgang. Along with many other people that I loved, he had departed from this world last winter. Tonight was a night to honor him. I last saw him when he came to Caserta during his Italian tour in 1770. Upon his arrival, I brought him to the safety of my garden so that we could speak freely. Arm in arm, we promenaded down the path toward the waterfall. With his large eyes and soft lips, he still had the remnants of the child prodigy I knew in my youth.

"How is Nannerl?"

"She is still composing her own music, but she is no longer allowed to travel with us," he said. "Though this was our father's decision, it has put a damper on our relationship."

Afraid I had ventured into troublesome waters, I changed the subject. "I am so happy we are reunited!"

"I am as well."

Returning his smile, I said, "How long will you be with us?"

"Six weeks."

"Six weeks! I must be exceptionally blessed!"

"You say that now, but wait until I begin working on my next piece. I will be absolutely abhorrent."

"Never. Not to me." We continued to walk. "Do you plan to go to France soon?"

"No. This trip will only consist of the Italian peninsula." He grew quiet, and I feared I had said something wrong.

"I am still cross you visited Venice before Naples," I said.

"Yes, but I save all my best work for Naples."

"Well, then, I suppose I can forgive you."

We continued to walk in silence, enjoying the late summer day. "I still love Antoinette," Mozart said suddenly. "I would have married her."

"I know."

"How ironic that the woman I love above all others moved to the one place where I cannot have my music heard." Paris was the hardest place for a struggling musician to perform. He had performed there several years ago, but he was not well received and had not been welcomed back since.

"Who needs Paris when you have Naples!" I said.

Thankfully, he laughed, the sound finer than any of his symphonies.

"And just so you know," I added, "she would have married you too."

"I'd like to think that," he said, squeezing my arm.

Now, in honor of Mozart, we had our private opera company perform my favorite of his works, *Le Nozze di Figaro*.

Glasses of wine from our very own fields were being passed around to the guests as moonlight spilled in through the arched windows of the vestibule. Off to the side, a string quartet was playing selections of Mozart's music. As I sipped the wine from our vineyard, I hated to admit I missed Champagne. However, Champagne was French, and that, too, was banned from my court.

Emma was in the midst of telling me a lively story about a recent dinner she had attended on Sir Hamilton's behalf when the Mackaus walked in, nearly causing me to spit my wine out. The wigs that they were wearing were twice as high as the ones that they had worn upon meeting us. Their clothing was a matching green silk trimmed in gold. They looked ridiculous.

"Haven't they been told not to wear wigs?" Emma asked.

"They're French. They think they know better," I said, eyeing them as they took a turn about the room. "They shall soon learn the ways of Naples."

It was a well-known fact that my husband had a phobia when it came to wigs. Not only did he refuse to wear them, but he refused to allow anyone else around him to wear them. It was never officially a royal proclamation. My husband was too creative for that. Anyone who entered his presence with a wig was soon to find it missing. We had been warned about it when I first came to Naples. I also knew that my husband was quite susceptible to suggestion, especially from me.

"I pity whoever has to sit behind them," Emma said. Like the rest of the court, she was keeping a wary eye on the couple, out of fear that they might approach.

"Emma, I have an idea. Follow me." I took my friend by the elbow and moved to stand by Ferdinand. He was well into his wine as he watched Signor and Signora Mackau try to talk to nobility too fearful to speak French.

"Emma dear, don't you think those wigs look a bit odd?" I said in his earshot.

"Terribly so," she replied .

"Why are the wigs always so curly? It's like twisty spaghetti, don't you think?"

Emma paused, contemplating, her head turning ever so charmingly to one side. "Yes, I think I do have to agree."

"I'm hungry," Ferdinand said, his eyes narrowing as he scrutinized the couple. He grabbed a poor waiter by the cuff. "Bring me buttered spaghetti from the kitchens. Now." He released the boy and proclaimed, "And make it a large bowl! The show does not go on until I have eaten."

I allowed a servant to pour me more wine as I waited for the scene to bloom just the way I had hoped.

Ferdinand's bloodshot eyes would not leave the Mackaus as they continued to try to speak to clusters of nobility. Each time they approached someone, they backed away with excuses that they did not speak French.

Baron Mackau then straightened his shoulders and strode up to me. "I know you speak my language," he insisted, speaking in French. "You must make this stop. We have gone out of our way to try to pay you, the queen, respect."

It was true: I understood every word he was saying. But instead of acknowledging him, I turned to Emma. "Did you hear something?"

"Not a word," she said, taking a sip of her wine. "Perhaps it was the wind?"

"Hmm, that would be quite hard. We are in the center of Caserta after all. Not many windows. Do you think we have a ghost?"

"A ghost! Oh, that would be fun. Perhaps we can arrange for a hunting party."

"Yes, dogs included. We cannot let ghosts get too comfortable; they can become pests."

Baron Mackau started to huff in frustration, but we were interrupted by a servant who wheeled a large bowl of hot buttered spaghetti up to my husband on a tea cart. Ferdinand dove into the bowl, making a great show of slurping up the noodles. A spot of melted butter shone on his chin in the warm light of the chandeliers. "Mackau," he called, with a mouth full of food. "Come, eat with me."

The whole room went quiet, and everyone looked to a very confused French ambassador, who didn't understand what was happening.

"Come," Ferdinand called, motioning like Mackau was one of his dogs.

Reluctantly, the ambassador came to stand opposite Ferdinand. In one swift motion, my husband lifted the bowl and dumped it over his head.

Mackau let out a yelp as greasy noodles slipped from his head down to his shoulders. In horrified shock, he picked off the pasta, leaving behind dark oil stains. Next, Ferdinand pulled the wig from the man's head, revealing black hair so thin that shiny patches of scalp showed through.

"Let this be a lesson," Ferdinand called, raising the wig in the air like a trophy. "No one, and I mean no one, is to wear a wig in my presence." Thrusting the wig into the ambassador's face, he scolded him, "No."

As Baron Mackau and his wife rushed from the room, the court broke out in laughter. The only one not laughing was Acton. His face was red as he strode up to me. "A word. Now."

We slipped into a side room, where Acton immediately began pacing. "How could you do this?"

"I didn't do anything."

"Don't." There were very few people in this world who were

allowed to yell at me. Acton was one of them. "You are behaving like a child," he hissed.

"I am behaving like the queen that I am."

"No. You are behaving like your husband. Antics from him are expected, but not from you. Never this from you." His reddened face was pained. "Do you have any idea what I have been going through while you are occupying yourself with your schemes?"

"Acton," I said. I reached out for him, but he pulled away.

"No." His voice was gruff. "While you have been busy playing your games, I have been doing everything I can to make sure that France does not invade. There are warships stationed just north of Rome as we speak. Admiral La Touche, the war hero from the American Revolution, is simply waiting for Mackau to give him word to come here. And after everything that you've put him through, I wouldn't blame him if he did." Acton took a couple of steps toward me, so that we were inches apart. "Can't you see that everything I do is for you?"

I picked my hand up and placed it on his pounding heart.

"All I ask for is some respect," he said, "and for you to be the woman I know you can be."

Tears swam in my eyes as I realized that while I was focused on my rivalry with France, I could lose the very thing I loved the most: *la mia bella Napoli.*

My Dear Sister,   *September 24, 1792*

I am not sure how much longer I will be able to write to you. All of my correspondence is being scruti-nized, particularly the letters that I send to leaders of foreign countries, regardless of whether or not they are to my sister.

It is official: France is now a republic. Louis and I have been flung from the throne. Quite literally, as they would have it. The people stormed Tuileries, intent on killing us all, but it was only our poor guards who gave their lives. The National Assembly took all of the king's powers away, for his own protection, they said. But I know the truth. All along, they wanted to take what was not theirs. They wanted to rule France. I can't help but wonder if the National Assembly put the people up to storming the palace. They couldn't take Louis's power away right at the very beginning. They had to beat it out of us, humiliate us. Make us believe that France was safer in their hands than in ours.

Well, they can have it. I simply want to go home to Vienna. To see the palace of my childhood one last time.

In the meantime, please know that I am safe.

Your sister,
Antoinette

CHAPTER FORTY-FIVE

August 1792

Following the spaghetti incident, as it became known, the Mack-aus' time in Naples was slightly less tense. People were allowed once again to speak French to them, but the shunning of Signor and Signora Mackau was still harsh. No salon was open to them. Other officials in Caserta avoided the ambassador.

"The funniest thing happened yesterday!" Emma said as we took our regular stroll through the English garden. "Signora Mackau walked up to me, Principessa Isabella Garlano, and the Marchesa di Cutrona. I say she walked up to us, but we could smell her long before she shoved her way into our circle. It is true what they say: The French really do stink." Emma gave me an amused sideways glance. "Anyway, she walked right up to Isabella and gave the deepest of curtsies and went on to speak to her in French, telling her what an honor it was to be among royalty."

"Do they not know that the title of prince and princess were handed out by my husband whenever someone pleased him? There are more princes in the Two Sicilies than there are in all of Europe."

"Apparently not. Furthermore, she completely insulted the marchesa. Everyone knows that the Cutrona line is far older than the Garlano line. What is even funnier is that Isabella doesn't even speak French! She looked down at this woman like a dog she wanted to kick."

I openly laughed. "I wish I could have been there to see that. What did the marchesa do?"

"The marchesa started waving her fan furiously and pulled Isabella away by the arm."

"And what, dear Emma, did you do?"

"I said, 'Signora Mackau, the next time you approach Italian nobility, you should really know who to insult and who to not.'"

"What did she say?"

Emma stopped short on the path and struck a pose like one of her Roman statues, only her pretty little mouth was contorted into a frown as she looked down her nose at me. "Madame, I do not need advice from a dirty English trollop."

Giggles rippled through us as Emma resumed her normal posture.

"Please tell me you said something clever."

"I always say something clever," Emma retorted, taking my arm again. "I told her that it was Lady English Trollop Hamilton to her, and that by the smell of her it was she who was the dirty one, not me."

"These French are the crudest of people. Their manners are the worst. Why, I got a letter from our ambassador to the Papal States just the other day. He was telling me that the Frenchman assigned to the pope is just awful. His manners are vile, particularly around the dinner table. Likewise, he has no respect for the Roman Catholic Church. One would think that whoever is running the government of France at the moment would see fit to not send an atheist émigré to serve as ambassador to the Papal States."

"Do you think the French ambassador to Rome is a Protestant?"

"Oh, goodness, that would be worse than an atheist."

I had returned to Caserta after my pleasant turn about the garden with Emma and made my way to the private dining room for lunch with Ferdinand when a breathless footman came skidding to a stop in front of me. "La Sua Maestà, an urgent letter from your sister."

I snatched the letter from him and ripped the seal off. The king had officially been overthrown, and there was to be a trial. As if a king could be tried in a court of man. A cold fury overtook me as I stormed to Acton's office.

"Did you know about this?" I asked, thrusting the letter from Antoinette in his face.

"I just learned about it." He calmly lowered my arm, not letting go of my wrist.

"What are we to do?" I asked, suddenly feeling dejected.

"I have a friend, Admiral Horatio Nelson, who fought for the English in the American Revolution. He and his men are sailing here as we speak. Their presence in our harbor will be a deterrent to a potential invasion. If there is one thing that the French military is afraid of it is the English navy." Acton turned me so that I was forced to face him. "We must make some concessions to the French ambassador."

"I have already allowed people to speak French to him. What more does he want?"

Acton leaned against his desk, crossing his arms. "Perhaps invite him to the royal salon. Allow others to send him invitations as well."

"I have not banned anyone from inviting him."

"But the nobility takes your lead. If you do not invite them, then the others will follow suit." Acton's calloused fingers of a sailor caressed my hand. "Let him come to the next salon. The least you can do is beat him at whist."

Acton knew I couldn't resist beating someone at my favorite

card game, and I began to smile despite myself. "Very well. But you must make sure he brings a lot of money with him. I plan on winning it all at the card table."

"Naturally."

* * *

A little over a week later, the nobility gathered at my salon. Luigi Medici strolled in with his wife. "La Sua Maestà, I am sorry to hear about your brother-in-law."

"Yes, we are all quite distressed," I said, trying to keep my emotions in check.

"We have all been watching the situation in Paris to see how this will turn out," he said, sipping his wine. "It is an interesting thing that the French are trying to accomplish."

"Interesting? More like barbaric," I said. "Who are they to decide who gets to lead their country when they have rulers ordained by God? Would you have the pope replaced simply because you don't like his sermon?"

Medici pressed his lips together in a thin, tight line. "What about your Freemasons? I seem to remember your having grand ideas about equal rights, justice reform, and an equal income for everyone."

"It has been a while since you graced us with your presence at council. If you had joined us, you would know that we are very close to instituting a basic income for all our people and we have adopted a number of the same reforms that my brother instituted in Tuscany when he ruled the region."

At the mention of Tuscany, Medici's eyes flashed. "Yes, we have seen what your family has done to our Tuscan region."

I was about to respond in turn when I saw, over Medici's shoulder, Baron Mackau strut into the salon. Steeling myself, I gulped down the rest of my wine, as he approached us triumphantly.

"Regina, I am glad that you have finally come to see that France only wants to offer you its hand in friendship."

"I find it hard to accept the hand of friendship from a country that seeks to destroy my family."

"We have done nothing to the royal family of Naples."

"My sister. The girl whom I shared a nursery with and who shared childhood confidences with me." I looked Mackau in the eyes, but he didn't seem ashamed. These men never did. They destroyed anything they couldn't conquer, including women, regardless of their station. "Of course, I would expect you to forget about such things. After all, you have painted Antoinette and any other woman with ideas to be as evil as the devil himself. You may say that you are friendly with Sicily, but I can assure you that neither I nor any of my family will ever call you or France a friend."

Feeling disgusted by my two companions, I left the men to find a place at a whist table.

⚜

Chère Tante Charlotte,   *February 20, 1800*

It is only now that I can find the strength to write to you, so that you should know what Maman's life was like in those final days. I can't bring myself to tell you all of this at once, as my memories dictate. And the pain, even after all these years, is still too fresh to express to you in person, but I know this is what Maman would have wanted. You were very dear to her, and she shared many stories of your adventures.

They told Father on the twentieth of January that he would be put to death by guillotine. However, we didn't hear it from Father; it was the town crier who called out the news of the imminent execution. Mother fell with a heavy thud onto the bed. She sat there, her eyes fixed on the wall before her. Chère Tante Charlotte, I had never seen Mother so despondent. While my brother and I clasped on to each other, openly crying, Mother could not move nor speak. She reminded me of a statue of the Virgin Mary with the miracle of her tears as they flowed from her cheeks to her lap.

In the end, we were allowed to visit Father in the apartments they had created for him. Mother curled into him, and grief took hold of us all. That was the odd thing. I wanted to enjoy the last moments with my family together, so I was trying to focus on the things that I wanted to remember about him: his scent, the feeling of his stubble when he hugged us. But grief is the great thief. All I could focus on was that my father would be gone, never aging on the throne like his grandfather. Instead, he would be ripped from us in his youth. I grew angry with him and with France. It was an injustice that I was powerless to change, and I hated everyone for it.

While they all held him and cried, I screamed. I screamed until my lungs gave out and I fell onto the settee. When Father came to me, I could not help but tremble. He was talking to me, but I could not understand the words that he said; they were a blur in my ears. When he stood up, the sound came back in rushing clarity. "You should go back to your room now," he told me. "I must prepare for tomorrow."

Maman protested, but Father was firm. Still, he promised that he would visit us in the morning.

The last promise Father made to his family lay broken at our feet. The hours ticked by, and no one came. The *grounds were so quiet that it scared me. Not even the birds chirped. Paris held its breath as they waited for the murder of my father.*

It was the drumming that broke the quiet. A rhythmic roll that gradually built into a crescendo ended the silence. Then the cheers of the people filled the air.

Maman closed her eyes as her face lost all color. Louis and I began to cry again. But Tante Elisabeth began yelling out the window. "The monsters!" she said. "They are satisfied now!"

But they weren't. The people's desire for blood would never be quenched.

It was not until later that I found out that the deciding vote in our father's murder came not from the revolutionaries who had imprisoned us in the first place but from our own family. A cousin by the name of Philippe Égalité. He said, "All who have attacked or will attack the sovereignty of the people deserve death."

Even our own family turned on us.

Your loving niece,

Marie Thérèse

CHAPTER FORTY-SIX

The stress of not knowing what would happen to our family in France led us to have a subdued Christmas. Outside, the markets were bustling with people celebrating the holiday, but inside Portici, we couldn't feel the same cheer as our people. The palace boasted the barest of decorations, and feasts became simple dinners. It was shortly after Epiphany when we received word from our ambassador that my brother-in-law had been found guilty of treason.

Louis-Auguste, king of France, was going to die.

I sat the letter down and looked up at Acton. "My sister is going to be next, isn't she?"

"We don't know for sure," he said. "It is highly unlikely that they will kill the queen. They are holding her as ransom. She is more of a political pawn."

The knot in my stomach tightened. I wanted to have hope for my sister. I wanted to believe that when this was all over, we would stroll through the gardens of Caserta, Schönbrunn, or whatever palace she called home when she escaped France, so that we could relive our childhood.

"My friend Admiral Nelson has arrived in Naples," Acton said. "We would like you and Ferdinand to come to dinner at Sir Hamilton's home. We would like to have a private discussion about France's foreign policy and their new commander by the name of Napoleon Bonaparte."

* * *

A week later, we arrived at the home of the English ambassador. Unlike past affairs, there were no large groups of admirers wanting to spend the evening with the popular official and his wife.

"I wonder if Emma will be doing her excellent parlor games," Ferdinand asked as we were escorted in.

"For some reason, I highly doubt it. There are far more pressing matters that need to be discussed."

"Yes, but we can have some fun, can't we? All this talk of revolutions and the affairs of the Two Sicilies has me quite bored. I would much rather be playing chess with my friends. They at least know how to balance the fun with the serious."

"I'll take that into consideration," I responded, feeling frustrated by my husband's constant whining whenever we had to do anything of importance.

Upon entering the spacious parlor, we found Acton chatting with the infamous Admiral Horatio Nelson. He turned to face me, and I was taken aback by Nelson's handsome features. His black hair fell in waves around his chiseled face. A smile broke out on his plump, perfectly shaped lips. "Your Majesty, it is an honor to meet you." He fell into a low bow, and I could feel my blush despite myself.

Ferdinand, having found a glass of wine, made his way up to Acton. "Well, it looks like you and I have new competition."

My eyes narrowed, warning my husband to behave, but Acton only smiled. "I doubt we have to worry about Admiral Nelson."

"All the same, keep an eye on him. I don't have the energy to accommodate a new favorite."

"I shall bear that in mind, my lord."

From my right, I heard a rustling. Emma was fidgeting with her dress as her eyes lingered on the new commander. Upon meeting my eye, she jumped, knocking over the empty crystal wine goblet sitting next to her. "Oh, I have been so absentminded lately," she said, catching the errant glass. "Now that the king and queen are here, we should make our way to the dining room, yes?" Emma took me by my elbow, not giving the rest of the men a chance to escort me.

"I feel out of sorts with him here," she whispered to me.

"The admiral?"

"Yes," she hissed. "Am I that obvious? He and I shared an evening in England before I met William, and…Well, anyway, he is here in my home now, and I am at a complete loss. I don't know what to do."

"I am sure you will find a way." I patted her trembling hand.

"Will you sit next to me for our dinner? I can't trust myself sitting next to him. As it is, his cologne makes my knees weak."

"Of course," I said, smiling as we took our seats. To be young and in love was a torture in and of itself. I sat at the head of the table, with Admiral Nelson to my right and Emma to my left. Next to her was Acton, with Hamilton as his partner across the table and Ferdinand directly opposite me. I pitied Acton; he would be privy to all Ferdinand's talk of volcanoes with Hamilton.

"La Sua Maestà, it is a pleasure to have you here at our home. As you know, there are far too many ears wanting to listen to our confidences. That is why we thought it best to discuss the situation here, away from Caserta."

"Thank you, Sir Hamilton," I said, looking around the table. "I agree there are far too many French in Naples for my taste."

"The same could be said for most of Europe," Nelson responded dryly. "We have reason to believe that this new French regime doesn't just plan on tearing their own country apart. They want to spread their propaganda and war throughout the continent. It was one thing when the Americans did it. They were able to keep their chaos in check, so to speak, but this revolution in France is dangerous."

Next to me, Emma sighed loudly. I could see her lean forward and rest her chin on her hand, her elbow landing squarely in a splatter of sauce. The poor child was doomed.

"Most of their troublemaking has been directed at the Netherlands and Prussia," Acton said. "What makes you think they will expand their reach?"

"They have their eyes set on the south," Nelson said. "I have it on good authority that the French have a resentment over the dominant rule of the Habsburgs. They believe your family has embarked on a bloodless war, infiltrating all the houses of Europe. They want to see every Austrian-controlled nation under a pseudo-republic rule."

"Pseudo?" Ferdinand questioned.

"Because the republic they are trying to create is nothing more than a power grab for men who want to conquer the world," Hamilton responded.

I turned to Nelson. "So does this mean that the English will finally get involved?"

"The events on the continent are quite troublesome. We cannot let the ideas of the Americans taint Europe. The imminent death of Louis has prompted England to prepare for war."

"Well, at least one monarchy has seen the error of its ways," I said as I brought a wineglass to my lips.

"I can assure you that we will not allow these acts of aggression to go unchecked," Hamilton added. "The war in Sardinia in not faring well. The French are ruthless. The country is on the verge of bankruptcy."

"You said that the French want to push back against Austrian rule," I said, "but the Sardinians aren't a Habsburg family." I knew this because I had my eye on marrying one of my daughters to one of Victor Amadeus's sons. It was a family that the Habsburgs had yet to have an influence on, and I wanted the Two Sicilies to have that opportunity.

"But they do occupy lands that France believes to be theirs. Land such as Nizza," Nelson said. "The commander Napoleon Bonaparte will be a problem if left unchecked. He is ruthless and has the backing of the French government, allowing him to do whatever he wants. There is a threat that he and his forces will invade Sardinia." Nelson leaned forward. "I know you have signed a treaty of neutrality, but England needs your assistance to keep this situation under control. We cannot have the violence of the French Revolution become the spark that creates violence for the rest of Europe."

"Admiral Nelson, I am at your service." I was delighted to finally receive the help I needed to destroy France.

⚜

Your Highness Maria Carolina,   *October 21, 1793*

This story I have been able to piece together is second-hand, but I thought it was important that you should know what happened to Antoinette. As you know, in August she was indicted on charges of treason, adultery, intentionally starving the people of France, and committing incest with her son.

You should be comforted to know that the prison war-dens, Monsieur Toussaint and Marie Anne Richard, took pity on her and did their best to treat her with respect and compassion. But the Jacobins made sure that she was under constant surveillance. Only a screen separated the queen from the soldiers stationed to watch her. And watch her they did. Those lecherous fools took every advantage possible to take a peek at the "immoral" queen.

Her final days were spent in deep sadness. The German melancholy, as she liked to call it. According to Marie Anne Richard, the queen's eyes were transfixed on the wall in front of her day and night, almost as if she were in a trance.

There was one last attempt to save the queen. The Chevalier of Rougeville left a carnation with a note for her. The following day, he returned and Antoinette al-most escaped. If it were not for a guard stopping her, she would have made it out alive with Rougeville. But yet again, it was another near miss for your sister's life.

Antoinette was given less than a day to prepare for her trial. Now, this part I was there for. I sat in the back of the room as they accused your sister of the most heinous of acts. At first for treason and for stealing from the royal treasury to pay for her expensive clothing and gambling. But then the accusations became dark. They put her on trial for acts they accused her of in the pamphlets, along with an accusation that she sexually abused her son. The women of the audience grew angry and yelled out on Antoinette's behalf. Pushing the people out of my way, I caught a glimpse of the queen, ever so briefly.

You should have seen your sister. She defended her-self against the accusations of the mob with all the grace and dignity of a Habsburg archduchess. But after hours and hours the trial ended and we received word that she would be sentenced to death by guillotine.

Please know that I loved your sister from the moment I saw her that fateful evening at the opera under the warm glow of the chandeliers. She was my angel. I did not attend her execution. As cowardly as this may be, I wanted to always remember her as my Josephine.

Yours,

Count Fersen

CHAPTER FORTY-SEVEN

OCTOBER 25, 1793

"Concetta, I'd like to wear my hair up today, in that style you told me about with all the loops and curls," I said, sitting in front of the looking glass as my servant started to work on my hair. My face freshly washed, I could see the wrinkles beginning to form. At forty-one, I was still lucky enough to hold on to my figure, though I was heavy with child again, this one due in December. This child would be my sixteenth, and I was hoping that this would be enough for Ferdinand. Though I enjoyed our marital bed, I didn't want any more children. I could feel the pull they made on my body. I loved them; there was no doubt about that. But a child took something of me with them every time they gasped their first breath.

While one servant was fixing my hair, another was performing my royal toilette. She lightly rouged my face and sprayed me with perfume. A soft knock interrupted our morning routine as one of the servants ushered Acton into the room.

"Acton, you're here early," I said. But the smile I had offered him through the mirror upon his entry fell.

From his deep frown to the heavy eyes that were locked on to me, not letting go, I knew. I knew without his having to utter a single word.

"Leave us," I commanded, and the servants scurried from the room.

"No." I didn't want it to be true. "No," I said, getting up from my vanity and taking a step back, trying to put as much distance between us as possible. The tears began to well up and choke me. "No."

Acton sucked in air, the way he always did when he was preparing to tell me what I didn't want to hear. "They executed Antoinette on the sixteenth."

"No!" I roared, flying toward him, my fists pounding on his chest. "No!" Blinded by my hair and my tears, I pummeled him. He stood there while my fury found its marks. Everything came rushing out: The vile treatment of my gentle, caring sister who deserved none of this. My loathing of the French people, who wanted nothing more than to see the woman who was my other half, my heart, sacrificed for their glorious revolution.

And then I lost my strength. My fists, suddenly too heavy to bear, drooped at my sides as I fell against him. The anguish was ripping out my insides, like a gutted fish at the market as my wails reverberated through the room. Strong arms wrapped around me, and we both went down to the floor. I gripped his arm, my fingers digging into the sinew and muscle as I expelled my grief. Acton wiped the wet hair from my face, his lips pressing into my head.

The rage turned to gulping sobs as he began to whisper in my ear. "You are stronger than this." He shook me slightly. "You are the queen. You are the queen that Antoinette wanted to be."

I struggled for air as he continued to hold tightly to me. My chest rose as my lungs spasmed. He rubbed my back as if I were a child while I fought for control of my sobs.

Ferdinand ran into the room, falling to his knees before me.

"I just heard," he said. "Do we need to give her a sedative?" he asked Acton.

"No," I managed in between the gasping breaths.

When I had my senses about me, the men helped me to my feet. "Gather the children at the chapel," I said. "I want to tell them personally. Once we've done that, we'll officially go into mourning, again."

Ferdinand rubbed my shoulder. "I will gather them now." Leaving the room, he gave a nod to Acton.

"Thank you," I said.

Acton cupped my cheeks. "You are the most capable woman I have ever known."

"Only because I have you."

"You don't need me."

Savoring the feeling of his hands against my face, I kissed his palm. "I should prepare to meet the children."

He nodded and left the room, and the servants returned soon after. Concetta swooped my hair to the top of my head, with curls wrapped in a braid.

Soldiers had their uniforms, and I had mine. My wardrobe mistress appeared, and we slowly began to craft my armor. Signora Gentile had dressed me for nearly twenty years, having apprenticed beside the lady I brought with me from Austria. She knew black mourning dresses were always a necessity and quickly had a new one brought up for me. I patiently stood there as she clothed me, from the bodice to the black satin petticoats that matched the plain black stomacher. Inspecting myself in the looking glass once more, I felt that I had the appropriate armor of a queen.

The Royal Palatine Chapel located within Caserta had become the center of every family celebration and funeral since it was inaugurated in 1784. The morning of its inauguration,

Ferdinand insisted on walking me down the aisle as if we were being married for the first time. "For once, I would like to make your mother proud," he said. "She can look down from heaven and celebrate that her daughter was finally married in a church!"

I took his arm as we made a great show of pretending to do a formal wedding march, much to the delight of the children as they giggled in the pews, their laughter ringing through the far-off cathedral-like bells.

"I declare that this will be a happy place for our family! Always!" Ferdinand announced as we reached the altar, which was still being constructed. At the time, it was more a lump of yellow marble, but eventually it would be decorated with precious stones, such as lapis, amethyst, agate, and jasper. Freshly painted angels had smiled down on our family. I should have known: My husband's predictions were almost always false.

I liked to think that Caserta shared in our sorrow, with every death our palace wept along with the family. That perhaps the gold sun at the base of the great domed ceiling that stretched all the way back through to the chapel entrance was just a bit dimmer. That Caserta had chosen not to reflect the sun that had the audacity to shine outside as if the world could still move forward without my sister.

Reaching the altar, I stared at the Bourbon sun being held by two white stone angels. The divine right was something that my mother had instilled in all my siblings, the knowledge that we were meant to be kings and queens of Europe. Under the Bourbon coat of arms, I wondered for the first time if my mother's wisdom was misplaced. Closing my eyes, I prayed for my sister's soul. Hoping that in death Antoinette would get the rest that she had long deserved.

At the sound of the great topaz door opening, I looked up and saw my daughters Christina, Amalia, and Antonia enter first. It was ironic that though Antonia was named for my sister, it was Christina who bore the greatest resemblance. Behind them were Francis and Ferdinand. I gulped looking at Amalia's large green eyes, thinking of the letter I had written to Antoinette about the prospect of marrying Amalia to the young dauphin. She had liked the idea, agreeing that when the boy came of age, we would make the match. Our other living children, Leopold and Alberto, were kept in the nursery. They were too young to share in our grief.

"Mother"—Francis paused before reaching me—"what happened?"

I looked for Ferdinand, who gave me a small nod, encouraging me to share the news. "Your zia Antoinette was murdered yesterday."

Amalia let out a little scream. "What of Louis? What will happen to him?"

"I don't know. We were hoping that we could foster him here, but…" Words failed me. My nephew was in the hands of the revolutionaries, and there was no guarantee of his safety.

"But I was supposed to marry Louis. I was supposed to be the queen of France," Amalia cried.

"Amalia, stop," Francis snapped. "Now is not the time. Can't you see Mama is grieving?" My eldest son turned back to me. "What does this mean for our position with France? Will we be officially joining the coalition?"

"Does this mean we are going to be thrown out of Naples as well?" Christina asked.

"France is going to invade us!" Amalia shrieked.

"No. No one is going to invade us," I told the children. "I will not lie; France is a threat. But this is our home, and we will fight as a family to stay here."

❧

Charlotte,   *May 12, 1796*

I write this letter to you in great haste. My family and I are safe, but the French have invaded Milan. We were able to escape to Parma and are comforted by Amalia's hospitality and our mutual grief over our dear sister. Soon my family and I will be returning to the safety of Vienna.

These French are a different breed of enemy than anything I have seen. They claim that they are coming here for the benefit of the people of Milan, but the reality is that they are here only to fill the French treasury. After taking control of the capital, I watched as they took priceless paintings and statues from the museums. They were like truffle pigs when it came to searching out our treasures. Bonaparte is the worst of them all. Before any of his soldiers could leave, he checked their loot. If there was something he wanted, he confiscated it for "the good of the state." This new French regime has no regard for anyone but themselves.

God help us if he makes it to Rome or, worse, Naples.

Your Brother,

Karl

CHAPTER FORTY-EIGHT

Everyone had always celebrated Antoinette's birthday on November 1, one day early, so as not to have it conflict with All Souls' Day, meant for mourning.

But Antoinette and I would celebrate when the clock struck twelve on November 2, at which point I would bring out my presents for her. Even when Mother separated us, I made sure there was a present delivered to her on the first.

There was no other day I would have wanted to remember my dear, sweet sister. It was a day intended for my closest family and friends.

Emma's sweet and gentle nature was a balm to my soul. I needed my best friend now more than ever. She was the one who had suggested the dinner and took over the preparations and listened patiently as I ranted about the injustice of it all. When we arrived at the dining hall on the given night, the smells of my childhood filled my senses. Plates of golden-brown Wiener schnitzel filled the table intermixed with giant bowls of *käsespätzle*. There were baskets of strudel, *kaiserschmarrn*, and *buchteln*. Off to the side was a small string quartet, playing one of Mozart's songs. Memories of our childhood friend and the time we had spent running around the grounds of the palace brought tears to my eyes.

"I didn't know what you and Antoinette liked, so I got a little of everything," Emma said.

"This is perfect. Thank you," I replied.

Sitting down at the table, I took note of all the people who loved me: Acton, whose devotion was unwavering, no matter my outburst of emotion. Emma, whose sweetness and loving nature was more than I could have asked for. Luisa and her husband, Joseph, who looked so much like my dearly departed brother. Having him here in some small way felt like I had my brother with me again. My son Francis, my future king; he was the one who would lead the Two Sicilies to her glory.

Next to me sat my husband, Ferdinand—he had put me through a lot, but he had also done what no one else could have; he gave me Naples, my love. When my sister died, I felt like I had lost my heart, but I was coming to find that it was never truly gone. I still had my beautiful Naples.

I stood and raised my goblet. "I want to thank you all for gathering here today. These past few weeks have been the hardest weeks of my life, but without all of you, I would never have survived. You are all—"

But the words fell from my lips. The great door to the hall had opened, and Baron Mackau and his wife had strolled in.

"What are you doing here?" I sneered.

My shocked guests turned from me to the French ambassador and his wife, standing by the doorway. At least Signora Mackau, in her hideous pink gown, had the decency to look embarrassed. Baron Mackau raised his chin in defiance. "I understand that you are having a dinner and have forgotten to invite us. But you need not worry: We are here now."

"This is a memorial for my sister!" I yelled, slamming my goblet on the table, the purple liquid sloshing out and staining the *buchteln* in its basket. "You know, the one whose head your country lopped off."

"The *English* ambassador and his wife are here. I will not be—"

"You will not be anything unless it is commanded of you! I am the monarch here, not you. Lord and Lady Hamilton are here because Lady Hamilton is a dear friend of mine. She is the one who arranged everything. Lord and Lady Hamilton have done more in support of this country than you could ever dream of." The heat of anger rose up my neck. "All I wanted was to have a day to mourn my sister on what would have been her birthday with the people I love, but apparently I cannot even have that without the French barging in. Will France ever leave me unmolested? Or do you intend on abusing me the way you abused my sister?"

Mackau began to sputter.

"You will leave my presence now!" I threw my goblet across the room, glass and wine splattering everywhere. "And if I ever see you or your wife in Naples again, I will make sure you know pain far worse than the guillotine, international incidents be damned."

I pushed through Caserta, opening and slamming doors behind me, startling servants as I went. As I closed the door to my bedchamber, a guttural explosion of anguish burst from my lungs, and bitter hot tears rolled down my cheeks. Was it not enough that the French felt they needed to warp all that my sister was, twisting her into some sort of deformed caricature of the woman I knew?

As the older sister, it was my job to protect her, save her. How many letters did I write begging her to come here? Better she spend her days in a convent overlooking the sea than to be sacrificed to the guillotine. Why didn't she see that we could have been together again? Did she not picture the same reunion that I did?

Wiping the tears from my face, I turned my attention to the box of letters sitting upon my table. All her letters of love. Her reminiscences of our beloved childhood felt hollow now. She didn't love me; she loved gambling and dancing and parties. Not once did she think about the family that had sacrificed everything to save her. I ripped each and every one of her letters out of the box as I wallowed in my animosity.

"You did this, Antoinette!" I scolded in the empty room. "You could have been safe. You wretched, foolish woman. I could have saved you." I looked at the pile of letters before me, and I hated them. I hated her. "When you arrived here, we could have found a way to save your son, if only you weren't so stubborn!"

The fireplaces in Caserta were always lit in November, warming the castle from the early winter outside. My black skirt billowed around me as I watched the flames twirling about the coals. With one swift movement, I picked up all my sister's letters and threw them into the fire. If she didn't want to let me save her, then I would not preserve her memory. She could die the despicable queen everyone believed her to be.

But then I remembered her hugging me when we were young, the way her bony shoulder dug into me. Her promises of what our lives would be like when we were grown. The way she would laugh, like a bird's song and hum when she thought no one was paying attention.

"Good Lord, what have I done?"

I reached into the fireplace and managed to save a single letter from my sister. My tears falling anew, I wiped the ash from its singed edges. Tucking it back into the box, I sat back and watched the last words of Antoinette climb up the chimney and out into the heavens.

⚜

November 3, 1793

The Kingdom of the Two Sicilies is demanding the immediate replacement of the French ambassador Armand

Louis de Mackau. During your ambassador's tenure here in Naples, he has gone out of his way to offend His Majesties, Ferdinand and Maria Carolina.

It is bad enough that your ambassador does not speak Italian, but he blatantly flouts our rules and customs. If that were not tedious enough, the ambassador and his wife barged into a private memorial for the queen's sister Marie Antoinette. Though we know your people had her executed, we trust that you have the decency to understand the queen's grief over the loss of her favorite sister.

Until such time as Mackau is recalled, we can no longer tolerate his presence at court and the royal family will no longer have any business with him.

Sincerely,

Sir John Acton
Prime Minister
The Kingdom of the Two Sicilies

CHAPTER FORTY-NINE

"How are you feeling?" Acton asked after I had had a few days to compose myself.

"France has yet to kill me. I suppose that is something. Do you have any news from Nelson?"

"He and his fleet are running a blockade outside Toulon. Bonaparte and his fleet have not been able to break it yet. The French have devoted a large part of their army to the northern provinces. Especially since everyone's attention is on Prussia and Austria."

I tapped my finger on the table. "Is there a way we can send England money or additional support without France knowing? We need to pretend we are neutral while doing all that we can to help the coalition's resistance."

"Yes. I can move some funds around in the treasury in order for them to get ammunition and other supplies."

"See that it happens." This game that I was playing was dangerous. One wrong move on the chessboard, and I could lose the whole game.

"We have another problem we need to monitor," Acton said,

sitting back in his chair. "There is a growing issue of refugees streaming in from France."

"I can't say that I blame them. They have started rounding up all their citizens and putting them to death. No wonder they are looking to invade the Italian colonies. If they keep going at this rate, they will have no one left to rule."

"My concern about these refugees is that there could be Jacobins among them. The Jacobins are dangerous. They carry with them the extremes of the Freemason beliefs, and we need to be careful that they don't spread their ideas."

"Yes, the last thing we need is for a revolution, particularly one in the French fashion." I wiped the crumbs of biscotto from my fingers. "The French have always had horrendous fashion sense. Monitor the refugees, however you deem necessary. Make sure there are no radicals sneaking in among them."

Later that day, I met Emma and my daughters for a stroll around the garden before supper. Amalia, Christina, and Antonia chattered on about court gossip as we promenaded. Meanwhile, Emma absentmindedly twirled her parasol.

"Don't you think the Marchesa della Rivero had the prettiest dress?" Antonia asked.

"Yes. I told her that I wanted the name of her seamstress because I was going to have her make two," Christina said. "But in different colors, of course."

"Well, I want her to make something different for me," Luisa added. "I don't want to look exactly like the two of you. If the seamstress can make a gorgeous dress like that, she must have a million delicious ideas up her sleeve. What do you think, Emma?"

"Hmm, what?" She looked up, startled from her thoughts.

"The dress, silly. Wasn't it wonderful?"

"Yes, a lovely shade of pink," Emma said, turning toward the pools.

"It was blue…," Antonia said, looking quizzically from Emma to her sisters.

"Girls, why don't you go on ahead. I would like a word with Emma alone.

"Out with it," I demanded as soon as we were away from the others. "Why have you been so distracted?"

"I'm not distracted," Emma said.

"So sighing and continuously twirling your parasol is nothing?"

"I don't know what you mean," Emma said.

"Since when don't you participate in gossip?"

"Can I tell you something in confidence?"

"Of course," I said.

"I have been having an affair with Lord Nelson."

"Lord Nelson? For how long?"

"I told you of the flirtation in England. And when he came here to Naples, we could not resist each other."

"And you are feeling guilty about keeping this from your husband?"

"No," she said, looking away. "William not only knows but he approves."

I stopped on the path. "He approves?"

Emma looked around the garden to see if anyone was watching. "What you have to understand is that Sir Hamilton and I have an unconventional relationship of sorts."

"How so?"

Emma gulped. "When William took me on as his mistress, it was more to have a companion. I was heartbroken at the time. My lover, Charles, had just put me aside with no promise of marriage. I had loved him—he had the most charming dimples—but he didn't even have the decency to tell me he was putting me aside. He passed me to William like I was a piece of property. Charles told me that he would come and visit me in Naples when the time was right, and I used to watch from the window, hoping he would come back, but he never came. Eventually his abandonment hurt less, and then there was William." Emma smiled at the memory. "He was so kind. Every day, we would meet for breakfast. He would show me his antiquities collection, and when I displayed interest, he took me to Pompeii and Herculaneum. He encourages my curiosity." She wiped a tear from her eye. "He was the first man to ever do that. It was so sweet: The first time he found me reading one of his books he got this large grin on his face. He sat down opposite me and started asking me questions about the book. We spent all night talking."

"And you said he approves of the relationship with Admiral Nelson?"

"William only asks that we be discreet. Nelson still has a wife back in London, and we have a reputation to maintain."

"Well, if everything is going so well, why are you so distracted?"

"I worry about Horatio," she said. "Napoleon Bonaparte is a fierce opponent. And I miss him."

I took Emma by the hands. "My dear Emma, your secrets are safe with me. Hamilton is right that you must use discretion, but you must also understand: Nelson is stronger than Bonaparte. His navy is better. And frankly, if the Americans couldn't kill him during their revolutionary war, then no one will."

Emma interlocked her arm with mine. "I'm sure you're right," she said, resting her head against my shoulder. "You always know the right things to say."

⚜

Your Honorable Majesty,   *May 20, 1794*

I am writing to inform you of the current status of Toulon. It is true that for months we were able to form a strong blockade to keep the French from expanding their naval campaign and reaching the island of Sardinia.

It has been a long and brutal campaign, but we have finally begun to see some success, much to the dismay of the English army, even though we are on the same side of the fight. They hate us sailors; we are too active for them. We accomplish our business sooner than they like. We have been told on more than one occasion that we are too gung-ho in our willingness to fire our cannons.

We pressed our advantage and sought to launch an offensive on the island of Corsica, which is a French stronghold. By attacking there, we knew we could weaken their forces in the Mediterranean. The French stationed at Corsica were sorely outnumbered by our British forces. Upon seeing our navy come to shore, the French troops immediately surrendered. The Corsican authorities made the educated decision to pledge their allegiance to the British, helping us to dispel the rest of the French. They, too, see that we will be victorious over this French aggression.

We would not be this successful without the financial support of the Two Sicilies.

Horatio Nelson
Admiral of the British Navy

CHAPTER FIFTY

JUNE 15, 1794

The news from Captain Nelson bolstered my spirits. The enemy was finally succumbing to the might of the English. The French had sent a ship to come and fetch Mackau, and I was so happy that I had my wardrobe mistress order a new frock. It was the same deep shade of green as the lush pines that protected Caserta from the rest of the world.

The heat of the day had faded into a pleasantly warm evening as I spent time with my family in the gardens after dinner. My youngest children, Alberto and Leopold, played chase on the lawn with other royal playmates. My daughters, lost in their own confidences, filled me with hope for the future. Ferdinand and the other members of the nobility played lawn games in the lamplight of the hundreds of candles that lined the pools.

Sipping my wine, I watched all this with joy. The fountains, fully completed, were finer than any of the fountains in Rome. There were the dolphins, with their catlike faces, and the nymphs and cherubs, forever frozen in stone, frolicking by the little waterfall.

This was what I had envisioned when I was just a girl. This was what my beautiful Naples was meant to be.

A blast ripped out like extended rumbling thunder, followed by an earthquake that jolted the ground. The goblet slipped from my hands, shattering on the pavement, the purple wine spilling everywhere. Lifting my skirts, I ran with the rest of the family through the palace to the southernmost point, where we all stood at the front gates, breathless, as thick black plumes of smoke rose into the air in the distance.

"Vesuvius is erupting," I gasped. After a moment of shock, I found Acton in the crowd. "Send scouts," I told him.

"Already done. The generals are mobilized. We will be making sure Naples is properly evacuated."

"Keep me informed."

Acton bowed and rushed to be with the rest of the military. The crowds quickly dispersed while I went to the parlor.

I stood at the windows in the same green gown that I had been wearing in the garden, watching the lightning stab the city, now blanketed by ash. The heavens were chaotic from Vesuvius's wrath. Francis sat in the armchair opposite his father, who was staring into the flames. Ferdinand's leg shook as he rested his head on his hands.

"Naples has to be all right," he said to no one in particular.

"There have been eruptions from Vesuvius before. We have no reason to believe that it will be any worse," I said, hugging myself. "The last one, in 1783, emitted very little lava. At most, there was a little stream that ran down to the coast."

Ferdinand shook his head. "In 1779, ash rained down everywhere. Hamilton himself said that if it had continued on an hour more, the whole city would have been buried."

A lightning bolt cracked just past the palace, bathing the parlor in an orange-yellow glow. Somewhere beyond the borders of Caserta, Acton was trying to save my city. In my mind, I feared the worst. I couldn't lose him or Naples, but if Vesuvius had her way, I could lose them both.

The door creaked open, and we all turned, hoping for news from Acton. But it was Christina, in her nightclothes. She padded her way across the room. Wrapping her arms around me, she pressed her head into my side, like when she was a child. "What are you doing awake?" I said.

"All of the children are awake," she said, trying not to yawn. "The governess is letting them stay up to watch the lightning."

I swept the loose hair from her forehead. "And why aren't you with them?"

"I don't like the lightning. I'm afraid for the city."

"Naples will survive," I said, kissing the top of her head. "She has survived thousands of years. She will be here long after we are gone."

"Excuse me." We all turned to find Acton standing by the door. Soot covered his face, and ash peppered his hair. Relief flooded me as Acton's eyes met mine. I wanted to release my daughter and run to him.

Ferdinand jumped up from his chair. "How is the city?"

"Naples is fine. The people close to the volcano were safely evacuated, but we lost Torre del Greco."

Ferdinand fell back onto the sofa. Torre del Greco was a town just south of Naples at the base of Vesuvius.

"The dome of the mountain collapsed," Acton said. "Lava erupted from the southwest, leading straight to Torre del Greco. The northeast flank of the volcano has opened as well, putting the town of Ottaviano at risk."

"Has Medici been notified?"

"Yes. He and a garrison of soldiers are riding to the town to lead the evacuation."

"Has anyone been hurt?" Francis asked.

"We don't know for sure, but right now our estimates are that about one hundred people have been killed in Torre del Greco alone, mostly from smoke and shard inhalation."

"Shard?" Christina looked up at me.

"When the volcano explodes, it releases tiny bits of glass," Ferdinand said. "In this case, it happened to get into people's lungs."

Christina gasped and buried her face in my shoulder again.

"Do what you need to do to protect the people," I said, holding my daughter close to me. "Give Medici whatever resources he needs."

Acton bowed. "As you command." He slipped from the room. As I watched him go, I felt a pain in my chest. Passing Christina over to Ferdinand, I followed Acton out of the room.

"Wait," I called after him.

He turned to face me, ash falling from his hair.

"I couldn't let you leave without telling you." My breath caught in my chest as I struggled to tell him that I would not be able to live without him.

Acton took my hands in his, and we stood amid the world crashing around us. He kissed my hand and left to save Naples.

THE COURT OF NAPLES
AND HER HATRED OF FRANCE

The court of Naples is primarily composed of enemies of the French Republic. Because of the queen's close relationship with her sister the late Marie Antoinette, she has poisoned the court's heart against the people of France. She wants nothing more than to see the glory that France stands for washed from the map. This is a common occurrence amongst the Habsburg nobility; they seek to undermine our glorious republic.

Queen Maria Carolina Charlotte, without doubt, favors her numerous daughters. They are allowed to get away with all sorts of mischief and follow their mother's penchant for gossip. Meanwhile, she is extremely hard on her sons, forcing them to study all hours of the day. Should she deem one of their activities as poor, it is swiftly and severely dealt with. The behavior that is tolerated in her daughters is beaten from her sons.

And what does the king think of this, might you ask? Well, he is emasculated, from the queen's oversexed tendencies. According to sources close to the royal couple, the king spends much of his time playing games or hunting while the queen rules the country. She devises strategies to get him out of her way, so that she can perpetuate her Habsburg agenda—an agenda that was ingrained in her from the time of childhood, for it is well known that Empress Maria Theresa used her daughters as agents for Austria.

One cannot blame all of this on the queen, for her mother was Machiavellian in the way that she ruled her kingdom as well. Maria Theresa had a desire to take over the European continent by marrying her children into the most prominent royal families of Europe so that she could spread her toxic belief in an absolute monarchy that deprives the people of their freedom. This is what comes of a woman who has ambition; she begets children who are morally weak and seek to dominate the people around them, particularly the men. Maria Theresa's husband was rendered as nothing more than a consort based upon the empress's own immoral sexual appetites.

I do not call you to be angry with the queen but, rather, to pity her, because she did not receive a proper moral upbringing.

CHAPTER FIFTY-ONE

JULY 17, 1794

Mount Vesuvius continued to erupt for the rest of June, spitting ash and fire into the sky, but the eruptions came to a slow end by early July. The people walked around the city with rags tied around their faces in an attempt to spare their lungs from the dangerous debris. In all, four hundred people were dead and the destruction was immense. The town of Ottaviano suffered even more damage when rain fell over the region, mixing with the ash. The ash formed a mud that slid down the mountain, taking with it whatever buildings were left. In total, twenty-four people died in the aftermath.

During our morning meeting in the council chambers, Acton met with me to deliver updates on the eruption. "The worst is over when it comes to the volcano, but we have another matter we must attend to."

"What is it? Is it something with the people of Naples?"

"No, it seems we have a problem with Mackau and Admiral La Touche, who was sent here to fetch him," Acton said. "Over the last few months, La Touche has remained in Naples, claiming first that his ship needed repairs. On the way here, his ship encountered a storm in the Atlantic and had a minor fire."

"How long does it take to fix a ship?" I asked.

"Not that long. He has been making excuses as to why he needs to stay. In the meantime, we have traced certain pamphlets written about you and the royal family to his ship."

"Pamphlets? What pamphlets?" My heart raced at what they might contain. Did they characterize me as being a beast, a dragon with sharp fangs ready to devour the country?

Acton slipped a piece of paper across the desk to me. My eyes quickly scanned the document. "Habsburg agenda?" I questioned aloud. "Severe with my sons? Do they not know what I went through with Ferdinand? Oversexed?" I slammed the paper on the table. "Who wrote this?"

"According to my spies, a man by the name of Giuseppe Gorani," Acton responded.

"Gorani?"

"You know him."

"Only in passing. He served under my mother for a number of years. He expected constant praise and went about as if he knew everything. He once even tried to argue with an Austrian about an Austrian custom. Of course, Gorani thought he knew more because he was 'an intellectual unlike any other.' He was constantly referring to himself like that. It was this title he wanted to force on everyone."

"How did he find his way to France?" Acton asked.

"When Leopold was reforming the judicial system in Tuscany, he discovered that Gorani was violating his laws for arresting and interrogating people. Leopold had him exiled not only from Tuscany but from every Habsburg-controlled land. I don't exactly know what Gorani did, but I know it had to have been bad for Leopold to react in such a way."

A burst of sadness grew anew at the thought of my brother. Choking back tears, I wished he were still here. He would know exactly what to do about this Gorani fellow and how to get rid of him.

"Was Gorani from Tuscany?"

"No. He was Milanese."

"So when he was dismissed, he couldn't even go home."

The pamphlet before me suddenly made sense. It was written by a man who was angry because he couldn't go home. The punishment he received was not common; Leopold had needed Mother's approval. When Gorani wrote that it was I who needed sympathy, it really was he. To be so bitter that you embark on a campaign against a woman who had nothing to do with his fate, a fate that he chose for himself, was a pitiful act.

"What do you want to do about it?"

"If all that La Touche is doing is distributing pamphlets, then nothing. The people know me and Ferdinand. They will see through this farce."

"Are you sure about that?" Acton's eyebrows rose skeptically.

"I watched my sister fight and flail over awful accusations like this. It was a waste of time when she should have been focused on governing the country. We do nothing. This will dissipate," I told him. "Is this all that La Touche is doing?"

"No," Acton said. "He is inviting people on his ship, people who he thinks would be sympathetic to the ideas of the Jacobin cause."

Anger began to burn in my chest. "Who is he inviting?"

"I don't know, but I can find out."

"Do it, and I want anyone who attends to be arrested. I will not have a revolution here like in France. My family will not lose its head to France's precious guillotine."

"I'll place spies in the right circles. We'll get them on the ship."

"When you arrest them, make sure that there is guilt beyond the shadow of a doubt. We cannot have the bloodbath that is occurring in France."

Officials began to stream in for our council meeting. "And keep this between us," I whispered.

Acton nodded as he began the meeting.

* * *

As the meeting closed and people began to make their way out, I pulled Francis aside. "Stay with me here a moment. I would like to have a word with you."

"Yes, Mother," he said, but immediately, concern grew on his face.

At almost seventeen, Francis held a strong resemblance to Ferdinand. Francis had his father's nose, of course, but he carried the stern face of a Habsburg. The look that knew there was work to be done and he was going to be the one to do it. Francis was the best of the Bourbons, and I wanted more than ever to leave him a country that was thriving. But I feared I was a detriment to my son.

"Do you believe that I have been too harsh on you?" I asked him.

"Where did that come from?" he asked as I slipped him the pamphlet that I had been holding on to. His eyes grew wide as he read it. "Is this what has you so concerned? This rubbish? Mother, you should know me better than that."

I smiled. "I wanted to be sure. Do you feel that you and your brothers have been unfairly treated?"

"Well, Leopold believes his governess is withholding sweets, and I have cause to believe him. And Alberto feels that it is a gross injustice that he has to bathe so much." Francis pulled out a chair and sat next to me, taking my hands in his. "Mother," he said, "those of us who truly know this country know what kind of man our father is. I know what a poor job Tanucci did. It is understandable that your greatest fear is that I, or anyone else who could potentially inherit the throne of Naples, would be as ill prepared as my father."

"Ferdinand is a good man...," I started to say, the involuntary need to justify my husband prevailing upon me.

"But he is a poor king," Francis finished. "He has always been a good father. If I want to take a break from my studies to hunt or play chess, he is the first one I turn to, but when it comes to ruling, you are the one I look to as an example. You made me into the man I need to be in order to be an effective ruler. You are the one who made sure that I can carry the burden of the Bourbon name when it is my time. And I will always be grateful." My son leaned over and kissed my cheek. "Ignore the naysayers."

Tears shimmered in my eyes as I watched my son, the future of Naples, get up and gather his things.

"Be sure to attend to sweets for Leopold, though," he said before he left. "He is preparing for a coup d'état."

I laughed. "I will see to it. But tell your four-year-old brother that he cannot topple countries until he is at least seven."

Standing at the window, I looked out over the immaculate gardens. The sun beat down over the pools that sparkled like gems. The trees and grass were a perfect shade of green, even in this heat. I wondered what my legacy would be. If Naples would remember me as the queen who tried to make things better. Who took on a role that seemed insurmountable and created something beautiful. Something lasting. Or would I be relegated to being just another name whispered in passing? A queen who reached too high and lost everything.

⚜

Your Majesty,   *October 17, 1796*

I am writing to you personally to advise you on the troubling turn of the war with France. We have been unable to stop Bonaparte in Corsica and Piedmont-Sardinia. I am sad to report that we also could not keep him from Milan.

One of the more troubling developments that my men and I have witnessed is the looting by the French army. They have taken every piece of art and treasure that belongs to the people of Piedmont-Sardinia and Milan.

These French may be espousing liberté, égalité, fraternité, but they are nothing more than anarchists.

Lord Horatio Nelson

CHAPTER FIFTY-TWO

OCTOBER 1796

The news of the looting by the French was troubling. I had spent years cultivating an art and antiquities collection for both Caserta and the public. I shuddered to think of all the treasures France could take from us. I strengthened my resolve. They may have taken my sister, but I would not let them take my beautiful Naples.

But before France made their way here, I had to make sure that they could not ruin all that I had built, and to do that, I needed to make sure their disciples did not take root in the Two Sicilies.

Acton's spies had found their way into La Touche's circle. He was mostly inviting the common people to his boat, but there were a few of the nobility, including my personal librarian, Eleonora Fonseca Pimentel, and one of my own council members, Luigi Medici. I seethed when I learned of their teachery. "Are you sure about these people?"

"Yes," he said gravely. "They are planning terrorist attacks in the city."

I gulped. Terrorism was a new invention of these French rebels.

They sought to cause the most damage possible while inflicting fear in the people and, worse, distrust in the government. "Arrest them. Arrest them all, but bring me to Medici. I want to talk with him."

The operation to arrest the traitors was planned by Acton. The police force was to sweep through Naples, rounding up everyone on the list, in the middle of the night. This way, they wouldn't be seen. I had only one request of Acton. "Make sure that none of them are harmed. I want each and every one of them to stand trial, publicly."

* * *

On the planned night, I waited with Acton in the family parlor while the police were making the arrests. I stood in the moonlit window, looking out toward Naples. "Am I doing the right thing?"

"You are doing what is necessary," he said, coming up behind me.

"Yes, but is it right? I feel like I am arresting half the city." I leaned into him, taking in the smell of fresh soap.

"Doing what is necessary and doing what is right doesn't always align when you are ruling a country. It is necessary to arrest these revolutionaries. If you were to let them take root in Naples, who knows what they could do?" He placed his hands on my arms. "You are being fairer than any one of your counterparts. If this were France or even Spain, they would not only have them arrested, but they would be killed. You are granting them the right to a trial; no other monarch would go to such lengths."

"I made a terrible Freemason, didn't I?"

"Freemasons are only men."

"Oh, well, that seems to be everyone's problem with me." I slipped from the window and found my way to the carafe of wine.

"You still hold to their ideals. It's just that some people have warped the belief."

I opened my mouth to respond, but the door opened. "La Sua Maestà, it's done."

"And Medici?"

"He is in the prison."

"Thank you." I turned to Acton. "Tomorrow I will go and pay my old friend a visit."

* * *

Early the next morning, I was en route to Castel Sant'Elmo. The early October sun beat down over the Bay of Naples as the carriage rolled over the cobbled streets to the castle on the edge of the sea. The castle, originally constructed in the fourteenth century, still had the scars from an invasion by the Spanish. But the Bourbons had turned it into a prison at some point in the sixteenth century.

The city was eerily quiet in the aftermath of the arrests. Normally during this time of day, there were people at the markets shouting about their wares, women throwing buckets of water to clean the sidewalks, and children walking in groups to school. But today there was none of that. The city held a collective breath as it waited for further actions from my government.

As we crossed the drawbridge, I steeled myself, preparing for what was to come. I wanted to know why Medici, one of my most trusted advisors, had betrayed me.

Inside, my guards led me to what was once a dining room. A long wood table was stretched out there, with a tray of wine and a small bowl of fruit in the middle. Windows all along one wall looked out to the sea just beyond us. I had to wait only a few moments before they ushered in Medici, his wrists clasped in chains.

"I wondered how long it would take before I was brought to you," he said.

"Why?" I didn't want to make small talk or hear any excuses. Medici was on my council; he was one of my first friends.

"Always quick to get to the heart of the matter," he said. He found his way to the wine and managed to pour himself a glass. "We Italians like to take our time. Even our language is slow." He pulled a chair out and sat down. "Have a seat. Share some wine with me. That's the least you can do for the accused."

Eyeing him, I made my way to the table and sat across from him. He watched me with a small smile as I poured myself a glass. "There," I said. "Now tell me why."

Medici drained his glass and then reached for more. "You know, I worked as the head of your police force for a long time. Maybe I will let my prisoners get wine. I never realized how much I missed it until I couldn't have it." He lifted the wineglass and examined it before taking another swig. "It is almost inhumane to deprive the people of it."

"You know how these interrogations go. Let's not play games," I said, trying to appeal to his sensible side. "I simply want to know why you betrayed me."

"I didn't betray you."

"You did. You conspired with La Touche against Naples."

"No!" He slammed his hand on the table. "Never have I acted against Naples. Everything I have ever done has been for Naples. And you, La Sua Maestà, are not Naples. You are just a Habsburg pretender."

"I don't understand." He was leaving me confused, and I didn't like it. "But you helped me get rid of Tanucci? You befriended me."

"You think we were friends? I used you. Tanucci was a puppet of the Spanish. He never had Naples's best interests at heart. And then you came along, and I knew that if I could assist you, I could oust my largest obstacle, get some proper reforms for the country. And then when you were no longer of use…Well, you soon shall see."

My fist tightened on the glass. "I will not lose Naples."

"Naples was never yours to lose."

"I've given everything for the Kingdom of the Two Sicilies. I am her ordained queen."

"Oh, La Sua Maestà, you are nothing more than a Habsburg whore, just like your sister," he sneered. "Your people took my home from me; Florence belongs to the Medicis. Your grandfather refused to sign the treaty naming Anna Maria Luisa de' Medici as the heir to the Tuscan throne, even though he forced Prussia to name your bitch of a mother as his heir in Austria. The Habsburgs forced their way onto the peninsula. You are an abomination."

I stood up abruptly. "I've heard all that I needed."

Medici began to cackle. "Go ahead and run. Run all the way back to Vienna. No one wants you here."

Medici's menacing laughter followed me as I exited the room.

"Did you get what you wanted?" Acton asked.

"Yes, and more," I responded, setting off for the entrance of the castle. Naples was mine, whether Medici liked it or not, I was not going to let these radicals take her away from me.

⚜

Dearest Sister,   *July 10, 1796*

Well, it has finally happened. Bonaparte has come to Parma. He is just as vile as everyone says he is. The man seems to think that he can push me out of my own country. When he stormed the palace, he and his troops threw open the doors to the throne room. It was a small pleasure to see the shock on his face when he saw me sitting on the throne, in my men's dress of course.

They demanded to speak with the duke. Weren't they shocked to learn that he had fled long ago, with the priests and women. I then informed General Bonaparte himself that no man has forced me from my kingdom and no man ever will.

I left the room with the men scratching their heads and have taken up residence in the abbey—with relative freedom, I might add. This Bonaparte has plans of not just conquering Italy but all of Europe. Beware, Charlotte. He is coming for Naples.

Amalia

CHAPTER FIFTY-THREE

Napoleon Bonaparte swept through the northern regions of Italy and was now preparing to invade Rome, a feat not accomplished since 1527, during the War of the League of Cognac.

"Can they even do that? Invade Rome?" Ferdinand asked as the family sat down to dinner.

"Absolutely," I said. "It's a kingdom just like anywhere else."

"Yes, but the pope can excommunicate the whole army," Ferdinand said as a servant set the first course before him.

"I don't think they much care about that," Francis responded.

"Well, they should," Ferdinand said, with a mouth full of food. "Napoleon Bonaparte should be more like George Washington. Now that is a great leader. Did I read you the thank-you letter he sent me?"

"Yes, dear," I said as I began to stab my vegetables.

"George Washington would never invade Rome. I am certain he is a man of faith. A good Catholic."

I didn't have the heart to remind my husband that George Washington was English and therefore most certainly a Protestant.

"If Napoleon invades Rome, which he most likely will," Francis said, ignoring his father, "what will our plan of action be? Do we invade Rome in turn? Or amass a heavy presence at the border?"

I thought for a moment, pushing my food around my plate. "We have to be cautious. We still have a neutrality agreement. For our safety, we can't be seen as breaking the treaty. Our forces are not strong enough yet, and we need to remain blameless. The more France looks the part of the aggressor, the better."

"But we have to do something," Francis said, letting his fork drop to his plate with a loud clatter. "We can't let France dominate us along with the rest of Europe."

"We have raised taxes on every class for the sake of the army."

"And what of La Touche? He is the source of the terrorists. Are we not going to put him on trial?" Francis asked. "He is breaking the treaty as well."

"Acton has personally seen to it that the supposed repairs are being made. Likewise, Admiral Horatio Nelson is on his way to Naples. His fleet will help to intimidate La Touche."

"There has to be something more that we can do. Can't we stage some war games or something that would help show the French troops how strong we are?"

"War games!" Ferdinand exclaimed. "Our son is a genius! Yes, we will have war games." My husband turned to me. "Make it happen."

"You both understand that this will take time, don't you? We are still building ships and ammunition. This will not be something I can pull together within a month's time."

Ferdinand waved his fork in the air as a new plate of food was brought before him. "You have a way of making these things work."

I chewed on my steak. Though I was not happy about having another task to worry about, I thought my son did have a good idea. Perhaps showing France what we were capable of would ward them off.

February 2, 1798

I was given a daily update on the trials of the rebels. In all, there were more than fifty men and ten women being tried for treason. It was important for me that each and every one of these people had a fair trial. We had created criminal justice reforms that allowed for the accused to be assumed innocent until proven guilty by officials, regardless of the outcome. Of the fifty men, six had already been found not guilty, and Medici's trial was coming up next.

"The unfortunate thing is that La Touche did too good of a job of making sure there was no way to trace those who were guilty," Acton told me. "We will have a lot of problems proving guilt beyond a reasonable doubt."

"But we must," I said, trying not to feel discouraged. "I do not want innocent people caught up in this nor do I want to be seen as a tyrant. I don't want to give France any ammunition against us."

"La Touche is calling the arrest of his friends a violation of our neutrality agreement. He is threatening a military blockade in the Bay of Naples."

It was not enough that France had taken my sister. They were trying to undermine me and my kingdom, taking away everything I had ever worked for.

"The jury has found one man guilty and has sentenced him to the gallows."

"Who?"

I had hoped that the man was going to be Medici, but I was soon disappointed when Acton said, "A man by the name of Tommaso Amato. He is originally from Messina. Shortly before our arrests, he forced his way into the church of Santa Maria del Carmine, punched a friar in the face, and proceeded to yell at the parishioners, telling them that they were fools for believing in a

God who did not exist. He went on to yell many other profanities as well."

"These people have been poisoned by France. Any news about Medici?"

"Our spy will testify on our behalf in Medici's case, but Medici is too popular. The jury believes that we paid the spy to slander Medici's honor."

"So Medici will be free and I will be seen as an unjust ruler, even though I am trying to do the right thing." I shook my head against the terrible irony of it all. It was as Acton said, doing what was right and what was necessary were two different things. If I wanted to do what was necessary for Naples I would have dealt with these rebels swiftly without this trial. But I needed to do what was right, even if it would tarnish my name.

⚜

My Good Lord St. Vincent,   *February 16, 1798*

I pray this letter finds you in good health. I am writing to you on behalf of our dear mutual friend Queen Maria Carolina. If you hear any lies about her, contradict them, and if you should see a cursed book written by a certain vile dog with her character in it, don't believe one word. She lent it to me last night, and by reading the infamous calumny, I put myself quite out of humor that so good and virtuous a queen should be so egregiously defamed. I have known the queen for some years now, and I can tell you that she has shown nothing but sisterly affection toward me and my person. She is too kind for all this, and though she does not show it, her heart breaks at the hatred that is being spewed from this man.

More importantly, we are concerned about the French aggression that is presenting itself in the southern Mediterranean. The French troops are, as I write this, invading the Papal States, and there is a force heading toward Malta. It is only a matter of time before France turns its eyes to the Two Sicilies.

In addition to the French refugees, we have welcomed poor souls from Piedmont, Milan, Rome, and Tuscany. They tell us that Bonaparte and his soldiers are openly looting not just from the governments but from the people themselves, and that the French are taking their liberties with the women, robbing them of their virtues. Without my lord Nelson and his fleet, we do not stand a chance against this enemy.

Yours Faithfully,

Lady Emma Hamilton

CHAPTER FIFTY-FOUR

I loved Carnevale. The festival took over the whole city. In years past, it was always a treat for us to walk among the people, to see them celebrate so fervently before Lent. The people dressed as if Carnevale himself bowed and danced through the street. The sweet, oily smell of fried dough drifted through the air as we dipped biscotti in sanguinaccio dolce. We would watch the Sicilian cart, from a safe distance, of course, as it rolled through the street. Its little brightly covered wagon was filled with every type of meat imaginable. The moment it stopped, the people rushed it, picking it clean of food. This was when Naples was at her finest.

But this year, things were different. There was a genuine pallor that hung in the air. La Touche's ships were still in the bay. Acton kept pushing to have him removed, going so far as overseeing the workers himself, but La Touche always found an excuse to stay.

"Do not vex yourself," Ferdinand said, preparing to go out for the festivities. "The people will cheer for us when we officially begin the celebrations."

"I wish I had the faith that you do," I said, watching Ferdinand examine himself in the mirror. "What game are you going to play today?"

"I am meeting my friends for chess, and then will wander about the stalls of the festival to see how many people I can fool into thinking I am not the king."

"I wish you would stay with me and choose this season's Carnevale king."

"Regina mia, I am always with you." He held my hands in his. "If you are in doubt or are at all unsure of yourself, look out amongst the crowd and you will see me." He kissed my knuckles. "Because I am Naples, and Naples is me!" he proclaimed as he left the room.

I wished I had his ease as I prepared for my part in the afternoon festivities. In preparation for an imminent war, we had raised twenty battalions of infantry, thirteen squadrons of cavalry, and a train of artillery. This was besides the Neapolitan fleet, which now consisted of forty gunboats and forty larger vessels, some of which had been secretly sent to the English in their efforts to subdue the French in the Mediterranean.

But it was not enough. France had twice this number, and it seemed an endless supply of soldiers willing to destroy our people. We needed more. I could not let them take hold of Naples. We had raised taxes and asked for donations from the churches and monasteries. The show of force that we now had planned for the people was to help inspire them, and to show the French that we would not be intimidated.

I ventured out into the populace expecting the worst. So far, the taxation hadn't been objected to, but it was no secret that the pamphlets were spoiling the people's minds.

To my surprise, the people responded well to my presence. My processional made its way to the stage that had been built for me in the center of the piazza as people cheered and threw flowers at me. Every year, I had the honor of choosing the human representation of Carnevale. The one to enjoy the first of the foods that the vendors prepared and who, when Lent began, would be "sacrificed."

"My fellow Neapolitans," I started, "we are here at another Carnevale, and I can guarantee you this will be the best one yet!"

The roar of the crowd rose up and echoed across the bay.

"But before we can commence with our festivities, we must find our Carnevale king. Who among you holds the spirit of the season?"

Men jumped up and down, pointing to themselves, to try to get my attention, but from the corner of my eye, I watched as a peasant was carried on the shoulders of men. He waved his arms in the air. "Regina mia, choose me!" The crowd parted, and I got a good look at the man calling to me. It was Ferdinand, dressed up as a peasant.

"With such devotion and enthusiasm," I said, "I have no choice but to choose such a handsome Neapolitan as the patron of the festivities."

My guards helped Ferdinand to the stage, and he bowed low.

"I shall do my best to serve you," he said with a wink before turning to the crowd. "And make sure my fellow Neapolitans have the most raucous of festivities ever in the history of the Two Sicilies!"

Everyone chanted for us as Ferdinand escorted me to the thrones put up in honor of me and our Carnevale king. As the merchants began to bring us their wares, I leaned over to Ferdinand. "Did you have this planned the whole time?"

He kissed my hand. "Carnevale is our favorite holiday. I wanted to make sure that we made this year special and that you would be happy. Are you?"

I smiled, caressing his cheek. This man throughout our marriage had never ceased to surprise me. He was not the most charming of princes, nor was he the smartest, but when he acted for me or the greater good of Naples, he truly shone. "Yes," I said, "I am happy."

* * *

In the weeks that followed, I let myself get distracted by the festivities and the preparations for our war games while the French ships sat in the distance off our coast. We were just sitting down for dinner one evening when one of our attendants entered the room. "Admiral Horatio Nelson to see the king and queen."

Ferdinand threw his napkin down. "Send him in! Don't make him wait outside."

Excitement filled me as the famed admiral entered the room. With his help, we would make the French think twice about invading the Two Sicilies. We made space for him at the table as he regaled us with stories of his adventures.

After dinner, we watched as our flagship held a pretend battle with the flagship from the English fleet. Our militia and artillery shone under the setting winter sun. The men in their new uniforms moved with precision as Acton looked on with pride. This military was very much one of his own design and creation. Watching them gave me hope that we could defend ourselves.

⚜

Madame,   *May 20, 1798*

I have in my hands several letters written by Your Majesty that leave no doubt with regard to your secret intentions of joining the nascent coalition. Will you risk your king-dom and the total destruction of your paternal house?

Should war break out because of you, you and your

offspring will cease to reign. Your errant children will go begging through the different countries of Europe. In order to avoid the inevitable, you must dismiss your prime minister, Sir John Acton, dismiss the British ambassador, Sir William Hamilton, and dissolve your militia. It has also come to my attention that you have sent an ambassador to Russia to plead your case. You must recall him back to Naples immediately.

I am sure you and I can come to an agreement regarding such matters, for your sake.

Napoléon Bonaparte

CHAPTER FIFTY-FIVE

MARCH 1798

The years following that Carnevale were filled with anxiety. The trials ended in the spring of 1796 with only six of the men being convicted for treason. As expected, Medici was found not guilty; we then promptly dismissed him from his position.

Meanwhile, I could feel France's noose tightening. Having invaded the papal states, it was now focusing its attention to the south with the invasion of Malta, the small island falling quickly.

"It's only a matter of time before he comes here," I said, reading the latest letter in front of me, an update from my daughter Theresa, doing her part to promote Naples's interests in Austria.

"We still have the neutrality agreement," Acton said, setting down his espresso. "As long as we keep that agreement intact, he can't invade."

"Bonaparte has no respect for anyone, particularly women. Men like him feel as if they are entitled to everything, and unfortunately the more you tell him no, the more, he will want it."

"Admiral Nelson left for Egypt yesterday with his fleet. Bonaparte is trying to expand in Africa, so the English are bringing the fight to him there."

"One can only hope that this time the English will be victorious."

August 1798

"He lost." I couldn't help but giggle as I read the letter from Nelson. The British had cut off Alexandria's access to the sea while the Turks marched on Cairo from the east. There was nowhere for the French to go. France tried to send reinforcements, but they were captured off the coast of Egypt, leaving Napoleon at the mercy of the plague that was ripping through the French forces, killing up to forty soldiers a day. For once, the noose was tightening around Bonaparte's neck instead of mine.

Napoleon had snuck off into the night, not showing his face until he made it back to Paris. For months, I danced around Caserta, knowing that Napoleon had been defeated. For years, he and France had managed to do whatever they wanted, without having to pay any consequences.

Russian troops were amassing in the north while the British were pressing in from the south. Our champion, Nelson, was injured in the back, and Bonaparte was looking at the Two Sicilies anew. We had what Napoleon needed: money. Upon news that France was regrouping, Ferdinand, Francis, Acton, and I met in the council chambers to discuss our strategy.

"We have to take the fight to them. They are focused on protecting their interests in the north; their forces will be weakened," my son insisted. "We'll have a chance to end this once and for all."

"No. We do not openly break our treaty of neutrality," I responded.

"You are a fool to think that we are still neutral," Francis snapped. "They have been seeking to conquer us for decades. Mother, you have played your chess match with them, and now it's time to fight."

"Acton, what do you think?" I asked.

He was quiet for a while. "England wants us to invade. They

have been a steadfast ally, and if we don't agree, we could lose their support. If there is any time to invade Rome, now is it. The French are distracted. Napoleon is losing. We need to openly join the coalition."

"We are going to Rome," Ferdinand said, crossing his arms. "And I am going with them."

"No, you are not going with them," I told my husband. "You have to stay here with your people, with me."

"I am doing what is necessary for my people. If it means going to war for them, so be it."

"Acton, will you please do something about this?" I pleaded.

"He is the king. If this is what he wishes, I cannot stop it."

"Ferdinand," I said, trying to keep my temper under control. "If this is what you want, then I shall not stay here and watch you kill yourself over it." I stormed from the room, disgusted by the men I had to deal with.

"Charlotte," Acton called, chasing after me. "Charlotte, wait!" He stopped and broke into a sputtering cough.

"What more do you want from me?"

"I want to talk to you about this. You have to see that this is the only way to end this once and for all."

"It doesn't feel right," I said. "If we go to Rome, we'll expose ourselves. France will finally have their reason to invade."

"France has never needed a reason to invade. They are going to do it, neutrality agreement or not. It's only a matter of time."

"No! We can't fight them. It's too much risk. I won't allow it." I started to walk away again, but Acton pulled me back.

"Do you think that you are the only one who cares about Naples?" He placed my hand against his chest, but the old gesture that had once brought me so much comfort now felt hollow. "Be the queen that you are, and do what is necessary for this country."

I took my hand back, holding it against my breast. "It would appear I don't have a choice."

CHAPTER FIFTY-SIX

The royal family came out in force to show our support of the soldiers and to say goodbye. Christina, Amalia, and I stood together on the stage as we watched the men march to Rome. Next to me, my daughter-in-law wrapped her arms around her growing belly, as if she could protect her child from all the sorrow that could befall them. Clementina, the young Austrian princess, and daughter of my dear brother Leopold, was a quiet but pleasant girl. She and Francis were fond of each other, but she tended to fidget and act scared whenever I came into the room.

Now as we watched the men ride away, silent tears rolled down her cheeks. I moved over to her, taking her hand in mine. "Don't fear. Francis will return, and until then you and I will be the dearest of friends." I leaned in closer to her. "You are going to be the queen when I am gone. It would be good to dry those tears. One day, it will be your job to take care of Naples as if she were your child." My eyes swept over the crowd. "They need a strong monarchy."

Silently she nodded, wiping away her tears.

My younger son Leopold stood behind us sulking. "I should be going with them." He and Alberto, my two youngest children, wanted so much to be just like their eldest brother.

"You are eight years old," Amalia said. "You can barely hold a rifle."

"I hunt with Father," he snapped. "You don't know anything."

"Both of you, stop," I ordered. "We have work to do."

I couldn't sit and worry about what was going to happen in Rome; I knew what happened when France invaded. They weren't this benevolent entity that wanted to share the gifts of democracy, as they so claimed. They never were. And Napoleon, that vile man, he forced everything he touched to bow to his will and took all he could.

I had to make sure Naples was taken care of, so that if France did come we would be prepared. Caserta and her treasures were too precious. Christina and Amalia supervised the staff as they crated everything, staging for the worst possible scenario. Meanwhile, I had Leopold study the evacuation route. It was the only way to make him feel as if he were of use. We needed to all be ready to face my greatest fear: the loss of Naples.

November 1798

In the early morning hours, as the sun was beginning to break over the horizon, a servant burst into my rooms. "La Sua Maestà, the soldiers are returning."

"Quick. I have to go see them." My maids dressed me in the simplest gown I had. As I ran down to the gate, I was devastated to see the state of our troops. They were disheveled, their faces smeared with blood and dirt. The number that had returned, it was a third of what we had sent. In the jumble of soldiers, I looked for the faces that I knew. I could see Francis and Acton in the royal entourage, but there was no Ferdinand.

"Where's Ferdinand?" I demanded when the officers made it to the palace.

Francis embraced Clementina as Acton approached me. "We lost him."

"What do you mean you lost him? Is he dead?"

"Our forces were divided by the French, and the king was on the other side. We don't know where he is." Acton wiped a hand over his tired face. "Charlotte, we lost."

I took a few steps back, reeling from the news. "How? Our forces were stronger. France was supposed to be distracted in the north."

"They had more troops than we thought."

"I told you!" I screamed. "I told you this was a mistake, and now we are exposed. Bonaparte is going to know that we violated the agreement. He has just cause to invade us!" I hit Acton in the chest. "This is your fault."

He took me by the wrists, shaking me slightly. "Napoleon is coming here. He is heading to Naples now. We don't have time to argue."

Napoleon was coming for Naples. I suddenly felt sick. France was going to take Naples. My bella Napoli, lost to me forever.

"We have to prepare our escape," Francis said.

"Not without Ferdinand," I said. "I will not allow him to be captured by that man."

"Mother, we don't have a choice," Francis responded. "They are coming, and we have to protect ourselves."

"The goods, the art, our history. It's all packed," I said. "Give the orders, but I'll stay here."

"Mother," Francis began, but Acton stopped him, whispering in his ear. Francis nodded and started to bark orders.

"If you told him that you would force me to leave with you," I said to Acton, "you are sorely mistaken."

"I would never dream of doing such a thing. You are far too stubborn, even for the likes of me." He tried to smile, but it turned out to look more like a grimace. "There is still a chance the other forces will come back, and if they do, I guarantee Ferdinand will be with them. Until then, please be ready to go with the rest of us."

"Go," I said, waiting by the entrance. "I want to stay here for a while."

Acton squeezed my hand as he went back into the palace.

The servants set out a bench for me to sit on as they traveled in and out carrying our precious treasures with them. Ferdinand had to live. After all these years and all the things he had put me through, I would not let him abandon me like this. We had been married for thirty years, and in that time, we had celebrated together and had mourned together. We'd created a partnership. Ferdinand had a duty to see it through. He needed to be here for his country. For me.

I was dozing off in my seat when I felt someone tapping my cheek. I smelled him before I saw him: the sharp tang of vinegar and dirt. My eyes flew open to find Ferdinand crouching before me in tattered peasant clothing. His face, though dirty as it was, had more wrinkles. The tip of his nose had grown redder and more bulbous. But even at forty-seven, his eyes still sparkled like when we were young. "Regina mia."

"You're home!" I exclaimed, launching into his arms. "And you stink." Immediately I took a step back, waving the air in front of me. "What happened?"

"My regiment was captured. I put on peasants' clothes and snuck away."

"The French are coming. We have to leave."

"I know," he said, kissing my forehead. "I know."

Ferdinand rushed into Caserta while I went to prepare my things for escape.

CHAPTER FIFTY-SEVEN

December 1798

Ferdinand and I stood at the stern of the ship, watching as Naples receded into the distance. Tears spilled down my cheeks as I watched my country fade away. My Naples, my beautiful Naples, was lost to me. Leaving her and Caserta felt like I was abandoning two of my children to that vile general.

When we could no longer see the shoreline, we slipped below with the rest of the family. In the royal cabin, set aside for us were two beds and not much else. It was the barest of accommodations, but we made do, since it was such a short voyage. Francis and his family were on a second ship, along with Christina, Isabella, and Antonia. On our ship, we had Leopold, Alberto, and Amalia. The Mediterranean Sea was rough, as if it were trying to keep us from leaving.

"Where are we going?" Amalia asked, rubbing Alberto's back.

"Palermo," I said, taking a seat on the other side of my youngest son. "How is he?"

Amalia shook her head. The last forty-eight hours had gone by in a flurry, with packing for our escape. We were all tired, but

Alberto seemed to be taking it the hardest. Since we left, he had barely had anything to drink and was regularly vomiting.

"Mama, I think I am expelling less," Alberto moaned as Amalia took a cool cloth to his head. My son rested against my shoulder. He yawned as I felt his forehead.

"No fever," I said. "Do you think you can keep a little food down? Maybe some bread?"

Alberto shook his head. "I think I just want to sleep."

I helped him lie down with his head on my lap. Stroking his damp hair, I looked to Ferdinand. "You haven't said anything all voyage."

"I lost Naples," he said, his voice thick with emotion. "What else is there to say?" Ferdinand closed his eyes and leaned back on the bed.

"Ferdinand."

"Wake me up when we get to Palermo," he mumbled.

I looked to Leopold, sitting in the corner, who shrugged and closed his eyes as well.

I focused my attention on Alberto. He had finally settled into a deep sleep. I closed my eyes and leaned back, letting the motion of the water lull me to sleep as well.

Twelve hours later, we arrived in Palermo. Alberto was still sleeping as the rest of the family prepared to disembark. I gave him a small shake, but he didn't respond. I shook him again, but still he didn't wake. "Alberto! Alberto, wake up!" I shook him harder. Panic sank in. "He won't wake up!" I yelled. "Someone help me! Help!"

Ferdinand fell to his knees, pulling Alberto into his arms. He slapped Alberto's cheeks, hard. And still, he didn't wake. I fell to the floor beside him, feeling for my son's pulse. But there was none. My eyes met Ferdinand's. Our son was dead.

* * *

We arrived at the palace in Palermo, ready to collapse. The family settled into the parlor as servants brought us food. But I didn't want to think about food or rest. France was systematically taking everything from me. First my sister, then my country, and now my son.

"We should get some sleep," Francis said after Clementina gave a large yawn.

"Yes, we'll sleep now," I said, "and in the morning, we'll plan on how we can exact our revenge on France. We have to get Naples out of Napoleon's clutches."

"Will you stop!" Ferdinand shouted. "Always with your schemes. You make these plans, and when they don't work out, we are the ones paying for your sins. Us, not you."

"I do what is necessary for the sake of our country!"

"You do what is necessary for you!" Ferdinand returned.

"France needs to pay!" I responded.

"Our son is dead! Charlotte, why can't you grasp that?"

"Because above all else, I am a queen."

"Not anymore," Ferdinand said, his voice suddenly growing quiet. "We've lost everything because of you."

"Because of France!"

"No, Charlotte, because of you!" Ferdinand roared.

"I'm leaving. If you insist on putting all the blame on me I'll go and have my own household."

Ferdinand came within inches of my face. "Go. I promise you I will not come and get you. Not this time."

CHAPTER FIFTY-EIGHT

I sat on the balcony, drinking an espresso and watching the sun rise over the Mediterranean. It had been a little over a year since we landed in Palermo. I had stopped waiting for my husband to send for me or for a servant to deliver a present from him. We'd always had our spats, and Ferdinand always took me back, because he said he could not bear to have our household divided, even if he did have another woman. I was always the wife he returned to.

The small castle where I had taken refuge was quaint enough, though it was no Caserta. Nothing could ever compare to my beautiful palace. Francis now ran our family affairs, so they didn't even need me. However, I enjoyed spending my mornings keeping vigil here, longing for my Naples.

On this particular morning, just as the golden rays slipped over the crystal-blue waters, my eldest son took a seat next to me. He and his little family had spent the night with me, a regular occurrence, when we pretended that living in Palermo was all perfectly normal.

"I see you are still keeping vigil," Francis said.

"Of course," I replied, turning over a second cup so that I could pour out some espresso for him as well. "Beyond those waters is my bella Napoli. I miss her more than you can ever know. It is a shame I will never see her again."

"Mother, do not be melodramatic," Francis said, taking a biscotto. "It doesn't suit you."

"What news do you have of home?"

"They are calling themselves the Parthenopean Republic."

"So, the rebels got what they wanted, didn't they?"

"Not quite. It's a puppet for France." He sipped at his espresso. "The Calabresi are putting up quite the fight."

"Thank God for the Calabresi. That is not a phrase I ever thought I would say." I took a long sip. "And what of your father? Is he still with that actress he found?"

Francis groaned. "Yes, and she is just as odious as you can imagine."

"What of the innkeeper woman? How are her children?"

"As far as I know, they are safe. The children are taken care of. The youngest is apprenticing with a mason."

"Oh, that's nice," I said. "She deserves to be taken care of."

"Mother, there is something I want to talk to you about."

"What?" I poured myself more espresso.

"I want you to go to Schönbrunn Palace."

"Am I not far enough away? Why do you want me to go all the way to Vienna?"

"I need you to go because you are the best advocate we have for the Two Sicilies. The coalition is still fighting against Napoleon, and we need you to make sure that when we win, Naples will not be forgotten."

"Don't you have ambassadors for that?"

"None are as good as you." He smiled. "Plus, you can be with Theresa. She is pregnant again, and I am sure you would like to spend time with her."

I looked back out over the water. "I don't want to be that far from Naples."

"You'll come back," Francis said, taking me by the hand. "Naples needs you to be her defender."

"Very well." I knew what Francis was doing, and I couldn't say I was surprised. The new generation was always trying to push out their elders. My son was no different.

However, there was one thing that I needed to do first. Say goodbye to Acton. He had been injured in the retreat from Rome. His health failing, he, too, was looking at a life in retirement.

I made my way to his family estate just outside Palermo, a home he shared with his young wife and son. She met me in the front room as we assessed each other. This young thing with mousy brown hair and doll-like features stared back at me. I knew Acton had married. I had heard that Admiral Nelson gave them a lovely party on the bay, attended by most of the nobility. Emma had even shared an amusing story about a drunk lieutenant accidentally knocking Principessa Melina overboard. I consoled myself with the fact that it was not a relationship made for love; it was an arrangement to preserve the money within the Acton family estate.

"He's in the garden," she said, after presumably making her own internal assessment of me.

"Thank you," I said.

Acton was sitting in a chair under the shade of an olive tree. He set down his book, looking over his spectacles as I traversed the garden.

"Since when did you start using a cane?" he said.

"Since my daughter seems to think that I am a fragile old woman."

He gave a little chuckle. "I remember what fifty was like."

"Not quite fifty," I said, correcting him.

"At least your family cares. I think mine would rather have me out of the way."

"That's what you get when you marry someone so young."

"Everyone is younger than I am. Even you."

I sat down opposite him. "And I will be sure to remind you of that."

"As you should." Acton smiled. "So, what brings the infamous Maria Carolina Charlotte to my garden."

"They are sending me to Vienna," I said.

"So Francis is looking to retire you as well?"

"It would appear so," I said, looking out over the golden-yellow grass covering the gently rolling hills. "He says I am to be an advocate on behalf of Naples, but I know that really he wants me out of the way so that I am no longer meddling." My eyes trailed a bird as it took flight across the sky. "Why does advocating sound so much like retirement?"

"Because it is." He moved his closed book from his lap to the small metal table beside him.

"You spend years in service to a nation, and they just dismiss you like a servant."

"I could go with you," Acton said.

"You could," I said. "But who would keep Francis in line?"

He smiled. "At least by you going to Vienna, you can continue to annoy our favorite Frenchman."

"Yes, at least there's that."

We were quiet for a long time as birds chirped in the distance.

"What will I do without you?" I asked.

"You'll beat every Austrian and Frenchman into submission."

"I should leave," I said.

We stood up in unison.

"I would have followed you," he said.

I put my hands on his lapels, attempting to smooth them out.

Gently he lifted my chin so that our eyes met. He didn't need to tell me how he felt. I knew. I had always known. Acton leaned down and kissed me with a passion that transported me back twenty years. When we were young, and Naples held so much promise.

"Goodbye," I whispered, breaking away from him.

Tears swam in his eyes. "Goodbye, my queen." He gave me one last kiss on my knuckles, and I left, not daring to look back—knowing that if I did, I would not have the strength to do what needed to be done.

⚜

Dearest Brother,   *December 12, 1809*

If I had to choose the moment when Mother's demeanor changed, it would be at the death of our sister Theresa. When we first arrived in Vienna, Mother was at her happiest, with all her daughters gathered around her, but when Theresa died in childbirth, Mother grew sullen. She was with Theresa when she passed. Did you know that?

I know many of our siblings have passed over the years, but it was clear that Theresa was her favorite. I have yet to be blessed with a child, but I can only imagine that something breaks within a mother when her favorite child dies.

It was after Theresa's death that the little vials appeared. She refuses to tell me what is in them, but I can spy her taking small sips when she thinks I'm not looking. I can't be sure, but I think she is taking laudanum. Francis, the mother we knew is gone. Servants run from her, and frankly, I don't blame them. Mother has also started harping about our sister Antonia's death again. She is convinced that Antonia was poisoned, telling anyone who will listen that her daughter needs to be avenged.

If Mother had her way, she would have Austria at war with every country on the continent.

Francis, I don't know what to do. I love our mother, but these new developments break my heart. I am afraid to tell her about my marriage proposal. I thank you for already giving your blessing, but I am still terrified. The only thing she rages about more than Antonia's death is France. It doesn't help that Philippe's father was the Duke of Orléans. The very man who betrayed zia Antoinette.

Your Sister,

Amalia

CHAPTER FIFTY-NINE

FEBRUARY 1810

My cane clinked in time with my footsteps as I stormed through Schönbrunn Palace. Ten years in Vienna. I had spent these ten long years advocating on behalf of Naples. Now that Napoleon controlled the whole Italian peninsula, we were in a fight to keep the rest of Europe out of French control. From my peripheral vision, I could see servants turning on their heels in an attempt to avoid me. They were afraid of me, and I had to admit, I kind of liked it.

It had taken years to instill this level of fear into the people around me, and it suited me well when I confronted my son-in-law. Reaching the doors of my son-in-law's office, I pulled my little vial from my pocket and took a sip, closing my eyes as I savored the feeling of warmth that spread, calming the pain in my side. Without waiting to be announced, I barged into Francis's study. For a moment, I thought I was back in Leopold's office, with all the papers and maps. It didn't help that my son-in-law looked like his father, even though he didn't have any of his brilliance. Realizing that there was a different group of men around him, I regained my wits and remembered what I was here for. Francis was about to make a huge mistake regarding my eldest granddaughter, Marie Louise.

"You are not doing this," I ordered, slamming my cane down.

Francis rolled his eyes. "We will talk about it this evening."

"No. We will discuss this now." I pointed a finger at all the men in the room. "You all need to hear this. My granddaughter's life will not be bargained for some peace treaty, which I guarantee will not be adhered to."

"Leave us," Francis said to the men.

When the men had left, he turned to me with the same tired face of his father, my brother. "My daughter's life is not yours to command."

"That's a funny thing. Do you even know who she is?"

"Of course I know my own daughter."

"That certainly surprises me, since you hardly ever visit her. When I was queen of Naples, I made time for my family."

"Say your piece and leave."

"You cannot marry her to Napoleon. What are you thinking?"

"I am thinking of the safety of Austria!" he exclaimed. "By creating a marital alliance with this man, I can guarantee that France does not invade here. It is us or Russia. And if I have to use my daughter to make sure that it is not us on the butcher's block, then so be it."

"My mother thought the same thing," I said. "The empress thought she could create an alliance with France by marrying Antoinette to the heir, but France knows no honor. They killed her daughter, my sister, just as they will Marie Louise. The French will forever be the antithesis of Austria. We can have no peace."

"Enough," Francis said, rubbing at his forehead. "You will not bully me the way you did my father. Marie Louise has already accepted Napoleon's offer."

Rage filled me. My granddaughter was to be married to that vile French pretender. My own family was betraying me. "Tell me you are at least putting provisions in the contract to protect her and your future children."

"Contrary to your beliefs, I am not a fool," he stated. "My daughter, like you and my wife, will become a regent when she bears him a male heir. She will have all the rights and privileges afforded to her to act on her son's behalf."

"And if France violates this?"

"Then there will be harsh consequences that I intend to see through."

"Tell me how that has worked for Austria, because from where I am, those consequences meant nothing to them."

"I will not discuss this with you further."

"Very well," I said, and I swept from the room.

Out of the view of Francis, I took another drop of laudanum. I wasn't sure anymore if the pain was real or just a figment of my imagination. Catching a glimpse at myself in the mirror, I barely recognized the woman that stood in my place. She was so thin that she almost looked emaciated, with dark shadows under her aging eyes. I stood up straighter. That woman would not stop me. I continued on my journey to find my granddaughter.

She startled upon my entry. Her quill fell to the floor, spilling ink as it went. "Grandmama, what brings you here?"

"I wanted to pay a visit to my eldest granddaughter." My old fingers warped with age caressed her smooth face. She was so young, only eighteen. It was hard to imagine that I had been her age once. This had been my and Antoinette's room when we were children. It still had the soft-pink drapes and the gold trim around the walls. I had sat on that very bed, contemplating marriage to a man whom I did not love and a future to a country that would forever hold claim to my heart. I walked over to the dresser, where an effigy of Napoleon lay. Picking it up, I smoothed out the worn tricorne and the cloth face. "I remember when your mother told me about this. She didn't want you to be afraid."

"He was the scary man in all our stories, all those times we ran from Vienna because his army was invading. His name alone terrified us." Marie Louise gave a sad smile. "Mother had one made for all her children."

"And now you are marrying him."

"I am doing what I must for my country," she said.

I pointed to a chair with my cane. "Move that chair closer. I wish to have a word with you." The girl did as she was told, and I settled myself in opposite her. "That is our burden as women. To bear the good of the country at the sacrifice to our wants." Marie Louise looked down at her hands while I spoke. "I was in your position once. I did not want to marry your grandpapa. He was everything they had warned me about, but I did as I was told for the sake of the Habsburg crown. My mother gave me advice that I wish to impart to you."

Marie Louise now looked up at me as I continued. "From the moment you marry *that man*, you will be French. You will speak French. You will gladly eat French food. You will make everyone around you think that you are the epitome of a French lady, but here"—I pointed the handle of my cane toward her breast—"in your heart, you will be Austrian. You will see to it that Austria is favored in all international dealings."

"Grandmama, did you love Grandpapa?"

I sat back and considered this. No one had ever asked me if I loved Ferdinand. "Love is not a requirement for marriage. That was another piece of advice my mother gave me," I said, fondly thinking back to her. "Make him believe he loves you. Men's egos, especially your betrothed, are fragile. If you can find love with your husband, then your job will be easier. When I first married your grandpapa, I didn't love him, I could barely stomach the sight of him. Then, after a time, we built a friendship. It was in the small moments, when we spent time with our children, found something to laugh about," I said. "Yes, I did love your grandpapa. Perhaps you will grow to love Napoleon, but, remember, it does not make you any less committed to your new country if you do not."

I took her by the chin. "Remember, you are the granddaughter of Maria Carolina. You are strong, determined, and quite capable of instilling fear in men's hearts with just a look."

Charlotte,   September 5, 1793

Do you often wonder if you could live your life over again if you would change anything? Or what would have happened to you if things had been different? What if Josepha had lived? She would have been the queen of the Two Sicilies and you would have been the queen of France. I think you would have been a lot better at it than I.

As for me, I would have been the duchess of a small territory. Maybe I would have been allowed to live in peace with my children.

As I look back on my life, I often think about all the things I would do differently. Perhaps listen to Mother's advice more. I would certainly ask her more questions, spend more time studying politics than learning to dance. Above all else, I would aspire to be more like you. More assertive, less gullible, and always, always following my heart. You always knew how to balance being queen with being a mother and wife. An enviable trait, if I do say so.

But within every realty, every choice that I make, there is always one constant. You are always there, close to my heart. Forever and always. My sister, I could never be parted from you.

Antoinette

CHAPTER SIXTY

Napoleon was defeated.

I breathed a sigh of relief when I learned of his failure. The fool tried to invade Russia during the winter. He had expected Austria's assistance, but my son-in-law had the shrewdness of his father, and in the end, there was no help for France. In April, the man who thought he could be an emperor abdicated the throne, and in May, the Treaty of Paris was signed. Napoleon was powerless.

Now I needed to restore Naples so that I could return home. After I left Palermo for Schönbrunn, Ferdinand led an army into Naples and took his city back. But a few years later, Napoleon invaded once more. This time, instead of setting up a republic, he had his brother-in-law, Joachim Murat, rule. Murat was a man who was as arrogant as he was cruel. He thought nothing of murdering my people if they did not conform to his rule. One thing he didn't know, though, was that the Sicilians were more stubborn than the donkeys they bred.

A congress was being held in Vienna, at the Ballhausplatz, where Austria and its allies were working out a peace treaty. Among

the questions put forth by the congress was whether or not the
Two Sicilies belonged to the new king, Murat, a pretender to my
throne, or to the Bourbons. When I appeared at the congress, I
was astonished to meet a Lord William Bentinck. He bowed low
when he met me. "I am here to represent the Kingdom of the Two
Sicilies in all matters as they pertain to this congress," he said.

"Well, that is not necessary. Since I am the queen of the Two
Sicilies, I shall be able to speak on behalf of the monarchy."

"Your Majesty, you must understand—we must also negotiate a
constitution for your people."

I openly laughed. "A constitution? You may as well hand them
another revolution. My people do not need your constitution;
they need their proper God-given king." I waved a hand in his
direction.

"Your Highness, you do not have the power to dismiss me."

I raised an eyebrow as I considered this man. Why was it that
these men always seemed to think they knew more than I did?
The sun did not rise and set on their orders. "Then who? I should
surely like to have a word with him. That he may know who holds
the real power in Naples."

"The regent of Naples, Francis."

I took a step back. Even my son was betraying me.

"Your Majesty, I will allow you to sit in the room. So long as
you remain quiet as I negotiate. I, too, want to see the Two Sicilies
restored, but you must trust me and let me do my job."

I considered the choices before me. Sulk in my rooms or watch
France's final defeat. I chose the latter. "Very well," I said, making
my way to the congressional chambers, not waiting for Bentinck
to keep up with me. "But don't think I won't correct you when
necessary. There is more than one reason for this blasted cane!"

I took a seat and slipped a bit of laudanum into my mouth as
I watched Bentinck argue fervently for a restored Sicily with most
of the provisions determined by the English. In the end, Bentinck

did what he had come to do, and I was relatively happy. I reached for my vial again as another pain rocked through me. Though I wanted to see the fates of Napoleon's comrades, I could feel the energy drain from me, after all the years of fighting.

My work was done. Naples was safe. I could finally go home. Returning to Schönbrunn, my eyes swept over the portraits of my family, past, and present. I liked to keep them close. A picture of my mother was on the desk in my chambers, next to my box of letters. She would have been proud. I fought for my country and prevailed. As no one would take Austria from her, no one would take the Two Sicilies from me.

And while I knew I now had a trip to prepare for, I took another sip of laudanum and sat down to pen just one more letter. But as I wrote, something else took hold. A strange tingling traveled from my head down to my fingers and back. My face, disturbingly, lost feeling. I tried to call out for someone but found I couldn't. I was able to stand, and thinking that maybe I could get someone's attention, I stumbled to the door, but my legs gave out.

As I collapsed, my hand caught the box of letters that had been gifted to me so many years before. Its once-shiny wood now cracked and faded, the box opened as it fell. My letters—all the words from Leopold, Acton, Emma, Mother, and Antoinette—floated down around me like leaves from a tree as I closed my eyes. For the first time in my life, I surrendered.

AUTHOR'S NOTE

In the midst of edits for my previous novel, *The Woman in Red*, bits and pieces of history that I learned about the Kingdom of the Two Sicilies started slipping into that story. As I began to dig into the history of southern Italy, I became fascinated by the antics of King Ferdinand, which did not require much fiction. This led me to ask: Who was his poor wife?

That was when I discovered Maria Carolina Charlotte. Within the first few chapters of *A Sister of Marie Antoinette: The Life-Story of Maria Carolina, Queen of Naples*, by Catherine Mary Bearne (1907), I came across a letter that Maria Theresa had written to her daughter:

> *You say your prayers very carelessly, without reverence, without attention, and, still more, without fervour.... Besides this, you have lately got into the habit of treating your ladies in a manner, which (and this I also know from strangers) has brought great discredit upon you.... Your voice and manner of speaking are also displeasing. You must take more trouble*

than others to amend this, and be careful not to raise your voice too much.

This was exactly the kind of woman I wanted to write about next. I began writing *Antoinette's Sister* at the very start of the pandemic, and I truly believe that it was Charlotte's fortitude that helped me get through it all. Maria Carolina Charlotte was an amazing woman who devoted herself to her country and her family—and, above all, her sister Marie Antoinette. Though the two sisters were born three years apart, they were raised as twins and kept a close relationship throughout their lives, even after the sisters' shared willingness to get into mischief together led them to be separated.

Perhaps one of the most surprising things that I learned when writing this book was that Maria Theresa, prior to the death of her daughter Josepha, had planned on marrying Charlotte—not Antoinette—to the Dauphin of France, a twist of fate that has caused everyone from modern historians to the sisters themselves to ponder the age-old question *What if?* Unfortunately, the letters the two sisters shared did not withstand the ages; whether Charlotte or someone else destroyed them, we do not know.

What we do know is that Charlotte was very concerned about her sister's well-being. She frequently wrote letters to her mother, to Countess Lerchenfeld, and to anyone else with ties to Marie Antoinette, asking after her sister. She negotiated to have Antoinette and her daughter brought to Naples; she made pleas to foster the dauphin after Antoinette's death and sent letters to every kingdom in Europe, imploring them for assistance. She was desperate to save her sister, all while France was using any excuse it could to invade.

And that was how Charlotte went from being a beloved queen to a reviled dictator. The same French writers who had smeared Antoinette turned their attention to Charlotte. They charged that not only was she "oversexed" but that she demasculinized her son Francis and her husband, Ferdinand. The lasting impact of this defamation continues to this day, even making its way into biographies of Marie Antoinette. Historians seem to have gone out of their way to give Ferdinand credit for finishing the Neapolitan archives; completing palaces and buildings, including the Fondo and San Ferdinando Theaters; planting olive trees in the wastelands; and regulating coral fisheries. Many people credit Joachim Murat for stopping the custom of burying the dead in church basements. All of this credit, however, must be given to Maria Carolina Charlotte. She even brought her favorite drink from Vienna to Naples: coffee. And she often uttered the phrase *la mia bella Napoli* when speaking of the city that stole her heart.

Charlotte didn't always help her situation. She banned the French language, expelled French artists, and snubbed French ambassadors to the point of creating an international incident—all examples of the petty nature for which her mother scolded her.

Her relationship with John Acton is one that has been perpetually steeped in controversy. Rumors swirled about Charlotte's supposed affairs, but the one alleged between her and Acton has never been fully confirmed. What we do know is that he was employed upon a recommendation from Leopold; he withstood accusations from Ferdinand, newspapers, and other council members; and he stayed with Charlotte and the Two Sicilies for the rest of his life. In my opinion, there has to be some truth to the rumors for him to have remained and endured the accusations and all the hardships that accompanied them. In actuality, he arrived in Naples in 1780, not 1776, which for the sake of plot worked out better. Likewise, some dates such as the when the traitors were prosecuted were moved up in the timeline for the plot.

During the pandemic, I spent hours online, virtually wandering the palace of Caserta while dreaming of a trip to Italy. It was this longing to be at Caserta while I was writing this story that made me keep my characters in Caserta more than at Portici, which was their home during the fall and winter months. In addition to all the contributions Charlotte made to Naples, she was the one who brought in much of the art you will find today in the gardens of Caserta (her son and grandson later contributed to this). Though I have visited Naples, I still hope to wander those gardens in person when Italy is fully open for travel.

We have a fascination and love for tragic historical figures. Maria Carolina Charlotte is one such figure who has been lost to the folds of history, misrepresented, and stripped of the acclaim that she is due. It is my hope that this story will help to reestablish her, even just a little, as the bold, fearless visionary she was, unafraid to raise her voice for her country, her family, and her sister.

For anyone who is interested in my sources, please feel free to visit my website. There you will find the books that I used for researching this fascinating story as well as a reading group guide.

ACKNOWLEDGMENTS

There was no way that I could create this book without the assistance of my wonderful agent, Johanna Castillo, and my editor, Karen Kosztolnyik. Your help in bringing Maria Carolina Charlotte and her world to light was invaluable.

To my husband, who patiently tolerated me during my deadlines, knowing when to offer support or tough love to this melodramatic writer. To my dad, who was willing to let me interrupt his own writing time to talk with me about Dante, *The Odyssey*, or whatever writing issue was bugging me. To my mom, for being the constant cheerleader.

Louis Mendola, for answering my questions and sharing your love of the Two Sicilies with me, which is now one of my favorite subjects as well. I look forward to sharing a drink with you in Sicily once travel to Italy can resume. Valbone Memeti, for your insights into the world of volcanoes, particularly that great mistress Mount Vesuvius. Patrick O'Boyle, thank you for your chats about Neapolitan culture and for sharing my love for food history.

My amazing critique partner, Alyssa Palombo, for your insights in creating Maria Carolina's world. Michele Leivas, for always sharing your opinion when I asked if something sounded right and answering my random questions. Thank you, Amanda Sawyer and Laurel Cole for being great early readers. Clorinda Donato, thank you for sharing your resources on the Freemasons. I look forward to more talks on Italian history.

A huge thank-you to my dear friends Brianna Anderson and Talia Arias for the emotional support during the roller coaster going on behind the scenes while I was editing this book. Also, Brianna, thank you for your patience when I asked questions about medical history and the difference between inoculations and vaccines.

Amanda Vetter: "After all this time? Always."

DISCUSSION QUESTIONS

1. What did you know about Maria Carolina Charlotte before reading the novel? Did you know she was the sister of Marie Antoinette or that she was the queen of Naples? What surprised you the most as you were reading?

2. In an age when men dominated the political landscape, Charlotte's mother, Empress Maria Theresa (1717–1780)— archduchess of Austria, queen of Hungary and Bohemia, and Holy Roman empress—was regarded as a shrewd, formidable, and influential ruler. Her dedication to governance, however, often took precedence over her role as a caregiver, as evidenced by the quote "I am a queen before I am a mother." Discuss the nature of Charlotte's relationship with her mother. In what ways was Maria Theresa a role model? In what ways did she fall short as a guiding influence—or do you not believe that she did?

3. When Charlotte was a child, her mother lamented her passionate and free-spirited nature, going so far as to call her "impetuous" and "selfish." Later in Charlotte's life, however, after she takes the throne of Naples, Maria Theresa describes her as "witty" and "charming." Describe the evolution of Charlotte's character, from her betrothal to Ferdinand at the age of fifteen to her death at the age

of sixty-two. What prompted Charlotte's transformation from rebellious teenager to headstrong ruler?

4. Charlotte and Antoinette are described as being very similar to each other in their youth, in both looks and temperament, yet their approach to their respective monarchies was very different. What were each woman's greatest virtues as rulers? What were their greatest vices? What do you believe were the pivotal factors that led each woman to lose her throne?

5. Maria Theresa gave birth to seventeen children during her lifetime; Charlotte gave birth to sixteen. The perpetuation of the royal line was paramount to both women, and most children in the family grew up and left to secure alliances with other dynastic lineages. Discuss the sense of home and homeland in the novel, the advice Maria Theresa and Charlotte dispensed to their daughters on their wedding days, and the push and pull royals often faced between personal and political duty.

6. In chapter 13, Charlotte says this of her first daughter, Theresa: "I wanted so much to simply love my daughter. To love her without any sense of duty. Without any sense that she needed to be something more than what she was." How did Charlotte's childhood in Austria impact her perception of motherhood? How would you approach raising a future leader of Europe? Would your approach be most similar to that of Maria Theresa, Charlotte, or Antoinette? Why?

7. In chapter 14, Leopold tells Charlotte that "chess is a lot like life." His first lesson: Always anticipate the actions

of your opponent. His second lesson: The queen is the most important player on the board. How did this scene foreshadow the events of the rest of the novel, especially regarding Charlotte's dealings with Tanucci?

8. In chapter 16, after giving birth to a son, Charlotte is finally granted her place on the council. Discuss the many ways in which Charlotte had to fight for her position as queen, despite the fact that she was a more prepared ruler than Ferdinand. At which point did she exert her influence for the first time to great effect?

9. What does it mean to be powerful in the novel? How is power wielded, seized, abused, and delegated by Maria Theresa, Charlotte, Ferdinand, Tanucci, and Napoleon? In your view, who is the most powerful character in the novel?

10. Describe the relationship between Antoinette and Charlotte. How did they influence and support each other throughout their lives? What challenges did they both face in their roles—and where did their difficulties diverge?

11. In chapter 19, Charlotte remarks that Ferdinand prefers to "play innkeeper or dairy farmer" away from the palace, rather than attend to his royal duties. Similarly, Marie Antoinette commissioned a private French "farm" for herself at Versailles, where she and her ladies would pretend to be milkmaids and shepherdesses. Why do you think Ferdinand and Antoinette gravitated toward this kind of playacting? How else did the monarchs in the novel escape from their royal responsibilities?

12. In chapter 20, Charlotte is exposed to the burgeoning Enlightenment philosophy of "poetry that sang of free ideas, of the relationship of science to art, of government's responsibility to its people." How did Charlotte incorporate these principles into her governance of Naples? How else did she aspire to transform her country into a "beacon of innovation"?

13. The notion of a monarch's divine right to rule—the belief that monarchs are chosen for their positions by God—is broached in chapter 19 and 20. How does this concept directly contradict the ideals put forth during the French Revolution, which ultimately led to the executions of Marie Antoinette and her husband, Louis XVI?

14. How would the events of the novel be different if they were narrated from Ferdinand's point of view? How does he perceive the world around him? Does he love Charlotte and his children? Do you believe Ferdinand had any wish to transform the society of Naples, or do you believe he was consumed entirely by the pursuit of selfish pleasures?

15. How did you feel about Charlotte's relationship with Acton? Do you believe the two loved one another? Would he have been a better match for Charlotte than Ferdinand?

VISIT GCPClubCar.com to sign up for the GCP Club Car newsletter, featuring exclusive promotions, info on other Club Car titles, and more.

 @grandcentralpub   @grandcentralpub   @grandcentralpub

THE
WOMAN
IN RED

THE FIRST NOVEL BY DIANA GIOVINAZZO
AVAILABLE NOW

When she falls in love with the leader of the Brazilian resistance, Giuseppe Garibaldi, Anna de Jesus is ready for adventure. Little does she know, however, that her first taste of revolution will lead her to cross oceans, traverse continents, and alter the course of her entire life—and the world.

PLEASE TURN THE PAGE FOR AN EXCERPT.

ONE

October 1829

I was eight years old when I was sent to school in the small trading settlement of Tubarão. But conforming was never my strong suit. I tried my best to be like my two older sisters, my hair in braids, my dress freshly pressed, but I couldn't sit still and pay attention. Our one-room schoolhouse was small and stale. I could feel the thick, hot air in my lungs making me struggle for breath.

This was once the justice of the peace's office, but the villagers' children needed a place to learn to read. He got a new building and we got the old one, yellowed with age and adorned with thick cracks that climbed the walls. Everyone was happy.

We sat at our desks, four rows across, every child dutifully listening to the basic lessons that would allow us to take over our parents' roles in the village one day. The teacher droned on, reading from a book.

Sighing, I looked out the window to where a cherry guava tree grew. One of the branches, thick with bright pink berries, bounced up and down in the morning sun. I leaned out of my chair to get a better look at what was making such a ruckus. The little black nose of a wild coati poked through the lush green leaves. I watched as the little creature carefully walked out to the edge of the branch, seeking out the ripe guava.

"Anna de Jesus! Get back in your seat!" the teacher yelled, snapping my attention back to him.

"But, senhor—"

He grabbed me by the arm to pull me in front of the class and made me hold out my hands. I tried to rip them away, but it only caused his grip to tighten. He slapped them firmly with his ruler. The sting resonated up my forearms into my elbows. "Do not speak back to your teacher. You are a girl. You should obey."

Hot tears stung my eyes. I wasn't going to reward him; I bit the inside of my lip to keep from crying out. Blinking back the tears, I could feel the other students' eyes on me. It wasn't until a giggle rippled up from the back of the room that my embarrassment led to anger. I grabbed the ruler from his hand and started to hit him with it. I could see nothing but my hand gripping the ruler as it made contact with my teacher's arms, raised in defense. It was the last time I ever went to school.

"What are we going to do with you, Anna?" my mother asked, red-faced, nostrils flaring like a bull's. We were in the safety of our small home with its thatched roof and mud-and-straw walls, away from the prying eyes of the village. My mother was always careful with what ammunition she gave the town gossips. I sat at the table, looking up at her, fear making my stomach clench.

"She will come to work with me." Neither my mother nor I had heard my father come in. He was standing in the doorway, wiping a damp rag under his chin and ears. Mamãe straightened her back as she eyed my father.

"You are too soft on her. This," she said, pointing to me, "this is all your fault."

"This is our daughter. We could use the extra hands with the horses." He looked down at me with his arms crossed, the hint of a smile on his face. I tried not to meet his smile.

My mother threw her arms up in the air as she walked in the opposite direction from my father. "I give up!"

I grinned broadly at her back as she stormed away. My father's face grew stern as he regarded me. "Wipe that smile off your face. This will be hard work." I nodded in agreement as he stalked off.

Working alongside my father with the horses and cattle was wonderful. Our area of southern Brazil, known as Santa Catarina, was a true Eden. No one loved the wild, rugged country like the gauchos, and Brazil couldn't function without us.

We spent our days taming the wild land of Santa Catarina. Every year more people settled here from Europe and northern Brazil, requiring more land, more cows, and more resources in general. When a rancher lost one of his cattle, it was my father and the other gauchos who went out to find it.

Santa Catarina would not be the country that it was without the gaucho, and the gaucho would not be the gaucho without Santa Catarina. We worked under a wealthy landowner, who was referred to as a patron. A patron would not think of muddying their boots to drive a herd of cattle from one clearing to the next. A patron would not rise with the sun to feed the horses and cattle that made them wealthy. A patron would not leave the warmth of their bed in the middle of the night to help a cow give birth to a calf, not caring about the blood and mucus that came with. But a gaucho would. We didn't need noble titles to know that we were the true owners of this land, with its lush green mountains that languidly stretched to the heavens. A wilderness that opened before us like the expanse of the ocean was better than any heaven promised to us by priests.

I was at my happiest when I rode out with these dirty, unkempt men who braved the wilds, through the downpour that attempted to cleanse all living things from the earth. No, I did not envy my sisters and former classmates. While they stayed in the air-less classroom listening to a useless lecture, I was getting a real education.

Working as my father's apprentice at first, I lined up his tools, making sure they were all in working order for him. I quickly became experienced enough to work alongside him, a full gaucho in my own right. At the end of the day, we cleaned the tools together, talking. My father told me stories about his people, the Azoreans who resided on the lush, exotic islands off the coast of Portugal.

"When I was a child, my parents couldn't keep me on the ground." He smiled as he wiped the mud off his prized *facón*, the knife that he had kept by his side since he first moved here. "There was this one bluff in particular that my friends and I liked to climb. It was so high that you could see for miles over the ocean." He put the *facón* away and picked up another tool as I sat on the stool watching him. "When you stand on a bluff like that, you understand just how small you are."

"What did you do after you reached the top?"

"We jumped." His eyes got big as he tickled me. "But don't you go getting any ideas now, little lady. I will not have you jumping off cliffs until you are at least…twenty."

"Twenty? Why twenty?"

"Because by then you will be your husband's problem."

I wrinkled my nose at the thought, but then another question struck me. "Papai, why did you come here?"

He thought for a moment as he closed the toolboxes. After a while, he finally answered, "I understood there was more to the world than my little island."

TWO

JANUARY 1833

As ran the course of my life, the omens came, and with them came trouble.

One morning while my father and I were preparing for our day's labor we heard my mother call out from the house. We dropped the tools that we had been packing and ran to her side. She was standing in the kitchen, staring at a little black bird with a bright red belly, sitting on the back of a chair, his little head rhythmically bobbing up and down.

"This is bad. Very bad." My mother crossed herself as the color left her face. "There are spirits here." She crossed herself again. "Something terrible is going to happen."

I slowly walked up to the bird so that I didn't startle him, setting one foot cautiously in front of the other. The bird turned his little head toward me. His eyes, as black as his feathers, shone brightly under his white-streaked brows. Gingerly I reached out toward him, stroking his little chest. The bird didn't move or flinch. Our eyes met and for a moment I felt a kinship with this creature. Moving slowly, I scooped him up in my hands and carried him outside, where I released him back to the wild where he belonged.

It was a hot January day when my father volunteered to figure out where the leak was coming from in the community storeroom, where our small village's produce and dried meats were stored during the rainy season. Any amount of moisture in that hut and we would all be starving for the rest of the season.

I volunteered to go with him, but he wouldn't let me. "You're too small. You might get hurt."

"Just last month I helped catch a wild bull."

"And you nearly got yourself trampled." He gathered his rope and hammer. "You are eleven years old. You will have plenty of time to risk your life chasing cattle and climbing on top of rickety sheds." He kissed the top of my head and left. I sulked, wishing I could go with him. They may have let me help rope the bull, but it was only because I was quicker with the lasso than the rest of the gauchos we rode out with.

Later that morning I was out at the stables, grooming the horses, when the news swept in like a rushing storm destroying everything in its path. The whole village went running to see the damage to the storeroom. Bile rose in my throat as I began pushing forward.

"He was walking on the roof," one of my neighbors murmured. "They say he fell."

"Of course he fell; that roof was so brittle that I don't think it could even support the weight of a bird." Their words died on their lips as they looked down, noticing me for the first time.

Weaving through the crowd that gathered, I made my way to the center of the room. It was only when I gasped at the sight— my father, white and waxen as he lay impaled by a beam through the abdomen—that I think I screamed. I couldn't tell. Lurching forward, I tried to grasp his outstretched hand. That's when one of the gauchos grabbed me. He threw me over his shoulder and carried me out the door.

The next day family, friends, and other kin gathered for the processional to bury my father. They hollered and cried, thumping their chests and pulling at their hair. My mother led the group, the loudest mourner of all. When the horse-drawn carriage came to a stop, she threw herself over the coffin, beating the lid as she exclaimed, "How could you leave me?" Two women pulled her away, her wails a low fog rising above the crowd of mourners.

I stood in the back, watching the spectacle that played out before me. People crowded around me as the whole village pushed past me to follow the casket. Clinging to a tree, I did my best not to get swept away by the current of faces that moved toward the grave-yard. Looking around, I could no longer see my mother or my sisters. Suddenly, I felt alone and scared in this sea of people.

Their noise was a cacophony that made me feel disoriented. Their sweat clung to my nostrils as I was jostled along the path-way. I had to leave. I was feeling myself go mad. Fighting through the procession, I made it to the river, my pulsing lungs on fire, and collapsed by a tree, gasping for breath. This world suddenly felt cold and dark without my father. He was the only one who understood me.

That was when I heard the footsteps behind me. I turned my head sharply, expecting it to be a wild animal, only to see Pedro, the village drunk. He smiled; half of his teeth were missing, and I could see his tongue in the gaps.

"Such a little thing. So sad that you are all alone now."

"Go away, Pedro," I said, looking back at the river but keeping watch on him from the corner of my eye.

He swaggered over to me and took one of my braids in his hand. "Such pretty long hair you have." He let the braid slip through his dirty fingers. "Such a shame that you don't have a father to protect you anymore."

"Leave me alone, Pedro." I went to move away but he grabbed me by the arm, throwing me against a tree.

"You do not speak to men that way." He was so close I could smell his cologne of alcohol and urine. "I should teach you a lesson." He pressed me up against the tree as he fumbled with his pants.

I began to struggle. He pinned me harder, licking my cheek. "Be a good girl." His words were thick and wet.

Instinct kicked in and I stopped struggling. I went limp, slipping through his clutches, and ran faster than I had ever run in my life back to our house.

Most of the guests were gone by that point, but my mother was just outside our front door, having said goodbye to someone. I ran to her and wrapped my arms around her, feeling safe in her strong embrace.

"Anna, what has gotten into you?"

I buried my head in her neck, unable to bring myself to speak. When I finally did, I told her everything. Her face went from pale white to crimson. "That louse. You are lucky you were able to get away." She held my head in her hands in order to look into my eyes. "You have to be careful. We no longer have your father here to protect us."

That night I lay in my bed with my older sister Maria snoring beside me. It felt like there was a chasm between us. Even though we were only three years apart, she acted as if she were one of the adults. We had never been close, but the ways we expressed our shared grief for our father felt like night and day. Where I felt stripped bare, she turned inward. Maria wanted to be left alone to the point that she would sneer whenever I came around. Now, as I lay beside her, I couldn't sleep, the events of the day racing through my mind. I stared at our thatched ceiling. Maria snorted and rolled over. I couldn't help but think, *Why do we need a man to protect us?* I worked alongside the men, doing the same work that they did. I could ride a horse better than most of the men of our village. I was given the most stubborn horses to break. My father was the one who taught me. The day that he had discovered that I had a natural affinity for horses was one of the best days of my childhood. And perhaps the most stressful for him.

I could taste the hay and horse sweat that the hot November air had carried through our encampment. The horse shook her black mane every few minutes. Her eyes were wild, darting from person to person, her breath loud and heavy with her anxiety. Whenever one of the men tried to approach her, she would rear up, kicking out in an attempt to defend herself against their whips. I stood next to my father, who sighed heavily. "That is not how you break a horse." My father had his methods, and this wasn't one of them.

When the men were preoccupied with their siesta, and taking a break from the horse, I approached the pen slowly, holding out my shirt like a basket in order to carry all the figs that I had collected. She stood there regarding me; with every step I took she stomped her hoof and let out an angry whine. I stood by the fence and watched her as I put one of the soft fruits to my mouth.

The horse stomped in protest again. So I turned my back to her and continued to eat. It took only a few moments for her to come to me. She nudged my shoulder with her muzzle. When I didn't respond, she nudged me harder, pushing me forward. I turned to look at her. We stared at each other until she quickly dipped her head. I smiled, holding one of the figs out in the palm of my hand. It was gone in an instant. Then another. Before I gave her a third she had to let me pet her. She shied away at first but by her seventh and last fig, her head was in my hands, letting me rub her as she sniffed for more food. At the sound of a cracking twig, she ran away, making laps around the pen. I turned to find all of the men, including my father, watching me. An old man leaned in toward my father, whispering something. My father grimly nodded and strode over to me. "It's time for you to get in there with her."

I had watched him break a horse a hundred times, horrified at the prospect of doing it myself. He nodded toward the horse as she nervously trotted around the pen.

"She's going to try to break you more than you are going to try to break her," my father explained. "Do not let her know she has scared you." The horse's ears were back as her large nostrils flared, releasing angry huffs. My father paused, staring down at the horse. "And for the love of God, don't turn your back to her."

Hesitantly I climbed over the faded wooden fence and stood there watching her. She shook her head, letting out angry huffs and snorts. Then she charged me. I stood my ground as she came barreling toward me, just like I had seen the men do. And at the last minute, she broke off, running the perimeter of the fence. I breathed a sigh of relief as I readied myself for her next attack. This dance between gaucho and horse was one I had seen many times. We continued like this for most of the afternoon, until she stopped, panting and huffing. She stomped her hoof into the dirt like an angry child. I made shushing noises as I approached her. Slowly I reached out a hand and stroked her sides. I was patient as I worked the rope around her. She trusted me and I wasn't going to violate that trust. I was my father's daughter.

Now as I lay beside Maria, I wondered if I would ever be trusted to work like that again. I could rope a calf in ten seconds, the fastest in the village. Was I not as good as the gauchos because I was a woman? I certainly did not feel that way. Why should I be treated any differently now that I no longer had a father to watch over me? I punched my pillow and rolled over. I needed to do something. That's when I decided that the next day, I would be the one to teach Pedro a lesson.

I spied the louse the next morning from a distance as he was doing his job, if you could call it that. He was a lazy farmhand who worked only if his boss was watching. He sat in the shade of a decrepit old pine tree, too focused on his drink to care about the oxen that were tied to the trunk with a thick rope. Years of termite damage made the pine slouch to the side like an old man in need of a cane. This was going to be too easy.

I kicked my horse in the hindquarters and she took off at a run straight for the oxen, who at this point noticed us. Their beady eyes grew large as they stopped chewing. The oxen pulled, trying to run away, bringing the tree with them, roots and all. Pedro, seeing this and seeing me, came right into my path with his arms raised in an attempt to stop me. He was just where I wanted him. I reached back and struck him with my whip, as hard as I could across his face. He cried out as if I had chopped off a limb. Blood seeped through his fingers and down his arm.

"Father or no father, you do not get to touch me." I turned my horse and galloped away.

A few hours later the constable showed up at my door. He brought my mother and me to the justice of the peace, Senhor Dominguez, to discuss my incident with Pedro. Senhor Dominguez was known as a fair man, but I didn't know if I could trust him. He was short and bald with a little black mustache that made him look official. My mother and I sat stiff-backed in our chairs on the other side of the desk. The air was thick and hot even though his windows were open.

"I understand that you attacked Pedro this afternoon and damaged a very old tree." He looked down his nose at me. "Do you want to tell me what happened?"

I stared at the dark spot on the wall above his head. He looked over at my mother, who shrugged. "I wasn't there but I am sure that *totó* got what he deserved."

He shook his head. "Luckily for you Pedro's reputation precedes him. I suppose you have to protect yourself somehow." He shuffled the papers on his desk. "Your father was a good man. I always enjoyed our talks. Just do me a favor and next time you try to teach someone a lesson, please don't make such a mess. We're still cleaning up after the oxen."

When we arrived home, my mother made the decision: We were moving eighteen miles away, to Laguna at the coast, to be closer to my godfather. We would be safer there.

THREE

JUNE 1835

I hated Laguna. The city was a crowded jungle of houses that ran along the horseshoe bay. I could feel the heat that radiated off the homes painted in bright hues of blue, green, and yellow. The only things the houses had in common were the clay roofs that were baked into a deep red from the Brazilian sun. The people always yelled, one voice over the other trying to make itself heard.

Though every village had its gossips, Laguna's were malicious. I was a favorite subject for them. *How can a fourteen-year-old girl with no father walk the streets with such pride?* Women whispered as I walked past them, their hands discreetly over their mouths, pretending they didn't want me to hear. *She doesn't talk to anyone; maybe there is something wrong with her?*

Wandering through the streets, I tilted my head to the heavens, praying to God to deliver me from such a wretched place. I missed my horse and our early morning rides. The smell of the woods after a rain. My freedom.

In a city so full of people, I was amazed to feel so...alone. My sisters, Maria and Felicidad, had been married off shortly before our move. I was left alone with our mother and our godfather, a shipping clerk. My mother took work cleaning the homes of the wealthy.

I ran my hands along my waist, feeling my hips, which had spread due to my newfound womanhood. My angular lines had softened out, giving me what many called a pleasantly plump profile.

One day as I was filling up the water jugs, I noticed a group of the village women talking in hushed tones, looking over at me in turn. When they saw that I was watching them they sauntered over to me, their baskets resting on their hips.

"It won't take you very long to find a husband." The lead woman wiggled her eyebrows as an amused smirk slowly spread across her face. "At least not with birthing hips like those."

A petite black woman placed her hands on my hips, sizing me up. "*Menina*, if my hips were as wide as yours, I probably could have gotten a better husband. I certainly wouldn't have had a twelve-hour labor for my last child."

I tried to pick up my water jugs, but my arm hit my left breast, making me spill water everywhere. I could not get used to these things. They were suddenly always in my way. The women doubled over in laughter. "See, Gloria, I told you some women have all the luck."

My new body was the talk of the gossips. Unfortunately, all of this led to men following me around asking to help with the most ridiculous things. As if I were unable to do anything for myself. They really were such a bother.

One morning, as the light from the rising sun crawled across the city, a sniveling, sorry excuse for a man by the name of Manoel Duarte approached me. Short and squat, at full height he barely stood above my shoulder. He looked as if he had just finished crying; his eyes were red, and he sniffled uncontrollably.

If I didn't know any better, I would think that he washed his hair with grease.

"May I carry your water for you?" he asked, out of breath from having to take large strides to keep up with me. I picked up my pace as he trailed behind me.

The next day he showed up at the well again. He asked if he could carry my water, and again I walked past him without saying a word. Surely if I continued to ignore him, he would go away like the stray dog that he was.

A few weeks later, while the sun set over Laguna, I sat down for our meager dinner of rice and beans with my godfather and mother. "I received a letter from your sister, Maria, today," my mother said with a grin. "She is very happy with her husband. Ship caulkers make a fine living. She doesn't need to work. Only tend to the house."

"Good for her," I said, reaching for more rice.

"I understand shoemakers make a good living as well," my mother said. "One, in particular, seems to have his eyes on you."

I looked up, stopping midchew. "Who?"

"A certain young man who likes to walk home with you from the well." My mother smiled coyly as my godfather stared intently into his beans.

"Mother, I don't know what you are talking about. There is only one person who likes…Oh no, Mother, you didn't. Please tell me you didn't."

"I was paid a visit today by Manoel. He is a nice young man. He says that you and he—"

"He and I nothing!" I roared. "I have no interest in that man at all. Whatever he told you is a lie."

"It can't be that much of a lie. He asked me for your hand in marriage today."

"Mother, no," I said, fighting the tears that were building in my eyes. "Please tell me you didn't."

"A woman without a father is nothing. You need to be protected and taken care of." My mother kept a controlled coolness that made me angrier.

"No," I said, feeling my world crashing in. I was only fourteen. I wasn't ready for this.

"The contract is already signed," my mother said, as if she were buying produce at the market.

"I can't believe you did this without my permission! I shouldn't have to marry anyone!" I yelled.

"Anna!" She dropped her food onto her plate. "I am your mother. I don't need your permission to do anything. I could have you dragged out into the streets and beaten for your disrespect. No one would even question me. Whatever notions you have in your head, you need to get rid of them right now. You have two purposes in life. One is to get married and the other is to make children with your husband. That's it."

"If that is to be my lot in life, then why not pick someone better? Why not let me marry someone of my own choosing?"

"Because you will be foolish and marry for love. You are a dreamer, Anna, always with your head in the clouds. I will not let you make my mistakes. Manoel will be a good husband." Her voice shook as she pressed her fists against the table.

"How do you know? Do you know anything about him at all?" I asked as my eyes betrayed me, letting tears trickle out. Manoel Duarte had a small, run-down shoe repair shop in the center of town. It was a well-known fact that the reason his shop was so badly kept was because all of his profit was spent at the tavern. The tavern owner's wife liked to joke that Manoel was a gracious benefactor. It was because of his patronage that she was able to acquire so many new dresses. And this was the man my mother expected me to marry?

"You haven't gotten any other offers, and he promised that he would take good care of you."

"Yes, because the promises of a drunk are always to be believed." I stormed out of the house, running as fast as I could. I made it down to the docks, where I grasped my sides, sucking in deep, jagged breaths. My mind raced. I couldn't believe this was happening. I paced, trying to control my breathing. I looked at the ships rising and falling with the gentle rocking of the ocean. Perhaps I could get on one and sail away to some other land. I took a step toward the harbor. For a moment, I closed my eyes, imagining. I could go somewhere exotic, like France or Africa. I could run away. Be a merchant, have adventures. Sail the seas. Get out of this horrible town. I could...

I shook my head, wiping away my silly thoughts. Even if I ran away, what would I do when I got there? I raised my chin as I regained control of my breathing. There was only one thing I could do. I turned on my heel and walked home. I was going to get married whether I liked it or not. Because as my mother said, I was nothing without a husband or a father.

FOUR

AUGUST 1835

August 21, 1835, was the day I married Manoel. Gray clouds blanketed the sky above the steeple. The gloomy afternoon mirrored my mood. The night before my wedding my mother slipped into my room and petted my hair. "Don't be sad," she said. "This marriage will be a good thing. You have the spirit of men's longing in your eyes. And that is so dangerous for a girl. It scares me. Soon you will come to see that a marriage will tame you. Keep you safe." She thought she was making me feel better, but my despair only grew.

I stood in front of a yellowed mirror while my mother fussed with my veil, waiting for the ceremony to begin. I wore a simple dress that had probably been fashionable when my mother was a girl. She'd purchased it from a newly widowed woman after being appalled by my plan to wear the same clothing I wore when cleaning houses. Just to be safe from any bad luck, my mother had the dress blessed by the priest.

"You look so much like your father," she said, smoothing out a stray wrinkle in my dress. "Such a shame his looks did not translate well to a girl."

She stopped and met my eyes in the mirror. "Try to be happy today, Anna. You will now be a woman. Your life is finally beginning." How could it be beginning when I felt like I was dying inside?

Standing at the altar, I looked over my new husband as he said his vows to our priest. Manoel's hair was slicked back with oil, and a thin trail of sweat rolled down his temple. He was even greasier than usual. *How can that happen?* I wondered. He was beaming, as if he had just won a hard-fought contest. I said the vows I had practiced like I was supposed to, not giving him the pleasure of a smile.

A middle-aged woman I vaguely recognized loudly whispered, "You would think she was at a funeral with that scowl."

As we hurried out of the church my shoe slipped off. When I turned back to retrieve it, an old woman gripped it in her hands. "I am so sorry, this is a very bad sign." She crossed herself. "You should get a blessing from the priest. Your marriage is doomed," she whispered.

"I know," I whispered back.

Dreading my wedding night, I kept passing goblets of wine to Manoel, hoping that he would become too drunk to perform his duties. However, when the time came, drink didn't slow him. I held my breath as he climbed on top of me, feeling slightly smothered by his weight. Manoel fumbled with his member and then tried to kiss me, but I turned away, squeezing my eyes shut. For a moment, he hesitated, but then he started pounding like I was a shoe that needed repair.

Thankfully, it was over as soon as it began. He rolled off me, lying with his back to me. Meanwhile, I lay on my back, staring at the ceiling. *Please, God, I will do anything. Don't let me be pregnant.*

* * *

SEPTEMBER 1838

For three years I dealt with Manoel. He worked making or repairing shoes; when business was slow, which it often was, he went out fishing. However, most of what he earned he drank away at the tavern. Somehow, we managed to pay our rent every month and were able to put a little bit of food on the table. I picked up work cleaning houses when I could, but it wasn't enough. I had to regularly choose between food, new clothing, and other basic needs.

I daydreamed of being out with the gauchos, reveling in my memories of riding through the hills as I stirred a pot of fish stew. We had been eating a lot of fish lately, given that it was the only thing we could afford. The deep red sauce bubbled, releasing a pleasant aroma through our little home. My husband was late again, but I didn't mind. I liked it better when I was alone. In those solitary hours I got to pretend I was my own person. I daydreamed about my time as a gaucho. As I stirred the stew, I tried to conjure the feeling of the air rushing past my face while I rode my horse. Unfortunately, Manoel stumbled through the door, bringing with him my miserable reality.

"Anna! Anna! Your prince has arrived!" he exclaimed with arms outstretched. He stumbled over his feet but caught himself on our table. "Where is my supper?" He looked around the room, dazed. "I demand that you have my supper ready when I come home, woman."

I helped him to a chair. "And I demand a husband who isn't a drunk. If only wishes were gold." I dropped a bowl in front of him. "Did you drink all the money that you earned today?"

He reached into his pocket and slammed a dirty fist on the table. Coins spilled from his fingers, spinning and rolling all over the table before he focused on shoveling food into his mouth. Half of it tumbled down the front of his shirt. I turned away from him in disgust. I heard his chair scrape along the floor. "I fought for you and I won. You are my prize. My prized jewel," he said, trying to reach out for me.

I pulled away, evading his grasp. "Well, it would appear that you were duped."

"Why do you not love me like other wives? They dote upon their husbands."

I rolled my eyes, knowing how this argument went. We had it every time he was drunk. He came home, complained about his life, and complained about me, culminating in a childlike melt-down. I sighed. "Because I never wanted to marry you."

"You shouldn't say such things to me. I am a good husband."

"If you say so." I walked into the bedroom, letting him follow me like a sick dog.

"Without me, you would be nothing."

I nodded.

He sat on the bed. "Why don't you make love to me? A good wife would perform her duties."

I walked up to him as he slowly blinked his bleary eyes. Reaching out, I poked him in the middle of his forehead. With a heavy thud, he fell back onto his pillows, asleep. I finished putting him into bed and went back to the kitchen to finish eating my dinner alone.

Two days later my mother arrived at my door. She sat down at my kitchen table with a heavy sigh. "Your husband came to visit me yesterday."

"Did he now?" I said, pulling my shawl tighter. A surprise visit from my mother required a gourd of strong *mate*. I went straight to the stove to begin brewing it as she went on.

"He tells me you are being a cruel wife again."

"When have I ever been a kind wife?" I asked, looking out the window. The sky was darkening with the onset of the after-noon rains. Every day at precisely the same time, the sky would open up and a torrential downpour would wash over us. It also meant that my mother would be visiting for longer than I would prefer.

"Anna, you have to be good to your husband. You don't want him to leave you, do you? Then you will have nothing."

"Mother, I have nothing now." I spread my arms out to show the expanse of my small kitchen with its tiny woodstove, wobbly table, and dingy cabinet that held what little food we had. I didn't even have a parlor. Below us was a general store; above us, another apartment, even smaller than ours. "I did as you told me and married the man. What more do you want? I cannot love a man I do not respect."

"Who said anything about love?" my mother said with a wave of her hand as I poured the *mate*. "A woman who marries for love is a fool."

"Why did you marry Papai?" I asked, setting the *mate* in front of her.

"Because he was exciting. I was just a girl in São Paulo; I wanted adventure, a new life." She sipped her drink. "Look at where it got me. If I had listened to my mother, my life wouldn't have been so hard. Maybe my sons wouldn't have died. A woman is nothing without her sons." She stared into her tea, scrying for what I could only imagine were the ghosts of the brothers I had never met—the two boys born in between Maria and I, the one who came out with the umbilical cord wrapped firmly around his neck and the other, who gasped for air but was too weak to live through the night. "Listen to your mother. Be good to your husband. You don't want to be a ruined woman."

* * *

November 1838

It had been over a month filled with tense politeness since my mother came to visit. Heavy rains rhythmically pattered against the windows. Manoel slipped into the apartment after a long day in the shop. His clothes were soaked, and water slid from his hair onto our floor, creating little puddles around his feet. I wrinkled my nose at the smell of mildewed old sweat that followed him. Manoel kissed my cheek before quietly sitting at the table. "I received a large order today."

"From who?"

"The Silvas." He refused to meet my eyes.

"Aren't they friends of yours?"

He shrugged. "What does it matter? An order is an order."

"Are you giving them a lower price?"

"I can't charge any less than I do already." He pushed his food around his plate: stewed fish and rice again. "Do you think we could—"

"No." I didn't even let him finish the question.

"It's been three months." He looked up at me. His eyes searched my features for a hopeful sign.

"I have a headache."

His grip tightened on his fork. "You've had a headache for three months."

I shrugged. "It's a constant ailment."

He dropped his fork. "I'm going out."

I watched as he stomped out of the room.

Two weeks later I was walking home from the market when I heard someone mention my husband. I paused, unseen by Senhor and Senhora Silva. "You can't keep giving Manoel money."

"I know." Senhor Silva turned from his wife's scorn.

"It is not your responsibility to take care of him."

"I said I know." Senhor Silva let out a loud puff of air. "We have been friends since we were children. I can't stand by and watch him become destitute."

"If he goes destitute it is his choice."

"Manoel has a wife he needs to take care of. Wouldn't you want someone to step in and help us if we were in that situation?"

I watched from behind a pillar as Senhora Silva kissed the palm of his hand. "You will never let us be in that position." Such a simple act, that kiss, but it filled me with immense jealousy. I wanted someone whose palm I could kiss in the middle of a busy street. Someone I could give little affections to, not caring who saw. Someone I could trust. I wanted a partner. My basket handle creaked under my tightening grip.

A few days later Manoel sat at our table, stinking of stale ocean and the pungent sour smell of iron and mud that comes from gutting fish. He wiped a dirty hand over his tired face as he watched me finish making supper. I dropped the plate of pan-fried fish and rice in front of him.

"Why do we have to eat this slop again? I know we have no money, but we don't have to eat the same food every day." He knocked the plate off the table with a swipe of his arm. "Pick that up and make me something else."

"No."

Manoel quickly stood up, throwing his chair back. "You will obey me! I am your husband and it is your duty to do what I say. I am tired of you defying me. Because of you I am an embarrassment! Now pick that up and make me something else."

"You can eat it off the floor for all I care. I am not your slave!" He reached his hand back to hit me. I stared at him without flinching. "Go ahead."

He lowered his hand without taking his eyes off me. "Why do you hate me so much? Why can't you be a good wife?"

"Because you picked the wrong woman. You are weak and

pathetic." My eyes narrowed, taking in his hangdog expression. "Look at you... You make me sick." I spit.

He stormed out of our house without saying a word. He was going to find comfort at the bottom of a bottle. I looked around me at my meager home, which I hated, living with a man I hated even more. This wasn't the life I wanted to live. It was time I made a change, even if it ruined me. I packed a bag and left the apartment, never to look back.

ABOUT THE AUTHOR

DIANA GIOVINAZZO is the cocreator of *Wine, Women and Words*, a weekly literary podcast featuring interviews with authors over a glass of wine. For more information, please visit her website: dianagiovinazzo.com.